DESTINY

THE SECRET WATCHERS
Book Five

Mairgrace,
May all your adventures
be wonderful ☺
♡
Lauren Lynne

LAUREN LYNNE

www.LaurenLynneAuthor.com
www.thesecretwatchers.com

ISBN: 978-1-68222-780-0 (Print)
ISBN: 978-1-68222-781-7 (Ebook)

ACKNOWLEDGEMENTS:

To my wonderful friends and family! With special thanks to the following people who helped to make *The Secret Watchers* series the best it could be: Nathan and Bryan Beals, Marge and Stan Walker, Cipriana and Sharon Mabaet, Cindi Etten, Amanda Wall, Julie Postlewait, Rachael Fetrow, Susan Chipman, Marty Herdener, Sheila Senger, Christy Slyter, Angela Theel, Sheila Johnson, Susan Hamann, and Lora Porterfield. You guys are the best and a simple "thanks" will never be enough! With a special thank you to the following Oregon retailers: Mail House Plus in Milwaukie and The Latest Trend in Clackamas!

A very special thank you goes to my friend Sally Paulson, who did not survive her battle with pulmonary fibrosis to see the end of this series. Sally had been with me every step of the way, from brainstorming parts I wasn't yet happy with, to reading many rough drafts. She will especially be remembered for her help with the cross country meet scene, in Visions, that we worked on together during our sons' cross country meet at North Clackamas Park. The park became the place where Owen discovers he is truly a *Secret Watcher*. You are missed, my friend - This final book in Owen's story is especially for you.

BOOKS BY LAUREN LYNNE

The Secret Watchers series:

Visions book one

Whispers book two

Insights book three

Perceptions book four

Destiny book five

ONE

I once read a quote. I can't remember who it's by, but I've been told it's John Ruskin's, though I can't prove it either way. Regardless, the words speak to me… "I believe that the first test of a great person is humility. I don't mean by humility, doubt of power. I believe that really great people have a curious feeling that greatness is not of them, but through them and they see something divine in EVERY other person and are endlessly, foolishly and incredibly grateful for that." I'm trying to live my life that way and every day it's a struggle, but that is the road I was given to walk. As they say, with power comes responsibility and I have both in abundance.

I'm not really an adult and I'm sure not a child anymore. I may be seventeen, but I remember being twice that old, though my life is quickly catching up to the memories Miles gave me. I looked at my watch. All that was *watcher* Miles had been contained in it by a spell cast by him and our mentor White Eagle. They had been experimenting, trying to build *good watcher* power and to pass gifts from *watcher* to *watcher*. Miles had felt the end screaming toward him like a military jet going Mach 8, or just over 6,000 miles per hour if you're not a math junkie. In desperation he had made a deal with a man known only as The Gypsy and now that man has contacted me several times to try to gain my trust and get me to partner with him to kill Evilia Malvada. If only that was as easy as it sounds. Just thinking it - makes me want to laugh. Last time I confronted her she nearly killed me and I still have to dye a chunk of my hair black to cover the white she left behind. Everything else healed up leaving nothing but scars, the marks of our trade.

In the cosmic balance of things I wondered what debts I owed Miles. I had his *watcher* gift and all his memories from about age twenty-one, when he became a *watcher*, to thirty-four when he knew his death was imminent. What a legacy. I hoped I wouldn't re-walk his path. Stephan Kraeghton predicted that I would and I lived in fear of that every day. Had I loved Lucie for no reason? Would either of us live long enough to have kids of our own and raise them? Would this *watcher* line end with me? Would I at least be able to pass on what I knew? These would be dark and unusual thoughts for a normal kid, but I'm not normal and now I wondered if I ever had been.

Miles had paid dearly to pass all that he knew on to me. He made the ultimate sacrifice and would never live to see for sure if it would even work. It was an incredible leap of faith and gave testament to his desperation. It had taken over twenty years for me to come along and activate Miles' watch. Now with my eighteenth birthday approaching I felt like I was almost communicating with him once more. I thought that I had absorbed all that he had to teach me but perhaps I was wrong and some lessons I had to be old enough to understand. I'm more or less used to being my real age and thirty at the same time, though it is strange. We believe that when I absorbed Miles, I wove the years he gave me into the fabric of my soul, making me a unique super *watcher*. I often wonder if I was really ever meant to be a mentor like White Eagle or if some of his gift got sucked into the watch too. I have since picked up or expanded many gifts that fit with my natural aptitude. Why I can do all these things, we don't know for sure, but I am thankful for it as I now know my destiny is to fight Evilia Malvada, the biggest threat any of us has ever known. This was my endgame and perhaps my final chapter. How could I enjoy anything about senior year with that racing toward me?

Now, strangely, I was the holder of Kraeghton's gift as well. Had it been his final act of defiance against Evilia or was it an accident? Apparently he didn't need The Gypsy to teach him how to force his *watcher* gifts into an object. Kraeghton put them directly into me or was it my fault when I broke the... phylactery... amulet... charm... jewelry? No, he had called it his talisman. White Eagle had the shattered remains locked away but hadn't been able to learn anything from the pieces so far.

Our best guess was that in the end, Stephan Kraeghton had believed that I was the best hope for finally defeating the monster known as Evilia Malvada. Part of the trick now, was figuring out how to use the ability he had forced upon me. I did not fully understand it and neither did White Eagle, but then we weren't used to dealing in *dark watcher* power in this context. Fight against it – sure, but fight with it – not knowingly. Kraeghton's dark energy had crippled me before, but not this time. Suddenly I seemed to be able to do more than just read body language, I could almost read minds, but in a different way than my brother, Alex, could. I gave people a headache when I did it and I didn't have to look in their eyes. Worse yet, where Evilia could manipulate emotions I could manipulate thoughts but I was out of control and a danger to people around me. I felt like I was back at the beginning except this time I was mucking around in people's heads without meaning to. I was dangerous. I had finally become the out-of-control thing that Bob feared. So really, who was the bad guy here?

There is a fine line between worrying about what might happen and planning for what could. I sighed as I sat in the stands, this time the distinctive crash of football pads was down on the field instead of filling my senses. I felt detached. I should feel sad or relieved or something, but I just felt... empty. I'm not lost. I know who I am and what I'm meant for and how many seniors know that? Maybe I was feeling a little melancholy and nostalgic or just plain worn from it all.

"I thought I might find you here," Marlo's friendly voice called softly.

"Hey, Mars," I replied without turning around. A part of me had sensed him coming before he'd even appeared at the stairs.

"What are you doing here?" he asked, sounding perplexed.

"Watching Adrian and thinking about roads not taken."

"Sounds like awfully deep thoughts for a sunny day."

"Yeah. Lately I can't seem to help it. Maybe I got a little more than Kraeghton's gift – maybe I've got a chunk of his dark personality," I sighed.

"Lucie and White Eagle have worked really hard to pull the darkness out of you."

"That doesn't mean they were successful."

"If you think that, then you still care and you're still you. I hate to suggest this, but you could go to Bob for help."

"You know I'll never do that. After all the things he's done. No one in my family will ask him for anything. The price is too high and the trust is too low."

"I know, but…"

"Mars, no… just… no. Did you do what I asked?"

"Yeah, but…" he paused and looked all around before continuing. "It's hard to hide it from Lucie and it bugs me. You know how she feels."

"It's because of that, that I asked you to do a little covert research. I don't want to hurt her any more than I already have."

Marlo looked really uncomfortable. "I hate lying to her."

"You're not really lying, you're just not telling her something."

"You used to think there wasn't a difference."

"A lot has changed."

Marlo's mouth turned down at the corners and his eyes narrowed. "Just to be clear, I hate this, but here goes. Yes, I found Piper and she's okay – probably not happy, but okay. She's at the University of Washington. She's living with two of Bob's people who pretend to be her aunt and uncle but are really her guards. They are still compiling evidence in the case against Caleb Carmichael and they have yet to catch him. There are warrants out for his arrest that even Evilia has not been able to bury and I bet that makes her very angry – though no one can find her either."

"UDub? Why? Piper should be in her senior year like us."

"Bob altered her transcript and pushed her on. Makes her harder to find, you know. He will also be incredibly pissed if he finds out I've been crawling around in his system."

"It will be on me. I just needed to know if she was okay. Communication with Bob tends to be one way and when I've had a chance to ask, he shuts me down."

"I don't like working for that guy. How can he consider himself on the side of good?"

"Is there a side of good? My view is changing. I think it's all shades of gray."

"Don't say that! That's Kraeghton talking, not you!" Marlo exclaimed sounding sick. "I don't ever want to hear you, of all people, say that. I've gotta go. I've got work for the right side that I need to do."

"Mars, wait," I said as I reached out and snagged his arm when he started to rise. "I'm sorry. I can't help it. I was being totally honest with you. I wasn't trying to be mean. I truly have lost sight of dark and light."

"I know you think that and it scares me. I just pray that you'll come back to us." I let go and he started to walk away.

5

"I don't know if I can," I whispered. Marlo paused, so I wasn't sure if he heard me because he didn't turn around.

My mind continued to churn as I watched the end of practice. Maybe I should have been on the field thinking about nothing but football. Maybe I could have pounded out all the dark and ugly places inside of me. On the other hand having less to do felt... freeing.

Even if Marlo didn't appreciate my new attitude, Adrian did. He got a kick out of this new and darker version of me. He told me that he'd always felt that Marlo and I were a little too Goody Two-shoes. What an expression, guess I could thank Adrian's grandpa for that one. Now I fit in better with Adrian's crowd where dark and reckless were admired.

I met up with Adrian as he exited the field. "Good practice. You guys should do pretty well this year."

"I hope so. I get tired of losing."

"It doesn't matter. You'll get noticed and get that scholarship you're hoping for."

"From your mouth to the right ears! Hey, the Trips have access to a boat. They were held back a year 'cause they were preemies or have August birthdays or something. Anyway the good news is that they are eighteen so they can drive the boat, so come with us to Detroit Lake this weekend. We've still got a spot for you and you don't want to miss the boat. It's our last chance before school starts and you never have any fun anymore. Come with us."

I thought again about my obligations and decided that nothing was worth missing some fun for. "Why not."

Adrian actually looked a little taken aback.

"Bet you thought I forgot what fun was," I quipped with a grin.

"Yeah, I did." He smiled back.

"Well, I haven't. Some stuff just got in the way."

"Well good. Our reservation starts tomorrow night. Maybe you want to ask Mitchell?"

"Nah, he's moving into White Eagle's old house this weekend. The renters moved and he feels safe enough. It will be monitored and warded like the rest of our houses, so I guess it's cool. It's gonna be weird to have my room to myself again. You sure I can't ask Marlo?"

"I guess you can. I like the guy, but he's even more of a Goody Two-shoes that you are."

"Whatever, Adrian, it's your party not mine. Still cracks me up that you use that phrase."

"Gramps says it all the time. Now there was a guy with a wild side. I love his stories. He was a greaser in the 50s; cigarettes in his rolled t-shirt sleeve, leather jacket, slicked back hair, jeans. He was like James Dean." Adrian gave my shoulder a friendly smack as he walked past.

"See ya, Aid." I watched him strut toward the locker room and I headed for the Kawasaki White Eagle had helped me rebuild a couple of years ago. I slapped my helmet on and swung my leg over almost angrily – it felt like Adrian was being unfair to Marlo and here I was letting him down in another way. Part of me hated myself and part just wanted to have a little fun for once. Besides I knew Marlo had to work for his mom this weekend and he'd have more fun not being around the jocks, right?

The sun beat down on my back and I forced myself to relax. I was tired of all the pressure. I parked my bike and hustled into the house. I was so mixed up, but I knew who could help. I found my mom in her room folding a mound of clean laundry. I cleared a corner of her bed and sat down to help.

She smiled at me. "Hey."

"Can I ask you something?"

"Yes?" she asked, stopping mid-fold to give me the full attention of her bright green eyes.

"I should be allowed to have fun, right?"

She just looked at me and waited.

"Because I want to, but I feel…"

"That right there is *why* you need some fun. What'd you have in mind?"

"Adrian invited me camping this weekend."

"And?"

"It's just guys, but Marlo's not invited." I paused again to gather my thoughts.

"And?" she asked when I paused too long.

"I feel bad – but it'd be nice to have a break, but I don't know if I can trust myself."

"You should go. You need it. Marlo's feelings may be hurt, but he'll understand. He and Adrian have been drifting apart for a while and he might be happy to be rid of you for a weekend. Why all the angst?"

"In a word – Kraeghton. Sometimes I don't know which are my thoughts and feelings and which are his. I start thinking things and they happen. Like the lady the other day… I don't know what her deal was or what's going on in her life and I made a judgment about her in my head, but I swear she heard it."

"She couldn't have."

"Then she believed the thought was hers – which is perhaps worse."

"You don't know that."

"Come on Mom. I looked at her… and… I wasn't being kind or understanding. I was thinking that she was fat as I looked at her and in my mind said, 'Stop eating'! Her fork hung in midair until the food fell off. She heard me. I… I feel like I kicked a dog."

"Maybe she sensed your thoughts, but I doubt it."

"She did and now I feel guilty. It wasn't my place to judge her. I hope she's okay but I wonder if I can trust myself. I don't want to hurt anybody and I don't want to become a bully."

"Owen, that incident happened almost two months ago, right after… right after Kraeghton died."

"Sometimes I'm scared that he's in here." I said tapping my head. "And only his physical form was left behind."

"That's not true. There is no sign of that. It's like Miles - just the gift and the memories, nothing more. So go. It would be good for you to get out of the house." I could see her worry even though her words sounded confident.

I hugged her and texted Adrian for the final information before I could change my mind. He was already at the grocery store. They'd be by first thing in the morning to get me and I could chip in on my share of the chow then. All I needed was my personal belongings 'cause Adrian "had my back" according to him. He'd even already packed all the camping gear at the shop which told me he must be excited to go.

I called Lucie next. I'd been wishy-washy on the subject of the great guy camp-fest for a month. I knew she had some of the same feelings but she'd tried to remain positive. After my incident with Kraeghton our relationship had taken an odd turn. I didn't trust myself and she was hell-bent on fixing all my broken bits. I wasn't sure who was whose supervisor anymore as all the team leadership had fallen to her. Mitchell wouldn't take it even though he was the oldest. He knew he was leaving when he finished his degree. He had taken three trips down to Nevada over the summer to work with Elliot Blackthorn. Elliot was a good old cowboy who kept up the property Mitchell had inherited from his former mentor Emiline. He was also the oldest *watcher* I'd ever met and had come out of retirement to cover Nevada until Mitchell returned. Mitchell, Eliot, Emiline – all easier thoughts than Lucie.

Her sweet voice caressed my ear through the phone line making me shiver. "I wondered when you'd call."

"Hey, beautiful, why's that?"

"You decided to go." She sounded so sure, so confident but then she seemed to know me better than I knew myself sometimes.

"Yes, but how…? Never mind. I should know better. You probably knew before I decided."

"I'll miss you, but I think you should go."

"What if I screw up? There won't be anyone there to help me."

"That is why you need to go. You need to know that you can control Kraeghton and yourself."

"How do you know?"

"Owen, how did you know to have faith in me? You just knew. You felt it. Now go pack, you Doofus, and enjoy your adventure."

"I guess."

"Love you."

"You too, Luce." She disconnected before I even told her a proper goodbye. Maybe I should go see her and… and what? Maybe I missed her already or maybe I was scared to go without her. Man up. I need to man up. Doofus – she only called me that when I needed it. She was right. I was a Doofus, so why did she stay with me?

I packed up and then did what I'd been doing most evenings all summer – I sat on the deck with our dog, Beggar, until after the sun had set. I'd been so still that our motion-activated back light hadn't even come on. I watched the branches on the trees sway in the gentle breeze and saw the shadows ripple. *I am in control.* I felt Miles, I knew him. I was him and he was me. Could I accept Kraeghton? Should I? Was it his darkness I had to embrace or was there enough good in him to sustain the being once known as Stephan Kraeghton. Suddenly I was incredibly tired. My body felt drained and my eyelids became heavy. A desire to sleep swept over me so strongly I'd swear someone had cast a spell. My whole body felt weary, heavy and achy. I wanted to lie down, right here on the deck. I didn't know if I could even make it inside. The feeling was almost desperate. My eyes burned and soon I could think of nothing but closing them.

I stood on a darkened street. Rain came down slow and lazy like it often does around here. Good thing I'd worn my overcoat. Wait, what? I turned my head to look in the plate-glass window to my left. My reflection was plain as day in the window of the closed art gallery – not me, Kraeghton or more precisely a memory of Kraeghton's had taken over.

I looked both up and down the street. I knew this place because he knew it. I was in a memory of Seattle, Washington and judging by the clothing the few people around here wore… it was the 80s or 90s. He looked young and fresh and felt powerful in this memory. He was waiting for someone. Past experience told me that Kraeghton had a lesson to share with me. I just wished he wouldn't take over like this. Miles never did it this way. It was disturbing and scary, like a nightmare you can't wake up from.

This memory was so vivid I could smell the acidic tang of fresh rain on asphalt. Kraeghton moved down the sidewalk. I could tell he was fully aware of everything around him – every movement, every sound had his mind busy calculating, but this Kraeghton was unaware of his passenger. I was lucky he'd looked in the gallery. What had he been looking at?

A black Mercedes-Benz pulled up. I couldn't make out the model but I knew it was the one he was waiting for. The driver's door started to open but the back passenger door was quicker.

Kraeghton quickly stepped out of the shadows. "Evening, Roberta. What a surprise," Stephan Kraeghton said smoothly.

"Why Erik, what are you doing here?" she said with a smile.

"I was meeting with Mr. Burk at the gallery and happened to see your car. Since you're here, how about if I bring you up to speed on the auction," Kraeghton purred.

"Ma'am?" The chauffer interrupted.

"I'm fine, Howard. This is a dear friend of mine. He'll see me in."

"Yes, ma'am."

Kraeghton took her elbow. I could feel the smooth, expensive fabric of her royal blue raincoat and the frail bones of her arm underneath. At their approach a uniformed doorman held the door. "Good evening Mrs. Stalworth, Mr. Alexander," he said touching his hat in respect.

"Charles," Roberta Stalworth replied back.

Then I felt it – an uncomfortable heat, right under my sternum. Kraeghton was using his gift. The doorman hit the button for the elevator and then the button for the penthouse the moment the doors opened.

Kraeghton, posing as Erik Alexander, kept the conversation light and friendly – asking about her day, her projects, and finally he brought up the art auction. I felt like he had taken his time with this one. He had researched and studied her intently before posing as someone from the art world. He had been patient and meticulous. These traits, I could learn from him. I could respect the process, but yet I was afraid. I knew what was coming and I could neither stop it nor stop watching. I was about to watch another innocent person die. I tried to wake up. I tried to rip myself away, but his hold was too strong. I was trapped again.

I watched helplessly as he poured wine and added a quick dissolving powder into her glass – yes, poisons – his signature. I could still feel him using his gift on her – manipulating her. Had he manipulated me in Florida? What about Mom and Alex? Maybe he couldn't. Did we block him? What was the lesson this time? He didn't block my thoughts in the dream but I could neither control what was happening nor communicate with him. It was so frustrating.

He rambled on. She was lucid enough to tell him he should go. She wasn't feeling well. "Yes," he told her. They could talk tomorrow. He silently lifted her keys and pocketed them. He left and took the elevator down.

He spoke to the doorman on the way out. He turned back. "My mistake," he said smoothly, his power burning in my chest. "I forgot to give her this." Kraeghton pulled out an envelope. "Would you please give her this tonight?"

"Yes, sir."

Kraeghton watched him walk to his desk and dial. The doorman nodded and headed for the elevator. Kraeghton smiled and walked down the street. At the corner he paused. He glanced around as if waiting for the crosswalk light to change and then turned and walked around the corner of the building. He walked its length to the entrance to the underground parking area and walked in with purpose to where he pulled a hat and gloves from behind a fire extinguisher. He put them on, turned up his coat collar, rounded his shoulder, affected a hitch in his step and kept his knees bent before walking right up to the back door like he belonged and used her key to enter, keeping his head averted from the camera. He could be any man from the building on this rainy night. With the gloves and hat anyone watching would not be able to get skin or hair color.

He turned and headed to a door labeled "no admittance." There were no cameras back here. An empty janitorial office sat to the right. Stale cigarette smoke and the musty odor of old stored items tickled my nose. Up ahead was a service elevator. I felt Kraeghton smile. He turned back and rummaged in the office until he located a key, hung neatly on a hook and conveniently labeled "service elevator." Key in hand, he headed to the doors and used the key to activate it. While he waited he glanced at his watch, just after ten. He rode up to the penthouse. He glanced around the corner in time to see the doorman leave.

He walked down the hall to an unmarked door, removed Roberta's keys from his pocket and entered the back side of a storage room. He moved silently to the opposite door, listened and turned the handle. He watched Roberta get ready for bed. It was clear she wasn't feeling well. He moved down the hall to collect the envelope she had clearly touched. It had contained another dose of poison on the sheet inside. Kraeghton carefully pocketed the letter and envelope and then moved to her office. He took a brief moment to admire the view before he broke into her safe. He used every pocket he had to take as much as he could, leaving the harder to sell items behind. He reclosed the safe and removed a painting from the wall. He quickly returned to the storage room where he cut it from the frame and placed it in a mailer tube. He picked up another painting, took it to the office and rehung it in the spot. Then he walked to Roberta's room where she appeared to be sleeping. He pulled a small vial from his pants pocket, opened it and poured a small, delicate, almost oily stream into her mouth.

She gasped once, her eyes rolled up in her head and she ceased to move. With one still gloved hand he held her mouth shut, with the other he pinched off her nose. He did not move until the second hand on his watch had made four revolutions. He closed her eyes and folded her hands over her chest.

He returned the keys to where he'd found them, put the mailer tube under his arm and left the way he came in.

TWO

Next thing I knew, the sun was rising and the blanket from the back of the couch was draped over me. How had I gotten inside? I folded the blanket and rolled to the kitchen. I ground beans and threw them in the coffeemaker as I thought about it. I was a blank. Damn. I rummaged for breakfast and was relieved to hear feet on the stairs.

"Hey," Alex said in a sleepy voice.

"What are you doing up?" I asked.

"Checking on you."

"Oh?" *Maybe uh-oh would have been a better response.*

"You had another Kraeghton-induced nightmare didn't you," Alex accused.

"Uhhh."

"Thought so. Mom told dad you were fine. She said your blood sugar was probably low. I don't think he bought it. He doesn't think you should go camping. In fact he thinks you need therapy. They had another argument because he doesn't think you can take care of yourself. If I were you, I'd get out of here before he's up and I'll pretend I never saw you."

"Why Alex? Maybe Dad's right," I sighed.

"When it comes to *watcher* stuff when is he ever right?" he asked, complete with eye roll.

"Occasionally?" I hedged.

Alex looked at me really hard and I felt the tingle of his gift. "No. Go." He moved past me, took down two mugs and poured from the sputtering coffeemaker. "Go get your gear. I'll make you a fried egg sandwich to go."

"Thanks, Alex."

"No worries. I like it when you owe me," he ginned back flippantly as he grabbed eggs from the fridge.

I silently sprinted up the stairs and grabbed my pack. Mom stepped out of her room in her usual eye-boggling night attire. How she slept in that stuff I'd never understand, but whatever floated her canoe, I guess. Who knew you could put grape, bright aqua blue and lime green together in a plaid and it would look okay? I guess it was the almost fluorescent lime green t-shirt that would have kept me awake. I wondered if it glowed in the dark.

She gave me a hug and gently pushed me toward the stairs. I moved back into the kitchen where my brother was busy with eggs, salt, pepper, butter and toast. I quickly texted Marlo the key points of what I remembered from the dream including names and approximate dates so he could add it to our ever-growing Stephan Kraeghton file. True to his word, Alex had the sandwich done and stuffed in a Ziploc bag. I could hear the distinctive sound of my friends' Suburban. With all that auto shop you'd think they could change the muffler but maybe they were saving up. I chugged the last of my coffee, hugged my brother and flew out the door.

The triplets or Trips, as Adrian liked to call them, pulled up in their big blue 70s vintage Chevy Suburban, hauling their boat. As I jumped down the front porch steps I could see that the back of the rig was already filled with gear. I hoped there was room for mine. I glanced down the street toward Lucie's. I sighed but I felt the sorriest for Marlo who was the only guy not invited. When I'd asked Adrian a second time he'd told me it wasn't Marlo's kind of trip. BS I'd said, but let it go. Mitchell mainly hung with his college buddies and he was busy anyway. He was one to use as a model when it came to separating work from the rest of his life which I seemed to be mostly incapable of.

I opened the door to the back seat and found another of Adrian's sports buddies. He slid out as he looked me up and down. I recognized him but I'd never tried to talk to him. Something about him made me wary and I've learned to listen to that.

Adrian hopped out of the front passenger seat. "Owen, Jon. Jon, Owen."

"Hey Jon," I said sticking out my hand to shake his. He hesitated, then reached for mine. His grip was firm enough but his soft hands told me he refrained from manual labor. His eyes, covered by dark aviators, gave nothing away. He had three day, movie star stubble and from my undercover adventures last summer I recognized the clothes. Boat shoes with no socks, a logoed polo and print shorts. "You shop at Nordstrom's or something?" I couldn't help digging at him a little.

"Maybe. What's it to you?" he asked with a curl of his lip.

"Nothin' Dude. You just don't look like you're from around here," I retorted back, playing dumb.

Adrian snickered. I looked down at my own tired rock band t-shirt, cargo shorts and scuffed Doc Martens, then back at him and shrugged. "We're camping, right?"

"Come on. Let's go," Adrian smiled as he pounded me on the back.

I threw my duffle through the hatch, slammed it closed and waited for Jon to push the lever on the seat or at least get out of my way. He chose the lever, then moved aside as he flipped his over-long bangs out of his eyes. A half smile touched my lips. This guy had to spend more time in front of a mirror than most girls I knew.

17

"Hey Joel," I smiled, ignoring Jon as I climbed in the back.

"Owen, zup?" Joel grinned.

"Not much, you?"

"The usual," he smiled bigger, "nothin' but trouble."

Now I laughed out loud. I like Joel, he's a good guy. I felt eyes on me and turned my head from Joel to Jon who was sitting in front of me. He looked away. He sat by Jesse, while Adrian navigated and Josh drove. Way too many J's on this trip. Once again I got that weird vibe I couldn't put my finger on and I knew it wasn't from any of my buddies.

An hour down the road Jon turned purposefully and looked at me again. He waited while I pulled out my earbuds. "So, tell me, Ryer. Why are you taking pre calc and physics this year? Are you a brainiac or nuts?"

"Neither. I plan to go to college and study forensics and law enforcement." I wondered why he cared what classes I took. Probably wanted to be sure our schedules didn't match up.

"I'm taking a light load so I can focus on football. I'm gonna play ball for the Ducks. I don't care what I major in, other than football."

"What will you do after college ball?" I asked, wondering why he hadn't looked a little further into his future.

"I'll play pro ball of course." *Well of course*, I thought sarcastically. "I hear you used to play. I hear you were good when you started. What happened?"

"I wasn't having fun anymore."

"Nah, really. I heard you were in some kind of accident last May and can't play anymore."

The rest of the Suburban grew silent. *And this, my friends, is why I don't like people.* "Nothing that exciting," I replied aloud, my scowl deepening.

"Is it true you date the hot girl who's crazy?" he asked with an intense penetrating look.

"You're half right," I growled.

"Which half?" he laughed maliciously.

Adrian turned in his seat. "Hey, let up will ya?"

"Why? Is he a little girl? Is he gonna cry?" Jon drawled.

"Are you trying to make friends or enemies?" I asked, my voice low and my eyes slitted.

Jon's eyes widened and then narrowed. "Hey, Dude, chill. I've heard interesting rumors about you. So I'm trying to figure you out."

I just looked at him. I really didn't care what people thought. I knew who my friends were and Jon would not be one of them.

"Some kids think you're some kind of a hero but all the under-classmen are afraid of you. Too bad you don't put that to use on the football field. Some kids say the end of last year you had some kind of a breakdown and barely passed your classes 'cause you missed so much school. Some kids think you're doing drugs and others defend you like you saved their life. I wanna know who I'm boating with – Bruce Wayne or a dopehead."

"I'm just a guy, Jon - nothing more."

Jon turned further around and leaned toward me. "I know that's not true. There is more to you than meets the eye and you try hard to cover it up. I know you do martial arts way beyond what Jesse, Joel and Josh do but you don't compete. You work out way more than Adrian. I know you swim, rock climb and run. What I want to know is what else you do."

"Maybe I'm just athletic," I scowled to let him know the conversation was over.

"No way. There's something about you that isn't right. I can't quite figure it out, but I will."

"Why would you be so interested in me? I'm nobody special."

"I think…" He stopped talking. He just froze for a moment, staring at me. A drop of blood formed by one nostril and ran toward his lip.

"Holy crap, Jon," Jesse exclaimed and the moment was broken. I realized I was overheated, angry and my jaw was clenched. *Shit, what had I done?* I turned and looked out the window, but I could feel Adrian's eyes on me as he, Joel and Jesse scrambled around for napkins.

What was wrong with me? All I could think about was how much I wanted him to just shut up. The bleeding stopped almost as fast as it started and he forgot his line of questioning for the moment and began to talk about the bloody nose and how weird that was. I put my earbuds back in to drown him out with a little *Hinder*, but that didn't stop Adrian from sending me a furtive glance.

We stopped at a convenience store for Jon to clean up and to get some snacks. The triplets looked at me warily as Josh gassed up and the other two headed inside. Adrian gave me a meaningful look over his shoulder as he walked in with Jon. I sighed and leaned on the back fender.

"Weird timing for a nosebleed, don't you think?" Josh said as he hung up the nozzle. "But then you couldn't do anything like that. Right, Superman?"

"You're kidding, right? Why would you even think I could?"

"I don't know, dude. I've know you for a while now and I've seen you do some pretty amazing stuff. Adrian doesn't say anything but sometimes it's what you don't say, you know?"

"I don't know what you're talking about."

"If you say so, but I don't ever want to get on your bad side."

The other guys were headed our way so we both stopped talking. Josh turned his attention to his brothers. "You pay for the gas?"

"No, Jon did."

Adrian spoke up first, "Can we chip in or get the next tank?"

"Nah, it's all good. You guys paid for the campsite and food. I got this and we can square up later," Jon replied flippantly.

"Thanks," we all said, but mine was more of a mumble. I handed Adrian fifty bucks for my share of the campsite and food. I didn't want to owe Jon anything so I figured I'd get the next tank of gas.

We got back on the road and made it to the lake without further incident. They wouldn't let us check in until 4 pm so we headed over to the day-use area. Jon continued to watch me, but didn't question me further. We had sandwiches for lunch and then explored the campground. Adrian and Jon found some girls almost immediately, but then I already knew Adrian was a magnet and Jon was just enough of a dick to really appeal to some girls. I overheard that they wanted help setting up their campsite. I was pretty sure they just wanted to hang out with some hot guys. *Whatever.* I wasn't interested, but I could play along. They seemed nice enough. They were friendly and flirty. Nine of them had come together. I let the others talk and hung in the background. Jon watched me but didn't say anything to me.

At quarter to, we packed up and headed back to check in and found our reserved spot. We set up camp while the triplets and Adrian joked around. Jon joined in but I stayed quiet. I could still feel the heat burning in my chest. I sure didn't want him asking any more stupid questions and I couldn't give the guy a bloody nose every time he pissed me off, although it sure was tempting.

It was immediately clear to me that Adrian and I knew the most about camping. Watching the other guys trying to set up their tents was killing me. I was working so hard at not laughing that my cheeks hurt and my breathing was ragged. I just hoped they were significantly better at driving a boat.

As soon as we had everything else done we took pity on them and helped out. I figured a little struggling was good for them, especially Jon. I found out that what I suspected was true. Although Jon liked to pretend that he knew everything – he had probably never camped a day in his life. He did not have a White Eagle who taught him life skills. Adrian took over the dinner preparations as I finished the canopy and hung the gas lanterns from the supports.

We ate quickly and then headed over to the girls' campsite, but it looked fine to me. I was pretty sure they didn't need any real help; they didn't want it to be just them alone all weekend. Or maybe it was the fact that they were stuck between four fishing buddies in their fifties and a young couple complete with two toddlers. I wandered off and sat watching the water. I figured the others could have their fun, but I hadn't left Lucie behind just to hang out with some chicks I didn't even know.

When I glanced back, Jon threw me a disgusted look and then I knew he was talking about me. I turned back around and stared at the water as I tried to calm myself by listening to the lap of the waves against the shore. I could have been gaming with Marlo, I mentally kicked myself. My cell binged. Jon posted some trip pictures, including one of me standing alone looking at the water, captioned "Sensitive or surly? Definitely douchy." I turned and looked back. He was watching me and smiling, so I flipped him off and headed to our campsite. I didn't need his crap. Bullies piss me off. Why was he picking a fight with me?

Adrian had cooked dinner so the least I could do was clean and hopefully burn out my anger. The guys didn't come back for a couple of hours. I had completely cleaned, organized our gear, and was reading our assigned summer novel by lamplight by the time they returned.

Everyone was talking in a low voice. If they spoke to me I answered but I initiated no conversation. I had to do something to keep it all inside. The triplets and Adrian took turns looking from me to Jon and back. I could tell they were wondering when I was going to blow. I turned in early, deciding the best way to restore my patience was with plenty of rest. I couldn't really sleep until I knew Jon was zipped in his tent. I listened for several more minutes before I let myself fall into a light sleep.

I had fully expected a prank during the night so the birds had me up first thing with their morning chatter. I started our campfire and took out our breakfast grub. I put water on to boil, stowed the rest, and went for a walk around the campground. I appreciated camp early in the day when most folks still slept. It was quiet and held the shiny promise of a new fun-filled day.

Jesse was up when I returned but clearly not yet awake. I took pity on him and made coffee. He hunkered down in a camp chair buried deep in his oversized hoodie. He stared off into the distance and didn't even flinch as his brother headed for the bathroom. Recognizing another morning hater by the scowl and slumped posture as he returned, I poured Joel a mug and said nothing. I started breakfast and the rest rolled out one by one.

By ten everyone was more than ready to go out on the boat. We dressed for swimming, gathered tubes, drinks and sandwiches and took the boat to the ramp. We started off with a grand tour of the lake, taking it slow and snapping pictures. The noise of the engine made talking unnecessary and I was glad. I kept as far away from Jon as I could.

As the lake warmed we stripped out of our sweatshirts. When it was finally warm enough we took turns being pulled by the boat as we rode on the tube. I pulled off my shirt for my turn and Jon had to open his pie hole.

"Geez Dude, were you in a car accident or what? Or wait, I know, you wrecked your bike, right? No, no wait, I know, you're a gang banger, right?"

"No."

"Then it was an accident. I was right the first time. Look at all those. No normal kid looks like that. How many stitches have you had? I thought it was just your ear that was a little tweaked. Tell me what happened to you."

"You don't want to know."

"Sure I do."

"Fine, I don't want to talk about it."

"Why not? Is it a big secret or does it bring up scary memories."

"Why don't you lay off?" Adrian spoke up, joining the fray.

"Hey, fine. I get it. He's private. Geez. I just wondered what happened to him. He looks like he's been in fifteen knife fights."

"Only three that I know of," Adrian said under his breath.

I gave him a harsh look and dove into the water before I lost it and shared some of my not so nice skills with Jon and his big mouth or Adrian for opening his. Yeah, I was private and for good reason. It kept us safe. The less Jon knew about me the better, but I couldn't have him so curious that he kept digging either.

The water was a rush. Joel drove the boat with skill, making for one hell of a ride on the tube. After a half hour I gave Jesse the signal and Joel slowed the boat. Jon was up after Jesse so maybe he'd drown, I thought with a smirk.

The sun glinted off the water throwing everything into a blurred haze. After all the swimming and tubing I was content to lie on a bench and soak up some rays. The boat bounced along pulling Jesse on the tube for his turn. The rhythm held a regular beat and voices were muted under the roar of the engine, the wind in my ears, and the slap of the water on the hull.

"What are you doing? Sit down," Adrian barked.

"It's fine, I'm doing my job. I'm watching the tube," Jon yelled back.

"You never stand in a moving boat," Adrian yelled back, "because you never know when you'll hit a wake and..."

"Relax, grandmaaaaaaah..." I felt the movement of the boat change, heard a thunk and then Jon's voice fading. My eyes popped open as Adrian yelled.

Josh cut the engine. I shot my gaze in all directions. Blood trailed off the back edge of the boat. Jesse had abandoned his tube to begin swimming toward Jon who acted confused and bewildered. Jesse tried dragging the tube but it slowed him down. I paused another moment in indecision and then dove off the side. Jesse would never make it in time. I carved my way through the water.

I paused to check my position relative to Jon and saw him floundering and swinging his head from me to Jesse probably hoping it wouldn't be me who reached him first. *Too bad, Dude. The guy you hate for no reason is gonna save your sorry ass.* I looked into Jon's wild eyes and the thought struck me that he was just as afraid of me as he was of drowning.

"Relax. I've got you," I said as I came in behind him. "Tilt your chin up and look at the sky."

Jesse continued his approach slowly as Josh carefully brought the boat closer. Adrian and Joel were ready at the side. Josh cut the engine and waited while Jesse and I helped Jon with the tube so he could catch his breath before we loaded him onto the boat. I figured he'd feel safer if he didn't have to hold onto me any longer than necessary. Jesse and I carefully pulled Jon over to the swimming platform where Adrian and Joel grabbed him under the

25

arms to pull him up to sit for a moment. Josh helped his brother into the boat. I waited, holding onto the rail as I treaded water.

"Come on Jon, let's get you in," Adrian said with a nod to the guys. They helped him and I swung myself up. The triplets were busy digging out a blanket, a first aid kit and a life vest to use as a pillow. Adrian spoke softly to Jon as I approached.

"Nnnnot him," Jon stuttered when I started to look him over.

"Don't be dumb," Adrian and Joel snarled together.

"Yeah," Josh added, "he's the best medic we've got."

"Besides, I hate blood," Jesse added with an appropriate cringe.

Jon's eyes skittered all around and then settled on me. "You won't… won't hurt me?"

Adrian and I looked at each other and then at Jon.

"Why would I hurt you?" I asked in my most soothing voice.

His eyes widened yet he kept his mouth shut. *Yeah, that's right; we both know you've got reason to wonder.*

"You find any damage, Aid?" I asked trying to keep the edge from my voice.

"Just a bump and a little blood."

"I saw blood on the side of the boat," I said as I continued to look Jon over.

"Bet that's where he hit his head," Joel added.

"I'm right here you know and thanks, I'm fine. If you'd given me a sec I'd have made it back on my own," Jon snapped, switching from scared to prickly in an instant.

"You're welcome," I snapped back.

Something warm touched my foot. I glanced at it and saw blood. Another drop splashed on the first. I threw back the blanket to get a better look. Jon had split open his shin. It wasn't bad enough to need stitches, but it did need to be cleaned up and bandaged. His time in the water would be cut off until it scabbed. Maybe he could practice sitting in a moving boat or better yet, remain at camp. I went to work on the wound.

The triplets looked at each other and then everywhere except at the two of us. By silent unanimous agreement they readied the boat and headed for the dock.

"What are you doing? It's still early." Jon groused.

"Need fuel for the boat," Josh said expressionlessly.

"Thanks a lot Jesse," Jon replied sullenly.

"It's Josh," he snapped back with a clenched jaw.

"Whatev," Jon replied sarcastically.

I worked hard at keeping my face neutral. The guys might be triplets but they had never tried to look exactly alike. Their hair was cut different and each was enough his own person that they weren't hard to tell apart or maybe I just paid better attention.

Back at the dock Adrian and I headed to camp to begin dinner prep while the triplets took care of their boat. Jon sat off to the side and watched them, not helping anybody.

In my head all I could think was... *day two*. As the rest of us worked, I glanced over at Jon now and then. He had remained so still for so long that I had ceased to watch until I realized something felt different. I looked over to Jon but he was gone.

"Hey, Aid, where'd Jon go?"

"What do you mean? He's right over... Oh." Adrian lurched to his feet. "Joel!" he yelled as he jogged over toward the guys. I couldn't understand a word from this distance but I could see hand-waving and shrugs.

Adrian jogged back toward me. "He's gone. No one saw him leave, but he won't go far. He left his cell on the boat and he's only wearing flip-flops, and a swim shorts. He even left his towel behind. Where would he go anyway?"

"Girls," we said simultaneously.

He didn't show until the rest of us had started serving dinner. He sat at the end furthest from me, making no eye contact and saying nothing. Finally I couldn't stand it anymore. "You really should ice your head," I said just loud enough for him to hear.

He glared at me.

"Trust me, it helps – personal experience."

Still he ignored me.

I sighed, got up and activated one of the insta-icepacks from my first aid kit that White Eagle insisted I keep around. We always took a full kit camping and had smaller ones in each vehicle and also one in a compartment on my bike. White Eagle and Saul could even do field surgery with those kits. Fortunately that wasn't the kind of help that Jon needed because I'm not that talented. I looked at Jon's eyes and his pupils looked okay though he smelled like beer. I handed him the icepack and then some ibuprofen and a Coke.

"Thanks, Mother," he said sarcastically.

"You're gonna be fine," I sighed and then I started cleaning up. I figured if I was working I wouldn't have to see him glaring at me.

"I need a drink," he whined.

I ignored him and kept working.

He tried again, "Maybe a cute nurse who's willing to do all the heavy lifting and a fifth."

The other guys laughed a little but kept up with their card game while Josh and Joel finished their last bites of food.

"Play a hand, Owen and we'll help you after," Josh offered.

"No thanks, I'd rather clean now."

Josh opened his mouth again but Adrian shook his head at him. He knew my moods.

I finished cleaning and wandered down by the water. I sat looking over the lake as the sun went down. Coming on this outing had been a mistake. Since I hadn't been thinking about how long I'd stay when I left, I was forced to wander back to our campsite before it was too dark to see. The guys already had a couple of propane lamps lit. We'd hung them from our canopy when we'd set up camp. As the sun left, the temperature dropped with a surprising quickness so I changed into jeans and a long-sleeved shirt. I fell into one of our camp chairs and watched the flames of our campfire flicker and dance. When I relaxed my eyes I could see the light streak out like starbursts. I was content to listen to the night sounds and soft conversation of the guys as I tried to clear my mind, but I was interrupted by giggling.

"Hey boys. Hey, Jon, are we on time?"

"You bet! I almost died today, so now I know I gotta live life to the fullest!"

"No matter how short that may be," I grumbled.

"Oh come on, Owen. Loosen up a little. Let's party," Joel said.

I shrugged and flashed a smile. The girls settled into the open seating and a new hand of cards commenced. Jon and Adrian dug out the makings for s'mores, chips, M&Ms, and cans of soda. The girls opened their bag and pulled out beer, pretzels and more chips. Two of the girls snuggled up close to Jon. Both had their hands on him. Now I knew for sure where he'd been this afternoon.

A brunette in a U of O sweatshirt, jeans and Keds offered me a Coors.

"No thanks, I'm good," I said, grinding my teeth.

"Yeah, too good," Jon sneered. "Unwind and have a little fun."

"You're gonna get us kicked out," I hissed.

"So what? Like I said, life is short, live a little."

"I can have plenty of fun without being stupid," I nearly snarled.

"Owen," Adrian warned.

I shook my head and grabbed a Coke before settling back into my chair. The girl to my left began roasting marshmallows and tried to start up a conversation. I answered her questions but didn't ask any of my own so she turned to talk to Jesse who'd plopped down on the other side of her. He was much more forthcoming and welcoming.

Jon's voice over at the picnic table was gaining in volume as he consumed his second beer since the ladies had arrived. There was only one group close to us and they were having their own fun so I guessed we were okay so far. As Jon's voice grew in volume and his lies more outrageous, I began to grind my teeth some more.

"Jon, seriously!" I barked in a low menacing tone.

"What's your problem?"

"You."

"Bring it," he growled, sounding tough.

Everyone turned to look at me, our campsite suddenly silent. "Have all the fun you want, Jon. I'm going for a walk so I don't spoil it."

"Yeah, that's it. Walk away," Jon slurred.

I grabbed a flashlight off the edge of the table and stalked away. I knew there would be another Facebook post about me shortly. I sighed and headed for a trail, any trail. I hadn't gone far when I heard a twig snap behind me.

The girl with the U of O sweatshirt was following me.

"You're the quiet one. I like that."

"I think you may have the wrong idea."

"It's still summer. You should loosen up and have a little fun, like your friends said."

"I am having fun."

"Not enough," she said moving closer.

"What do you think I'm missing?"

"Me."

"I have a girlfriend."

"She's not here."

"It doesn't matter."

"It does. What she doesn't know won't hurt her."

"I love her. I would never hurt her like that."

"She doesn't have to know."

"I would know. I'm a one girl kind of guy. Please go," I said firmly.

"Too bad. We could have had fun. She's lucky to have you. Jon was sure you'd cave."

"Jon put you up to this?" Even I could hear the anger in my voice.

"It was just a joke, okay?"

"You need better friends."

"My friends are fine. I think you need to look at yours," she replied, sounding a little mad herself.

"Jon is not my friend. We share some friends."

"What is it with you two? You both seem nice enough, but get you together and it's like a flame to fuel."

"We just can't find common ground I guess. Why do you care anyway?"

"I'm not what you think. I was just supposed to see if I could get you to kiss me and flirt a little. Jon likes your girlfriend and wanted to send her some pictures. I see now that you're not that kind of guy. I'm sorry. Okay? I'll play nice. Can I just walk with you? I promise I won't make trouble and I'll tell the others to leave you alone too."

"I guess. I'm Owen. What's your name?"

"I'm Fey and I know who you are. Jon may be an ass, but he did admit that you saved him today. Is it true?"

"What did he say?" I asked, feeling curious.

"He said he stood up and fell overboard and that you were the guy who jumped in to pull him to the boat. He said he'd hit his head and cut his leg."

"And you ladies let him have beer?" I stopped walking to stare at her.

"Not me - that was Jenny. She finds him strangely attractive somehow."

"But you don't."

"I have an older brother just like him. I don't need a one night stand, nor do I need that kind of trouble."

"Me either."

We laughed and walked on. We stopped and looked at the lake as the last of the light crept out of the evening, turning it to full night. She told me about University of Oregon and I told her she should talk to Adrian because he really wanted to go there. We talked about growing up in Portland and our favorite restaurants and then we wandered back to camp.

Fey smiled at me and then went over to sit by Joel. I took my seat by the campfire, gave it a stir, added a log and went back to watching the flames. I caught movement at the table. Jon was glaring at Fey who was shaking her head. A small smile touched my lips but I looked away before Jon could catch me.

I checked my watch. After being shushed once by our neighbors my friends and our visitors quieted down but the girls stuck around. Just after midnight the two sitting on either side of him took a wobbly Jon away with them. The triplets were all talking to a girl and so was Adrian, but I really hadn't seen him flirt much so Brenda must mean more to him than I'd guessed. I went and brushed my teeth. When I came back no one was in sight but Adrian was setting up his sleeping bag in my tent. I raised my eyebrows at him.

"Who knew? I have this great opportunity and all I can think about is Brenda. I wish she was here."

"I'm glad to hear you say that, Adrian."

"I've liked lots of girls but none of them were her. I don't know where this thing with us is going but I don't want to be the one to wreck it."

"Good thinking. Now sleep off those beers you drank or I'm not letting you out on the water."

Adrian smiled. "I can't believe you haven't killed Jon yet."

"Can't say I haven't thought about it."

We laughed and then we slept.

It was no surprise I was the first one up. I went through the same routine as the day before except now I was serving coffee to three ladies, the triplets and Adrian. Jon was a no show but this time I wasn't going looking. Fey wandered by as I was dishing up breakfast. She looked like she could use coffee too.

"Did you forget to sleep last night?" I asked with a smile.

She gave me a fantastic stink-eye and propped her elbow on the table to rest her chin on her hand. "Too um… noisy," she said sounding disgusted.

I snorted. "Funny, it was quiet here."

"Maybe folks here had less alcohol and have a little more respect and self-value."

She had said it with such a straight face that I couldn't help laughing out loud. "I like you Fey, my first impression was totally wrong."

She grinned at me. "Yeah, mine too. You're not the tight ass I thought you were."

"No, not a tight ass - Adrian will tell you I'm a…"

"Goody-two shoes," Adrian and I finished together and we all laughed a little as the coffee began to do its job.

Fey and her friend Kendra stayed to help clean up while the other two ladies left to take showers. When our camp was all spiffed up and all the recycling and garbage taken care of, we headed over to the girls' camp where the fire pit was cold and only one lady was up, looking at it dismally. Fey and Kendra left for showers and their two freshly showered friends helped Josh and me set up their camp again. In ones and twos, the rest of girls crawled out but there was no sign of Jon. I was just about to get worried when a snuffling snore erupted from the largest tent.

A huge smile split my face. I pulled out my phone and activated the camera feature. Fey, Josh and Kendra gave me huge grins. Fey helpfully held back the flap. I was about to snap and thought better of it. I tossed a piece of clothing over Jon's privates and then snapped my picture. The drool running from the corner of his mouth had to be my favorite part.

I got his email address from Josh and sent the photo only to Jon with the message that cyber-bullying wasn't okay and to play nice or I'd turn him in. I suggested that he not make any more Facebook posts about me or anyone else. I did not include another threat of any kind in case he decided to turn me in. I guessed he wouldn't with the pink eyelet shirt over his crotch and an aqua bra still wrapped in his fingers. I just hoped he'd remembered to put a helmet on that soldier because more little Jons running around would be a great tragedy.

Day three and I was feeling better already.

THREE

Jon hung out with the girls the rest of the day. I was surprised they'd have him, but I was not-so-secretly glad. I gave up my boat privileges so that the triplets could take the girls instead. I worked on the last of my summer's homework and thought of Lucie. Fey hung out with me for a while and we tried some of the trails in the daylight. Adrian and another girl joined us so that someone else could go on the boat.

I was ready to go home. Jon didn't join us for dinner or even sleep at our campsite. I repeated my ritual from the day before. Fey met me at her fire pit where she had it started and handed me coffee for a change. "You're a nice guy, Owen. It's been great getting to know you. Lucie is a lucky girl. I'm really sorry that I fell for Jon's lies and tried to trick you."

"It's okay, he's quite the salesman."

"He's good looking too, but it's all show with nothing underneath. He's jealous of you, you know."

"He'll figure out that he doesn't need to be."

"Maybe," she said. She stood and walked over to a tent. She silently opened the zipper and slipped inside. She was back in less than two minutes with a cell phone. "It's Jon's and I don't trust him. Will you look and wipe out anything that shouldn't be on it?"

I looked into her eyes and could tell she was worried. She cared about her friends. I took the phone. It was locked. I channeled Marlo and thought about what I knew about Jon. I had it open in only three tries. Other than inappropriate pictures it was pretty clean. He hadn't posted any of them, so I wiped the pictures, turned on his GPS, and sent Marlo a text from my phone so that he could capture all Jon's phone information. This guy would be on my radar for as long as I could keep him there. He wasn't the biggest threat out there but he was going to be a problem - I'd bet my Kawasaki on it. The tent rustled. Fey caught her breath but her friend Traci stepped out. Fey tossed the phone back in the tent while her back was turned and then came and sat innocently by me.

"You look good here for the time being. I'm going to go see what I can get ready to go at our camp site. I'm sure I'll see you again before we all leave."

"I hope I see you again after camping. You can never have too many friends," Fey replied with a smile.

"Thanks, Fey."

I went back to our camp where Adrian was finishing up breakfast dishes and Joel was taking down a tent. Jesse wandered back into camp and started rolling sleeping bags in the next tent. Josh grumbled a little as he came out of the third tent. He got a big smooch from the lady who followed him out. He watched her longingly as she flounced down the road back to her own camp. His brothers started laughing; he blushed. Adrian and I joined in on the laughter.

We had camp cleaned up and nearly all the gear stowed by the time Jon appeared looking rumpled and lost.

"Where's my stuff?" he asked, sounding confused.

Jesse gave him a not so friendly smile and threw it at him a little harder than he needed to.

"I'll uh, go take a shower, grab a bite and then help," Jon said sounding almost sheepish.

"You do that," Joel grumbled and then left with Josh to finish getting the boat ready for the trip home.

We had to check out even though Jon had not returned. We waited in the parking area. Jon took so long in the shower, that he ended up not helping at all and we had to wait for him so we could leave. I handed him coffee in a travel mug and a granola bar. We loaded up the last of his stuff and headed for home. This time Jon got the way-back and slept all the way home. We dropped him off first and then the rest of us went over to the triplets' house to wash and stow their boat. I guess they didn't want Jon's help though nobody said a word about it. We helped them unload their gear and settled up on the remaining cash.

Next we took all the gear from the shop over to the back room and set it up in the empty bay to dry and be spot cleaned. I asked the guys to leave me at Lucie's house. I thanked them all and smiled. "Well guys, it was… memorable. Thanks for having me along."

At least my comment was met with laughter. "Thanks for your help, Superman," Josh smiled.

"And remember," Joel threw in, "what happens at Detroit Lake, stays at Detroit Lake."

"Until those ladies call you," I flipped back.

I slammed my door, grabbed my gear and headed up the driveway. Jesse tooted the horn and started to roll forward.

As I walked up the driveway, the front door burst open and Lucie ran out. She lunged at me, giving me a huge hug.

"How was your weekend?"

"Okay, I guess."

Adrian interrupted. "Okay? Okay? He was amazing."

Lucie gave me a hard look. Adrian laughed, pounded the side of the Suburban and Jesse pulled away, beeping again as he drove off.

"I don't want to talk about it," I mumbled.

"Yes, you do," Lucie said gently.

I sighed. Her irritation melted into sympathy. If she could have just stayed mad, I would have been okay. Lucie moved in and hugged me again. I caved. "I met a new guy; he's a friend of Adrian's and the triplets'. He tried to push me into a bunch of stuff. He opened his yap to piss me off, tried to get me drunk and even found a girl for me. I'm not interested in that crap. He thinks I'm a kid. We know I'm not. Anyway, I gave into his verbal prodding. I know better. I just can't seem to control... you know... the heat and anger that flashes through me. Kraeghton still has too much leverage. I made Jon's nose bleed without even touching him." I paused and sighed. "On the flip side, he fell overboard and almost drowned. It was the old Owen who pulled him out. Kraeghton thought I should let him drown." I paused again. "I'll own that – the hesitation, but I did pull him out."

Lucie kissed me. She should have been angry. She was doing it again, she'd connected to me. I knew she was doing it to help me beat back Kraeghton, but she was causing my temperature to rise for a whole other reason that had nothing to do with anger. She wanted to help, but she needed to be more careful when I was like... this. Miles and I were so much alike and nearly always saw eye to eye but Kraeghton was a whole other beast - beast, being the operative word.

"Luce," I breathed, unsteadily.

She ignored me and came closer yet. My brain shut off and all I could do was... feel... every part of her pressing into me. I drew in a deep shuddering breath – mistake – she moved her lips to my neck and I was lost. Lucie's hands pulled my hips into her. *Driveway. You're in front of Lucie's house. But Lucie...* I ran my hands over her and my other voices vanished. No Miles and no Kraeghton, just me and her.

"Now that's what I call making up," Alex interrupted.

"Go away Alex," I huffed.

"Can't, we've got work to do."

Lucie pushed away from me but gave me a dazzling smile. "Later," she whispered and then she smiled at my brother.

"He hasn't even made it home yet. How'd you know he was here?"

"The Suburban," Alex replied with a *duh* kind of look.

"So what is this work?" I asked him.

"We get to do some heavy lifting. Max cleaned out an estate sale in Northeast Portland. He just pulled up at the shop in a U-Haul and claims he needs us all over there like five minutes ago. You'd think he would've called before he left the sale. Besides," he added dropping his voice, "Dad says you're not staying here – alone – with her."

Busted. Had he seen us? "Isn't this the guy who was handing out condoms a few months ago?"

"Pretty sure. Not that I've had use for mine."

"I would hope not!" Lucie huffed indignantly.

"Come on Luce, I'm in eighth grade, I'm not a child."

"Yes, you are. Don't you dare fool around with girls. You're too young. I want you to keep your pants zipped until you're at least seventeen and maybe older."

"Are you my example?" he asked wiggling his eyebrows.

"Not that it's any of your business, Nosey, but yes, I can still be your example."

"The way you were kissing him, that won't last long."

"Alex! You can't... don't talk to Lucie like that!"

"What? She's the only sister I've got. Who else am I gonna ask girl questions? Not our parents. They're old. Besides, she can hold her own."

I was speechless but Lucie laughed. "Okay Alex, enough about this subject for now. Let's get to the shop and burn some of this... energy out of you. When you have an appropriate question, I'll answer it."

Alex grinned at me and I couldn't help but smile back. Just what I needed – my girlfriend giving my brother *the talk.*

~ ~ ~

Alex was right. It looked like Max had cleaned out the entire estate; just looking at the jam-packed back of the truck made me sigh. I didn't have a clue where'd we put all of it. Max was in a hurry to get the U-Haul back before he had to pay any more for it. Max and Adrian had it partially unloaded by the time Alex, Lucie and I showed up to help. We threw open the bay door at the back of the shop and went to work on all the camping gear to get it out of the way so we could move our new acquisitions in. Between customers White Eagle lent a hand. Mom and Lucas showed up and were a big help. Before we were done with the camping gear Max and Adrian took off to return the U-Haul.

Marlo took the quieter moment with everyone busy to tell me what he'd learned about Jon. Lucie came over, listened to my story of the weekend and soon Adrian, who'd returned with his uncle, added his two cents worth.

"I'm sorry. I feel like this is my fault. He's been curious about you ever since he came to Milwaukie. I thought maybe if he got to know you... I didn't think it would be a big deal to camp with him. He moved here last year during baseball season. The triplets and I had some classes with him and hung out a few times this summer. I guess I didn't know him as well as I thought. I just thought he was trying to get to know people around here; not cause trouble and knock you down so that he could be top tough guy."

"It's okay Adrian, but just so you know - I'm going to be watching him from now on."

"I figured."

"Did you get to see Brenda?" Lucie asked, changing the subject.

"I was just getting to that when I got hijacked by my uncle."

"Invite her over here. She can help and we don't have to talk shop around her," Lucie said kindly. "We're just finishing the camping gear anyway."

Adrian smiled at her and started texting. He'd barely finished when his phone rang. We just smiled at him so that he knew it was okay if he wandered off to talk to Brenda. Lucie, Alex, Marlo and I began moving the heavy furniture into the bay now that the camping gear was put away. When we got to the dining room table, we froze. All four of us had touched it at nearly the same time and it had something to tell us.

A splash of red wax. A dark candle dripped and oozed. A burning flame. A ring of dried herbs. Black fabric with gold painted symbols. Bone and blood. More symbols in chalk or ash. *What was this?* Images, sound and feeling flooded us. Marlo dropped to his knees. I knew how overwhelmed he felt. We had all been through this at some point, but Marlo usually did the recording and rarely experienced events first hand like Lucie, Alex and I did.

Lucas came out into the sunshine but stopped cold. His expression and body language flipped from joyful to concerned in the beat of a heart. "What's wrong with Marlo?"

"Fine, I'm fine. I ah, got overheated. I must not be drinking enough water," he answered with a crooked smile for my brother.

Marlo rose to his feet as Lucie went for water. He and I shared a look.

"Lucas, lend a hand would you? Let's get this piece inside," I said more to distract him than anything.

He took Lucie's spot and we started to move toward the bay door. Lucas had a funny look on his face. Lucie came up and hip bumped Marlo, trying to hand him the water and relieve him of his position.

"No, no that's okay. Maybe you should help Lucas," he said with a flip of his head to get her to pay attention. One look and Lucie was quickly over by my little brother.

"Hey, Friend, what's up?" she asked him.

"I don't like this table."

"Really, Lucas? Why not? It's kind of pretty with lots of nice carvings."

"The carvings may be nice but the table isn't."

I couldn't laugh that one off. He was right. "Why do you say that, Lucas?"

He gave me a look. "Seriously? Marlo saw something, didn't he? I mean, if even *I* can feel it then it had to hurt you guys."

We all looked at him.

"I know, okay? Get over it. I'm tired of pretending I don't know about you guys. I know you try to keep things from me and I'm not one of you yet, but I know I will be. Why do you think our cat loves me so much?"

I looked at him dumbfounded. I hadn't thought about it. Ron did seem to like him more than anybody else at our house these days and Beggar, our dog, spent more and more time in Lucas's room, though it was clear she was still Mom's dog. "What are you saying exactly?"

"If I was anybody else I would think it was a coincidence, but with a family like ours I have to assume I'm gonna be one of you. This sounds nuts but I understand Ron. It's like I can almost read his mind."

In any normal situation, people would have laughed, but not here and not now.

"Okay Lucas, I give up. I'm tired."

"Owen, no!" Marlo and Lucie said together.

"You won't like it," Alex added. "It's not nearly as cool as I thought and sometimes it's scary."

"I know, but I'd rather know and be included when I can and not be left to wonder. I have a pretty good imagination and sometimes that's worse than… well, the real thing, you know?" he exclaimed showing his excitement. To him it was still just a game.

"Yeah, we know," I replied glumly. "Let's get to it. Pull up a chair Luke, but if it gets to be too much you have to go up front and find something else to do."

Lucas rubbed his hands together. I remembered the good old days when he got that excited over Marla Saggio's cake.

Marlo looked at Lucas and back at me, his lips compressed. I nodded at him and he finally spoke, "I think it *is* black magic, voodoo, or both. I recognize it from gaming; Dungeons and Dragons, Call of Cthulhu and shows like *Supernatural* all have images like we saw. Just seeing that stuff, a normal person would think it was nothing, but we all felt that dark energy, even Lucas.

It was really powerful. The only dark magic that I can imagine being that strong is blood magic."

"So you're saying, in your expert opinion, that blood magic is real?" I had a hard time keeping the sarcasm out of my voice.

White Eagle came into the bay to see what was taking so long. He must have overheard. He looked around at us and then focused on me. "Most people wouldn't believe that *you're real* either and yet here you are."

"We're not trained for this," I grated, really beginning to feel fear.

Lucie took my hand. "I bet Evilia is or… what about Kraeghton? That thing of his you broke…" she walked away from me and over to where we kept Kraeghton's amulet or whatever it was. She handed it to Marlo who promptly dropped it.

"I don't really know anything about this stuff but I feel it." Marlo's normally calm and confident voice came out panicky and tight. "That thing of Kraeghton's feels like the table. It gives me major creeps."

Lucie looked determined. "How could we sense the table like we did without touching each other?"

"Maybe it's the nature of the table?" Alex suggested.

"Keep thinking. I'm going to check the other pieces. I'll have your mom tend the shop so we can figure this out. And Lucas, maybe you better wait in the shop with your mom."

"No way, White Eagle. I'm in with my brothers on this one. I game and watch *Supernatural* too. I can help."

White Eagle gave him a long steady look, jerked around like he'd heard something and then hurried over to shut the bay door with a bang. He turned back to us looking grim. "The folks behind us were in their backyard. I pray they thought you were just kids talking about computer games or didn't hear you at all."

What could we say? He was right. We needed to be more careful and we knew better. Wasn't that why we'd finally gotten around to replacing the back curtain with an actual door over the summer?

Marlo took the bull by the horns. "I doubt they'd believe a single thing they may have heard so why speculate. What's done is done. I know one thing for sure... I hate feeling that stuff like you guys do. It was that jolt of malice more than the images that got to me."

"Evilia," Alex jumped in, "she has that feeling about her."

"I'm sorry, Alex. I forget how much she's hurt you. Here you are treated like a kid but she took that away from you. You haven't been a child for a long time."

"It's okay, Marlo. You guys have always been... you've been my friends even though you're really Owen's friends."

Lucie moved over to hug him while he and I shared a look. I knew how he felt. I'd been there back before I'd confided in Adrian, back when only Marlo knew about me. It hurt, lying to your friends about who you really were, but we all knew how dangerous this life was.

"Now," Alex said getting back to business, "touchy-feely time is over. Let's get this bad boy recorded and start some investigating."

"Yeah," Lucas enthused.

Marlo started laughing. "This really is *Supernatural* 'cause Alex is sounding like Dean."

"Never disrespect Dean Winchester! He's my hero. I love *Supernatural*," Alex exclaimed very seriously and then looked at Marlo from under his brows and quoted his self-proclaimed hero, "We know a little about a lot of things; just enough to make us dangerous."

"Ain't that the truth," Lucie added.

I decided to bring the situation back to reality. "Before we all panic or worse and start thinking we're no longer part of the real world, let's think: this table holds evil but we don't know for sure that it is evil magic."

"What?" Alex sounded frustrated.

"How can you of all people..." Lucie cut in.

"Magic is cool," Lucas added.

"I don't want to believe it, but..." Marlo said at the same time.

White Eagle chuckled. All voices stopped as we turned to look at him. "I see what you're doing there," he said with a smile for me.

Acid churned in my stomach. I swallowed and focused on White Eagle. The smile slid off his face. "Or not," he added.

"I'm afraid – petrified, really. I'm not Harry Potter or even a Winchester. I never thought this stuff was real. I don't want it to be real."

"Whether or not it's real is beside the point. Other people believe that voodoo and black magic are real so now our job is to find out everything we can about this table and research all the images it showed you. Then we will decide what to do next," White Eagle said, using his sensei voice.

"Yes, White Eagle," we replied as one.

I bent and picked up the trinket Marlo had dropped. It was unnaturally warm but not uncomfortable.

Marlo watched me. "That thing gives me the creeps."

"There's something about it. It's almost like it whispers to me." I stared at it willing it to communicate.

"What are you doing?" Lucie asked. "Hoping it will start talking to you."

"Yeah, I am."

Everyone else grabbed a computer and set to work. I continued to stare at the pieces in my hand. I closed my fist around them and squeezed. A burst of pain shot through my palm and… *suddenly I was standing outside a rundown motel. The Twin Pines Inn looked like it had been built in the 1940s or 50s and had never been remodeled. It was a one-story, sixteen unit, drive-up affair. After market A/C units had been sloppily added and the stripes in the parking lot were in serious need of paint. I glanced back towards the sign where the "y" in vacancy was burned out and one of the two pines from which the establishment had taken its name was clearly dead. Kraeghton pulled his hat low over his eyes and shrugged his duffle higher on his shoulder.*

He pushed open the door to the office and took two steps to the desk. A wizened old man looked up and squinted through thick bifocals.

"Yes?" he wheezed.

"A room for three nights. I don't want maid service. I like my privacy. I want to be as far from everyone else as possible." I felt the burn of Kraeghton's gift.

"Yes, sir. No service. Do not disturb."

He pulled out a driver's license and a credit card. As he did, I caught a glimpse. The photo was of a white haired man with glasses. The height was listed as 5'9" and the weight at 145lbs. It was so clearly not Kraeghton that I wanted to laugh and run at the same time.

The myopic clerk looked up at us and blinked in the dim light. I felt Kraeghton's power surge. "Remember, I like my privacy."

"Yes, sir. Make, model and license of your car?"

"I won't be parking here."

The clerk stared at us for a full minute. "Room 16, far end. No car, huh? How'd you get here?"

"You're not interested in me."

The clerk blinked. Who'd Kraeghton think he was? A Jedi or something?

"Have a nice stay." The clerk picked up a newspaper dated October 9, 1983 and resumed reading.

Kraeghton walked to his room and looked around before entering. Once inside he dead-bolted the door and closed the drapes. Finally he unloaded the contents of the duffle onto the room's only table. He felt satisfied as he looked at the array of items, but I was confused until I registered the small decorative vile that lay broken in my hand in my reality.

He lit a black candle and sliced his arm with a silver knife, letting the blood drip into a silver bowl. He sprinkled some herbs and whispered an incantation I could neither really hear nor understand. He picked up a small piece of parchment on which the ink appeared to squiggle as he lit it from the black candle and let the burned bits fall into the blood mixture. What had once been so dark it was almost black, flashed to brilliant red. Kraeghton was suddenly excruciatingly weak. It took all the energy he had to pour the blood into the vile, cap it and then seal it before he passed out. I could feel myself falling.

When I hit the floor I was too weak to do anything but lay there for a moment. Lucie and Alex helped me to sit up, but I still felt light-headed and almost dizzy. Alex peeled my fingers from Kraeghton's talisman. Then he tipped my hand and the pieces spilled into a Zip-loc bag Marlo held open. Lucie took my other hand. I watched Marlo set the bag by his computer and pull out the first aid kit. He handed it to Alex and stepped back. Alex gave him a questioning look.

"I don't do blood," Marlo exclaimed, blanching.

Lucie giggled, "With Accident Man, here – you'd better learn to deal, bro."

Alex poured the wash over my hand and Lucie gave it a serious looking over. "Well, I've seen worse. I don't think you need stitches and I don't see any glass. The liquid bandage is gonna hurt."

"What happened to you?" Alex asked me as he dabbed at the cuts.

"Kraeghton's talisman was showing me… something."

The three of them looked at me expectantly.

"Where's Lucas?" I asked instead.

"Mom took him home to help fix dinner," Alex answered and then reminded me. "About the talisman?"

"I saw how it was… OUCH!" Lucie snuck up on me and had begun swiping on the liquid bandage. I tried to pull away but she held fast, blew on it and added more. I gritted my teeth. "I saw how it was made."

"Why didn't it talk to you before?" Marlo asked this time. Before I could answer he answered himself. "It was your blood wasn't it. It was blood magic and it needed blood to… to reactivate it." He shuddered.

"Black magic," Lucie added.

"Yes, I think it was."

"Has it been there all along but it took the table for us to see it? Because as far as we can tell, the table had nothing to do with Kraeghton." Alex contemplated aloud.

"Maybe," I answered. "Why can't Kraeghton just work with me like Miles does?"

"Lucky I guess," Lucie said sarcastically.

"Yeah, that's it," Alex threw in. "You're cosmically lucky."

"What about the table? Anything?" I asked, wishing something would go our way.

"It's a bust. It was purchased in 1942 and has stayed with the same family. Now we need to look at the family," Marlo answered.

"Whether or not we or anyone else believes in dark magic, someone has done bad things and needs to be stopped." Lucie was taking her new leadership role seriously.

"Agreed," we replied.

Then Alex added under his breath, "Yay. More research."

"What are you complaining about?" Marlo asked. "I, for one, love research."

Alex rolled his eyes. "Of course you do."

Blood dripped off my hand. Lucie took it again, her lips pressed into a thin line. I took a paper towel from the kit and gave my hand a swipe.

Max popped his head through the inner door, wearing a huge grin. "Wonderful news... the table has sold as is. Open the bay and get ready to load."

"No!" we all shouted at once.

Max looked taken aback. "Why not?"

"It's broken," I lied.

"Doesn't matter. As is, is as is."

"But we haven't finished research..." Marlo began but I interrupted.

"He means refinishing it."

Lucie's voice overlapped mine, "We need to finish authenticating it so you get the best price."

"What is wrong with you kids? The buyer is paying $3000. Now load it up."

I tried one last time. "What did White Eagle say?"

"I don't understand why you're acting so weird. He's the one doing the paperwork."

I felt my eyebrows go up. So much for my poker face. We all looked at each other as the door swished shut, and shrugged. Questions bounced around in my head and I'd bet my next pay-check I wasn't alone, but we moved the table into position and reopened the bay door. The neighbors were nowhere in sight and all was quiet at the back for the moment.

"Where's Adrian?" I couldn't believe it took me until now to notice his absence.

Lucie smiled at me. "He went to see Brenda. She was just finishing her shift at the mall."

"Did someone photograph the table?" Now that my brain was working, it was in overdrive.

"Of course," Alex responded giving me the look you'd give someone who's not all there.

I threw him a half smile. I lifted my end of the table and the others jumped in so we could move it outside. I almost dropped it when an unfamiliar wave of darkness brushed over my skin. All my hair stood on end and I suppressed a shudder.

The unmarked panel truck backed to a stop a few yards from us. The emaciated driver stepped around the back. His hair was thinning and his eyes reminded me of… death. He opened the back of the truck with a hand covered in long thin scars crisscrossing all over like a crazy road map. He reminded me strongly of an old-fashioned undertaker, right down to the smell. Who in today's world would release a puff of formaldehyde and mothballs? Maybe it was the white shirt, stark against the black of suit that gave the feeling. The modern slim cut trousers made him look even more skeletal, but it was the eyes that drew me back. This man was no ordinary mortal.

Marlo had taken a step back. This man was no *watcher* but he was definitely dark. The sensation was emanating from him. There was no mistaking it.

"Well? Are you all going to stare or load my table?"

His words seemed to break the spell. We positioned the table behind the truck. White Eagle came out to help. Alex and I held steady while the other three lifted the end. Then Marlo and Lucie held it steady, while we lifted and pushed it forward. Lucie and Marlo couldn't seem to get out of the truck fast enough.

"Lovely doing business with you. Until next time." He looked me in the eye as he spoke. We were the same height but I had to have forty pounds on him. His enormous sharp nose stood in stark contrast to his small black eyes. He reached out a bony hand to shake mine, but he turned my hand to look at the palm instead.

"You should be more careful"

I wasn't sure what to say, but he was done. He climbed back in the truck and drove off.

"I don't like it," White Eagle stated, bringing me back to the present. We moved inside and shut the bay door. "That was one fast turnaround and he didn't negotiate. He also way overpaid."

"Maybe it's not our problem?" Marlo hedged.

"It is. I just haven't dealt with it in years. I wish Emeline was still around." He sounded contemplative and then he turned his gaze to me. Now it was his turn to grab my hand and look at it. "Maybe you should ask *him*." No need to ask which him.

"I've tried. He tells me what he wants, when he wants. It's not like with Miles."

White Eagle dropped my hand in disgust. "I don't know what else to do. It's Kraeghton or Bob. Both are bad choices."

"I may hate Bob, but at least I don't fear for my soul," I said, trying to be funny but falling flat.

"Maybe you should," White Eagle returned sounding serious.

"Why the change of heart? You've always backed Sarah and her defense of him."

"I thought Sarah could handle him, but… now… I'm afraid he's using her."

"Now that doesn't surprise me. After what he did to me and Lucie - I think he'd be willing to do anything."

"That's what I'm afraid of," White Eagle said, sounding sad. "Let's get out of here. It's late and some of us have had a long day."

We locked up and went home. I kissed Lucie good night and Alex and I headed to our house. All I could think was… dinner, a little TV, and bed. I was bone-tired and there is nothing like coming home and sleeping in your own bed - not only after camping but after moving six rooms of furniture and household goods - let alone Kraeghton and that darn table.

My room was too quiet and half empty without Mitchell. I'd rearrange it later but right now… sleep. I fell across the bed sideways and was gone.

I could hear branches slapping and the thud of feet. Piper ran past like I wasn't even there. She looked over her shoulder and screamed, tripping as she ran on. I waited another beat and still seeing and hearing nothing behind her, I followed. I could hear Piper panting as she ran. She skidded to a halt at the edge of a cliff and windmilled to keep her balance. She dropped to her knees and I could hear her whispered words, "Jesse, where are you? Help me Jesse." She opened her eyes and looked right through me. "No!" she screamed. I looked to see what she saw but nothing was there. I looked back and the cliff top was empty.

FOUR

I awoke with a start, sweating and breathing heavily. I couldn't put it off any longer - I had to see her. The sight of Bob shoving her into his car and whisking her away as I stood by helplessly was still raw and fresh and now more nightmares. Ever since Kraeghton had darkened my soul I hadn't been the same. I couldn't sleep through the night and the darkness held shadows. I went ahead and wrote up the nightmare for Marlo who would run it through his programs in the morning. Maybe this time he'd find something. We had to find an excuse to go see Piper.

I looked over at the empty half of my room where Mitchell used to live and felt alone. I put my hands over my face for a moment and then moved them to my sides. Breathe. I shed yesterday's clothes and crawled under the covers. Peace. I needed peace.

Marlo had a text waiting for me when I finally got up at ten. There was one last college information session and tour available to high school seniors this coming weekend. Now I just had to figure out how to get away from Lucie for the second weekend in a row and figure out what to do about… wait, that was it. Get her going on the table from one direction and Marlo and I could work on another angle and go up to UDub. God, I was gonna owe Marlo big - maybe bigger than I could ever hope to repay.

Information on the owners of the table, the purchaser and the table's provenance were trickling in. Marlo convinced his parents that a trip to the University of Washington was worth the time. They were hoping for a more prestigious school but Marlo insisted he had a chance at a full-ride academic scholarship. Sold

- one visit. They also bought that my parents were busy and that I was truly interested.

Lucie thought we were investigating relatives of the Wright family who had owned the table and Mitchell and Alex were on board to help her scout out some local family and to learn a little more about the table's buyer.

Marlo's folks picked me up at 6am for the drive up. That early in the morning no one was big on conversation. We parked the car and followed the signs for the open house. I checked my watch for the fiftieth time and went over Piper's schedule again in my head.

Marlo slid me a glance and whispered, "What if I'm wrong and she's fine?"

"Jesse!" Piper practically screamed as she threw herself into my arms. Marlo's parents looked on in utter shock.

"Old friend," Marlo muttered and pulled them away across the commons or as they called it up here, the HUB yard, for the open area by the Husky Union Building.

"Did you get contacts?" Piper asked.

"Owen wears contacts?" Marla asked perplexed as they walked away.

"Long story, Mom. Come on or we'll be late for orientation." Marlo gave her another tug. She gave me one last look and moved away, a wrinkle still stuck between her brows.

"Where is your hearing aid?" Piper continued, "And who were those people?"

"Piper, we need to talk."

"I know a coffee shop not far from here."

"Okay. Lead on."

Piper gave me a dazzling smile and took my hand. We walked without talking. It was a surprisingly nice day for a place that got close to forty inches of the wet stuff each year. Heck, they were known for having even more gray days than we got. We arrived at a cute little coffee shop called of all things, Ugly Mug Café, ordered, and sat.

"Look, Piper, I want to apologize. I thought we'd have time to talk before they took you away."

"I missed you. You're all I think about. I kept waiting for you to find me and here you are." I felt instantly uncomfortable. I had led her on. I was a jerk and worse.

The barista called, "Jesse." It was the name Piper had provided. I went and picked up our coffees, the whole time struggling for what to say. I set down our cups and took a deep breath.

Piper took a sip and smiled at me. "So why no glasses and no hearing aid and why are you here? Not that I'm not happy to see you."

"Piper, I want you to… understand. I was doing what I had to do. I help people. I wanted to tell you before but…"

"I know you help people. I saw that. Did you know they wouldn't let me go to Quentin's funeral? I wanted to see you but they said for my safety that I had to stay here," she interrupted.

"I'm sorry, Piper."

"Quit saying that and tell me what's going on. You look guilty and hurt."

My gut clenched. *Had her coffee cooled enough that when she threw it at me, I wouldn't get scalded?* I took another deep breath and then a sip of my Butterscotch Latte to kill a little time.

"Piper, this will be hard to hear, but here goes. I don't need a hearing aid or glasses. Those were my communications devices to help me to fit in and to find the drug dealers on campus."

"You're an undercover cop?" she asked sounding intrigued.

"No, nothing that exciting."

"I don't understand."

"I'm... uh..." *Oh help - how to tell her?*

"That man wasn't even your dad, was he?" she said, narrowing her eyes.

"No, he's my mentor, coach and friend."

"So, he's the undercover cop." Now she sounded emphatic.

"No, he's not one either."

"Spit it out already."

"I'm trying. There is part I can't tell you, but know that I wanted to see with my own eyes that you were okay and to tell you who I really am. My name is Owen Ryer and I live in Milwaukie. I help people with... with the things they can't fix on their own. I'm part of a group who... rights wrongs."

"Oh well, that answered it all then didn't it." Her voice dripped with sarcasm.

"I care about you, but I can't... I can't be what I think you want."

"What do you know about what I want?"

"I..."

"Then why are you here?" she interrupted again

"I told you, I wanted to be sure you were okay."

"If that was all, you could have called."

"I had to see for myself."

"Don't lie," Piper breathed in a sadly resigned voice with an edge of anger to it. She clutched her bag to her, probably hoping it would protect her.

I gave her a hard look. "Don't you get it? I had to do it. It was my job. Now I'm trying to tell you the truth."

"Why should I believe anything you say?"

"Because deep down, no matter what, you know me, the real me and not the guy I looked like on the outside. I let you in. You're my friend."

"I thought I knew Jesse. I liked Jesse. I don't know who you are."

"Then let's start over. I'm Owen, and I'd like to be your friend."

"Friend... I see." Her eyes looked watery and sad but she had to know.

"Piper, please. I care about you, but you should know that I have a girlfriend. Her name is Lucie. She knows about you. I thought it was only fair for you to know about... us."

"You lied!" she hissed. "How old are you anyway?"

"Almost eighteen, why?"

"You said that you help people. You said that being Jesse was your job. You're too young for that kind of job. I'd think it was a huge practical joke, yet here I am. Mr. Bruner said you worked for him. He implied you were lots older and when I asked to see you... forget it."

"Bruner?"

"Your boss, Bob Bruner. The man who took me away."

"Oh him." *Did she mean Robert "Bob" Bowman?* "He's not exactly my boss."

"He said he was, but it doesn't matter. I don't like him. He asks lots of strange questions and doesn't give direct answers."

"That's him alright."

"I want this to be over. I may not want my old life back but I don't want this one either."

"I don't know when it will be over. Until Caleb Carmichael and his boss are caught, you are in danger."

"I miss my mom. She wasn't much, but she was all I had."

"You have a chance for a whole new life. You can be whoever you want."

"Except I'm not really free. I live with people I hardly know. All friends have to be approved. They monitor the GPS in my phone and watch my laptop. I wouldn't be surprised if they tapped into surveillance everywhere I go. They seem to know an awful lot about me. There are even days that I feel watched and I'm pretty sure they follow me sometimes."

I tried to remain calm and keep up my poker face. "Your testimony is important."

"I'm doing it for Quentin and nobody else," she said, raising her chin. "Why did you tell me about Lucie?"

"You had a right to know about me. I hated leaving things hanging. I felt like I led you on. I wanted to tell you but I didn't get the chance."

"So I was just a job."

"No, Piper. I really do care. I truly believed we were friends. If things were different… maybe we could have been more, but I love Lucie."

Piper's expression turned sad again. "You two are… it's good. You're solid."

"She saved my life once."

"Tell me about it."

"I… I can't."

"It has to do with your job?"

"Yeah." The hair on the back of my neck stood up. Two very angry looking people approached our table.

"You don't belong here," the male agent whispered gruffly as he moved to stand over me. He was good but I knew intimidation tactics too.

"Piper, it's time to go," the female agent said, grasping her arm.

Piper tried to yank her arm away but the burly agent's grip was firm. I met her stormy gray eyes. She was what most people would consider a handsome woman, certainly not beautiful. She had probably been striking once, but now that her dark hair was turning to gray she looked washed out. The male agent looked like he did more office work than field work. Was this what I had to look forward to or would I even live to be their age. Anger burst through me, I could feel Kraeghton taking control. Before I could get myself under control the male agent was clutching his left arm and half falling, half sliding onto the bench next to me. I was so startled that I automatically grabbed him and in the moment I was distracted, the other agent was out the door with Piper. A barista came to see if we were okay.

"I'm fine. Just water please. I don't feel well," the agent said sounding only slightly shaky.

The barista hurried away.

"Are you okay?" I asked, afraid I was the cause.

"Like you care. I've been warned about you, kid. You stay away from Piper or next time I'll shoot you and if you ever pull your *watcher* crap on me again, I'll kill you slowly." He had released his arm, but he felt overly warm without my even touching him and a sheen of sweat now beaded up on his forehead and lip. His color was coming back though.

"What are you talking about?" I asked, half afraid to hear the answer.

The barista slid him the water. He thanked her and chugged it down. She hovered for a second but he waved her off.

"You squeeze my heart like that again and so help me, I will crack open your chest and squeeze yours manually. You understand me?"

"I hear you. Tell your boss I don't like games and I want to be left alone."

He snorted. "I'm leaving. You will wait here five minute before you return to your friends."

"And if I don't?"

"We shoot the caterer."

My jaw dropped open. "Do you even hear yourself? You're supposed to be the good guys."

"Sometimes collateral damage is necessary." With that horrible statement, he left and I sat. I sat for ten minutes just to be sure. It did not stop me from texting Marlo under the table and warning him to be extra careful.

I tipped the barista and walked out half expecting to feel a bullet slide into my body. I moved quickly to get away from the coffee shop and then entered a crowd of students. I pulled off my jacket and turned it inside out. I messed up my hair, rounded my shoulder and affected a limp. I entered the nearest building, found an alcove where I could see out but not be easily seen, and placed a call to White Eagle.

"Hey, how's it going up there?" His voice was so cheerful and enthusiastic I felt my own heart squeeze and it had nothing to do with Kraeghton.

"Not good. I made a terrible mistake."

"Talk to me."

"I sent Marlo and his folks on ahead to the campus tour and I uh…"

"You found her didn't you," he sighed.

"Look, I know I let you down. I just had to see her, to explain, to apologize, to make sure she was okay. I don't know. I guess I was sick of Bob not answering my questions and… I'm sorry. I've made things worse."

"What happened?" A part of me wanted to cry but I sucked it up and told him everything.

White Eagle let me talk and didn't interrupt even once. He paused for so long after I stopped talking that I pulled the phone from my ear to see if I still had a signal.

"Are you still there?" I finally asked.

"I'm here," he said wearily. "I'll always be here. Why don't you go find the Saggios and join them for the rest of the time up there? Try to fit in and look interested. I'd say that was your second warning from Mr. Bob Bowman. I don't recommend a third because I doubt there will be one."

"I was afraid you'd say that."

"I'll talk to Sarah." I could hear his sadness and worry.

"I'm sorry. I really thought it would be okay. I didn't think it was a big deal."

"I understand. Bob does not. Be safe, be smart and for heaven's sake, lock down Kraeghton before he gets you into any more trouble."

"I'll give it hell." I disconnected first, put my phone in my front pocket and turned my jacket back around. I saw a men's room on the way in so I hit it on the way out. I ran my hands through my hair until it was back to almost normal. I looked at myself in the mirror for a moment. *What had happened to the kid I used to be?*

I knew I had a tail five minutes after I hit the HUB yard. I wasn't surprised, so I played it cool, found Marlo and his parents and pretended to pay attention to the orientation, but I really watched the guy in the leather jacket. He kept his eyes on us and not on the speaker, his hat low over his eyes, failing to take it off indoors. I lost him when we walked back to the Saggio's van to do a little sightseeing.

By Pike Place Market I realized he was watching us again and he had a partner. This agent was a woman but her clothes gave her away. She was wearing a blouse and slacks with lace up shoes. I even caught a flash of her badge on her hip. Maybe they wanted me to see them. They stayed with us through dinner. It was way too much of a coincidence to be in the same three places that we were in. When we got into the Saggio's van to go home, I saw them pass by in a dark blue Audi. A few miles down the road I saw the same car behind us. When we hit Olympia they finally turned off.

Marlo kept watching me, saying nothing. I just couldn't bring myself to tell him that Bob's people had threatened his mom.

The Saggios dropped me off and I walked wearily toward our front door. Dad about jumped me when I walked in.

"How did the visit go?"

"Okay"

"Are you going to consider UDub?" he asked sounding enthusiastic.

"Not really."

"Why not?" I could plainly hear his frustration. "You need to do something besides mope. Are you becoming one of those emo kids or something?"

"What? No! Why do you assume I'm not doing anything about my future? Just because I don't want to go to the University of Washington doesn't mean I don't have plans."

"You don't talk to me. How should I know what you're thinking? You need to communicate."

"*I* do? Of course the problem is me," I said sarcastically. I was picking a fight and I knew it, but I was so sick and tired of this kind of crap.

"Don't you take that tone with me!"

I clenched my jaw, trying not to snap. Mom came in from the kitchen. "What's going on?" Of course she sensed the tension in the air.

"Owen just wasted the Saggio's time, wasted a day he could have been working and spent our hard-earned money for no reason."

"Brad, don't be like that, please. Give him a chance to explain."

"Of course you're on his side. He has got to have a plan. He is not going to live with us for the rest of his life. He needs a quality education and a good job," he seethed, then turned his ire back on me. "Once you are eighteen and graduated you are either in school full time with good grades or you are out of here. No exceptions."

"Dad, why do you believe I don't want those things? What makes you think I don't have a plan?"

"You are lackadaisical, your grades are crap, and you're not even playing a sport. You spend all day at the pawn shop and with Lucie. What happened to you?"

"You know what happened," I said through clenched teeth. Mom said nothing. She twisted the dishtowel in her hands and watched my dad.

Dad looked from one of us to the other. "I'm going to check on my father."

"Now? It's after ten," Mom questioned.

"Yes, now." He walked out the front door. He neither hurried, nor slammed it behind him. Mom and I turned to look at each other in confusion.

"What was that really about?" I asked her.

"Darned if I know. How was the visit?"

"Piper's okay, but Bob's people caught me. I don't know if she forgives me, but at least I got to apologize and explain my side. I'll have to be happy with knowing I tried."

Mom hugged me. We said goodnight and went to our rooms. Maybe it was time for me to reclaim mine as my own. I moved some furniture around and vacuumed with the door shut so I wouldn't bug my brothers. It still looked empty. At almost midnight my father still wasn't home. I texted Lucie but she didn't answer. She always had been smarter than me. She was probably asleep.

FIVE

The days until the first day of school ticked down. Research on the table continued. Nothing else spoke to us like it had. There were hints but no real messages.

Labor Day weekend we were slammed at the shop. Marlo and I hid in the back. He needed quiet to do the bookkeeping and I was processing product and refilling shelves as fast as I could.

Marlo looked up from his computer and the shrinking piles of paperwork, his jaw clenched. "It's been a long week. I'm tired. I've lied for you. I went on a campus tour for heaven's sake! Something happened up there. I know it. Why won't you tell me? It's selfish, you know; to ask so much and give so little."

"I told you everything about the meeting with Piper."

"I'm not stupid. You were gone longer than that. What happened after? She couldn't have just walked out of the coffee shop. And you sure didn't come right over to meet us. And you better not tell me you got lost. You don't get lost. I also know someone followed us. I caught you watching the guy in the leather coat and I caught him taking a greater than normal interest in us."

"You're right," I sighed. I dropped onto the stool next to him. "I'm sorry Mars. I had a run in with Bob's people. They threatened me and when I didn't react like they wanted…"

"They what? Threatened Lucie, Piper… me?"

"No Mars, worse; they threatened your mom."

"What?"

"I'm sorry. I tried to tell you, but…"

"All you did was warn me to be careful. What's wrong with you?"

I looked at him and then hung my head. If I were him, I'd be mad too. I wanted to apologize again but it didn't look like he was ready to hear it. How could I tell him I'd done it for him and his mom? She was like family to me.

Lucie walked in and looked from one of us to the other. "What's going on here?"

"Nothing," we said at the same time.

Lucie scowled and looked at me. "What did you do?"

"Why does everyone always assume it's me?"

"Because it usually is," Marlo said sounding grouchy.

"Well thanks a lot for the vote of confidence." I probably felt more hurt that they were actually right than the fact that they'd said it out loud.

"Am I wrong?" Lucie asked.

I looked from Marlo, who would not meet my gaze, to her. "No," I finally answered, "You're not wrong." I threw down my rag and walked out the back door. I slid down the outside wall and sat staring at my hands. I could hear them talking but I couldn't make out the words. Marlo was probably spilling his guts and I deserved it. Now they would both be pissed at me. What was it Mom's father always said? "No good deed shall go unpunished." Well, I was about to get my punishment.

My phone pinged in my pocket. I considered ignoring it for a full minute and then I sighed and pulled it out.

Piper had texted. "I've thought about what to say since I saw you. I want to hate you, but I can't. They grilled me for hours. I believe you now, but I'm still mad. Don't contact me again."

I dropped my phone and put my head in my hands. Everyone hated me. I heard the back door bang but I wasn't in the mood to talk to anyone.

"Owen, how could you?" Lucie snarled in my head.

"How could I? I thought she was in trouble," I whispered without looking at her.

"All I ever wanted from you was the truth! I think I deserve it – I know I've earned it." I could both see and feel her hurt and anger. It was true that she never really had asked me outright to leave it alone, but I knew it was what she wanted.

"Maybe I'm not sure what the truth is anymore."

"Oh, Owen, what has happened to who you used to be?"

Now I was angry. "That guy is gone. It was bad enough to share memories with Miles but now I have Kraeghton in here too," I whispered harshly, thumping my temple with an index finger. "You have no idea what it's like trying to sift through... all these jumbled memories. It's almost like having a split personality or something. Now I'm seventeen, thirty-four and... like sixty." I sucked in a breath. "Who do I listen to? I don't even know who I am anymore."

"I'm sorry," she whispered sounding helpless. Maybe that summed it up – I felt helpless too and I hated it.

"And then there are his thoughts... dark, creepy," I paused, shuddering. "Sometimes I feel like he's turning me dark from the inside and there's nothing I can do to stop it. I'm good and bad and there is nothing in between."

Lucie sank down beside me and took my hands. "Breathe. We'll figure it out. Can I still have a ride to school tomorrow or have I burned that bridge?"

70

"Of course you can, Luce. I'm not mad at you. The situation... Marlo... Here..." I said, shifting gears. I handed over my phone. "You may as well hate me too. You won't be alone."

Lucie took the phone and read the text. "You should at least let her know you got the message," she said softly.

"You tell her. I'm not in the mood."

"I'll text her for you and then I have something for you. A peace offering."

"You don't need to make peace, Luce. I'm pretty sure that's my job."

"Owen, as long as I've known you, you've always tried to do what you thought was right."

"Lucie, I've been trying to tell you. I don't believe I'm that guy anymore. I want to but... I remember doing horrible things even though I've been an unwilling participant when Stephan Kraeghton kills. It's changing me."

"You are not a participant. You are a witness. I believe in you. You will survive this."

"Marlo hates me."

"He doesn't hate you."

I gave her a look that said, *Yeah, right.*

"He's frustrated, disappointed and hurt," she replied to my silent communication.

"I would be too, but I can't change the past."

"See, I knew you were in there. Come on."

Lucie stood, took my hand and pulled me to my feet. She led the way inside where Marlo gave me a halfhearted smile and turned back to his computer.

71

Lucie pulled a small box from under the counter and handed it to me. "Happy early birthday."

I looked at it and then at her, then I shrugged. I lifted the lid and looked inside to find a nice pair of vintage Ray-Bans aviators. I smiled, reaching for them, "Nice, Lucie, they're…"

I froze. These weren't any old pair. I met her gaze. They had belonged to Miles. "How?"

"White Eagle and Marlo helped me track them down. We thought they might help you."

"Help me remember who I am or who Miles was?"

"Both. We all want what's best for you."

"Thanks guys. Really, thanks."

"You're welcome," they replied together.

"I'm sorry, Mars. I never meant to hurt you."

"I know, but you did." His look was steady and calm. Lucie was right, he was more hurt than truly angry.

I started to step towards him but he turned back to his computer. "I, ah… I'll just leave you be for a while then." I turned to Lucie. "Thanks again. I need to go pick up a couple of things for school tomorrow. I'll see you at eight?"

"I'll walk you out."

"Did you want to come with me?" I asked as we walked through the shop.

"Not this time. I have some work to finish and I believe you need some time to think."

She kissed me but it was fast and fleeting. She probably needed time just like Marlo did.

I put on my new dark glasses and waved at her. Heck, I wanted a minute with the Ray-Bans to see what they could tell me. They did have something to say, but not what I expected. They'd been a gift from his wife and it was the happiest I'd ever seen Miles. It made me feel happy too. I shrugged, started my bike and pulled out of the lot. I'd almost made it to the middle school when my phone began to vibrate incessantly. Normally I ignored it when I rode but someone had to be desperate to get ahold of me since they must have called at least three times in a row. I pulled into the bus loop and checked the readout as it vibrated a fourth time. I was perplexed to see it was Lucie calling again. What could be so urgent?

"Hello?"

"Where are you?" She sounded breathless.

"At the middle school, why?"

"Take off the Ray-Bans right now!"

"What? Why?"

"Just do it, please. Mitchell is on his way." She disconnected. I stared at my phone. Having Mitchell headed toward me could only mean one thing... something bad was about to happen.

How do you prepare for the unknown? I shut off my bike and moved away from it. I carefully set my dark glasses in my helmet and put them on the ground. Nothing felt out of the ordinary. I did some slow breathing with my hands loose at my sides.

Mitchell's junky car rounded the corner and halted next to me. He didn't even shut it off.

"You're okay!"

"Well, yeah. What's up?"

"I saw... I saw you get a vision and wreck your bike."

"You're mistaken. I only saw happy stuff."

My phone buzzed.

"Hello?"

"You're okay?"

"Yeah."

"Is Mitchell there?"

"Yeah, Luce. What's going on?"

"He'll tell you. Promise you'll be careful."

"Always."

"And Owen?"

"Yeah?"

"No matter what. I love you."

"I love you too, Luce." She clicked off without waiting to see if I had anything else to say. I turned to look at Mitchell. "Talk to me."

"You are about to… experience an event. It's not good, but it will help you. Try to remain detached."

"What are you talking about?"

"The Ray-Bans Lucie gave you belonged to Miles, right?"

"Yes."

"He has something to tell you."

"But the watch…"

"After he and White Eagle enchanted it or whatever they did, he didn't wear it or not as much, right?"

"I guess."

"I saw you crash because Miles' Ray-Bans showed you something devastating."

I cut my eyes to the glasses and then picked them up and moved over to the grass. I sat down and put them on. Nothing happened. I looked at Mitchell and waited some more. I was just about to give up when my reality vanished.

Kraeghton stood before me. "You take from me and I take from you. That's how this works," *Kraeghton snarled at me.*

I felt my own lips twitch and then I was saying, "You and me. May the best watcher win."

"So ready to throw it all away?" *Kraeghton sneered.*

"I've got nothing left to lose." *Miles sounded so calm and certain.*

"Just your dignity."

"If you say so." *I felt my shoulders move in a shrug.*

"Seems to me you should have seen this coming." *Now Kraeghton sounded a little unsure.*

"Maybe I did and I just don't care."

Kraeghton lunged at me. I could feel us fighting. Every punch thrown and received vibrated through me. This Miles seemed different than the Miles I knew. What was he doing? There was something... a strange peace. He wasn't afraid. He was ready to die – suicide by dark watcher. Kraeghton tried to drain us but pulled his hand back in surprise. I felt my lips pull into a smile.

"I forgive you."

"No, you don't."

"I do. You can't help what you are - a soulless monster. When I leave this earth, I'll go to heaven. Where will you go?"

Kraeghton tried to drain us again but Miles just laughed. "Don't you see? There's nothing for you here. I have nothing left to lose. I've made my peace. Have you?"

Kraeghton made an inarticulate sound, beat at Miles until he had him in a headlock and then snapped his neck. The vision did not fade there. Kraeghton kept ahold of Miles as he sank to his knees and wept. I felt angry, hurt and confused, but so did Kraeghton which looped back on me, revving my feelings into high gear. Images swirled. Everything was mixed up. Brother, enemy... "I need to know. What did you do with your gift? How could you take this from me too?!"

A wave of raw emotion so strong that it knocked me to the ground had me vomiting on the grass. A hand touched my shoulder and without thinking I hurled out a blast of energy to send Kraeghton away from me.

Sound rushed in. I could hear moaning. The grass around me looked scorched and Mitchell was on the ground at the edge of it.

"Mitchell, I'm sorry. Are you okay? What did I do?"

He stayed still with his eyes closed. His hands rested over a hole burnt into his t-shirt. I reached for him and tried to heal him but I was empty. I pulled out my phone, but it was fried and so was Mitchell's. I heaved him up into a fireman's carry and dumped him in the backseat of his car. I threw my helmet in the passenger seat and sped back to the shop.

White Eagle rushed out followed by Lucie and Marlo. I opened the back door and stepped back. I had done this. I had blasted my friend with all of my power. Who would I hurt next? Maybe this was why Kraeghton was a lone wolf.

Mitchell was able to walk into the shop held up between White Eagle and Marlo. Guilt sat heavy making me sick.

Lucie touched my elbow. "I'm sorry."

"You are?"

"The Ray-Bans that belonged to Miles - I had no idea. Mitchell called. He was so worried about you, but it was him that got hurt. How did that happen?"

"How did he not see that coming?" I asked.

"Maybe he did and he wanted to help you anyway."

"God, I hope not. I'm not worth it. I'm a horrible person. Look what I do to people." I felt pressure in my chest and my hands began to shake.

"Owen? What's wrong?"

"I'm having a heart attack." In my mind I thought I was getting what I deserved.

Lucie pulled me to the back room and pushed me into the nearest chair. She took my pulse. I watched her walk over to the sink and take out a few items. She put a cold pack on my head and another on the back of my neck. Then she handed me an aspirin and some water.

I looked over at Mitchell on the cot. White Eagle was sitting on the edge with his hands on Mitchell as he murmured. My heart gave another spasm of pain and I gasped. White Eagle turned and looked at me. He patted Mitchell's shoulder and then walked over and stood before me.

"What is this?" he asked Lucie.

"It's not a heart attack," Lucie replied. "It's something else."

"I can see that. Help me here." Lucie stepped next to him and I felt them slip into my mind. I could hear their voices in my head as they went back over the events at the middle school.

"Interesting," White Eagle said.

"Yes, very," Lucie replied.

White Eagle snapped the connection closed and then knelt in front of me. "You have connected yourself to Mitchell. You are taking his pain."

"What?"

"Find the connection to Mitchell and let it go."

"No. If I feel his pain then he isn't. I did this. I deserve it."

"No, you don't," Lucie said firmly.

"I'm a freaking wreck. How's Mitchell?"

"You hit him pretty good but he'll be okay. He's resting. You should be too. You did everything you could. Now let go. He doesn't need you anymore." White Eagle gave me his best stern father look.

"I bet he's pissed."

"Nope," White Eagle answered, warmth glinting in his eyes.

"He should be."

"Did you do it on purpose?" he asked like he already knew the answer.

"Of course not!"

"Then it was an accident. Let it go." That was definitely his teacher voice.

"Seems to me, I'm having too many of those."

"You just need to control Kraeghton."

"Yeah, I know."

I tried to do as White Eagle asked and gently remove the connection to my friend. I was pretty sure no one hated me more than I did myself right now. Even Marlo looked like he was afraid of me. Lucie probably should be, but instead she pulled a stool up next to my chair, took the icepacks and without a word, ran her fingers over my scalp as we watched Mitchell sleep.

SIX

School started with the minimum of fuss, unlike last year. Marlo had scheduled us all together again and how no one noticed was beyond me but it did make my life much easier. My dad was not happy with my school choices this year. Since I had taken a full load each year to date, I had some holes for electives; I didn't need the credits and I could use the extra time at the shop to work and train. It also gave me more time for *watcher* business. I had to have English and economics, but then I went ahead and took pre calc and physics. That made my dad happy but it was the fact that I could squeak by on the minimum credits and take nothing else that made him grouchy, since he believed that I should make the most of my free education and take a full load. Marlo worked it so that I had two classes a day and could then leave. Lucie did the same thing except that she and Marlo continued with Spanish. Marlo put himself back into orchestra so that he could spend some time with Caitlyn. Their on-again, off-again romance continued. Most importantly, he made sure that Jon wasn't in any of my classes.

I walked Lucie to Spanish and kissed her goodbye. I was riding my Kawasaki to school this year. In the mornings I'd take Lucie and in the afternoons she would come to the shop with Marlo. On the days he had orchestra she would wait on campus for him and do her homework. Better her than me. I'd do my homework at the shop away from all the other students. Being around them was getting to be almost more than I could stand. It wasn't like how I'd felt back in eighth grade so it had to be Stephan Kraeghton's influence. Marlo had been working extra hard to find information on him. He found a tiny bit more than we had in our own files, but the man had been, and now always would be, a ghost. I took a deep breath and tried to access him once more even though I knew it was pointless. He surprised me by responding. It was almost like a tap on the shoulder.

I detected a presence behind me but I kept walking across the parking lot, waiting to see what would happen. There were too many people around for this to be an attack. Students were heading to class and the buses were unloading from the satellite campuses.

I sent out a pulse of energy to test for *dark watchers*. She was not one, but I didn't like the feel of her intentions. I let her move up beside me because she had me curious. "Mr. Ryer, we need to talk."

"Oh?" I asked lazily, just to be irritating, as I put on the retro Ray-Bans from Lucie.

The agent looked both ways and then snarled in a low, quiet voice, "About Stephan Kraeghton."

"I gave my statement last May, so... no."

"I'm afraid it's not a choice."

"And you are?"

"I'm Doctor Anita Moretz. I work for counterintelligence. We need to evaluate you."

I snorted. She wasn't as sneaky as she thought, doctor or no. "You work for Bob."

"I do," she replied, sounding smug.

I was surprised she'd admit it. "Then you know there is no way I'm letting you pick around in my head, Doctor," I replied with an unfriendly smile.

"Like I said, you don't have a choice. You cooperate or you will be shut down," she growled.

"Shut down?"

"You are a rogue asset, Mr. Ryer. You play by your own rules. Even your handlers have trouble with you."

"Handlers?" I asked. *Who was she kidding?*

"Sarah Lando and Earl White Eagle."

I laughed. "Clearly, you don't understand…"

"Maybe I understand more than you, boy."

"You're telling me that Bob thinks I'm out of control and that he wants to psychologically evaluate me. What game is he playing now?"

"It is a game of dollars. You have become a big ticket item. Are you worth it?"

"The man does not pay me, so I can't cost him that much." I let my disgust show.

The shift in her eyes was the only warning. I'd let someone else get too close. I felt a sting in my back. Her arm quickly came around me and pulled the dart free. I should have paid closer attention to the van parked next to my bike. My vision shrank to a dot and flashed off and in my head I heard Kraeghton laugh, "I told you so."

~ ~ ~

I took a breath. My shoulders, upper back and neck hurt. I shook my head to get my bearings. And then I remembered. Bob would pay dearly for this one. I was hanging by my wrists, attached with chain to a hook in the ceiling. My feet touched the floor, but not enough to relieve the pressure in my shoulders. I noted the empty room and the one-way glass. This was just like all the interrogation rooms I'd seen in the movies, so of course Bob would have one. I could not think of a strong enough expletive.

Doctor Moretz walked in with a syringe in her hand. I gave her my best stink eye.

"What is this?" I snarled.

"This is how we question uncooperative assets."

"What's that?" I asked, indicating the needle with a jut of my chin.

"A psychoactive medication."

I shook my head and laughed a mean laugh. "Like truth serum in a bad movie? Why?"

"Because we don't trust you to answer our questions truthfully." Her voice had become silky, making my skin crawl. She sunk the needle into my arm.

"You don't trust me... Just so you know... I don't trust you or Bob." *And so help me, when I got loose they'd both pay.*

While I was out, they'd stripped me down to my boxer briefs; my clothes had been tossed off to the side. Bob's psychiatrist seemed to be waiting for the drugs to work. An agent came in and photographed all my scars and noted their positions on a chart. I could see enough of the nearby computer screen to see a speech conversion program was running on half the screen and a video log on the other.

"If you create files like that on me, you are putting me, and everyone I work with, in danger." I wasn't slurring yet but I could feel the drugs beginning to work.

"Oh, how do you figure Mr. Ryer?"

"You create files and someone will hack them. It's what happens to those who think they're superior."

"No one can get into our system."

"So says the over-confident. You should know better than to make that assumption, Madame PhD."

"Maybe we just don't care anymore if you do get captured. All we want for now is to know what you know."

"You should ask nicely."

"We are done with niceties."

"Well, it's nice to know where I stand, I guess. At the very least I'd think you would care about the people I work with."

"Do you?"

"Of course I do. Why would you ask that?"

Dr. Moretz allowed a sly smile to cross her face. "You ask them to do things you shouldn't."

"Oh?" I asked innocently, but I was instantly worried about Marlo more so than anyone else, even though he was still mad at me.

"You've tracked down Piper and that was a no-no. Shame on you Owen, Lucie would be so sad. What do you think she'll say when we tell her?"

"'Go to hell' would be my first guess," I said with a slight slur. My vision was beginning to show halos of light.

She laughed. It was a deep rich laugh that I would have expected out of a chronic smoker. She reminded me of Tess, tough, except Tess had a good heart and I was pretty sure the doctor's was black.

"You will come to appreciate me, Mr. Ryer. I have so much I could teach you."

"Oh, like what?"

"I am an artist in my own way. I can remake people and Bob has assigned me to see if you qualify for the program."

"Sounds like playing God."

"Not at all. I'm a Behavioral Psychiatrist, not God, but I can reprogram you."

My vision blurred further and shrank to a dot. Soon the only voice in my head was hers. Truth and lies swirled together into something I would never be able to separate. I saw things in flashes as I drifted in and out of consciousness.

"You are going to spy for us," her voice said.

"No," I slurred.

"You don't have a choice."

"There is always a choice," I babbled. "I won't."

"You'll do whatever I say."

"I make my own choices." In my mind I said it with conviction.

"Not anymore. You work for us."

"No."

"If not you, then Alex and Lucas will suffer. What a shame that would be." I heard the click of her heels and then the sound of other voices. A block of ice formed in my belly and my lungs forgot how to breathe.

"No," I whispered. I was begging. I felt helpless. "Please, no."

"I will teach you everything you need to know to be a quality spy; how to dress, walk, talk, eat and even sleep. Haven't you heard the saying, 'you have to fit in to get in?' I own you. You will do it for your brothers. You will fit back in like nothing is wrong and you will tell us everything you observe. You will be the best one I ever made and if you so much as put one toe out of line or give one hint about our time here someone will pay."

"You don't own me and neither does Robert Bowman."

A slap stung my cheek and I hadn't even seen it coming. "We don't speak his given name!"

"You won't hurt them, it's unethnic...unethnical... unethical."

"We can make it look like an accident," she purred.

"Why are you doing this to me? To them?"

"We need to make you reliable."

"I am loyal to those who earn it. I respect my family and friends."

"So you say, but understand this, if you let no one in, then there is no one who can hurt you. You love people. That gives us leverage. It also gives your enemies leverage."

"I won't live like that and I won't be your puppet."

"Then you may die if you're lucky. You'll watch others die if you're not."

"What do you want? I don't understand." My voice caught.

"We want obedience. I will break you, to remake you."

"What do I have to do?"

"Learn the skills I teach you and show your loyalty to us when it counts."

"What does that mean?"

"You will know when the time comes."

"What do I need to do right now?"

"Listen and learn. Earn someone's trust and you can do anything, but first you need to earn mine."

"I think you have that backwards. You should earn my trust."

"I don't need you to trust me, just trust that people will get hurt if you don't follow instructions. Now hold still and be a good boy." I tried to glare at her but I wasn't in a position to do anything yet. I watched her out-of-focus form measure a dose of a clear liquid and inject it into my other arm. I would never trust her. The room began to spin.

"I think he's had enough for now. Let him down."

My arms were released and I crumpled to the concrete floor. My wrists were still cuffed but I reached up to hold my head, willing my stomach to behave and trying hard not to pass out.

People walked in and out of the room. Voices blended together into babbling, like water over stones in a creek. Time passed and I was confused. They made me drink water. They talked on and on. I passed in and out of awareness. Some words formed into sentences but I couldn't tell who was talking.

"What is he doing?"

"I've never seen anything like it."

"How is he doing it?"

"I don't know but be sure you record it."

"It's running all the time like you asked, doctor."

Somewhere someone screamed. An agent landed on the floor by me. His nose was bleeding and he stared at me sightlessly.

"Carl!"

"Just finish the watch. Then help him."

"That kid is dangerous. He should be put down."

"He is a weapon we need to aim."

"If he killed Carl, so help me, I'll kill him."

"That is not for you to decide. Who do you think you work for?"

The room went silent as they cracked open my watch and slipped a microchip inside. I closed my eyes and her voice returned to my head.

"You are everyone and no one. You hide among friends and tell me everything. You can trust no one."

"No," I pleaded again.

"You will be who we want you to be."

"Leave me alone."

"You are ours to control."

"I'm a minor with parents."

"We can take them away."

My vision blurred further and my eyes burned as if I was having a bad reaction to chopping a strong onion. I felt so confused. "Why would you do that? What have we ever done to you?"

"Perhaps you are being treated like a terrorist."

"I'm not a terrorist. I'm just a guy."

Dr. Moretz laughed. "You are not. I don't believe you are even human. Your kind must be monitored at all times. You are just a tool. A dangerous tool."

"You're crazy. I'm no terrorist and I most certainly am human."

"Give him water and put him back in his cell."

I was picked up by my armpits. I didn't even try to resist. What was the point? It felt like I was completely drained. I was tired and thirsty. I couldn't even think straight.

I heard the thunk of a plastic water bottle hitting the concrete floor and then the clang of a metal door. I squeezed my eyes tight. They burned worse, but then they began to water and clear. There was a single cot in the room with a blanket folded at one end and my clothes were in a jumble at the foot. Dr. Moretz was nowhere to be seen, but I could hear her voice. What she was saying sounded familiar, like I'd heard it many times before. My head was pounding and my mouth was desert dry, I felt like I'd been eating sand and dirt. This had to be what a migraine was like. I pulled on my clothes, drank the bottle of water dry and waited. What time was it? I tried to look at my watch but it looked like it had stopped. I slowly looked around. There was nothing in here but the cot and the blanket.

With nothing better to do, I put the cot to use and took a nap. I don't know how much time passed but I wasn't fully rested when the clank of my door awakened me. It was the two guys from earlier - Carl's friend, the one who hated me and a tall dark man who reminded me of the heavy muscle in a modern day military film.

"Stand up." I did. *What was the point in fighting at the moment?*

"Come with us." Again I complied. This time they led me back into an exam room. Whether it was the one they'd had me in earlier I couldn't say. Dr. Moretz was waiting for us. The two men stood to the side.

"Have a seat," she said expressionlessly. I looked skeptically at the weird chair. One of the guards took a step forward so I sat.

She slapped a cuff on my arm and took my blood pressure. "It's high."

"I'm not surprised."

"Your blood work looks normal."

"I don't understand what you want."

"I want answers," she said as she hooked me up to electrodes coming from a machine next to me. The two agents cinched me down with the leather straps attached to the chair. I wasn't going anywhere. Dr. Moretz sat at the monitor and began to ask her questions.

"Where is Evilia Malvada?"

This again. "I don't know."

"Have you threatened her?"

"Not in a long time. How can I do that when I don't know where she is?"

"Where is Stephan Kraeghton?"

"He's dead." I could feel him move within me; watching, waiting.

"How do you know?"

"I told you last May. I saw him lying on the floor without a pulse."

"Did you kill him?"

"I... I don't know..." and so it went. On and on as machines whirred, recorded and took my vitals. I was past hungry. That was my only clue that I'd been here for a long while. I was taken to a bathroom and then back to my cell where another bottle of water waited. I drank it all and sat with my back to the wall.

I started to nod off, but someone was paying attention because the two agents came to escort me to another room. This time Dr. Moretz was sitting at a conference table with a file in her hand. She watched me for a long time, but all I wanted was to put my head down on the table. I closed my eyes and hung my head, trying to stretch my neck and relieve my headache, but bending forward just made it pound worse so I straightened back up to look at her.

The doctor's voice was sharp. "Sit down."

The agents forced me into a chair and stepped back.

Dr. Moretz ignored them. "Parts of your mind are especially resistant to penetration. I'll get in eventually. I always do. You are our best lead to Evilia Malvada and Caleb Carmichael but we have to keep you in line. We will find out what happened to Stephan Kraeghton. Your memory will come back and you will share it with us. You can't hide what you know forever. For now, a little incentive to behave... ." She picked up a remote and hit a button.

A screen activated and a clip began to roll. It was being shot inside Lucas's fourth grade class. The person wearing the camera pointed it at Lucas and then held up a spiral notebook that said. *I am in Lucas' class. I can get to him at any time. You can't get here soon enough and no one will believe you.* The person set the spiral down and the view returned to Lucas.

"What do you want?"

"Stay away from Piper. We can't have you ruining our legitimate legal case against Malvada, Carmichael and their underlings."

"I can do that, if you leave my brother alone."

She ignored me. "For now, keep doing the other things you normally do. We'll be in touch. Just remember. You are never alone. We're always watching. You won't be able to blow your nose without my knowing it. Best behavior."

The agents each took an arm and pulled me from my chair. "Wait. I don't understand."

"Don't forget to wear your watch or I will find a more permanent solution."

"A solution to what?"

She picked up her phone and sent a text message. The camera in Lucas' classroom moved. The person walked toward Lucas. I felt drawn in, afraid to look but too frightened to look away. The person set down a pencil and picked up the one Lucas had been using. Lucas looked questioningly at the person but then picked up the pencil. The person moved away but then looked back. Lucas was pale and visibly sweating. I watched him drop the pencil and raise his hand.

"Stop," I begged. "Help him."

"It is you who must help him. Do as you are told and tell no one. Wear your watch and live your miserable life. We'll bring you back when we think you have more to share."

I gave her a brief nod and was half dragged from the room. The agents took me by elevator to sub level three where we got off and walked to a car. They put me in the back, with an agent sitting with me. What had I told them? I watched downtown float by my window.

Yikes, just yikes. Had I been gone a day? A week? I didn't even know. The trees still had leaves so it hadn't been forever. I looked past the trees to the eastern horizon. It was hazy enough that the distant mountains were nothing but a darker smudge against the sky. The trees in front of that were nothing more than the spiky texture of a bad haircut. Lights began to appear though the sky was still an odd shade of pale greenish blue with a splash of peach along the horizon.

Neither agent said a word the entire trip. I refused to give them the satisfaction of asking them anything. I was half surprised that they really were headed to my house. As they turned the corner onto my street I caught a glimpse of White Eagle standing in the front yard, his smart phone in his hand. He studied the car for a brief moment and ran toward his house. Before we reached my driveway he was running up the street.

Mom burst through the front door with my brothers right behind her. The driver put the nose of the car in a driveway and did a fast turn. My door flew open, my seatbelt unlatched and the other agent put a foot in my hip, shoving me out of the still moving car. I stopped rolling in time to see White Eagle try to stop the driver but he was smarter than to throw himself in front of the car. He leapt nimbly out of the way and came to me. Alex snapped a picture of the car but I knew it wouldn't matter. I rolled to my knees and dry heaved onto the street. I could hear Sarah, Lucie and Dad converging on me.

All the noise was making my head hurt. "Water?" I rasped at them.

They all spoke at once making me feel like I was back in that awful interrogation room again and I began to shake. A water bottle was shoved in my hand. Lucie, Alex, White Eagle and Mom tried to heal me. This wasn't an injury – well except for my hands and knees – this was chemical.

They got me on my feet and Dad and White Eagle helped me into the house. I tried to take another drink and found the water bottle was empty. Lucie handed me another as soon as I was seated on the couch. I put my head back and took a breath.

"Ice?" I begged.

"You need to keep the water down," Mom said, trying to sound calm and failing miserably.

"Icepack for my head?" I tried again.

As soon as the coolness touched me, it began to ease the pain. I opened one eye when someone grabbed my wrist. When I realized it was Saul, I relaxed into a less aware state. I could hear him talking to Lucie mainly to get assistance like you would from a nurse. I felt the prick of a needle. Saul put in a hep lock to draw some blood and then he attached a bag of IV fluids.

"You are horribly dehydrated. I could barely get a vein," Saul griped angrily. "What did they give you?"

"I don't know. Doctor Anita Moretz said it was a psycho… a… psychoactive… a truth serum and another clear liquid. She gave me around 5cc of it twice that I know of. Plus they hit me with a dart when they took me from school. Whatever they gave me, it made my eyes burn like nobody's business."

"As soon as you can pee, I need a urine sample so I can try to puzzle it out."

"Don't you want to know who…?"

"Oh we know who," Sarah snarled.

"What about why?" I asked.

"We will find out and we are going to do something about it. He can't treat people like this." I had never heard Sarah so angry.

"How long?"

"Four days," Sarah growled.

"Help me get him upstairs, Luce. The rest of you do whatever you need to. We've got this." Saul waved everyone off, except Lucie and put my arm around his shoulder. Lucie took my other side and we headed upstairs.

They took me to the bathroom and helped me undress. I took a shower without them even leaving the room, my arm extended through the curtain. Saul sent Lucie to my room for clean clothes. She took my dirty ones with her. She was back in a flash, giving me just enough time to get Saul his sample.

He evaluated me from the top of my head to my toes. He found six needle marks and bruising over most of my body. Nothing was broken – well nothing he could fix anyway. He helped me to my room and reminded us that he was not a psychologist. He thought I could use one. I told him there was no way in hell I was letting anyone else play around in my head. He took it good naturedly and left with his samples, promising us that he would use a secure outside lab.

I was too wired to sleep. Every time I closed my eyes I was back with Dr. Moretz. Lucie stayed and even replaced my IV bag. I could hear talking downstairs but I couldn't focus. Mom fed the crew dinner, Lucie brought me my plate. I smiled crookedly at her, remembering when I had taken care of her when she'd had her wisdom teeth out.

"You're going to be okay, Owen."

"I know. I just feel like I was run over by a truck. I don't know what I said or did or anything. Worse I don't know what the doctor said to me. It's all jumbled. I wasn't supposed to say who had me, but you already knew."

"You heard Sarah. Bob won't get away with it."

"Was I really gone four days?"

"You really don't know?"

"I don't."

"You were gone for the four longest days of my life. They took you after second period on Wednesday and now it's Saturday night."

"No way."

"For the moment, just rest. I'm taking the first shift with you. I want to be sure you're okay."

"You're my guard?"

"Yeah, that's it." she smiled at me and I didn't care if she was guarding me from harm or guarding everyone in the house from me.

I fell asleep with my head on her shoulder.

Something scared me awake. It took a second to realize where I was – at home, in my room. Lucie was next to me and the bedside lamp was on. She blinked sleepily at me. I started to say something but a knife of pain shot through my head and I was sure I was going to throw up. I bolted for the bathroom and made it just in time. I rinsed my mouth and looked at myself in the mirror. I looked like hell – bloodshot eyes, dark circles, sickly pale and sweaty – not my best look. Bob and Dr. Moretz were going to pay for this. Lucie knocked on the door and asked if I was okay.

"I'll live," I sighed.

"Saul is on his way."

"You didn't need to bother him."

"Trust me, he would want to be bothered."

I staggered back to my room, waving off Lucie's offer of help. I tried to close my eyes but I didn't like what I saw when I did. Saul was over in less than fifteen minutes. I was pretty sure he'd slept in sweats just for me because he looked like he'd rolled out of bed, into his shoes and grabbed his medical kit on the way out the door.

"Good job on the IVs, Lucie Lou! You barely left a mark."

Oh yeah, I did have one of those didn't I. "Did you take it out too, Luce?"

"I did it while you were asleep."

"Wow."

"She's good huh? Maybe she should be a doctor," Saul smiled at her like she was his best pupil. She probably was.

Lucie blushed. "Did you learn anything yet, Saul?"

"We're getting there. I don't want to ask Bob or that team directly. They are acting like nothing happened. We need to be careful here. When you disappeared and we started investigating... let's just say things didn't look right to me. I was afraid I was going to have to treat White Eagle for a heart attack."

"And when Marlo and I found your bike still at school... White Eagle called both of us when you didn't answer your cell. They blocked everything. Marlo and I skipped class and headed out to the parking lot. That's when we saw your bike. Did they forget that I can hear it when something bad happens? I could hear you like you were right there. Marlo helped me get all the information I could. I called White Eagle while Marlo drove to the shop so he could get into his system, but not even he could track you. Sarah tried to call in her team but they had all been dispersed onto assignments. All but Saul were hours away and Rick was unreachable by cell. They all came back as fast as they could." Lucie's eyes looked a little teary and her heart was beating fast. I could see goose bumps all over her arms. It had been a rough four days for more than just me.

Saul took back over then. "Like I said, things didn't look or feel right. I have some results on your blood work. A friend of mine can do most things we need under the table and out of Bob's view. What she found so far definitely shows drugs - fancy, synthetic ones."

"Do you know how to get them out of my system? They don't..." my stomach turned and I belched, "seem to agree with me."

"Damn, looks like a drug allergy. I'm still not completely sure what they stuck in there, how fast it metabolizes or what the side effects are."

"Awesome."

Lucie brought me the plastic waste bin from the bathroom and Saul set me up with some chemistry of his own to counteract the work of Dr. Moretz. "Again," he said calmly, "your body I can heal. Your head is another matter."

97

I gave him a look and then put my head in my hands while I waited for the pain and nausea to ease. Lucie put more ice on my head and I prayed for time to pass. I finally was ready to go back to sleep, so I told Saul he could go. His answer was to raise one eyebrow at me. *Okie, dokie then. I hoped Saul liked pancakes, 'cause that's all I'd be up for cooking come morning.* I tried closing my eyes again.

Doctor Moretz was coming at me with a needle. I was restrained. I begged for her to leave me alone, to go away and not to hurt anyone. She laughed and then she started shaking my shoulder. She was making my head hurt again and I whimpered. My shoulder was shaken more strongly and reality and the dream world slammed together. I opened my eyes and it was Lucie standing over me and not the doctor.

"I'm sorry," I whispered.

"It's okay. It's not your fault. We think you have PTSD."

"Post-Traumatic Stress Disorder?"

"Pretty sure."

"Oh man, Luce, I don't want to see a shrink."

"I know. Come on. I smell muffins."

She took my hand and led me downstairs. I looked over at Saul who was snoring softly in Mom's chair. I realized I could hear Mom and Sarah talking quietly in the kitchen. Lucie was right, I could smell muffins. Everything was going to be okay - eventually.

SEVEN

Lucky for me, the head help I needed, White Eagle thought he could handle. Everyone treated me gently, but in a leery fashion that was frustrating. I escaped to the shop on Sunday to get away from the house and work with White Eagle. Lucie came too and had either forgiven me or felt so sorry for me that she was acting like she had. Marlo was still a little cold but the more normally I behaved the better he did. When Mitchell dropped by he acted like he always had. I had hurt my friends and now I had helped Bob without wanting to. My guilt was so strong that I couldn't shake it. By two in the afternoon I was so tired that I couldn't resist the cot we have in the back of the shop. I thought I'd just shut my eyes for a few minutes and recharge.

I woke up shaking and sweating again. Flashes of Dr. Anita Moretz, Bob and Kraeghton all swam in my head. White Eagle must have sensed I was up because he picked that moment to check on me.

"It's going to take time you know."

"I know. I was just about over the whole Kraeghton thing and then… it just seems like the hurt goes on and on. No matter what I do, I make things worse. I want to tell you what happened to me but when I try… ." On cue my hands began to shake and I was sweating again.

"She really did a number on you, but you are strong."

"I don't even know what all she did or what I said. I feel like I'm watched all the time and I feel… fear… all the time." I dropped my head and stared at my trembling fingers. "How's Lucas?"

White Eagle gave me a peculiar look. "Why would you ask?"

"I'm really scared for him."

"That's not your ability."

"I know it's not. I just can't shake.... Was he sick while I was gone?"

"Yes."

"Out of the blue?"

"Yes."

"Mom... she's okay, right?"

"Yes."

"She would know if there was anyone new at school. She'd know if there were new hires or volunteers. We have to talk to her but we can't let anyone know. If I... If I don't do what Bob wants then, ... Lucas will pay."

"You're remembering."

"Just enough to be dangerous. How do we protect Lucas without them knowing?"

"Maybe your dad should take him to Cuba."

"No. He'd be easier to get to there. We need to stick together. They told me to trust no one but I can't do that. I can't do this alone."

White Eagle put his arm around my shoulders. Remember the pact you made with Lucie, 'Together we are more'? It's still true. Bob has underestimated us before."

"I hope so."

White Eagle called Mom and to my surprise, Evelyn. White Eagle had me tell them everything and then he grilled Mom. Sure enough, a new aide had been hired. Evelyn would put someone in the classroom. Her plan involved a substitute teacher. Lucas' real teacher was about to win a trip. It was the most we could manage; a job change was out of the question. Mom and Evelyn went to work with Marlo and Lucie came over to work with me.

Mom kept Lucas home on Monday. Sarah stayed with him. He thought it was a pretty great adventure. Mom told the school he had a fever and she wasn't sure when he would be back. Mom was at the building extra early and swiped the new aide's personnel file with Marlo's remote help.

Mom wanted her arrested, but Evelyn convinced her it was better for us to spy on the spy. If we had her removed Bob would have her replaced with someone we might not know. This was safer for now. On Thursday, Lucas' teacher was notified of her win and the wheels were set in motion for Evelyn's sub to take over the class.

My nightmares were occurring almost nightly. Maybe I needed Alex to come and sleep in my room like the old days except this time it would be for me, not him. No one had bothered him at school.

White Eagle worked with me intently every day after school and that felt like old times too except that we hardly ever saw Adrian any more. I was doing better at controlling Kraeghton when I was awake, but Dr. Moretz would not leave my nightmares or occasional day terrors. Marlo recorded it all and we began to piece together my time with her. We figured she'd picked clean everything I knew and was busy analyzing it. I allowed Marlo to fully track my phone, not just the GPS, but the texts and phone calls too. Not even I, thought I could be trusted. She said I would spy for her but we couldn't see what, if anything, I was doing... yet. Evilia's words flashed through my mind – she told me I wouldn't know what was real anymore. I wished they'd all get out of my head.

Two weeks flew by. Lucas' teacher returned and there had not been any threats on Lucas. We coached him on what to do in an emergency. What more could we do without raising suspicions. My father grew more and more distant as it became apparent to him that the whole thing was a figment of my imagination - all the while my mom argued. Then where had I been for the four days I was missing? Did Dad think I had run away from home or something?

By Halloween, I had convinced myself that it was my imagination and I began to relax back into my life as much as I could. All except the sleep thing. At some point I had quit working on my English essay and had fallen asleep on it. Well, until I jerked awake from another nightmare that was.

Marlo turned on the stool to look at me as I sat up. "It happened again didn't it?"

"Yeah."

"Anything new?"

"Not really, I still think Kraeghton is trying to teach me through dreams. Miles has a different way. I get a… mini vision while I'm fully awake. Sort of like… let's say I was holding my hand the wrong way for a punch. I see Miles doing it the right way. Kraeghton is completely different. I'm not sure what he's trying to tell me. I get these little vignettes and I know there is a message in them, but most of the time… I just don't get what he's trying to tell me. Then there's Dr. Moretz – she had me so doped up, I don't know what I said or did or even what was real and what was a hallucination."

"Then we need to do more than write them down, we need to add what you think the message is and see if there are patterns. I've been doing more research on them, which isn't easy, I might add. Let's keep working up profiles. Soon everything will start making sense." Marlo looked way more confident than I felt.

"I sure hope so, Mars. I can't keep living like this."

"I know. Now, cheer up bucco, it's Thursday and that means tomorrow is?"

"Friday?" I paused and thought. "Of course, English project and you're partnered with Caitlyn."

"Life is sweet." Marlo grinned at me. It was the friendliest I'd seen him since our argument.

"Marlo, I want you to know that… that I'm sorry about everything. I know I'm not myself."

"I know you can't help it. I'm sorry too. I haven't been a very good friend. I can't imagine what you've been through."

"Thanks, Mars. It means a lot."

I could breathe a little easier as we worked in companionable silence. I felt the door between the shop and the back room move, more than I heard it. I looked up to find Adrian, but he didn't look happy. He looked incredibly sad, hurt and almost angry. He glanced right and then left as if waiting for someone to pop out at him.

"I want out," Adrian hissed. "I want a life. I want to be normal. I'll always be your friend and I will keep your secret but I don't want this. I want some distance. I'm tired of being asked questions I can't answer. I thought it would be so cool to be like some kind of super spy or something but it's not. Not when you can't brag about what you do."

I glanced at Marlo, but his mouth was hanging agape. "Um," I tried.

Adrian gave me one last hurt look and then turned and left without giving me a chance to really reply. I looked back at Mars, torn between following my friend and leaving him be for a little while.

Clearly he was hurting but what had I done? I started to rise but Marlo shook his head and turned back to his computer screen.

A variety of thoughts and feeling swam around in my head like fish in an overcrowded tank. What was I going to do? Finish my work and get out of here I guess. It was nice to leave at closing time and take in the distinctive autumn bite of withering leaves in the air. It was still daylight, the sun trying to peek under the layer of heavy clouds giving everything a surreal brightness. Fall had kissed the edges of the trees golden, deep orange and brilliant red. I usually loved this time of year. It wasn't too cold or rainy yet and nature's colors were vibrant against the deep gray sky. It was the kind of day that helped me to put all the ugliness in my life out of my mind.

~ ~ ~

The weight Marlo had lifted off me lasted all the way through classes but I worried about Adrian. Maybe he could be his own problem for a while. I convinced myself that I felt nearly normal by the time Lucie met me in the parking lot. We were skipping the shop today to work on the project for English which normally I wouldn't have loved, but since it meant Lucie time, I felt like smiling. We hopped on my bike and rode to my house.

"You know," she said as soon as she'd pulled off her helmet, "we're going to have to start taking my car or carpool with Marlo when the rain gets serious. Your mom will never let you ride the bike."

"True." I pushed the bike into the garage and shut the door behind us. Lucie and I were still smiling at each other as we entered the kitchen.

I came to a halt and stared at Mom.

"What are you doing home?"

"Bad day," was her clipped answer. She didn't sound mad though, she sounded defeated.

I really looked at her. She had tempera paint on her slacks and dry erase marker on her shirtsleeve. Her hair was a mess and she had a reddish purple smudge under each eye, telling me that she wasn't sleeping well either.

"What happened?"

"Why do people treat me badly?" she asked instead.

"Because you let them," I answered and then I bit my lip. Maybe today was not a good day for brutal honesty.

"I'm afraid not to be nice. What if I lose my job, my friends or the people I love?"

"You should talk to us. Even if we can't help, you can still unload. You seemed fine this morning before you left for school," I said gently.

Mom sighed, "I'm still worried sick about Lucas. Your dad and I had an argument about your grandfather. He still wants to take all of us to Cuba for a month to see family. He wants to go during Christmas. I asked the principal just to feel out the situation and I won't get the time off. A student threw up in class yesterday and now they are dropping like flies from the flu. I sent two more students home today. The principal got mad at me regarding another situation that was completely out of my control and my teaching partner just got the word that she's leaving. Her husband got a great new job out of state. I'm thrilled for them, but I was also informed that I will be teaching full time from when she moves to the end of the year or I quit and they hire someone who will. I can't work full time. I have to be here for you and your brothers."

Mom put her head down on her arms and cried. Lucie talked to her softly and rubbed her back. I wasn't good at this. Mom was my rock. *How could I help her?*

I sat down next to her and rested my shoulder against hers. "It's going to be okay, Mom. You don't need to solve it all today. We'll figure this out. You stood up to Caleb Carmichael. You can stand up to Dad and your principal. I believe in you." But in the back of my mind I couldn't help wondering if this was Bob's doing. That had to be crazy, right?

She raised her head and wiped her eyes. Lucie went to fix a pot of tea and then came and sat across from Mom.

"Why are you so kind and supportive of me and so hard on your-self?" Mom asked me. "Look at you, taking my advice and par-roting it back to me. What you need to do is get to where you can admit that you are a good person no matter what terrible things have happened to you. When you achieve that, you'll be able to forgive yourself and let it go. All the hate and all the fear… all the anger will melt away. I worry about you, Owen. One frost does not make a winter and I guess my pile from today doesn't either."

"I guess none of us has to be strong all the time. There will be other jobs, other friends and you'll always have us. Don't be afraid to start over," Lucie said. "Owen, I'm afraid, is a work in progress."

"Maybe we're all works in progress," Mom replied to Lucie and then she looked at me. "You were in such a dark place and then it seemed like you were better. Alex grows and improves every day, yet I find I'm worrying more, not less. It's not even Thanksgiving and I need a sick day. A mental health day, I mean. I need to… think because I sound like a crazy person"

Lucie smiled at her. "You're not."

"Mom, the day or so off is a good idea. You deserve time to think about a big decision like this and I can't go to Cuba for a month right now either. Maybe Dad could take Lucas and Alex? It would get them out of here."

"I guess. What a lot of pressure to put on Alex. You know he'll feel responsible for everyone."

"He might. Maybe it will be good for him. He'd learn things we could never teach him here."

"I suppose," she paused and then looked at me startled. "Why are you here?"

"English."

"I'm sorry. You told me. I forgot."

"It's okay, Mom. You've got a lot on your mind."

"Why don't you go clear your head. Owen and I will take care of English and dinner. Marlo and Caitlyn are working on the other half of the project so we may need to see them later but we have plenty of time."

"That would be lovely. Thanks, Lucie."

They hugged each other. It was probably the thing my mom needed most. Now if I could just figure out what I needed to fix myself.

EIGHT

Days passed. We weren't getting anything useful on the table. The man who bought it was a ghost but his cash was good. Lucie began scouring estate sales to see if she could find more items to fit our lonely puzzle pieces to help us find the table and its vanished buyer. The only happy side effect was that it was taking so long that Lucas was losing interest. He even lost interest in the shop and was spending more time with his friends. I for one was thankful – he needed to be a kid, away from us and hopefully out of danger.

The timing was good because Alex was digging up news from the middle school that would have gotten Lucas interested all over again. This year Alex was skateboarding to the shop every day after school like I had in eighth grade. He was so far ahead of where I was back then, it was scary. Maybe if I'd been as good then as he is now – I wouldn't have gotten in so much trouble, but maybe I would have gotten in even more.

Alex had texted me at lunchtime that he was on to something. I promised I'd be here when he arrived after school. It was hard for me to treat my little brother like an equal. Just a short time ago he was a little kid but not now. He was nearly as tall as me and stick thin. Mom struggled to find jeans with a 28 inch waist and a 33 inch inseam.

He came into the back where I was refinishing a desk from the same estate sale we got the table from. Alex glowed with enthusiasm. A fresh case can do that for you.

"Well?" I asked.

"I know there has been increasing gang activity. I've been following the police logs. Did you know tagging is way up? Anyway it's not just the quantity that has increased; there is a new tag out there."

"Oh…kay," I drew out. I knew this couldn't be all he had. Spray painting symbols on trains, containers, buildings and fences had been going on way before my time.

"I saw it last week on a kid's binder. I was curious enough to follow him. Turns out there are nine kids using the symbol that I know of."

"Be careful, Alex."

"Of course, but anyways… these guys are good - our kind of good. They've got to have a club and outside help. I need surveillance done."

"They're not on to you are they?" I asked, with a worried frown.

"Nah, I get no sense that they know about me. The leader even asked one of the guys if he'd been followed. When he answered 'no,' he was being honest. They don't know about me."

"Are there any rumors going around about you?"

"A few kids know you're my brother and a few know about my karate, but no one knows how many kinds of martial arts I really do or what I really am. Not even Tyler knows that. Not that I wouldn't like to tell him."

"I'm impressed."

"It's no big deal," Alex smiled. "I have you guys to talk to about this stuff."

"So, do you have a plan?"

"Where are Lucie and Marlo?"

"They got a table lead. Why?"

"I need to talk to them too. I need their help." He paused. "What table lead?"

"Mitchell talked to Tess who has a women's studies class this term. In her class is a woman who admits she's a white witch. They are interviewing her and she's going to take them to a shop she buys components from."

"Really?"

I just smiled.

"Okay so when will they be here, do you think?"

"They'll be gone as long as it takes, but you know they'll be here to leave notes about the interview."

"Okay." Alex actually sounded disappointed. "I'm going to practice. Want to join me?"

"I need to finish the desk. We have an interested party coming in tomorrow."

Alex nodded and went to change.

I watched him glide over the floor as he worked through several katas. He had a gift - that was for sure. It made me feel… proud and a little jealous. He turned and paused… too long. Something was wrong. I took a step toward him as he fell over sideways like a lawn chair tipped by the wind. My breath froze in my chest. "Alex!"

I rushed to his side and knelt down. I barely noticed White Eagle bursting through the swinging door that covered the opening to the front of the shop.

Alex looked up at me with terror in his eyes, his body momentarily locked. I watched him swallow and try to work his jaw.

His hand fought its way to his heart. "My chest," he gasped in a breathy whisper.

White Eagle knelt down too. We each put a hand on Alex, who sucked in a deep breath and relaxed. "It's going away," he sighed.

I couldn't tell what was going on with him but I knew it wasn't medical. "Was it her?"

"I don't think so," Alex replied calmly. "It doesn't feel like her. Or, it is, but not in the way you think. It wasn't a direct attack - it's an after effect."

Lucie and Marlo found us still squatting by Alex.

"What's wrong?" Lucie asked with a frown.

"It's Evilia," Alex answered calmly.

"She attacked you?" Marlo queried.

Alex sighed. "Not exactly; what she did to me... years ago... damaged me. Sometimes I get these weird... I don't know, attacks or something."

"Oh, Alex." Lucie moved in to hug him. She turned her gaze on White Eagle. I knew that look. She was desperate for a solution.

White Eagle looked grim.

Alex glanced from him to me and then put his attention on Lucie. "I'm not dying today but since you're so concerned and all, I could use your help."

"Okay, what do you need?" Lucie asked in a tone that let me know she was eager to fix everything.

I listened to Alex retell his board warriors story and add that he needed Marlo for remote surveillance and Lucie to volunteer at the middle school to be another pair of eyes.

"I don't understand. What am I looking for? Just kids using a gang symbol?" Lucie asked.

"The guy I've pegged as second in command has the same social studies teacher you did. I want you to schmooze your way in and spy. There's some intergroup arguing. I want you to teach him something other than social studies that will make him think he can become the leader."

"I follow - you want to stir the pot. So, what do you think I should teach this guy?" Lucie was sold. I could tell by the way she leaned in toward Alex and gave him her full attention.

"What about Kav Maga or gymnastics? They do Parkour. I've seen it. Either skill would have him drooling."

A slow smile spread over Lucie's face but Marlo was frowning. "You want her to teach her skills to a gang member? Are you crazy?"

"Crazy good!" Alex insisted.

White Eagle smiled. "You sound like your brother. It could work."

"You want Lucie because she looks less dangerous and you think he'll like her." I added.

"Well, duh. She's hot and she's older. He won't know what hit him."

Marlo returned to his laptop, shaking his head. He called Alex right over to discuss the surveillance plan. White Eagle indicated the desk with a look. I stood, kissed Lucie and went to show my work to my boss. Lucie got on a computer to email her former teacher and looked into volunteer forms.

I talked to White Eagle about the desk but kept my eyes on Alex.

"It's okay to let him do this you know," White Eagle said softly.

"It's hard sometimes. I want to protect him and I'm proud of him." I watched Alex some more. "I understand why he can't use me, but I want to help. I imagine that's how Adrian feels a lot of the time."

"I'm sure you're right and speaking of Adrian... has that Jon kid been giving you any more trouble?"

"He watches me warily and I watch him. He seems to be busy enough with girls, football and school in that order, of course.

"Of course."

"It's been bugging me for a while. I have to know… Why'd you let Max sell that table so fast?"

"I wondered when you'd get around to that. There are two reasons. One, I don't want to upset Max and get him any deeper into our business and two, I couldn't risk getting the buyer too suspicious."

"But he got away," I hissed, frustrated.

"Did he?"

I paused. "Didn't he?"

"I know who he is, Owen. I heard today. I took his fingerprints and Evelyn got back to me."

"Evelyn – not Sarah?"

"Sarah knows, but if we use Sarah's resources, Bob has access. If we use Evelyn, he doesn't. It just takes longer."

We smiled at each other.

"So, who is he?"

"Let's hear what Marlo and Lucie found first."

White Eagle put up the closed sign and Marlo got the deposit ready and squared away the register. The new system of having Max open and White Eagle close was working well so far. We all did our parts, but we about needed another person so that White Eagle didn't have to be here six days a week.

"Mom," I burst out looking at White Eagle.

"What?"

"You need more help here and Mom's job is changing. She can't work full time with Dad gone so much. She wants to be home for Lucas. Maybe she could work here?"

"She loves teaching."

"She loves working half time with her friend, and the kids are a bonus. Her friend is leaving and they won't let her stay half time. There is a new principal this year with different ideas. She and Mom have not hit it off."

"What? Everyone loves your mom."

"Clearly, not everyone."

"I'll talk to her."

Everyone finished their tasks and we huddled up around Marlo's workspace in the back.

"We had an interesting day," Lucie began.

"I'll bet," I added.

Lucie slid me a glance. "We met Mitchell and Tess at Seattle's Best Coffee near the PSU campus. We decided that it would feel less intrusive if only the three of us went so Mitchell walked us to the Library and did his own thing while Tess took us to the basement and we used a room she'd reserved. Her wiccan friend, Meegan, met us there."

Lucie looked to Marlo and he resumed the tale. "Meegan is an interesting... person. Ze believes in equal ... everything - right down to the balance of darkness and light."

"Did you say, 'ze'?" Alex asked.

"Yes, not he or she but ze is how Meegan identifies. Ze referred to self that way and explained that the term 'ze' is gender neutral."

"Ah," White Eagle and Alex intoned together.

"Ze knew what we were," Lucie added.

"It was amazing," Marlo cut in. "Meegan had a crystal and held it out to Lucie and then me. It started to glow when it came into contact with us."

My eyes nearly popped out of my head.

"It's okay," Marlo said soothingly. "Meegan took us to the shop ze works at and took us into the back room. Ze had a special table with all kinds of sigils, you know, symbols used in magic, from the Latin meaning seal, inlaid in it. You would have loved the craftsmanship, White Eagle," he added as an aside.

I had to stop and think about what he said, he threw so much together. *Leave it to Marlo to over-describe.*

"But anyway," Lucie took over again, "Ze laid out a tarot deck for us and then used a map and that crystal to locate the darkest magic in the city."

"And you believe... ze?" I asked.

"We do," Marlo said. "Meegan did not feel like a *watcher* - good or bad - yet there was power and knowledge that we can't explain."

White Eagle took a turn at questioning. "What does Mitchell say?"

Lucie replied, "He was not with us and has never met Meegan."

"It's worth a look at the location she… I mean ze, identified," I said

"And I have a name. Any bets as to whether or not the name and location are a match?" White Eagle asked.

All eyes turned to look at him.

"Our purchaser was one Abner Grolier."

"How'd you get that?" Marlo asked.

"I lifted his prints while he was here."

Now Marlo's curiosity was piqued. "You didn't run them through Sarah, so you must have used Evelyn. If she found him in AFIS then he has a record. What did she say he was arrested for?"

"Oh little things like art theft, the importation of illegal exotic artifacts and… ingredients."

"Did Evelyn send us a profile?" Marlo asked, sounding excited.

"She's meeting me in," he paused to look at his watch, "about ten minutes."

"So we'll have two things to scout: A location and a guy on the table front and for Alex, we need to profile some teenaged hoodlums." Marlo was into it now.

"You do know that nobody uses that phrase anymore, right Mars?" I asked.

"Hoodlums," Alex laughed.

"Well I beg your pardon," Marlo huffed. The twinkle in his eye let Alex know he was only half serious.

"I believe 'hoodlums' sums it up just right," White Eagle added causing Alex to burst out laughing. White Eagle smiled at him and left to meet Evelyn.

We finished the close-up routine, but White Eagle was back before we had escaped out the back door. He handed Marlo a mini flash drive. Marlo restarted his computer and we all hovered over his shoulder to see the file. Yep, it was our buyer. We agreed we could do more tomorrow and locked up the shop for good. Marlo went his way and the rest of us piled into White Eagle's truck. Alex took shotgun which left me the opportunity to sit in back with Lucie; the tradeoff was worth it.

The next day we used our shop time to plan our mode of attack. White Eagle took Lucie and Marlo to scout the building where Meegan had identified the darkest energy in the vicinity and Sarah went with Alex and me to check out our perp. Sarah loaded his data onto her laptop and read aloud his pertinent information while we watched his last known address for signs of activity.

Hours passed. I thought I saw the same car pass us twice but I told myself I was nuts. Sarah looked at her watch and sighed, "Do we set up real surveillance or start questioning people?"

"I think the less Bob knows the better. At least we should give him as little access as we can get away with. We're in too deep."

"I agree," Alex added. "We should start with interviews. Besides that's why I'm here. I'll know what's what."

Sarah smiled at him but it was the look in her eyes that made me pause. She loved him like her own. We weren't her biological children but it didn't matter. She loved us like our own mom did and whatever was going on with Alex was killing her a little bit every day too.

"Come on you two. What are you waiting for?" I could hear his enthusiasm.

"Alex, I want you to know that I appreciate your taking time away from your board warriors. It means a lot."

"Why wouldn't I? The table is ours, not just yours – besides I help you and you help me, right?"

Sarah put her arm around his shoulders, "Yes, that's what family does." Then she put on her brusque business face. "Let's start with his place."

We knocked on the door to Abner Grolier's condo but no one answered. One neighbor was home or at least willing to open the door. Sarah showed her badge and gave the usual spiel.

"What's with the kid?" the burly man asked instead. He had to be the hairiest human I had ever encountered. With his dark brown hair, bushy beard and dark eyes he had to be a logger, biker, bartender or woodsman. Now I was profiling.

Sarah glanced at Alex, "He's my student intern."

"Really? They start younger and younger all the time. So whadda you want?"

"I would like to ask you a few questions about your neighbor, Abner Grolier."

"Older guy, skinny, quiet and lives in 18753? So that's his name." He seemed to answer his own question but watched Sarah's face for confirmation. He nodded and went on, "He never smiles or waves."

"Does anyone live with him that you're aware of?"

"Nope, seems to live alone."

"Do you know when he'll be back?"

"Nah, I'm about to leave for work. Sometimes I see him when I get home, which is kinda strange seeing as how I work swing shift and most folks are in bed when I get home."

"Do you know where he works?"

"Sorry lady, I haven't got a clue. I've never actually talked to the guy."

"Does he socialize with any other neighbors?"

"Not that I've ever seen. Hey sorry, but I really need to get going."

"I understand. Here's my card. If you think of anything you left out, would you please give me a call. We appreciate your time today."

"Sure, no problem." His big beefy hand took the card from Sarah. I'd thought of her as a little old lady once and now I was seeing her as little again, but old...not so much. We turned and his door gently clicked shut.

We were still walking to Sarah's car when he drove by in a big diesel Chevy truck with an extended cab. He had his window rolled down and waved to us. "Hey one more thing," he said loudly over the diesel's rumble.

"Yes?" Sarah inquired.

"He drives a BMW 6X in a dark green color. Seems like an odd car for a guy I never see wearing anything but a black suit." He smiled a big teddy bear grin, slapped the side of his Deep Ocean Blue 3500 Silverado and pulled out.

"Well, Alex?" Sarah asked, knowing he would know what she was talking about.

"He's a grizzly bear with a big heart and completely honest."

"I hope Luce, White Eagle and Marlo had better luck."

We headed for Sarah's house where we had previously agreed to meet. I missed having Marlo running home base so that the latest intel was plugged right into my ear. The wait was torture. We had alerted Mitchell to be paying attention tonight and to call if he even had a twinge of good or bad news, but we had not alerted Sarah's team. As much as we trusted them, Bob had lost our trust and we needed that man off our backs.

White Eagle, Lucie and Marlo came in the front door looking tired. "Well?" Alex burst out before I could open my mouth.

"We came, we saw, we did not exactly conquer," Marlo said in a sad, resigned voice.

"What happened?"

"We watched the location for hours. We never saw Grolier nor could we get inside. The address is a warehouse," Lucie said in the same kind of voice.

"If Grolier owns it, it's hidden well. All we know for sure is that table is inside."

"Are we back to B and E?" I asked hopefully.

"Now is not the time to get caught," Sarah advised.

"No, without Bob's support it's too dangerous," White Eagle agreed.

"Then what do we do?" Alex asked, sounding disgusted.

"We let Marlo do what he does best - research and we work on your board warriors."

Alex grinned at my suggestion. "Now that, I can live with."

"Lucie is in at the school; she starts on Monday. What did Marlo get you on your guys?"

"He was able to get video footage from the busses the kids ride. We'll be watching that and the video from the outside entrances to the school. Until we figure out where they hang, it's all we've got.

"Watch your back."

"Don't I always?" Alex shot back.

"So that's what we're calling it now?"

"Oh like you are any better at that than I am. We're both reckless. I own that, and so should you," Alex said sounding superior, but I knew he was mostly teasing me. Maybe I should wrestle him to the ground to remind him who was boss. I tackled him onto the carpet. I'm a brother – fighting fair is not expected.

White Eagle broke up our mock fighting at dinner time. At least I had Alex flat on the mat more often than he did me.

It was Alex's night to cook. Personally I was glad that I could spend time on our latest novel that I'd been neglecting for English. I like to read more than most kids, but I'm tired of having to read what other people choose for me. I also get tired of all the deeper meaning stuff. I mean come on – can't a character just wear black because they think they look good in it? Maybe sometimes a story is just a story and deeper meaning is just crap.

Sure enough, in English we got to discuss the deeper meaning of the novel. At least I'd read it. Days like today I was actually looking forward to college. I had to get undergrad stuff out of the way and then I could focus on what I wanted. Which was what? Forensics or law enforcement? I knew I needed to be a field guy and not a lab guy. Lucie kicked me under the table. She was right, I wasn't paying attention.

When the bell rang, she put a hand on my leg before I could rise. "You do know that reasonable and realistic do not mean the same thing, right?"

"What?"

"It is a reasonable expectation for you to pay attention in class, but for you it just isn't realistic. You've been this way since eighth grade. Where do you go when you leave?"

"I don't know… anywhere but here. I get bored and my mind just takes over. I can't help it. If I'm moving or doing something, it's different."

"Yeah, I guess. Well Goober, I'll see you at work." She said it with a sweet smile and a big kiss so I knew *Goober* was a term of endearment. "And don't forget to finish the book."

"Yes, Mother."

I headed for the shop. The weather was getting brisker and the clouds darker. It was about my last week with the bike. I'd have to ride with Lucie and get stuck at school for an extra hour each day or I could run to the shop in the rain. I hadn't been doing much running lately. Without Tess around to bug me, I'd gotten lazy. I rode to the shop for the last time this year and promised myself I'd do better. I even sat in the back and finished the novel like Lucie suggested. I could be a whole new me; we'd see if it was only for one day.

Lucie came in with Marlo and hugged me when she saw me reading. "Yeah, I know, good boy and I'm not even sleeping."

"Or drooling," Marlo quipped and then laughed.

"Now that's saying something!" Lucie lightly punched me in the arm for emphasis. "I'm headed up front. I want to rearrange the glassware and antiques."

"You want help?"

"Nah, I'm good. Mars is on the register, so I'll grab him if I need it."

I returned to the last chapter of the book. Luce and Mars had left the swinging door open. I overheard White Eagle and Marlo talking about going to install some surveillance cameras to focus on the warehouse that held our mysterious table. Lucie said she had the register until Max returned.

A little time went by. It was quiet except for Lucie moving around up front. The bell rang over the shop door and I assumed it was Max but the voice was wrong. It was familiar. I had to be mistaken. Please let me be wrong.

"Hello?"

"Piper?"

"You must be Lucie."

"I am. It's nice to finally meet you."

I dropped my novel without even marking my place and moved toward the open door to the front of the shop.

"Really? I didn't expect you to say that. It even seems like you mean it," Piper replied.

I peered around the corner trying to decide if I should come out or pretend I didn't hear. I watched Lucie smile at Piper. "You don't have to be afraid of me," she said softly as if Piper were a scared rabbit.

"I thought you'd be mad about Jess, I mean Owen."

"You didn't know he had a girlfriend."

"But he did. Nothing happened though," she quickly added.

"I know."

"How can you be so confident?"

"I'm not positive about anything other than the fact that I love him. We've been through a lot together and right now he needs me."

"I see."

"Are you here to see him, Piper? I thought you weren't allowed."

"Even without Caleb Carmichael or Evilia Malvada they are proceeding with the case against everyone else involved. I testified today. They are releasing me from protective custody."

There was silence for a moment. "Why would they release you if they're still out there? It makes no sense."

I couldn't stand it any longer. "It makes perfect sense if Bob signed the paperwork."

Piper gave a start and blushed. "I didn't know if you were here."

"It's good to see you Piper, but it's dangerous for you to be here."

She sent a nervous glance to Lucie, "Um, thanks, it's good to see you too. Why does it make sense about Mr. Bruner?"

"His name is actually Robert Bowman. He's a division chief. We are pretty sure he has lost his way because all he seems to care about anymore is his rise to power or something. He wants Evilia Malvada and he has the crazy idea that I'm the key to her capture," I answered.

"Are you saying he's so single-minded that he'll do anything even if it's against the law he swore to uphold?" Piper's eyes had gone wide but her brain was still hard at work.

"Pretty much," Lucie added, "and it sounds like he wants to use you as bait."

"How would that work? I've never seen nor had I ever heard anything about Evilia Malvada until today when I gave my statement. I didn't even know who Caleb Carmichael was until they brought the case against him. I only saw him on the video with the other dealers."

"Easy, Bob's people are watching Owen; so are Malvada's. You've been seen here. Each side is waiting for Owen to make a move, but Bob must have gotten impatient and tried to speed things up. He knows you're Owen's friend. It won't be long before she figures that out. Then all she has to do is snatch you up. Then Owen will save you. She gets Owen and Bob gets her. You are collateral." Lucie's words were true if a little harsh.

"I thought it was over. I wanted to believe I was safe."

"You're not," I said firmly. She had to believe us.

Lucie turned to me. "How are we going to hide her?"

"I'm done hiding! It's no way to live and I want to spend some time with my mom. Besides, who do you think provided my ride here?"

"You don't know *what* you're up against," I said as I moved next to Lucie.

Lucie spoke before Piper could respond, "You don't know *who* you're up against."

"Forget it. I came, I saw, and now I'm leaving."

"Piper, no," I tried.

"Let us help you," Lucie added.

"There is nothing for me here. You're crazy. You can have each other."

"Piper!" I yelled at her retreating back. I rushed around the counter but she was out the door. At least she didn't slam it. She got into the back of a black sedan. I stopped and Lucie nearly ran into the back of me. I looked at her for help.

Lucie wore a thoughtful expression.

"What should I do?" I asked.

"Let her cool off or at least give her time to think. That was definitely one of Bob's cars she got into, so they can't hold you responsible."

"I guess."

"Owen, she was a message. Bob wants you to move faster."

"I don't know where Evilia is and he won't help."

"I know. I also know that I believe in you and we will figure this out."

I hugged her close. At least I had her. We were just heading back in when White Eagle's truck pulled into the lot.

"How'd the install go?" Lucie asked.

"I just hope it doesn't get noticed. I didn't realize how much Bob was helping until now. We had to use some cheaper old-school outdoor equipment. I'm not happy with our view. White Eagle and I could only cover about seventy-five percent of the warehouse. I'll let you know when I catch sight of Grolier." Marlo went on inside to put away his tools.

I cut my eyes to White Eagle who shrugged at me. I hate waiting. We followed Marlo inside and then told them about Piper's visit. White Eagle agreed that we couldn't force her to accept our help. I was beginning to wonder if anything would ever go right for us but Lucie felt positive. She told us how things were going with Alex and the boy he'd targeted. Lucie helped Alex monitor what was happening in the building and had gotten herself assigned to the boy. She quickly formed a connection with him and next week she and Alex would meet with him after school to practice some gymnastics and Krav Maga. We finished at the shop and I went home with Lucie. I owed her some quiet time to just chill. It was our night to cook so we drove past Safeway for a roasted chicken, fresh French bread, a chopped salad and Marionberry pie.

Without real planning it's tough to do school, work and cook. No one complains at the White Eagle's house; we're all just happy when we don't have to cook, I guess. Sarah's rule is anyone who says an ugly word, cooks the next night. I like that. It's quiet down here too, without my brothers around or anyone arguing.

After dinner, White Eagle and Sarah retreated to their office that had been remodeled to accommodate them both. Lucie and I cleaned the kitchen and then she headed to her room to change. I wandered into the family room and began to scan Netflix for a movie to watch. Lucie came back in yoga pants and a tank top. She pulled the blanket from the back of the couch and snuggled in.

"Good job at the shop today," Lucie said softly.

"Thanks and good job with Alex."

"I liked the way you talked to Piper."

"I like the way you're handling Alex's classmate. Tell me, are you my reward for good behavior?" I asked with a big smile.

"Pretty sure I am," she said sliding onto my lap, "and you can be mine."

"You're missing the movie," I said against her lips.

"What a shame," she replied, not meaning it.

For the moment all the sleepiness left my body. She had my full attention. I couldn't even tell you what movie we weren't watching. I hated to leave when it was over, but there was always tomorrow. Lucie even had me feeling a little more upbeat.

NINE

I awoke with a start and that was happening way to often these days. Something didn't feel right. I scanned my room, the house. Nothing. I forced myself to relax and then... *I was standing in the shadows, my hat brim tipped low and I was waiting. I pushed up the sleeve of my charcoal raincoat; my watch gave the time and date but not the year. I pushed off the wall, turned the corner and walked through the first door on the left. I took in the asbestos tile floor and chrome chairs, showing their age in their cracked maroon vinyl seat covers. The chipped Formica counter was another hint about the era and so was the manual register. A waitress escorted me toward the back. She flipped a mimeographed menu on the table and left. Her uniform was nylon hideous complete with a foofy fake handkerchief next to her too wide lapel. Her name was... wait for it... Doris, stitched in the same maroon as the seating. I shook off my raincoat and hung it on the coat rack. Dear God, I was wearing a leisure suit of baby blue. Shoot me, shoot me now.*

White Eagle's grandmother entered, walked to Kraeghton's table, hung up her own coat and sat. Her spine was stiff. Her skin appeared stretched over her bones and looked almost papery. Her color wasn't good either.

"Nadie," Kraeghton greeted. I could feel a cat that ate the canary smile tug at his lips.

"You win," she sighed in a resigned tone.

"I'm sorry for your pain, but I knew I would."

"You care about my pain? I doubt that." Nadie Black Feather looked deep within my eyes to my very soul. Her hand came down on mine

gently like a falling leaf and then her lips began to move. "Your world will grow darker and darker. At the moment things are at their worst, you will be given a choice. Choose the light and there will be hope."

I felt my lips move, "What light?"

"You will know it because it will shine like no other. Resist the urge to covet it or destroy it. It is not yours. Help it and all will be forgiven."

"What are you saying?" Kraeghton begged, but the memory faded away.

Sunlight streamed through my window and slapped me in the face. Well at least I'd only had one nightmare. Was I late for school? I checked my cell. It was Saturday. Saturday and sunny in November; it was an appreciated oddity, but it was also time for chores and work. I started mumbling to myself as I headed for the bathroom – gutters, cover faucets, cut the grass one last time.

I stirred up some pancakes to motivate the troops. I scrounged up some frozen bacon and was defrosting it when Mom staggered over to the coffee pot. "Why are you up so bright and early, Tiger?"

"I forgot to close my blinds and the sun got me. Besides, today is chore day, right?"

"Yay, chores. I'll go start a load of laundry while you get those pancakes going."

Mom disappeared for a bit, but when she returned she smiled.

"What?" I asked, infected by the smile.

"I won, for now," she grinned wider.

"Won?"

"No visit to Cuba until this summer."

"Nice going. How'd you manage that?"

Then her smile wobbled a little. "Everyone's grades are slipping."

"I guess you can't win 'em all."

Five hours later I had finally made it to the shop. I figured I'd worked out plenty so I met up with Lucie and we rode over in her car. I got right to work on a leaf blower that was barely wheezing and Lucie took a turn watching the feed from the monitor on the warehouse while she cleaned some glass pieces that had come in.

The door to our workroom in the back swung soundlessly and my jaw dropped open. Julie stood just inside the doorway looking fully recovered on the outside, but her eyes told me a different story.

"Hey, Julie. This is a surprise. I thought that Bob wanted to keep you away from us," I said bluntly, still in shock.

"He does," she replied looking all around the back area as if he would pop out at any moment.

Lucie elbowed me in the ribs and moved forward to hug her. "I'm so glad to see you, Julie."

"You too. I'm here on business."

"Oh?" Lucie replied, giving her an opening.

"Bob won't help me," Julie blurted, her annoyance clear, "but I knew you would."

"What is it?"

"She's at it again. Bob says he's looking into it and is watching for her, but he doesn't really try. It's like he doesn't care. He's busy with something else. What can be more important than children?"

"Nothing," Lucie agreed.

Marlo got up and stood by us.

"Julie, this is Marlo, our tech expert."

"Nice to meet you Marlo," she said reaching for his hand.

"You too, Julie. Are you saying that Bob can't find her or won't find her? We've, ah… been a little cut off lately," Marlo hedged.

"He tells me otherwise, but I know he isn't really looking. He has everybody on something else but I don't know what. I never hear from him anymore unless I contact him. I'm sick of sending him information and getting nothing in return. I hoped you all would know what was going on, but from your comment… I'd say he's treating us about the same.

"So, you want our help. What's up?" I asked to divert her because I was afraid Bob's latest project was me.

"Bob got me a job at a hospital in Vancouver. I've seen some strange stuff lately - our kind of strange, but Bob won't send any help. Some of the kids that have come in have *her* mark on them. I can't do this alone," Julie said as she pulled a flash drive from her pocket.

Marlo was quick to snatch it, plug it in and pull up her files. Julie had patient files, with photos and notes on abuse. She translated anything we couldn't understand from *medical-ese* into plain English.

Marlo was wearing his thinking face. "What do all of her activities have in common?"

"They're evil because she's evil," Lucie tried.

"She only cares about herself," I added and Julie nodded.

"Her activities are all about power and power is money. I've just got to follow the money," Marlo exclaimed.

"I have some intel Bob shared, that you may not have. It's from when he blackmailed you two into working for him. He got it from the facilities you were kept at. Not everything was destroyed like I think he led you to believe."

"I'm going to be like Eliot Ness and his pals and catch our own Al Capone the only way we can!" Marlo returned to typing and flipping his attention between monitors.

"What's he saying?" Julie asked.

"He's going to hack into the FBI's files and find out what Bob really knows about Evilia, add it to what he knows and then track her through her funding. It's genius. And that, my friends, is why we call him Marlo the Magnificent."

Marlo beamed at me and then began typing with a flourish. Julie bit her lip, trying to hide a smile. "I did come to the right place."

Lucie glanced at Marlo and then back at Julie, "We are nothing if not enthusiastic."

"Yeah, that's it," I laughed. "Have a seat Julie and catch us up. I need to finish this today."

Julie looked from me to the workbench. "You're a mechanic too?"

Lucie laughed. "Yep, that's how I think of him."

"What Lucie means is I do a little repair on odds and ends around here. Now spill. What's up?"

Julie stared hard at the leaf blower but started talking, "All I wanted was a little help with Evilia Malvada. I'd never actually seen her. The only reason they kept me around was for my medical skills. I admit that I'm not the *watcher* you guys are, but we all do our part, right?" Julie sounded both sad and proud.

"Yes, ma'am," I answered.

"Bob kept blowing me off. I didn't get it. I went to his office one day to confront him because he had very specifically told me that anything I did, I was supposed to run through him. He had me in therapy for months with a Dr. Anita Moretz..." I dropped the wrench I was holding. Julie gave me an odd look but continued. "I don't think he trusted me even when she released me for work. What's with the wrench?"

"Owen has seen Dr. Moretz too. Only his visit wasn't voluntary." Lucie spoke for me.

"I take it her therapy with you was not the couch sitting kind."

I shook my head.

"She had such a way with people. Did she make you listen to her nattering on for hours on end while you tried to sleep?"

"Yes."

"I feel for you, buddy. Don't worry. Her crap seems to wear off. She may think she's da bomb diggity, but power has gone to her head."

"Tell us what you know about Evilia and I'll add it to the files while Marlo does his thing," Lucie said over Marlo's mumbling to his computer screens.

"You saw some of the files. I've seen her mark eight times now. I believe Evilia is trafficking children now too. I just wonder what Bob's motivation is? My theory is that he cares less about Evilia, who he is sure he will eventually catch, and more interested in keeping you guys under his thumb." Julie paused and then snapped her fingers. "How I get these ideas is from the day I went to his office. I didn't check in with reception. I went in our way... you know." We nodded and she went on. "I went past his tactics room and guess who was on the big screen?"

Marlo and Lucie had on surprised, expectant looks but I went straight to frustrated. "Me." Mars and Luce both turned to look at me and Julie refocused on my face, her look thoughtful.

"I got right back out of there. I stewed for three days before I came to you and I'm sorry about that. You had a right to know sooner. I just couldn't figure out why you. I wouldn't be here now except... it felt wrong."

"Thanks, Julie."

"I can tell you're not surprised. You... knew. At the time, I tried to tell myself he had people watching an op., but then the view changed to this little guy... the name tag on his desk at school said Lucas Ryer. So I had to ask myself...Why would Bob be watching your brother?"

Marlo and Lucie gave me sharp looks.

Julie looked around. "You knew... they didn't."

I hung my head for a minute. "When Dr. Moretz had me, she drugged me and threatened me. Even now, I'm not completely sure what was real and what was just my imagination. We know we are watched by Evilia and we are sure that Bob watches us too, but threatening my family was a new low even for him. Part of me refused to believe it was true. So far, they've only told me to stay away from Piper. They haven't contacted me and they've cut us off. But Piper came by the other day and nothing has happened to either of my brothers... yet."

"Oh Owen," Lucie said softly making me feel even worse.

"It's fine," I said gruffly, "I'll be careful."

Julie gave me a hard look and then turned to Lucie, "I hardly recognize you anymore – all blond and blue-eyed. You are not the girl I last saw. I'm proud of you Lucie, you've really turned yourself around. Now what? Senior year, right? College plans? How's your dad?"

"Way to change the subject," Lucie smiled. "He's the same – a pain in my backside. He's getting married this summer. They have a prenup and everything. May he and Chloe Tate live happily ever after and out of my hair. They very much deserve each other."

"And still feisty I see."

"Every day," Marlo added from his computer.

"I like him!" Julie smiled while hitching a thumb in Marlo's direction.

"We all graduate this year and we are all going to Portland State so that we can stay in the area," Lucie added as she forced Marlo into a headlock.

"So what's the plan?" I asked Julie.

"All the kids came from the same house. I've driven by. It's an old farmhouse type place far away from its neighbors. Even from the road I could see bars on the windows and it's got a bad vibe. I know better than to go in alone."

"It's almost Christmas break and we need a few days to dig up what we can anyway. Guess what our vacation plans are now?"

Julie smiled a crooked smile. "I wish it could be sooner but you're right. We need to be prepared. Everything I've got is on that drive. Do some reading and give me a call." Julie grabbed some paper from the desk. "I bought a burner cell. I don't trust Bob anymore." She wrote her number down. "Are your phones secured?" Marlo just gave her a look. "Apologies, Marlo. Of course they are."

"Too bad we won't have Mitchell," Lucie lamented.

"He needs to spend that time in Nevada working with Mr. Blackthorn and reconnecting there," I reminded her.

"Yeah, he's just handy to have around."

"Yes, but we can't rely on that. One day soon he'll be gone for good. We are the team here."

Lucie smiled at me and touched my face. For a moment everything else disappeared and then Julie cleared her throat. "We need to plan. I'll be back when you're ready to chat. Call me."

Lucie and I saw her out while Marlo got going on researching the house and compiling Julie's data on all the patients that had come through her E.R. It would be strange to work on this. It wasn't that I didn't want to help; it just seemed weird that it had not come to us. Was Julie just in the right place at the right time?

"You're better today," Lucie said softly, taking my hand.

"What do you mean?"

"Some days I can almost feel Kraeghton in you but today it's quiet."

"Some days I think I have him under control and other days I know I don't. I don't even know how this works. Is it using my energy or his? Am I winning or losing? I finally decided I'd just fake it until I made it but that isn't working either. I do feel better in the sense that I haven't hurt anyone lately. I'm trying really hard to stay calm because when I get upset…"

"Shhh, I know. You are going to win. I believe in you."

"I'm glad one of us does."

I could tell she wanted to say more but she hugged me instead. Maybe she thought she could shield me from the world. I knew that as much as I wanted to do it on my own, I could use all the help I could get.

"Let's go see a movie and grab a bite to eat like real people," I offered.

Lucie threw me one of her more brilliant smiles. "Sounds like a wonderful idea. We need Mexican food 'cause I'm feeling a little spicy."

Now she had me smiling. I like spicy.

TEN

It had been two and a half weeks since Julie's first visit and we were finally ready to make our move. Bob had been silent except for a video clip of Alex at school. He had not hurt anyone, yet, but the threat still loomed. I figured he had to know what we were up to. I had no proof except for a strong feeling in my gut. Thunder rolled in the background, muted by the drip of water off the eaves – something I'd have to check later. They were probably clogged with some leaves I'd missed on the last go-around. The thunder drew closer and the dripping more insistent. I could hear the croak of one the many little frogs we have around here and the occasional passing car. If ever there was a perfect night for an op, this was it. No one wanted to be out in this muck, including us.

We hadn't solved the table or Alex's board warriors and here we were working on Julie's case. I won't lie, I was interested too, and no matter what else went on, Evilia would always be my top priority – she had hurt too many people not to be. Yet I was torn. Why did everything always come at once? I supposed that was just life.

Julie, Lucie and I had geared up. White Eagle and Marlo would take the van and Sarah would play cover-up at home. We also decided to stick Alex in the van so that he could learn the other side of operations and he hated it. We all recognized it was because we never knew when he would have one of his strange attacks, but no one said it. Saul had pow-wowed with Julie and White Eagle over him and still we had no answers.

Today the van sported logos for a plumber. The drive over was uneventful except for Alex's grumbling. I guess hanging out with

Marlo just wasn't as cool as it used to be. Marlo did a little grumbling of his own. It was getting really difficult for him to hide things from his parents. With the holiday season in full swing there was lots of catering to be done and he wasn't around to help tonight. Lucky for Julie, we'd booked our techno wizard in advance otherwise Marla would never have let him go.

We pulled up out front and surveyed the house for a minute while White Eagle pretended to hold a conversation on his cell phone. It was not in the best part of town, but still it was a little unusual to have bars on every window from the basement to the second floor. The front door sported a keyed padlock – the kind you'd use to keep someone in and not what you'd expect on the outside.

Everything seemed to be quiet - perhaps too quiet. It was going to be strange to hear Alex in my ear but I was ready if the rest of them were. I turned and made eye contact with each of them. "Let's go. We have darkness to extinguish."

Even Alex cracked a smile, his teeth flashing white in the darkness. White Eagle moved the van to the spot Marlo had determined to be the best. The ladies and I hopped out and walked back to the house in question. Alex ran a quiet running commentary of what was happening in the neighborhood. I signed to Julie and Lucie to move on up the right side of the house as we'd planned. I took the left.

Lucie's voice whispered over my earwig that each window on their side was locked and barred. The only light they could see was in an upper window. The basement and first floor were in darkness. The strange quiet was bugging her too. No dogs barked, no frogs croaked and no humans were around. Only the constant patter of the rain kept us company.

"I hope they didn't move them. What if they moved them?" Julie whispered, sounding both scared and frustrated.

"I've got nothing here either. No water, no footfalls and no lights on my side," I whispered back.

I made it to the kitchen door first and set to work on the lock. I had it picked in less than five minutes. I carefully checked for alarms. Finding none, we eased into the kitchen and listened again. Only a faint creak met our ears. I nodded to Julie, who led Lucie into the main hall toward the front stairs.

"Kitchen clear," I whispered as I headed for the back hall. I checked the pantry and finding nothing, moved forward. A sound came from behind me. I melted into the shadows and turned to look. A man stood blocking that end by the kitchen. His stance and night vision goggles told me he was no surprised homeowner. Another sound behind me alerted me to someone at the other end of the hall by the living room. Super. I swiveled and ran forward. Kitchen guy started to lunge, but I quickly flipped to my hands to kick him in the face. I landed on my feet and ran toward the guy behind me. This time I used the wall for a one-armed handstand to kick him in the side of the head. Kitchen guy was staggering down the hall toward us. Fists flew and were blocked in rapid succession. These guys knew what they were doing. Both men were on me. I dropped low and tried to leg-sweep living room guy.

I could hear Alex talking through the com but I mostly ignored him. "Lucie, Julie, you've got company," I barked.

My lack of attention netted me a hit to the side of my head so hard that lights flashed and my neck popped. I shook it off as kitchen guy delivered a kick to my lower back. I spun and kicked in return. My foot connected with his temple. I resumed my fighter's stance, hands at the ready but, a strange thing happened. He just stood there for a moment and then fell straight over backwards, his body stiff. His head bounced twice on the floor before he began to twitch. I was horrified yet curious. Had I just caused a seizure? He gave one last twitch and was still. Did I kill him? Spectral visions of Kraeghton flashed, haunting me.

A dart flew past my ear and thunked into the wall. Living room guy was cheating. Too late – the poison had me too. It had to be some kind of neurotoxin or something. I could feel the paralysis flow from skeletal muscle to skeletal muscle. How did that happen? Living room guy ignored his buddy and trussed me up. I couldn't even speak. I prayed my grunts would be understood but where were Lucie and Julie? When had I last heard a sound from upstairs?

Another man appeared and helped to carry me down the stairs to the basement. I was dumped on the ground, landing hard on my right side. My other attacker landed with a thud next to me a few heartbeats later. I watched them sink a needle into him and my suspicions were confirmed when he began to move. It sounded like the other two, who had walked away, were barring the door. I realized that it was weirdly quiet down here - muffled. There was no sound of water running or even a furnace. The floor was covered with a thin layer of dirt. I could smell the earth, sweat and fear.

Without waiting for their buddy, who'd made it to his hands and knees, the other two hoisted me back up and then secured me to a cleared off workbench. It was musty and moist down here but the workbench was sturdy and it held. I could see the cobwebs hanging between the floor joists, wires, pipes and bare bulbs. I couldn't have moved anyway, but they tied me to the workbench using three loops of rope over my chest and arms and three more over my legs. The room was small and dark and I could barely make out the corners. They slapped a piece of duct tape over my mouth but never checked my pockets or touched my tactical ear piece.

A man entered through a door out of my line of sight. It was frustrating to only be able to see what my eyes could provide without movement. Had the guy been waiting down here or was there a way in we hadn't seen. He sure didn't come in a window. They had looked blackened by paint from the outside but down here I could see that they had been cemented off. I felt his dark energy wash over me. It was not the crushing wave I was expecting. I had never seen or felt his power before. When he entered my vision, I saw he was as ugly and scarred as his energy felt. He had suffered a bunch of abuse in his life but he wasn't a very powerful *dark watcher*. I'd have to pray that he didn't know who he had.

A tingling began in my fingertips and toes letting me know that the feeling was beginning to come back. Now I just had to last until I could do something or help came.

With my peripheral vision, I watched him move to a utility sink and wet a towel. He started to place it over my face but stopped and set it aside. Instead he dipped his fingers in a jar of goo he pulled from his pocket and made a mark on my forehead.

"Nod if you can hear me," his voice grated, soft and deep, like he'd gargled with rocks this morning.

I tried to comply and managed only a very small movement.

"Then let's begin."

He placed the towel over my face, blocking my vision and filling me with terror. Water immediately hit the towel. My breath froze in my chest as fear seized me. I fought not sucking in a startled breath. I couldn't even turn my head more than a fraction. Just as the panic took hold, the towel was whipped off. I frantically sucked in some watery air through my nose. I choked and snorted. I tried blowing hard out my nose so I could take another breath.

"Do you believe that I am not afraid to kill you?"

I gave him the same small partial nod, but he seemed to understand.

"Why are you at the house?" I widened my eyes. I tried to shake my head. The tingles had spread up to my elbows and knees. I was probably burning out the drug faster with my rapid heartbeat.

He yanked the tape from my face, leaving a stinging trail behind. "Who are you?"

"I heard you had my cousin here," I gasped.

"How did you find me?"

"I…"

"Too late." He slapped the towel back over my face and poured water over me again.

The towel came off just as I was about to lose it and suck water.

"Who are you?"

"My… my name is… Owen." I thought I heard a muffled thump overhead.

"We need to go," one of his men said in a worried tone.

"Not yet."

"It's just a kid."

"This is no kid."

My heart kicked up its erratic beating by another notch. Rage and fear battled within me and then Kraeghton was there gathering my *watcher* powers and preparing to throw them. I felt the swell and expansion, but then things got crazy. It was as if it hit a barrier and came back. A flash of light blinded me, warping my perceptions. My back arched and I shook and shuddered on the workbench.

"Told ya," he said to his buddies in that same strange voice.

A louder thump shook the basement door; they looked at each other and ran the way the *dark watcher* had come from.

"Someone wants you back." I felt a small smile pull at my lips but that made him angry. His fist hurtled toward my face and I could barely move. I felt the punch through my entire skull and my head exploded with pain as the door flew inward.

Lucie burst through and launched herself at the *dark watcher*. She swung up to wrap her legs around his neck and took him down to the floor. Julie stumbled down the stairs only to be shoved out of the way by White Eagle and Alex.

My body spasmed again as Bob and a team came through the basement door. Agents flooded the room grabbing each member of our team and the *dark watcher*. The moment quiet reigned, Bob pulled himself up to full stature and looked to the *dark watcher*.

"Who are you?" He asked in his best interrogator voice.

Bob's question went unanswered. He waited but I could feel his impatience. Lucie kept looking to me as did Julie, but no one let them move. Feeling was returning to the rest of my body and I could feel my eye swelling shut as blood leaked from my nose and mouth.

"How many of you are there?" Bob asked sounding a little angrier. "And where is Malvada?"

The *dark watcher* tore his eyes away from Bob and looked at me. "I have so many surprises waiting for you. How does it feel to be victorious – to kill the villain?"

I lay there, looking at him perplexed. I heard a crunch and foam began to pour from his mouth. The agents released him in horror. He dropped to the ground. His eyes rolled up in his head and bloody spittle burst out in a final gush.

Bob turned to me with murder in his eyes, then a slow smile slithered over his lips and he slid his eyes to White Eagle. "You are under arrest for breaking and entering and murder. You have the right to remain silent and do please try to test me. I'll learn the truth and right now, the hard way sounds like way more fun. You'll be lucky if anyone can find you to serve as your attorney. Take him out of here," he ended on a scream pointing at White Eagle.

"Sir," Julie begged.

"You – are a failure," Bob sneered, turned on his heel to leave. Julie looked listless; Alex and Lucie fought to free themselves, but White Eagle shook his head *no* at them. The click of the handcuffs was overly loud in my ears. The agents trooped out behind Bob and a handcuffed White Eagle. Three others carried the body of the *dark watcher.*

The moment they were up the stairs Lucie cut me free. Tears rolled down her cheeks as Alex took out a support beam in frustration with one impressive kick. I tried to sit up and collapsed on Lucie. She caught me before my knees hit the floor.

"Julie, help me," she begged.

Julie shuffled forward, looking sick. "I'm so sorry," she breathed. "I... I..."

"You called Dr. Moretz didn't you?" I asked, but I already knew the answer.

"What did she do to me? I locked Lucie in a closet to call her. How could I do that? I don't trust them. I would never hurt you, but I did. It's my fault they took White Eagle. How will we help him?"

"It's not your fault, it's mine. Bob is punishing me," I said, feeling sick.

"How did you know I called? I turned off my com. It was like I was watching a dream. I could see it but I couldn't control it," Julie croaked as a lone tear escaped.

Lucie and Alex were looking at her like she'd sprouted another head but it was Lucie who spoke, "When you pushed me, I thought you were trying to save me from them. You... you did it on purpose? I thought it was an accident. How could you?"

"That's why your com went down," Alex added. "You were concealing your actions."

"I didn't want to… the doctor…"

"She couldn't help it." I defended.

"How do you know?" Alex snarled.

"Because they got to me too. The stuff the doctor does is… bad. I don't know. I know I haven't been myself but I haven't had an episode like Julie's either." Lucie and Alex looked at me like they had at Julie a moment before. I started to add to my story when a creak upstairs alerted us. Alex went into combat mode, ready for anything, but it was Marlo and Sarah creeping down the stairs.

"Well, my dear, you look like hell," Sarah said looking right at me. "We should get you out of here."

"Not before we go over this house. Bob let three men get away." I turned to look around the room. "They didn't just vanish. They went somewhere," I added, staring into the dark corners.

"Bob let them get away, did not investigate this house and took Earl instead of doing his job. He has lost it." She shook her head. "Fine. Owen, back on the workbench. Julie, fix him. The rest of you open the passage."

"But Julie…" Lucie burst out.

"She's fine now, dear. She is only programmed to do certain things. She won't hurt him and I think she's learned her lesson."

"How do you know she's not programmed to kill him?" Alex growled.

"Because Bob wants Owen alive," Marlo answered with a side-long look at Julie.

"How do you know?" Lucie asked.

It was Sarah who answered, "We heard everything. The minute I heard Julie make her call to Dr. Moretz all the pieces fell into place and I headed right out."

145

"I thought Julie's com was down." I said feeling confused.

"It was but…" Marlo looked to Sarah who nodded back. "Sarah was worried about Julie and her status with Bob."

Sarah cut in, "When Bob stopped communicating with me like he normally did, I got suspicious. Even Saul can feel that things aren't right. I was concerned that Bob had gotten to Julie while he was supposed to be helping her, so I had Marlo… um, adjust her phone."

Julie looked at Sarah with a stricken look on her face. She looked like she was about to cry, throw up or both.

"I promise you, we only kept track of your calls to Bob's offices," Sarah added in a soothing voice. "I wasn't sure – I just suspected. Over the past three weeks, you only gave the standard weekly report, but my gut told me I was missing something. Today's call was different and just so you know - all she said was that the house was empty and the children were gone."

"What's your trigger, Julie?" I asked, but she looked blank.

"She heard you being attacked."

"What? How do you know?"

"It makes sense. When the first blow landed she shoved Lucie in the closet and cut her com. Then she made the call. I've worked with the good doctor before. She knows what scares people most and uses it to her advantage."

"She's afraid of Owen getting hurt?" Lucie asked. I watched jealously, hurt, anger and confusion roll over her beautiful face.

"Not just Owen. She cares about both of you. You saved her life. I believe that if either of you were being hurt she would be triggered to call in."

Julie looked broken-hearted and small. Alex looked at each of us. "It's true. I want to hate her but... I can't. She truly feels guilty and hurt. She can't control it and she can't help it."

"Your time with Dr. Moretz - that's how you know that White Eagle will be okay. She won't be able to find what scares him, but I was easy. That's why she targeted Lucas. In my mind he's the weakest and least able to defend himself. She also threatened to take away my parents but that didn't have the desired effect. I know that the rest of us at least have a chance of taking care of ourselves but not Lucas. If something happened to him it would have been my fault."

"Because Bob wants Owen alive, he triggered Julie to protect him," Marlo answered with another look at Julie.

"Shouldn't we do something for White Eagle?" I couldn't help but worry after what they'd done to me.

"He'll be alright. We have time."

"How do you know we have time to worry about White Eagle?" Alex persisted.

"Marlo has him tagged. They're headed to the downtown offices. Not where they took Owen and Julie. They are going to question him the right way. They are more afraid of him then they are of Owen. Besides, I've made a few threats of my own and Bob is not quite as free to do as he'd like."

"You're playing a dangerous game, Sarah."

"Aren't we all?"

"So who were these guys?" Alex asked of no one in particular.

"I'm not entirely sure but I know they weren't Bob's. He doesn't use *dark watchers* – even with his faults." Sarah replied with conviction.

I took a step and almost fell again. Lucie still had her arm around me and that stopped the motion. She hugged me tightly.

"I'll be okay, Sunshine. We have bigger problems."

Everyone turned to their assigned tasks. Lucie moved away from me reluctantly to help Marlo and Alex search for the passage. Sarah continued her overview of the room. Julie popped an ice-pack from the emergency kit Marlo had brought from the van and started to put it over my eye but stopped.

"What's on your forehead?" Julie queried.

"I thought it was dirt," Lucie exclaimed.

"Let me see," Marlo said getting in front of Julie. "I can't believe it. Luce, take a look at this!" Marlo said as he pulled out his cell to snap a picture. "I'm texting it to Meegan."

"Meegan? You think it's…"

"Dark magic," Lucie ended.

"What? There is no such thing," Julie insisted.

"You only say that because you haven't seen it before," Alex said in a snarky voice.

Sarah swore. "I found a concealed door but we aren't getting this open without an explosive. Let's check the rest of the house. Julie, take a sample of the foam on the floor when you're done with Owen. I'll have it checked for cyanide. Alex, leave Julie be. Marlo, when you hear from Meegan, ask if she knows of anything special we should do to eradicate the mark." Sarah, always cool in the face of a storm. Someday I would do better. Clearly I could still learn from her.

We headed upstairs, me more slowly than the rest. We gathered as much evidence as we could. Without help we could not search beyond this house. I knew I was damaged both inside and out but what could we do?

Meegan finally texted that ze knew of similar marks and thought it was for protection or containment. Ze conferred with Marlo and Lucie on what they thought the material it was made from could be and finally decided it was a block of some kind. She told them it wasn't her kind of magic, yet she understood the properties. Ze explained in general how binding symbols work and suggested removing the ashy mixture with a salt scrub to weaken it and hopefully remove its power.

While Alex, Sarah and Julie finished checking the house, Marlo and Lucie set to work on Meegan's salt and herb concoction with components from the van.

"I wish White Eagle was here," Lucie said softly.

"We'll get him back."

"I know, I just think he would be better at this than me."

"He has taught you about as much as he knows on the subject. You're the chemist, herbalist and magician now. You know what to put together and what they mean. Maybe you should learn Meegan's lore too. You never know because it looks like we've stepped into a whole new realm."

"I guess. I just…"

A loud thud sounded above our heads. "Alex!" Sarah shouted, both through the house and over the com.

We stopped what we were doing and bolted for the stairs, my salt smear dripping off my face.

Alex lay on the floor in the bedroom above the kitchen. I knew this… he'd been here before and then he began to speak, "You are a fool, Owen Ryer. You can't catch me that easily. I know where you are and where you're going. My offer still holds; come work for me or die. The choice is yours. Just know that the greatest darkness ever known is coming and you will not survive the outcome unless you come to my side." Alex convulsed one last time and held still except for the steady rise and fall of his chest.

Julie knelt by his side but I knew there was nothing she could do. He just needed time. She turned her haunted eyes to me with an intensity that blocked everything and everyone else out. "I'm so sorry, Owen. I swear I didn't understand the consequences. I was supposed to let the doctor know if we were close to getting Evilia Malvada. She was the only one who seemed interested and I fell for her lies. Now I see how truly dangerous Madame Malvada really is. One minute he was fine and then... I've made everything worse. I took away your tools... I..."

"Julie, stop. Evilia saw us or sensed us. Maybe Bob is mad because he missed her. No matter what happens, this is not your fault."

"What does Bob want from you?" Julie begged. "I don't understand."

"He wants results," Marlo said sadly. "All the available data points to his needing a results-focused outcome, no matter what it takes or who he has to sacrifice."

"But he's not helping. How can he ask us for results?" Julie's voice cracked as she spoke.

"Because he thinks I'm part of the problem and now he's angry because he's lost *her* again."

Lucie put her arm around me for a moment and then we moved forward to get Alex to the van. Alex moaned a little as we lifted him. He came around faster than I expected and was ready to walk before we made the van. Sarah's car was parked right behind it, but she had us all get in the van. Julie took Alex's vitals as Marlo documented what we'd learned from the house.

"The house has been empty for a couple of days. They knew we were coming. I could hear the kids and I can confirm some names that match missing kids around here," Lucie said aloud.

"And I could see some of it," I added, "but I'm pretty goofed up right now."

"Nearly all the physical evidence was wiped clean," Sarah added sounding frustrated. "Marlo, that concealed door lead somewhere. Why don't you see if you can tell where its tunnel might lead."

Marlo whipped out a tablet and began tapping away. The rest of us took a collective breath but then Lucie grabbed my wrist. "When did your watch stop?"

"I don't know, why?"

My memory kicked into gear and I could remember a chip being placed in it while I was in Dr. Moretz's care.

"Let me see it," Marlo said, dragging his gaze from the tablet's screen. "I couldn't figure out what my equipment at the shop was reading. It was reading you! You're bugged."

"They've known your every move since September," Alex said angrily.

"I told you it wasn't just Julie. Well played, Bob. So which of my pawns is he going to remove from the chess board next?" I sighed.

"Piper or Lucas," Lucie commented, sounding angry. "If he would just help us! Why does he make it harder!"

"Let me see what I can do," Sarah said with gritted teeth.

"What about Julie?" Alex was a dog with a bone.

"She needs to hear this. Marlo, put Bob on speaker, would you please? The rest of you say nothing." We nodded at her and Marlo set up the call.

Bob answered on the first ring. "What do you want?" he growled.

"Well hello to you too, Robert. Do tell me. Why didn't you let me know that Evilia was gone instead of wasting my time? Or didn't you know?"

"Of course I knew she was gone. I'd had that house watched since Julie first told me about it." I watched Julie's jaw clench at his words but she remained silent.

"Help me out here," Sarah said in a syrupy voice. "I'm a little confused as to why you'd waste our time. Why on earth would you let us go into a dangerous situation for no reason?

"It is you who is wasting *my* time with that... that boy... he doesn't know what he's doing – he's cost me valuable resources! He is dangerous. That kid is exactly what we swore we'd protect people from and you insist on helping him. He's no better than Evilia Malvada or any of her people. Your husband had nothing of value to share and I know you alerted my boss. You've made me look stupid. I'll never forgive you, Sarah!"

"You did that all by yourself, Robert." Sarah still sounded calm but I could feel her anger.

"Really? Well here you go then. I must be too stupid to keep you. You're fired. You hear me? Fired. You are cut off. No help, no lab, and no backup. You get nothing and I will give you nothing. You, your husband and those kids you think you're protecting are your problem. Not mine. I'm done with you and the whole mess."

"You've made some bad choices lately that need to be reviewed. I feel that this is another."

"This is my division – not yours. I am your boss – not the other way around. I make the decisions. I don't need to explain myself to you or anyone else."

"Is that what this is about – you think I want to lead your division?"

"Of course you do, you power hungry bitch. I see your plan. I won't let you do it." Had he been able to slam down his phone, I felt he would have. I could clearly visualize him throwing his cell across the room and it shattering on impact.

"Well… at least we know where we stand." I hoped a little levity would help.

Sarah laughed a little but it wasn't the happy kind. Julie was quietly crying and Alex, of all people, had his arm around her shoulders. I guess he finally believed what his gift was telling him.

Marlo's tablet gave its electronic notification noise and he scrambled to decipher it. "We should look to the rear of the house."

We piled back out and walked around the side of the old house once more, flashlights in hand. I led the way as we tromped into the backyard and then we fanned out and entered the woods. We kept each other in sight as we moved forward. Time crawled by as slowly as the moisture wicking its way from our feet up our legs. The rain had stopped but water still dripped from the Douglas firs and ferns.

"Guys!" Marlo called from his end of the line.

We made our way to him. He shined his light on a pair of old-fashioned cellar doors hidden in the ferns. "*Athyrium alpestre.*"

"What?"

Lucie smiled. "He's saying it's American Alpine Lady Fern. He has botany this semester, remember?"

"Nice," I said, rolling my eyes. The door was relocked with a brand new padlock. Marlo dusted for prints and then I unlocked it. The tunnel was empty all the way back to the house. At least they'd left a couple of prints and Alex found fresh tire tracks on the dirt road just past the cellar doors. We snapped pictures as Sarah tried to call White Eagle and when that didn't work she called another contact. Sure enough, Bob had to let him go. We headed for the shop to wait for White Eagle's release. I closed my eyes as Lucie drove. I was beat and I figured it was a good opportunity to grab a twenty minute or so nap.

ELEVEN

I watched her gnarled hand move, tracing the symbol for strength. I felt a laugh brewing in my chest but clamped down on it. It would not be a good idea to laugh. She was very serious about her beliefs and had no patience for mine. I watched the mark form and had to admire her work and dedication. It almost moved with a life of its own but that couldn't be, could it?

"Stephan, I know you want things and I can help you get them."

The laughter died and the image faded to be replaced by another.

Hatred burned through me, white hot. I had never hated a watcher as much as I loathed this one. Why should he have a normal life when I could not? He had what I wanted – a home, a family and he was happy. My lip twitched into a sneer. Look at him, dancing with his pretty wife. The way she smiled at him – like she worshipped him - I should have that. I deserved that. Why don't they look at me that way? "Because they see the killer in you" A voice whispered in my head. I jerked so hard I woke up.

"What did you see?" Lucie asked calmly.

Julie was riding with Sarah so I saw no reason to hide anything. Hiding things clearly wasn't helping so I spilled. Marlo jotted it all down.

"It sounds like it's time to let Kraeghton free," Lucie suggested.

"No."

"He has things to teach you and we are running out of options. In fact, I think the option well has gone dry. Except for that."

"No, Luce. It's too dangerous."

"So, what? We wait around for you to die? I'm not making that choice. Not for you and not for Alex!"

"How'd I get drug into this?" he asked Lucie in a grumpy tone.

"We can't let her win and Kraeghton is our last hope," Lucie shot back.

"No," I said again.

"You have another idea?" she asked.

"No." They just weren't getting it.

"Well that's helpful," Lucie said sounding irritated. "Anyone? Ideas?"

"Let's talk to White Eagle before you go all crazy and try throwing gas on a blaze," Marlo said before I could speak. It was probably a good thing, because I'd bet money, marbles and chalk that Lucie would take it a whole lot better from Mars than she would from me right now.

White Eagle was there waiting for us. Sarah hugged him tightly and they whispered to each other. We held back to give them a moment of semi-privacy.

White Eagle turned to us. "Bob had too many witnesses, so he couldn't hold me. In addition, our arrival was met by a very serious looking man in a gray suit." White Eagle was looking right at Sarah. "He had to be about sixty and about five foot eleven, slim build with piercing blue eyes and graying hair. Am I ringing a bell? Bob was not at all happy to see him. I think I like this man."

Sarah smiled.

"What do we do now?" I interrupted.

"We may be without help, but we are not without resources. We proceed with Alex's board warriors, our mysterious table and we keep our eye out for Evilia Malvada," White Eagle replied calmly.

"What about those children?" Julie's voice was filled with both anguish and resolution. "If you won't help…"

"No one said we wouldn't help. Bob is busy right now but agents will work on the evidence they have. They won't stop looking. Trafficking is everyone's problem. You should keep doing what you do best. Help the people who come into your E.R. and inform us if anything looks like our kind of problem. We'll keep looking as well and let you know if we need you."

"So that's it then. You really are angry with me."

"Not at all, but we can't entirely trust you either. Until Robert Bowman and Anita Moretz have been reviewed by the appropriate authorities we need to keep our thoughts to ourselves just in case. We seem to have a leak and I mean to find it. I would think after what you've been through you would understand." It was Sarah who did the talking for our group now.

"What about Owen?"

"He is my *watcher* and his problems will be addressed in-house." White Eagle spoke softly but firmly.

Julie bit her lip. "I only ever wanted to help."

"You did help. It just didn't go the way any of us thought. Go with a light heart, not a heavy one. You have friends here but our problems are deep and wide," Sarah said, sounding an awful lot like White Eagle.

"You're saying I'm another problem." I could hear the hurt and tears in Julie's voice.

"Your gift is not here at this time. You can do the most good at the hospital. You'll see that. If you need us, we will be there."

"But you don't need me, right?"

"Not never, just not at the moment."

"Okay," she replied in a sad voice and then hugged us each good-bye. I knew she wanted to say more but she kept it to herself. I watched her go, my own heart heavy. I couldn't help but feel like I was the biggest problem here.

Lucie sensed my mood. She came up behind the stool I'd dropped onto and hugged me from behind, resting her chin on the top of my head. I took ahold of her arm and held it to my chest as I closed my eyes. I just needed a few moments of this, of her. I needed to let everything else go.

"Come with me after we're done here," I begged.

"Okay," she whispered in my ear, close enough to tickle it. I loved how she didn't ask where or why – she would just come.

I let go of her arm, turned on the stool and pulled her between my knees. "It's Christmas break. We have a tree and only a few decorations up. Please help me make it a nice one for Lucas. We are getting dangerously close to a time when he won't care any-more. He still needs to care."

"You have a big heart buried in there somewhere," she said tapping my chest. "I would be happy to help. I know it's hard at your house because of your grandmother. I know you miss her. Lucas... no little kid should have to be there when their grand-mother dies that way."

"No they shouldn't. He was very brave. He had nightmares for a long time."

"What I would give to make it all go away."

"Oh Luce, don't say that out loud. One day someone may try to take you up on it."

"You're in a strange mood."

"Well, yeah, Julie's gone and I can't help but feel like the problem here is me, not her."

"You are the problem White Eagle has chosen to resolve. We can't have two of you running around waiting to snap."

"You don't think I'm the leak do you?"

"No, I don't, but someone is and if not us, then who?"

I didn't get a chance to reply to Lucie. White Eagle snagged our attention. "Sarah is going to take Alex home. It's late."

We watched him. He didn't want us to say anything; I could tell by the look he gave me. I watched him lock the back door behind Sarah and my brother and raised my eyes. Surely he didn't think that Alex was the problem.

"Marlo, I want you to do a sweep and then lock everything down and shut it off. I can't afford any mistakes."

Marlo gave him a single nod and went to work. Lucie also gave him a nod of understanding and went to help Marlo.

"What's this about?" I asked in a hushed voice.

White Eagle looked exhausted. His whole body slumped and then he turned to look at me. His eyes held wisdom, worry and years. Eyes that had seen three lifetimes looked at me solemnly. "Madame Malvada contacted you through Alex."

"Yes," I answered wondering what he was getting at.

"I need to be sure that she isn't hijacking him, like you did to her. Our other problem is that Bob knows way too much. We have clamped down about as far as we can go and yet... he knows. How does he know?"

I felt guilt well within me. "What if it's me?"

159

"That is what we are going to find out and I want every safeguard in place before we do it."

"We're clear, White Eagle," Marlo interjected.

"You've had a plan in place regarding me for a while, haven't you?"

"Yes."

I hung my head. "I'm sorry," I whispered. "I am the problem."

"We're not completely sure. It's time you let me in your head. I need to see everything that happened with the good doctor and I think we need to go back to the day Kraeghton died. We're missing something. We need to look at it again. Maybe Kraeghton is ready to help us."

"You know it doesn't work that way."

"He's been in there for over six months. It's time he shared his plan. Will you let us try?"

"I don't want to hurt you."

"You won't."

"I hurt Mitchell and... and Carl at Dr. Moretz's office."

"Let us try."

I turned my lips in and nodded. *He was right; I couldn't keep going it alone and pretending I was okay.*

White Eagle had us sit on the mat. He had allowed Marlo to use one laptop as a recording device and they set to work. I tried to relax but I was scared. Lucie came first and then White Eagle; they slid in easily and I felt a calmness glide through me. Then I was back in the cell with Dr. Moretz. It all replayed in my mind complete with the same physical reactions. Then everything flashed to the day Kraeghton died. Fear pierced my chest, my heart raced and my throat seized up. The connection broke and I found myself lying on the mat panting. Without a word Lucie lay down behind me, fitting her body to mine and wrapping her arms around me. She held me until I quit shaking.

White Eagle spoke softly to Marlo. If I was going to break down, these were the people I would want to do it in front of. I vividly remembered not only what we had just seen, but also the time in Florida when I nearly lost everything but gained Lucie. I knew now I would be okay. I just needed a little faith.

"We know one thing, Owen. You are not the leak. It looks to me like you, Kraeghton, Miles or all of you held Dr. Moretz off. She only got in around the edges. I don't even think she learned much from you. Perhaps we should be thanking Kraeghton."

"I still believe that what Kraeghton does is for Kraeghton," I sighed.

"Are you saying that you believe he has conscious thought within you? He's dead. You have his memories. That's all, right?" Marlo gasped.

"I can't fully explain it, Marlo," White Eagle began calmly, "but I believe it is more than that. Think of it as his essence. Kraeghton is not really a thinking being within Owen, but what he shoved in there was too much for Owen to process. It's the same with Miles: when Owen needs to know something it floats to the surface. It's kind of like when you connect a memory to a book you're reading or like how you remember a math fact that you learned in fifth grade and it sticks with you."

"I guess," Marlo said. I could almost see him thinking.

"Let's call it a night. I mean morning," White Eagle said looking at his watch.

White Eagle and I loaded up in Lucie's beater and Marlo hopped in his car to follow us home. We made sure Marlo was inside before we went to the White Eagles'. He called my mom himself to say that I would be home later but that I was safe for now. *Safe... well at least I hadn't blasted anyone. I didn't think we had any real answers. Didn't they realize I'd been mulling it all over in my head ever since it had happened? What did they know anyway without Alex around to tell them what was the truth?*

Lucie put on a movie in the family room but I didn't watch it. I watched her and then I fell asleep. She made me waffles when I woke up. Her silence was killing me.

"Are you mad?"

"No, why?"

"You're so quiet."

"I've got a lot on my mind. I want to help and I'm trying to figure out how."

"Luce, you do help. Every day. Who else would have put up with me for this long?"

Her smile lit the room.

Sarah and White Eagle must have smelled waffles because they showed up before we finished. Lucie poured more batter in the waffle iron and I started some eggs for them. We made plans for decorating both houses at least a little and set to work.

Christmas was quiet at our house. Dad brought my grandfather over for a short time. I could tell that they were not happy about the Cuba trip being postponed. I wondered what the big draw was anyway. I knew I had family there but I had never met them. Did it make a difference in the cosmos if I never did? Besides my "Cuban" was terrible.

We were back at the shop bright and early the next morning. I was expecting a quiet day seeing as how we're not a big retailer. I about fell over when Adrian walked in. I realized that other than school I hadn't seen him at the shop much in weeks.

"Hey, Stranger," I greeted.

Marlo looked up. "Yeah, Stranger. We only ever see you at school."

Lucie came in through the swinging door and smiled at Adrian. He shuffled slightly from foot to foot. The room was coolish yet he had a sheen of sweat on his forehead and upper lip.

"Yeah, senior year, guys. I wanted to have fun. I used to think this was fun but not anymore. You three are great, but you've become the biggest bunch of killjoys I know. Sometimes I wonder how you stand each other.

Lucie looked at him appalled. "Did you really just say that... out loud?"

Adrian put up his hands palms out. "I'm not trying to be mean or hurtful. It's just not fun at the shop anymore. I'm hardly here anyways what with year-round sports and all. On the weekends I wanna kick back and ya know, have a weekend."

"Why are you here exactly?" Luce asked as she stepped next to Marlo in a show of solidarity.

"I uh, just wanted to explain is all. I owe you that, right?"

"And you should do what you think is right," I said, trying to channel White Eagle but not doing a very good job.

"My dad is getting me a job at Denny's as a busser. That will get me money over the summer to use for stuff at college."

"So you're saying you're going to see us even less and be even busier," Marlo said with a strange mix of sadness and disgust.

"Uh, yeah. That's it. No hard feelings, okay?" Adrian hurried to reply.

"Sure, Aid. You do what you need to do. We'll be here when you figure it out."

"Okay. So good. Thanks. See ya." We watched him go. As I looked at Marlo and Lucie I saw the same looks of confusion that I was pretty sure I wore.

"So what on earth was that really about?" Lucie asked.

"How should I know, he's been ignoring me for months," Marlo grumbled.

"Something's up. That's for sure."

"Let's forget about Adrian for now," Lucie said. "I got ahold of Meegan and ze has agreed to work with me a couple of times a month or so to teach me some of her... Wiccan lore."

"That's great Luce."

"I also plan to hit Alex's board warriors project hard. It's eating at Alex, yet he can't seem to catch them at anything. So far I've been able to keep him from joining the group to catch them. The main guy I'm stalking is Toby. I think we're close to encouraging him to stand up to the group leader. To me, he seems like Calvin, you know, alpha male douchbag, all over again, just an upper level bully with a following. Alex would get him eventually, but I'm happy to help.

My thoughts turned to the elusive table and Abner Grolier. The warehouse just sat there. No one came and no one went. No furniture moved. Marlo could find no trace of any other holdings by the man and without a "get out of jail free" card we didn't want to attempt any more breaking and entering.

Vacation slid on with no further sign of Adrian. I probably should have at least texted him but he didn't contact me either. Lucie and Marlo helped Marla with a huge post-holiday flurry of catering gigs. They even roped Alex and my mom in, but White Eagle wouldn't let me go. It felt like he was spending every waking moment with me to fix my head and perhaps my soul. It was more important than ever that I control Kraeghton, but the more

I tried the less control I felt like I had and I was just too scared to let him take over completely.

Mitchell swung by the second week of January after he got settled into his winter classes. "How's it going?" he asked after watching White Eagle work nearly silently with me for almost five minutes.

"Slowly," was White Eagle's reply.

I snorted.

"You gonna be okay?" Mitchell asked me.

"We're working on it. He's lucky to be alive after a blast like that," White Eagle said grimly.

"I wish I'd seen it coming."

"Don't beat yourself up," I said to my friend, hoping to make him feel better. "And just so you know, White Eagle wasn't even talking about that one. I just took a hit that imploded inside."

"I'm sorry I couldn't be there." I could hear the remorse in Mitchell's tone and it made my chest hurt.

"You're spreading yourself too thin. You just need to focus on you," White Eagle advised after giving Mitchell a long hard look.

"That's not very 'team' of you, White Eagle."

"We are a team, but I'm beginning to think that we are doing this wrong. We all worry about everyone else all the time and thus, leave ourselves open to not taking care of ourselves."

"I don't know," Mitchell said in a far off voice, like he was looking at the future and now at the same time.

"You can't watch everything, Mitch. You've got to focus on your future. You look tired and worn. We are doing that to you. It's not right." White Eagle's look was firm but kind. The educator in him was speaking.

"I feel guilty every time I miss something, yet I know in my head that I can't do it all."

"Let it go for now and tell us about our new friend Elliot Blackthorn."

Mitchell smiled a real smile. "He's good. He has done so much work on Emiline's old place, I hardly recognize it. He and I have cut a deal. It's too much property for me anyway so he's bought half. Turns out he loves it in Fallon and is starting a whole new life. He's been helping me get permits and design blueprints for my own place. He's gonna keep her little old house. It really wasn't fit for expansion but the new place will be. You won't believe what he's done to the barn and he had his horses shipped over from Wyoming. I'll miss you guys but I'm really looking forward to working with him."

"Good for you Mitchell. You deserve good things."

"Yeah, now I just need to graduate and find a job. I can't live off of what Emiline left me forever."

"You mean I can't live off White Eagle forever?" I laughed.

Without missing a beat White Eagle gently smacked the back of my head and replied, "No, you may not!"

TWELVE

Monday I woke up before my alarm. I scowled at my clock. It was almost too early to get up but it really was too late to go back to sleep. I threw back the covers and rolled out. I began with some stretches and then did some sit-ups and pushups to wake myself fully. Whatever I'd been having a nightmare about lingered, but in that foggy way where you can't remember anything but the feelings of helplessness and fear.

By the time I got downstairs Lucas was leaving for school. Watching him, I felt something strange shift within me. He was almost ten. I remembered being ten. I could smell the elementary smell and see the classroom. I remembered my teacher. Lucas has the same lady, full of energy and love for her kiddos.

"Hey, Lucas. I think I'll walk you in today."

"It's bad enough I have to go when Mom goes in. I want to go by myself," he huffed back at me.

"Yes you can, but I want to see Mrs. Martin."

"Well, I guess that's okay. You all just get so… in my business all the time. I have too many bosses."

"You know we do it for a reason, right buddy?"

"No one walked you to school in fourth grade. It's embarrassing."

I smiled sadly at Lucas. "The world has gotten a whole lot more dangerous in the last eight years."

He sighed heavily. "Well come on then."

Mom locked the door as Lucas and I started out. At least it was trying to be daylight. This early the walk to school was peaceful and few cars were on the road. Lucas told me all about the report he was doing on the Kiwi bird for his animal report. Mom smiled a distracted smile as we walked along.

She let us all in with her key card, signed in at the office and then we headed to the room she shared with her friend and teaching partner. I was shocked to see just how tiny the kindergarten tables and chairs were. It felt like the whole room had shrunk since I'd been here. Lucas walked over to a table group and put down the chairs so I did another for Mom. I continued on but Lucas sat down and went to work on the report he'd been telling me about. Apparently this was his usual homework time. It made me happy to think that at least this part of his life was routine.

I told him goodbye and gave him a half hug and then I walked over to Mom.

She tilted her head to the side as she often did and gave me a good once-over. "Something is bothering you."

"Yeah, I had the usual nightmares but this one still has a hold on me."

"You want to talk about it?"

"I can only remember the anxiety and frustration, but… it almost feels like…"

"Something is coming," we finished as one.

"I hate it when you do that," I groaned even as I smiled at her.

"Be careful."

"I will," I said as I hugged her.

I walked to Mrs. Martin's room. Her whole face lit up when she saw me.

"Owen Ryer! How the heck are you?"

"Good and you?"

"Super-de-dooper and better after seeing you. What brings you by?"

"I was feeling a little nostalgic and just wanted to stop by and say hello."

"Senior year does that to a lot of kids." She waved her arm around the room. "As you can see, not a lot changes here."

She was right. The tables were still in groups and her desk was in the same place. Her bulletin boards were still covered with happy, bright fabrics and friendly posters about social skills, positive attitudes and fourth grade subjects. Currently the animal unit was taking up a huge section.

I glanced at the clock. "I should go or I'll be late for school. I hope you have a wonderful day and thanks for... being you."

"Aw, Owen. You're a great kid. I miss you, my friend. Come see me again."

"I will."

I left with a smile on my face and headed for Lucie's to catch a ride with her and Marlo. Lucie was fine but Marlo was twitchy.

"Something's coming," he stated in a grouchy tone.

"What is?" Lucie asked.

"That's just it. I don't know. I just feel... the wrongness. I can't tell you how frustrated that makes me. I'd rather not know than be plagued by... feelings with no direction."

"So you have no hints at all?" I asked him.

"I can tell you that it feels like Evilia."

"Oh good. That's a relief," I said sarcastically.

"Exactly!" Marlo lamented.

The drive to school was quiet, each of us wrapped in our own thoughts and growing tension. First period started fine but by halfway through, the hairs on the back of my neck were quivering.

I snagged Adrian between classes. He yanked his arm out of my grasp with a frustrated look.

"I need to talk to you," I insisted.

"Not now," he answered firmly.

"But Adrian."

"I said, not now." He spun away from me and didn't look back.

I just stood there. The bell started to ring before I could really evaluate my feelings but I guess number one was hurt. I dashed into class and slid into my seat. My wariness had not lessened. I looked up toward the door and caught a glimpse of Jon turning away from the window.

Marlo, Lucie and I walked to third period feeling like we were about to be attacked. I looked over my shoulder again, sensing... something. A flash of fabric turned the corner. Wasn't that the color of the hoody Jon was wearing?

"Mars, do you have a way to see if Jon has been in class today?"

"Yeah, I could do that. It will take a few minutes. Cover me."

I knew what that meant. Lucie and I put Marlo between us and both opened our textbooks wide, covering the desk in front of the three of us. Marlo got out his tablet and tapped away under the desk. He was even able to do that and answer the question the teacher asked him. Lucie and I started our group work. When our teacher drew near, Lucie started talking as if we were already in a conversation.

"I don't know, Marlo," she said loud enough for the teacher to hear. "I think…" she dropped her voice as he moved past.

"Got it," Marlo breathed. "He's absent. That's all I can get so far. Oh, and it wasn't pre-excused."

I mulled that information over. I was sure I'd seen him, so what was he up to?

Class ended and it was time for me to head to the shop. "You two watch out for each other," I told them unnecessarily, but I couldn't help myself.

I had to smile when they replied, "Be careful," at the same time.

I kissed Lucie goodbye and hugged her tightly. I went to the locker room to strip off my pants so I could run to the shop. I could almost feel something closing in on me. It was almost as if Miles was with me. Guys were getting ready for PE and nothing seemed off.

I loaded my jeans into my backpack and hit the road, my senses on high alert. I often run with at least one earbud in so that I can listen to music, but not today. Today I wanted to…

I was slammed from the side. I went down hard on my right hand and knee. At the moment I couldn't even feel it. I sprang to my feet and spun to face my attacker. Jon.

He was panting, sweating and had a wild look in his eyes. He snarled and lunged at me again but I knocked him to the side.

"What are you doing?" I half yelled at him.

"I hate you!" It came out broken and disturbed sounding.

The neighborhood behind the middle school had grown quiet. No cars passed. It was as if it was holding its breath.

"I thought we resolved this. I don't want to hurt you," I said, feeling confused.

171

"I have to. I don't want to. I want to. You can't make me," Jon babbled.

"What?"

Jon's eyes had gone open so wide that I could see white all around the irises. "I should be in class. You are keeping me from class," he said as he swung at me.

I blocked him easily and moved past him to throw an elbow between his shoulder blades. He didn't have my skill and I didn't want to hurt him. I tried to decide on my next move but the game had changed. I watched in horror as he pulled a NAA Guardian pistol from his hoody's pouch pocket. He held the small handgun unsteadily in front of him. I automatically put my hands in front of me.

"Jon, what are you doing? Even if you hate me, it's not worth this."

"I... leave me alone."

Sweat sparkled all over his face and an uneven flush tinted his cheeks. The moment he wiped the sweat from his eyes I lunged, taking him to the ground. He landed hard and my weight knocked the air from his lungs. His right hand smacked the pavement and the pistol popped free. Jon's eyes rolled up in his head and he went slack. I checked for a pulse and finding one, I quickly moved to kick the NAA Guardian out of sight. Then I called White Eagle.

A car finally came by and the driver paused to roll down the window. I gave her a quick once-over but couldn't sense anything. I pulled the phone from my ear so that White Eagle could hear too.

"Do you need help? Shall I call 911?" she asked.

"It's taken care of. Thank you."

"I'll wait with you for them to get here."

I felt Kraeghton writhe within me. "*No, you won't. You're late. Get moving.*" Power surged through me with the words. Suddenly I was afraid for the good Samaritan.

"Are you sure you're okay. I'm running late and need to get moving."

"Yes, we'll be fine," I replied in my own voice.

The driver reluctantly left.

"What was that?" White Eagle asked as I moved the phone back to my ear.

"Kraeghton," I replied wearily.

"Well today that was useful I guess. I'm almost to you."

Chills ran up my spine. "You're not alone," I breathed turning to face the new danger.

A black SUV pulled up and two *dark watchers*, followed by a third, spilled from the vehicle. Now I was sorry I'd kicked the gun away.

I moved the phone to my left hand and left the line open. I stepped back from Jon, feet shoulder-width apart and arms loose at my sides.

We eyed each other warily. One guy moved his hand slightly without taking his eyes off me. The other two surged forward but they didn't attack me, they moved toward Jon.

"No," I said taking a step.

They converged on me instead. I changed the grip I had on my phone and used it to hit the first guy in the throat. While he coughed and gagged, I kicked at the other *watcher*. The third one moved forward but instead of joining the melee he picked up Jon and threw him in the back of the SUV.

I took a hit to the eye that was still bruised from our assault on the trafficking house. It was a fair trade for the guy whose nose I think I broke. Another hit and my phone flew out of my hand. The third guy moved toward me.

I was holding two off but barely. I felt the burn of adrenaline as sweat ran into my eyes. Anger flashed through me. Kraeghton was trying to seize control. I tried to push him down but that only made him push back harder.

A *dark watcher* laid a hand on me to begin a drain. I put my hand on his wrist to shove it away, a motor cut behind me, a flash of white light blinded me and the nothingness took me.

I felt my body hit the ground. What was black, shifted to gray and red. I blinked and saw a slash of gray sky. I blinked again and saw that, plus Douglas fir branches. Sound whished back in, an engine was running and doors slammed. A rock dug painfully into my hip and then I heard the crunch of gravel. I rolled quickly off the road, the SUV narrowly missing me. A hand came down on my shoulder.

"Holy heck, Owen. What did you do?" White Eagle gasped.

"Kraeghton," I croaked through my gritty throat. I wanted to flop back onto the wet grass and just lie there but I wasn't safe here. White Eagle and I struggled to our feet, threw an arm around each other and limped to his truck.

He started to pull out. "Wait!"

I threw open the door while the truck was still moving and limped over to the vicinity of the tossed pistol. I dug around in the overgrown grass and wildflowers at the side of the road. White Eagle came to join me.

"What are we looking for?"

"My phone and Jon had a NAA Guardian. I can't risk anyone else getting their hands on it."

"What was going on with that kid?"

"I think Evilia had him under her control. I don't know how. It was kind of like what she did to my grandfather."

"Do you think she was trying to hurt you?"

"Hurt me? Maybe. Catch me? Definitely. Sometimes I wonder about the elaborateness of her schemes but then I suppose she can't just march into school and take me."

"I suppose not. She has got to be close if she is focusing on you again."

"It's payback for her house and the loss of her interrogator."

"You're probably right."

"Here," I said. I covered my hand with the cuff of my long-sleeved t-shirt.

"Hang on. I've got a glove," White Eagle said, returning to the truck to retrieve it.

He gently picked up the pistol and slid it into an evidence bag. I found my phone a few feet away. The screen was cracked. We loaded back up and he drove us to the shop without a word. We staggered into the back and hauled out the first aid supplies. I didn't even complain when he stitched up the side of my head. There was nothing to stitch together on my hand or leg, but he picked no less than twenty-six pieces of gravel out of me.

I don't think I fully appreciated how awful I looked until Lucie's gasp brought me back to the present. "What happened?"

"Other than Jon trying to kill me?"

"What?" Lucie nearly screeched.

"White Eagle and I haven't even begun to puzzle it out yet but I think maybe Jon is being controlled by Evilia. I must have missed it because of our focus on Bob. I think that Jon has been stalking me for a while."

I paused for breath and Marlo jumped in. "That would fit with the number of absences and tardies he's had. They've been building over the last couple of months. His parents have even gotten a warning. It's all in the file."

"Part of the time I swear he was either talking to *her* or to voices in his head. *Dark watchers* came and picked him up."

"I take it that you didn't let them just take him?" Lucie said eyeing me critically from head to Nike covered toe.

"Of course not. Kraeghton sort of helped and hindered. I even blasted White Eagle."

"What are we going to do with you?"

"I wish I knew."

"So where's Jon?" Marlo asked.

"They took him," White Eagle answered.

"Are we going to save him?" Lucie asked.

"We will do what we can but our resources are crippled by Bob at the moment. I did manage to send a call in to Evelyn and she'll be here shortly to retrieve Jon's pistol. An anonymous tip has been entered that a boy was reportedly abducted. His parents should report him missing anytime."

"I know the school will call his parents and report his absence. The system always does but not until later in the day."

"So... we wait," I said to no one in particular. "While we do that. Do you think you can fix my phone?"

"Not again," Marlo whined like the mother of a chronically naughty child.

THIRTEEN

I tried to relax and breathe. Through my window I could see the clouds that flecked the sky glowed hot pink and the horizon burned orange as the sun crept higher. Why not just get up? I wouldn't be able to sleep now anyway. Instead of easing, my heart rate increased. Things felt wrong. Evilia and her team had to be on the move again but what were they after this time? I wasn't surprised when my cell chirped, though it wasn't who I was expecting.

"What's up Mitchell?"

"Run! I got a bad Lucie vibe. Get her! NOW!"

Lucie... at dawn... where would she be? The gym... she was going to help her old coach today. I left the line open as I flew out the front door and didn't even shut it behind me. I vaulted our front steps and jumped over every shrub in my path as I ran. I could see Lucie's car parked at the curb and she was already in it. The engine gave a halfhearted clicking sound. I heard it from two houses down. I saw Lucie cock her head to the side and release the key through the dew collected on the rear window. I sprinted on toward her as she pressed the accelerator in a sharp burst that matched her temper. I slid over the trunk just as she started to flick her wrist again. Her hand left the key as she jerked in surprise. I yanked the driver's door open, released her seatbelt and dragged her from the car.

"What are you doing?" Lucie demanded, her voice angry. "You scared me to death!"

"Bad feeling," I answered roughly as I pulled her further from the vehicle.

"I'm going to be late."

"Mitchell sent a message."

"What?"

"When has your car ever not started?"

"Well…"

Boom. The blast was deafening, knocking us to the ground. I covered Lucie with my body. Heat washed over my back and shards began to rain down on us. All sound was warped and distorted.

I felt Lucie gasp. Our eyes met and then White Eagle was yanking me to my feet. I could see Sarah on her phone and vaguely hear sirens in the distance. He gave me a slight shake to get my full attention. "You just got here." Then he turned to Lucie, "And you tried to start the car but then were coming back to the house to get your school bag."

Lucie and I nodded. Marlo sprinted up the street as Mom and Alex ran down to meet us.

"Luce, you went off the grid!" Marlo wheezed as he grabbed her and pulled her into a huge bear hug.

We all gave him an odd look. He pulled back from her and seemed to realize we were staring at him like he'd lost it.

Lucie slapped a hand to her forehead, "My cell was in the car. My purse was in the car. My gym bag too, but you're right, my school stuff was still in the house."

Sarah jumped in, "Rick is on his way."

"I know it is," White Eagle interjected, ignoring Sarah for the moment, "I tripped over it when the windows shook."

The sirens grew louder. A fire truck was the first to arrive followed closely by the paramedics and police. Firemen went to work on the car blaze while a police officer approached us. Sarah stepped forward to meet him.

"Can someone here tell me what happened?" the officer asked.

"Yes officer," Sarah said immediately, showing that she was both in charge and in control. "My daughter was going to take her car to meet with her gymnastics coach. Thank the Lord, she ran back toward the house for her forgotten school books. Had she still been in the car..." she trailed off looking pretty devastated. *I knew it wasn't an act.*

"Young lady?" the officer queried looking toward Lucie.

"It's like she said. The car door's still open. My purse and gym bag were in there. I can't imagine what on earth..." she too trailed off and turned her eyes back to what was left of her car.

"And you are?" he asked looking at me.

"Neighbor," I replied.

"Did you see what happened?"

"No, sir."

"Then why is your shirt smoldering?"

White Eagle came up next to me and clamped an arm around my shoulders.

"He lives up the street and goes to school with our daughter. He was one of the first on the scene. He must have gotten too close. Probably wanted to be sure his classmate was alright. Good kid this one. His mom's right over there," he finished pointing to my mom and shoving me behind him the minute the officer's eyes were off me.

"Ma'am," the officer called to her, "is this your boy?"

"Yes, sir."

"And you are?"

"Lila Ryer."

"Where do you live?"

"Just there," mom said pointing.

He turned back to White Eagle, "And you, sir, what's your name?"

"Earl White Eagle."

"Do you have ID on you?"

"Yes," he replied, pulling it out.

The officer looked carefully at him, the ID and back, and then at the house. "Your wife's name?"

"Sarah," he answered. I watched Sarah's eyes narrow. She had started the conversation but apparently wasn't worthy of finishing it. *A big mistake on his part.*

"And your daughter is?"

"Lucie."

He wrote each comment down in his notebook and then looked up. "You have any idea what happened here?"

"I wish I did. My daughter's safety means everything to me." I could tell he meant it. I knew that we were all his kids.

I saw Rick pull up and I could see Sarah relax just a little. He looked over the situation carefully and got on his smartphone without leaving the car.

The officer kept asking questions and taking notes. He was nice enough but a little crisp for my taste and there was something.... He finally stepped away to call in on his radio keeping his eyes on us. The fire appeared to be out and the firemen were starting to clean up. The ambulance had left and I hadn't even noticed. When I looked back to the officer, one I'd never seen before today, he was almost right next to me. He studied me as he handed some information to White Eagle about what to do with the remains of Lucie's car and told him to call his insurance adjuster. Then he gave him a case number. I'd had about enough. Something about this guy was off. I had a sudden idea and it probably wasn't a good one. I looked hard at the officer and thought "*These people are not interesting. I have all the information I need.*" I repeated it over and over for good measure while staring at his forehead.

He had turned his attention from me but was still looking skeptically at Lucie. I repeated my mantra. He began to pinch the bridge of his nose like he was getting a headache. One corner of my mouth quirked up until I saw his wrist where his sleeve had fallen back just enough to reveal the edge of a tattoo – one I recognized – one of *hers.*

"Well I think that's all for now. Let me get your numbers and I'll get back to you if I have more questions."

I started at him harder. "*There is nothing here. There is nothing here.*"

Hoses were reeled up, firemen got back in their seats and the police officer finally left, now rubbing his temples. Before he was even around the corner, Lucie grabbed my cell to call her old coach and let her know she couldn't make it today because of car trouble. *Boy was that an understatement.*

She hung up and turned to us, "I didn't love that car but it was mine and it was all I had." Her voice sounded soft and forlorn.

"Don't worry. We'll get another," White Eagle offered.

"I can't afford another one. I saved for eleven months to buy that one."

"Have faith, Honey, "Sarah interjected, "The insurance will come through. I'll make sure of it. Besides we have two vehicles and only three drivers at our house and Owen has his Kawasaki. You'll be able to go wherever you need to go."

Lucie hugged her. "You're right. Thanks for reminding me to be positive."

"You may not be my biological daughter, kiddo, but I love you like you were and I'd adopt you in a heartbeat if you'd let me."

Lucie laughed and cried. "That would be such a waste of money!"

"It would be worth it to us," White Eagle added.

Now that the coast was clear, Rick got out of his car. He indicated with a tilt of his head that we should follow him into Sarah's house.

With one last look at her dripping burned-out shell of a car, Lucie headed inside and I followed. We all crammed into the living room and Rick looked at each of us in turn. "The good news is… it wasn't us. The bad news is I'm not supposed to be here and I'm not allowed to help you. I'm not telling you that someone was spotted messing with Lucie's car at school last Friday. We caught a little something on the school's camera. I'm also not telling you that you are being watched and tracked. I don't have details because I'm no longer allowed access to the inner circle."

"Slow down," Sarah pleaded. "I can't believe what I'm hearing."

Rick moved into parade rest. If he was reverting to military habits, he must be stressed. "I'm an idiot, ma'am."

"You're not!" Sarah insisted vehemently.

"I am because I couldn't keep my yap shut and stood up for the kid. I should have known better and I should have seen it coming," Rick added with a glance to me.

He relaxed his stance a little and continued, "Notice I wasn't on the raid at the trafficking house and that you haven't seen me in weeks. I was sent away on a wild goose chase. I wanted to warn you but my task was conveniently out of cell range. I'm not sure what is going on. Things at the office… they aren't right. Bob has brought a few unquestioningly loyal folks close. Melody, Neil, Saul, Joy and I are being left out. I think Neil especially has been pushed out because he has shown loyalty to you over Bob more than once. Mel, Saul and Joy are keeping their heads down and mouths shut. They don't like what's going on either."

"What exactly *is* going on?" White Eagle asked in a surprisingly calm tone.

Rick turned even more serious. "Secrets mostly – odd secrets. It's not a clearance thing, it's more of a personal opinion thing – we are left out of everything that has anything to do with you. Most importantly you need to know what I saw. I walked by the conference room to get a file. An agent I don't know left the room while I was in the hall. I glanced in and you were on the big screen. The room was set up for four people to sit with laptops. Dr. Anita Moretz was on a video conference with them."

"I'm sorry, Rick." He shot his eyes to me.

"Why?" he asked perplexed.

"They told me to behave. She, I should say. The doctor also told me to follow the rules and that someone would be punished if I didn't do what I was told. She said…"

Sarah's living room took a sudden spin and I was back with Dr. Moretz. Fear seized me. I began to shake. She was coming at me with another needle and a determined look on her face. I hate needles. She was questioning me again and then she began to threaten me…

I closed my eyes in despair and reopened them to find I was once again lying on the floor of the living room, feeling shaky and sweaty.

"Is he alright?" Rick asked, sounding scared, which was so unlike him.

"He'll be fine," White Eagle replied. "This happens sometimes. He gets too close to a Dr. Moretz memory and he flashes back. As you saw today, sometimes her name is enough to do it."

Rick's voice held an edge of anger, "I don't get what Bob is after. Why did he let you go to the trafficking house when he knew Malvada's crew had cleared out? Why did he turn you over to Moretz in the first place? Until recently she'd only been used for suspects in extreme cases. She is a little known secret weapon of Bob's and a very dangerous one. When she started seeing *watcher* Julie Barnes, I believed it was because she didn't have enough to do and was trying to help, but then she got her talons on Owen. I have got to play it cool and find out what I can. This is not how we treat friends and allies."

"Be careful, Rick. Whatever is going on, it's bigger than all of us." Sarah looked at each of us in turn but I wasn't sure if it was for confirmation or for signs of argument. I knew two things for sure: We were about to be late for school and I didn't want to show up in my red plaid jammie pants.

We left Rick and Sarah to plan out Rick's next move. Lucie and I hurriedly got ready for school. White Eagle dropped us off on the way to the shop since we'd all agreed that leaving a vehicle at school was asking for trouble. I just hoped we wouldn't have to go back to riding the bus.

Lucie pretended to be unfazed by the loss of her car, but I couldn't fake it. I was freaked out on many levels and couldn't concentrate no matter how hard I tried. Trying to concentrate had become like trying to catch smoke in your hand. I could feel Bob and Evilia pressing in on me. Although I had known for a while that it was just a matter of time before Evilia had a few good guys on her side, it made me sick to think that she had gotten to someone in law enforcement. She had to have something on the poor guy that he didn't want exposed. Maybe Evelyn would know something, though White Eagle was probably already pursuing that angle. Getting information from her would be secondary to warning her to be careful because she was in a pit with at least one viper and she was likely being watched.

School and shop time oozed by with the speed of molasses in winter, meaning that dinner with Lucie would be a bonus in an otherwise crap day. We decided on pizza. Lucie and I swung by Safeway to pick up a cheese pizza for a base and bought mushrooms, onions, tomatoes and olives. Sarah kept some awesome Italian sausage from Otto's Sausage Kitchen in her freezer. A beautiful pizza was about to hit my taste buds.

We got it put together and baking, its mouthwatering aroma filling the house while Lucie and I tried to conquer some homework. We got very little done since I was more interested in kissing her than I was in working on English.

Sarah and White Eagle showed up in the kitchen when the buzzer sounded on the stove. Lucie put the salad we'd made on the table while I sliced the pie. We dished up and sat around the table pretending to be a normal family. They began talking about school but I was more interested in food. I was just ready to bite when I felt something shift. The hair on the back of my neck was standing at attention again. I dropped the pizza without tasting it and lurched to my feet. Lucie and White Eagle were just behind me. Sarah took a beat longer, probably taking cues from us more than anything else.

White Eagle and Sarah silently headed for the back door and Lucie and I took the front. I could no longer sense anyone and visually the coast seemed to be clear. Luce headed left and I went right toward the garage, where I met Sarah. We nodded at each other and she went back her way and I went back mine. I was just ahead of Lucie. My eyes moved from her, back to the front door. An off-white, square envelope had been taped to the surface.

I carefully peeled it off, touching only the corner. Nothing was on the outside. I took it in the house and laid it on the kitchen counter while Lucie relocked the front door. I got out gloves and Sarah's special tweezers just like I'd been taught and pulled the note from the envelope. "You take from me – I take from you. E."

"Should we even bother with prints?" I asked Sarah, who'd just come back in the sliding glass door with White Eagle. They came and looked over my shoulder.

"Couldn't hurt," Sarah answered. "Maybe it will give us a lead on who's helping *her.*"

"I know we've been trying to ignore the gorilla in the room, but why us? Why are they both gunning for us? I wish they'd just go after each other and leave us out of it."

"We couldn't get that lucky," Lucie said, sounding exasperated.

"Maybe we are – maybe that's what this is – we're in the crossfire – Bob is turning you into bait and it's working."

"He has a funny way of asking for my help," I snarled.

"Be honest. If he asked, would you help?"

"Not for a million dollars."

"So you made him mad and he went about using you in his own way. He tried using Dr. Moretz to break into your mind to get the information he needed and when that didn't work he set you up."

Now I had clarity but did I feel better or worse?

FOURTEEN

Anxiety made my gut churn. I was getting sick of feeling sick to my stomach and having my head ache right above my eyebrows, let alone the tension living in my neck. It felt like weeks since I had slept through the night. I could fall asleep but not stay asleep. At least once a night I had a nightmare involving Bob, Evilia, Carmichael, Anita or Kraeghton, and every morning I dragged myself out of bed still feeling exhausted. Maybe that was Evilia's trick... wear me down. I would be too weary to fight. Jon returned to school. He looked terrible but so far he was avoiding me. One thing was for sure – I was cranky. I had no patience for anyone, especially Jon, so it was best that he steered clear. Every time the need arose I took a deep breath, but it felt like I was removing the last bit of brownie batter from a bowl with a rubber scraper every time I dealt with someone. So much for my well of peace – it was virtually empty. I knew this was no way to be but I seemed to be helpless to stop it.

When Jon took one look at me and turned away, it made me smile but when Adrian did the same thing between classes, I sighed. I finished my last class, grateful to be headed to the shop and thankful that I'd left my textbooks at home so that my backpack was lighter for the run.

Marlo had taken over chauffer duties to school since Lucie was carless and the weather was its usual winter crappy. Marlo kept his car in a locked garage so we figured it was secure by night anyway. Marlo even had the garage set up with a motion detector that ran a camera when it was tripped. His house seemed to be clean for now.

I got to the shop feeling no less grouchy and set to work on the pile of repair tasks that White Eagle had lined up for me. I was clanking away on a riding lawnmower, trying to take my aggressions out on the extension cord that the previous owner had run over and twisted mercilessly around the shaft of the mower's blade when Marlo walked in.

He frowned at me, his brow deeply furrowed. "What's with you? You look like you're about to pop."

"Everyone's avoiding me and treating me weird. They're afraid to talk to me and then there's all these expectations of me. Where did the myth about me begin? I'm just a guy," I groused.

"Are you kidding?" You've been face to face with three of the most powerful *dark watchers* known to *watcherdom*. It's changing you. All that and you think you're not a myth?"

"Well right now I'm failing. I can't convince Bob I'm doing all I can and Evilia wants to kill us – for all I know, Bob does too. If they don't succeed, then Kraeghton might or, and this is my favorite, I will finally snap and get arrested for killing an innocent civilian."

"You need a project."

"Thanks, Mars. In case you hadn't noticed, I've got one," I belly-ached, indicating the dreaded mower.

"Not that kind, you dope, the *watcher* kind. Has it never occurred to you that you may be right where you're supposed to be? Maybe this is a process you are supposed to go through."

"Thank you, Mother Marlo. So tell me, is that your gift talking or are you channeling White Eagle?"

"White Eagle, I know, right? I'm getting preachy after my years of experience and deeper understanding of life and *watcherdom*."

"Full of bologna is more like it."

"What do you want me to say? We both know your life sucks and it's not fair. You're awesome and I'm glad to call you friend but I wouldn't want to be you."

"Me either. Can I be you for today? Or maybe Adrian or one of the triplets?"

"You miss him don't you?"

"Yeah, I understand but it feels like one more price I have to pay."

"You think someone got to him?" Marlo asked with a tilt of his head.

"I do, but I haven't looked too closely because I don't want him to have any more heat on him."

"I hope he appreciates you."

"How would he know?"

"I don't know. I just thought he'd know you well enough to, I don't know… see past it all. We were never as close as you two so when he started shutting me out… well, it was what it was – but you? Why?"

"Like you said, 'it is what it is,' Marlo. I figure I've got to fix me before I can work on anyone else. I know I'm not fun to be around right now."

"Then I guess we need to focus on something we can fix. We've got nothing on Grolier beyond what Evelyn provided. He's a ghost. We've also got a warehouse with zero activity, so I started going at this thing from the other end."

"What did you find?"

"The table was originally crafted in Massachusetts around the turn of the last century. That part was easy from the records and the stamp burned into the underside of the table. There was nothing else odd about the load it came with and that sent up a red flag for me. I looked into the folks who sold the stuff. They were the Lockners and long story short, they got the table from an aunt's estate. You know the kind of aunt I'm talking about - the interesting kind, who lives alone, has no spouse or children and few friends. The kind who makes her nieces and nephews feel uncomfortable but then divides all her worldly goods up among them, leaving them amazed."

"And this helps us how?" I queried.

"Guess what the old aunt's name was?"

"You got me, do tell."

"Grolier."

"No way."

"Yes, way. Who's the best researcher you know?"

"You, Mars!"

"So with you missing Adrian and me not fully buying into his being afraid and all... I mean seriously, why would they bother to threaten him? What's the point? Anyway... I rounded him up to go check the warehouse in person."

"He actually agreed?"

"Well yeah, I was quite convincing. That and he has started missing our kind of fun."

"So the warehouse is a ploy to get us to talk?"

"Sort of, but I also noticed something about my feed."

"What?"

"I think we've been made. I'm pretty sure I've been looped."

"What did you see?" I asked, narrowing my eyes.

Marlo wiggled his fingers at me in a "come here" kind of motion. He led me to his laptop, where he signed into three different places before the feed popped up. We watched silently for several minutes before I couldn't stand it any longer. "I don't get it."

"Check out the lower left corner."

I stared at the screen some more. "Holy hell, the plastic bag - it wouldn't blow through the same spot over and over for days like that! When did you notice it?"

"I took me until day before yesterday but I think on some level I noticed it just before that. I talked to Adrian today after he snubbed you."

"You saw that?"

"Yeah, I see a lot of stuff. People don't notice me. I blend."

Yeah, right, I thought, taking in his spiky hair, plum colored converse and symphonic metal t-shirt atop his black, skinny jeans. He blended liked sprinkles on ice cream.

"So what's your plan, super spy?"

"We can pick Adrian up at 5:30 and give it a look."

"Deal."

I went back to the mower with a better attitude and I think it knew it because I had the cord untangled, the blade sharpened and the whole thing put back together with the motor purring by 5:00. Marlo filled White Eagle in and I convinced Lucie to spend some time with Brenda. Marlo and I hopped in his car and headed for Adrian's house.

Adrian came out before we could even get out of the car. "Don't forget our deal, Saggio!" he said, sliding into the front passenger seat I'd left for him.

"I haven't," Marlo sighed as he backed out of the driveway. The conversation was a little awkward at first but it was gaining momentum as we rode. Marlo drove to the expressway but surprised me when he turned off at the Milwaukie Market Place.

"What are we doing here? I thought we were headed for the warehouse."

"We are taking care of Adrian's bribe first," Marlo groaned.

I raised my eyebrows at Adrian. "I thought that was a joke."

"It's no joke. I take Taco Bell very seriously. My help will cost you a couple of Crunchwrap Supremes."

I busted up laughing. "Okay Aid, we'll 'get your Bell on' and then we've got to hit the road. Some of us still have homework."

We parked and rolled in so that Marlo could read the menu. He decided on a burrito that he could munch on while driving and I tried an Adrian special. Adrian loaded up on goodies and it seemed to make him really happy. He had loosened up and was chatting normally until we got back to the car with our bags of chow.

Adrian paused near the back tire and then quickly bent down. He was out of sight only a moment before he was back with a small black, rectangular box with a silver antenna in his hand. "Who knew what kind of good that auto tech class last year would do me, right?" he asked triumphantly.

"Right. What is it?" I asked.

"Don't you want to know how I knew it was there?"

"Sure, okay, Adrian. What is it and how did you know it was there?"

"Not here, drive on and I'll tell you," Adrian answered.

"Oh... kay?" I said as we hopped back in. Adrian took a huge bite of his Crunchwrap before he would tell us anything. By the time he'd chewed, swallowed and guzzled some Baja Mountain Dew, Marlo had pulled back onto the road.

"They adjusted it poorly. When I walked past the back of the car I saw an antenna. Of course Taco Bell's parking lot lighting helped. The antenna caught the light. How do you guys function without me? Aren't you glad we stopped?"

"I know what it is!" Marlo crowed, interrupting Adrian's moment, "It's a tracking device. Shall we ditch it at a junction so they don't know which way we went?"

"You ruin all my fun," Adrian said with a scowl which turned immediately to a grin. "I do kinda miss this stuff. Too bad I'm not supposed to do it anymore."

"Instead of ditching it maybe we should make use of it. I'd like to know who put it here. It's obviously not ours... so... Evilia or Bob? Maybe we should lead them on a wild goose chase instead of just dumping it," I suggested, ignoring Adrian's other comment for now.

"A wild goose chase it is," Marlo agreed.

"Maybe they'll kill each other yet," I grumbled.

"Maybe we should go through a car wash or something so I can crack it open and see if there are any identifying marks. We could leave it there if I get anything on it." Marlo suggested.

"Why not?" I said, as I got out my phone to Google the nearest drive through wash. As soon as the car was on the tracks Marlo hacked the signal from the unit with his laptop. Adrian read him the serial numbers and manufacturer information.

Marlo mumbled for a bit and then spoke up, "Hey guys, it's not Evilia. It can't be. This is technology our government uses. She would go cheaper and foreign so that she couldn't be traced. Bob is watching you."

"Of course he is," I replied glumly. "Except now he's watching you to watch me."

"I don't want to think of it like that and I sure don't want to be watched like that. I've changed my mind. Let's dump it."

"Wait, leave it, he wants me to lead him to Evilia. I want to be sure I do that, but I also want to know how and where else he's watching us. Let's check all the cars and get everything you can off of that transmitter. Maybe we can start watching what they're watching and start sending them false information."

"Are you sure we shouldn't ditch it right here? This was a carefully chosen car wash. The beauty to this place is that the entrance and exit are on two different streets," Marlo argued as Adrain's head swung between us like he was watching tennis.

"We can park in a spot over by the exit that is partially obstructed by low growing Junipers – our view will be clear, but theirs won't be. The range on this thing would be what?"

"About a mile," he replied glumly.

"I want to see who's following us."

"Okay, Owen but I still want to check the warehouse and more importantly I want to know who hacked my camera. You know how I feel about being out-teched."

I started to answer but stopped as a black Lincoln pulled into the lot. The driver looked right and left and then pulled off to the side to check a tablet. He looked toward us and I about had a heart attack. The driver was the goateed man who had tortured Lucie. He looked both ways again and slammed his fist against his steering wheel. Then he got on his phone and within minutes another car pulled up, but it wasn't Madame Malvada; it was Mica. My Crunchwrap Supreme rolled over in my stomach and threatened to come back up. I swallowed hard to keep it down. *It would be a horrible waste of good food and I hated to wreck Marlo's car. Mica! How could she betray us?*

Marlo suspected Bob but we couldn't prove anything right now. He had outsmarted us before but now I wondered if he'd lost it. Was Dr. Moretz feeding his paranoia and crazy obsessions? I couldn't help but tell her everything. What had I said that made us worth following? I'd blocked most of my nightmare inducing Dr. Moretz memories out but now I remembered more and more. Maybe I was the monster here. I wondered again if Kraeghton and Miles had protected a part of my mind. Maybe that was why Bob was so persistent. How had he drug Mica over to the dark side? How better to get to Kraeghton than through Mica. He knows.

"WTF," Marlo breathed breaking into my jumbled thoughts. "Mica! I never would have thought she'd roll over on us."

"Disable that thing for now but don't kill it. For now, let's get out of here, Mars. We can decide what to do with it later, we might even be able to use it to our advantage. I'll call Sarah and let her know to look into Mica and we have a warehouse to check."

"Roger, boss."

Marlo played with the transmitter for a few moments and then deemed it safe. We left the back way. After I hung up with an appalled Sarah, I turned to Adrian. "I'm curious. You've stayed away from us for weeks. I can't believe that the bribe of Taco Bell changed your mind. What's really up with you?"

"I'm sorry. I've been kind of a jerk and I did miss you guys."

"That's not all of it."

Adrian looked angry but he stared straight ahead for a beat before he turned and looked at me intently. "I don't like anybody telling me what to do."

"Ready to tell us about it?"

"I don't know who did it. I got notes in my locker. They came in square off-white envelopes made of thick paper and they were signed by E."

"Do you have them?"

"The first few, I threw away. I thought they were a prank. All they said was stuff like, 'Choose your friends wisely' and later they let me know they were watching me. Some mentioned what grade I'd gotten on an assignment or how many points I scored in a game. Later they included pictures. I never saw anyone watching me or leaving notes. When I stopped hanging around you guys they stopped coming. I was scared at first but then I got mad. Mad is a whole lot better."

"Lucie got notes for a while too but they quit coming. Do you want our help?"

"Yeah, but I think I should make it look like I'm not with you guys just in case. It's why I left the house so fast. I don't want her hurting my family, Brenda or my other friends."

"We will have to be careful."

"Speaking of... crap, the unit is sending again," Marlo interrupted.

"What?"

"Mica's not dumb, Owen. She probably rebooted it and changed the signal pattern. I didn't turn it all the way off. I just scrambled it like you asked. It was all I had time for. I could have smashed it you know."

"Well, I guess they're just going to have to find out about the warehouse then, but I bet they already knew. Heck they may have been the ones who looped your feed."

"I was wrong," Adrian cut it, "you all are in it deeper than ever. I came along, why?"

"You're here because we need to get up on a rooftop without a ladder. You've got skills."

"Great and you've got both sides after you. Things have gone to hell around here. I feel like a duck in a shooting gallery."

"Welcome to my world."

"How can you joke."

"It's better than crying."

"Amen," Marlo added.

The warehouse was completely dark and utterly deserted. Even the plastic bag from the video loop had long since blown on. We parked a short distance away and approached with caution but it even felt forsaken out here.

I watched Adrian and Marlo. Adrian hadn't lost any of his skills. He still moved with an athlete's grace. He had left behind the letterman jacket he usually wore in favor of a black hoodie. I suppressed a smile when I realized he was wearing the black camo pants from our old adventures. Tonight he'd skipped boots and was wearing black athletic shoes.

I was thankful that the rain was giving it a rest tonight but a little extra light from the moon would have been nice over the thick gray clouds.

We glanced around looking for cameras and seeing none decided to retrieve Marlo's gear before we checked on the warehouse itself. Adrian leapt gracefully onto the nearest dumpster. I followed suit and turned to look at Marlo. He ran at the dumpster, hit it with a thud and slid back off. He shook his head and ran at it again with the same results. I scowled at him to let him know he was making too much noise.

"Okay, okay, I got this," he whispered loudly. He jumped and put his elbows on the edge and scrambled to his feet.

"Some things never change," Adrian said with a big grin as we reached over the edge to haul Marlo up by his belt.

A big smile found its way onto my face. I missed working with these guys. I put my hands to the wall of the building and scrunched down into the ladder position that Lucie had taught me. Adrian quickly climbed to my shoulders, his shoes cutting in uncomfortably. Marlo tried to help steady me as Adrian grabbed the edge of the building and pulled himself up. Lucie was a whole lot better partner for this stunt I decided as I imagined the blood blisters forming by my neck in a partial Adrian shoe print.

Adrian got on his belly and waited for Marlo to climb me. He was lighter than Adrian but less sure of his footing. As soon as Adrian reached down to grab Marlo's arms and haul him off me, I stood and cracked my back and neck. I tossed up the bag of tools Marlo had brought along and sat down to wait.

I closed my eyes for a moment and just listened. I could hear the swish of car noise in the distance and the closer crunch of tires on gravel. They were here already. I sat very still, hoping I blended into the shadows. I opened my eyes and watched the same black Lincoln pull up by Marlo's car. Two people got out. It had to be Mica and Goatee but I couldn't see well from this distance. They shone a light in Marlo's car and then began to walk toward the warehouse.

Well that answered one question for sure. They knew where they were going because they knew about the warehouse. It was probably how they showed up so fast. Mica moved her hand to her Ruger and her badge flashed in the street lamp. I watched Goatee stiffen.

"He's here." His voice was soft and as smooth as I remembered. It carried across the space between us like it was magnified.

I stood silently and prepared to jump. "Yes, I am."

I jumped from the dumpster. Mica and her pal jerked and turned in my direction.

"What are you doing?" Mica barked.

"I could ask you the same thing," I snarled back and then shifted my gaze to Lucie's torturer. "What's he doing here?"

"He works for us now."

"He should be locked up."

"Maybe you should!" Mica shouted back. "I said, he works for us now. Deal with it."

Anger shimmered through the space. I could feel it spiraling up and I could feel it gaining power over Mica's pet. "Works for you as what? A bloodhound or a blood thirsty pit bull?"

That was all it took for him to lunge at me. Mica shrieked but we ignored her. Goatee went for my neck but I deflected his strike with my right hand and punched his throat with my left.

He stumbled back clutching it and I spun and kicked his head.

"Wait!" Mica screamed.

Behind me I heard a bang as feet hit the top of the dumpster, immediately followed by a second.

Goatee lunged again trying to grab my arm. I dropped down fast as I turned to face him, smashing my elbow into his nose. Before he could recover I front kicked into his sternum, forcing him back.

"I said, STOP!" Mica yelled even louder. She threw an elbow at my temple. My vision blurred and Kraeghton roared within me. Adrian punched Mica as Marlo jumped on Goatee's back.

Pain. Excruciating pain burst through me. I grabbed my head and fell to my knees and then onto my side. "Make it stop."

And then it was gone. Blood dripped from my nose. I tried to rise but Mica put a foot on my head.

"I... said... stop," she wheezed. "Christ, Owen. What's wrong with you?"

"Get off me."

The pavement was digging into the side of my face one moment and the next there was a thud, the sound of a smack and I was free.

"He was mine," Mica cried.

I rolled onto my hands and knees. Adrian had Mica flat on the pavement, his body stretched over hers from his spectacular tackle.

"He was mine," she said again with less vehemence. "I hate you."

"What is she talking about?" Adrian asked.

"Me."

Marlo was panting and Goatee appeared to be out for the moment. A car door slammed. I tried to get to my feet but fell back to my knees.

"Damn it Mica. I warned you not to provoke him." Bob's voice slid over the scene like a slithering serpent.

Agents jerked us to our knees and held us with our arms pinned.

"Can you at least tell me if it's Kraeghton's power he holds?"

"I..." her voice trailed off as a strange sound filled the air. Time seemed to slow and stretch. I could feel gravel biting into my knees. My shoulders, elbows and wrists complained about the way they were being torqued behind me at odd angles. I glanced at a defiant Adrian who looked none the worse for wear. Then I looked over at Marlo. He was dirty and scraped yet he looked angry. This was not the old Marlo. Goatee was sitting up, his legs splayed out in front of him. He held his head like it still hurt. Good. I glanced back at Mica, she stood frozen, staring at a dart that protruded from her chest.

Slowly she reached a hand toward it and then she was falling over sideways, no one fast enough to catch her. With a pop everything returned to normal and then exploded with a cacophony of sound as the agents scrambled to protect their boss.

I heard the strange whistle begin again and yelled, "Get down," to Adrian and Marlo.

Thunk, thunk, thunk. A dart hit Goatee in the leg and one of Bob's agents in the back and another in the neck. The remaining agents' weapons were drawn and they swung them around looking for a target. They had to be coming from more than one place.

"Playtime's over, Robert."

"Sarah! So help me, if you weren't fired already, I'd do it now. I think I'll arrest you for interfering with..." He stopped talking when the agent to his right dropped, a dart protruding from his shoulder. "Damn it, Sarah!"

"Go home, Robert. Collect your garbage and leave." Sarah yelled back. I turned toward her voice but I couldn't see a thing through the darkness.

Bob changed his demeanor like a chameleon changes color. "Come out. Let's talk."

Around the dark edges of the perimeter Sarah, White Eagle, Alex, Mom and Lucie emerged. All held tranq guns I hadn't seen before and they all were pointed at Bob.

"I believe you are done here for tonight, Mr. Bowman," Lucie sneered. "We don't work for you anymore."

"You don't understand. I'm trying to help. He's dangerous. He needs special treatment you can't provide, but I can. I want to help you get Evilia Malvada. He's in no shape to do it now. Let Dr. Moretz..."

"No!" Lucie bellowed. "Leave."

"At least tell me why you're here," he begged. "Is this warehouse hers?"

"We don't owe you a damn thing, Robert. Not anymore," Sarah said harshly.

"Did you kill Kraeghton? Do you have his powers? How did you do it? You'll need them you know - when you face her. You need me to beat her. Don't you see? If we get rid of her, everything changes."

Silence stretched to the breaking point. I could once again hear the swish of car tires in the distance.

"Sir?" the last agent asked.

Bob looked from me to each of the others, settling on Sarah before he finally spoke. "Load them up, we're leaving."

I saw Mica's fingers twitch; whatever they'd used, it was fast acting. Soon she was moving her legs. One by one Bob and his goon helped their fallen comrades into the company Suburban they'd arrived in. Bob gave us one last hard look before he climbed in and started the engine.

He paused by the Lincoln for his last untranqed agent to hop in before they both drove away. The minute their tail lights flashed out of sight, Lucie about knocked me down again.

She didn't say anything. She just burst into tears. I fell back onto my butt and just held her. I didn't even care what the warehouse held anymore but over the top of her head I could see White Eagle did. He was picking the lock while Sarah held a light. Mom hugged Adrian and Marlo and spoke to them in hushed tones. Alex hovered by White Eagle and helped to pull the door back as soon as the lock was removed. The three of them stood in silence, gazing within. I hugged Lucie, stood and walked over.

We went over to stand by Alex to have a better view of the dust sparkling in the lamplight. The only sign of the table were its footprints and those of the men who'd moved it.

"Fan-friggin-tastic," Adrian said from behind me. *Yep, that about covered it.*

FIFTEEN

I fell onto Sarah's couch with a weary sigh. "You know, you just held him off, right? You should have just let him have me. Don't you think he'll be back with more people?"

"Not now," Sarah said with a soothing voice. "He has plenty to explain to his own boss after tonight."

"You went over his head didn't you?"

"He is in over his head and he's making bad choices."

Lucie had changed out of her gear and brought me some clean dry sweats. "Go take a shower."

I gave her a smile and followed her instructions. When I came back she had a snack ready for me including a glass of ice and a can of Pepsi.

I sat down on the couch again and she went into nurse mode.

"What happened to your neck?"

"Adrian stood on me. His shoe pinched me."

"If that was the look you were going for, I could have given you a hickey. It would have been lots more fun."

I gave her a pained smile.

Sarah walked in looking better in her own version of casual wear, but even more serious looking. White Eagle was right behind her. It didn't take a super genius to realize they weren't done talking to me.

"Now you fully understand why they say, 'with great power comes great responsibility.' If you abuse power enough then eventually something will come back for vengeance. Always think before you act because desperate people make desperate bargains." Sarah sounded so calm, so sure, but I felt her pain and then I saw a glimmer on her cheek. It was quickly followed by another. "Be careful." Sarah had spoken softly but from the heart. I could almost hear tears in her voice. She was scared – scared for me.

"I'm sorry," I whispered. "What did I do?"

"You didn't do anything. I just feel… *she's* coming. You know that and you accept it. I can tell that you do, but I don't. It's not fair and what Bob is doing… I don't understand. More than anything I don't want to lose you. I can't."

I looked at White Eagle. He should know what to say, but I could tell that he didn't. Lucie sat next to me without touching me and pulled her knees to her chest.

"Sarah, if I knew what to do, I would do it in a heartbeat if it saved all of you. It's okay. I'll be careful but never doubt that I'll do whatever it takes."

"No, it isn't okay," Lucie added softly. "We've got to find another way."

"Until we know what that is, I'm going to keep living my life like nothing is wrong. I need to be like Alex in that. I won't just hide and hope it all goes away. If I'm going down, I'm going down fighting and I plan to take care of every problem that comes my way until the end."

It was better that we'd had this talk with Mom and Alex safely back home and Adrian and Marlo being none the wiser, thinking we'd done all we could for tonight. I wanted Adrian out of this life. Marlo, Lucie and Alex were beyond my ability to do much about. I'd had a dream once about trying to save both my brothers and being unable to do so. I couldn't trust Evilia to make a good trade; she was only in it to win it. I had to take her down but I'd have to find her first and she wasn't ready for me to do that yet. For now I would hold Lucie and listen to her breathe.

"I don't know what else to say, Owen, except that I love you." Now Sarah was crying. "Sleep well and think about what I said. Goodnight."

"Goodnight, Sarah, I love you too."

She gave me a hug and walked toward the hall. White Eagle put a hand on my shoulder and gave it a squeeze before he followed his wife.

I pulled Lucie toward me and just held her until I could forget today, until I could think of nothing but her, until I could think of nothing at all.

Dark and light flickered across my face. I cracked an eye to find the sun coming up in a virtually cloudless sky, the sun's rays broken by the swaying branches of the tree in Sarah's front yard. I picked up a lock of Lucie's hair and watched the sun move over it, spun gold in my fingers. She drew in a deep breath and stretched before settling back in. She looked up at me with those deep blue eyes I loved so much. She didn't say anything; she just smiled a small smile. She ran her hands over me and I knew that she was trying to forget, at least for a while. It was so easy to get lost in her. I could kiss her forever. Her hand moved to my zipper and I froze. We were not alone. I heard Kraeghton in my mind, *Don't stop on my account. I always found her...*"

"Shut up," I hissed aloud. Lucie was already giving me a strange look. "We're not alone," I added looking deep into her eyes.

The muscles bunched along her jaw. Her expression was unreadable, as if she couldn't decide if she was angry or sad.

"I'm sorry," I added.

"I want us to figure out how to fix this. I thought you were getting better."

"Maybe he just wants me to think so."

Lucie gave me one last heartbroken look and then left me on the couch without another word.

I wasn't sure how I felt either, so I left. I went home and grabbed some clean clothes and took a shower, I left a note for my mom and headed right to the pawn shop. Max stopped dead when he came in the back door, his hand over his heart.

"What are you doing here?"

"Hey, Max. Sorry if I startled you. I just needed some space."

"Okay. Well, um, don't let me interrupt. I'll ah, just head up front and um, open."

Awesome. Now Max was afraid of me too. I started to throw the carburetor I'd been cleaning but stopped myself. Heat shimmered over my skin. I felt Miles take over for a moment and then Kraeghton was back. I could feel my whole frame shaking as I switched from one of us to the other. Each persona took over as fast as an old style film projector flashing frames. The carburetor fell from my fingers and I dropped to my knees. I clenched my jaw and fought the scream lodged in my throat. Then it was over as quick as it began, but I was left sweating and shaking. "Damn it, Kraeghton. Leave me alone!" I breathed in a harsh whisper.

I was calm by the time White Eagle made it to the shop. "You look like hell."

"Thanks. I feel like it too."

"How can I help?"

"I don't know. I wish I did. I can't keep living like this. The only things keeping me going is you guys and… and this horrible driving need to get Evilia out of our lives."

"I know."

I couldn't stand to look at the fear, frustration and sorrow in his eyes. It was like looking at Lucie but different. "Just let me work okay?"

"Sure, Owen. I'm here. You know I'm here."

I worked hard at putting everything out of my mind and focused on the many mindless tasks that awaited me around the shop. My stomach growled reminding me that I hadn't eaten today so I grabbed a protein shake out of the fridge and went right back to it. No one bothered me until late in the afternoon when my cell vibrated.

"I need your help tonight, please. I'm desperate. My new hires have the flu. I need servers. Marlo, Lucie and I can't do this alone and Melvin is out of town. Marlo suggested you. He said you could stand to get your mind off other things."

"Okay Marla, I understand. Let me go see Max and find out if he can cover the shop for me.

Marla had to be in trouble if she was scraping the bucket clean down to me. Maybe Max could use the money. He'd been taking most Saturdays off since before he got married but with a baby on the way he might want a break or at least the cash. I just hated giving him such short notice. I wasn't sure if it was lucky for me or not when he jumped at the chance. I just couldn't leave White Eagle here alone.

White Eagle threw me a look of concern but let me go. I headed home to shower and change. I walked down to the Saggios and jumped right in to help load the van. Marla was unusually somber and stiff. Marlo kept watching her with worry written all over his face. Lucie tried to exude a steady calm but Marla couldn't quite seem to pull herself together. I was surprised Lucie could after the way I'd treated her this morning.

We made it to the venue fifteen minutes later than Marla had planned. I couldn't decide if she needed an antacid or maybe some Excedrin or both. Her hands held a slight tremor I'd never seen before and a fine sheen of sweat glimmered on her forehead. It was as if she was channeling me.

We set up in record time with Marla doing an unusual amount of dithering. I wanted to ask her or at least Marlo what was up, but I was afraid to mention it. We each took a corner of the room and went to work as the guests began to enter.

Once the crowd was served, it was my turn to take a brief break. I moved to the hallway just outside the gathering room and rolled my head around on my neck. I let the sounds wash over me, trying to listen and relax. If you've ever sat and listened, really listened, you can take in the mood of a room. You don't have to hear the words. In happy times, voices bubble and bounce, punctuated by laughter or even squeals. I've listened at the airport while people are waiting for someone to arrive. Those folks are mostly looking forward to a happy reunion. Some read, some nap, some fluff their hair or bounce from foot to foot. It really wasn't so different here at this reunion. These people were happy to see each other and all wanted to impress each other. Was that what life was all about? Fooling people into believing your life was perfect or at least better than the next guy's? Maybe it was faking it until you finally tricked yourself into being happy.

"Hello Owen." I jerked around at the sound of my name.

"Why are you here?"

"We need to talk," The Gypsy said calmly in the smooth way he had of speaking. He was dressed like he was every time I'd seen him, all black with a long trench coat, leather bands and other jewelry he favored.

"Kraeghton is dead. Leave me alone." My voice sounded weary even to my own ears.

"I know he is, but it changes nothing."

"How did you even get in here?"

"What? You think I can't enter a church? I'm not evil. Besides that stuff's just for books and movies, right?"

"Whatever."

"People have been messing around in your head."

"Yeah, it seems to be a popular pastime these days."

"Don't be flippant," he snarled.

"What else have I got? Help me and I'll help you, is that it? What have you ever really done to help me? I can't tell what you've actually done, and what is just a made-up story for your amusement."

"You amuse me."

"Great, glad I could help. Now go away. I'm working."

"You're on a break. No one will miss you for a few more minutes."

"What do you want?" I sighed.

"You should know. I'm always watching, just like Bob and Evilia are watching. If that doesn't make you a pawn, I wonder what does? What I want to know is, how many times am I going to have to save you before you get serious?"

"Get serious? She's all I think about but we can't find her."

"She knows where you are. Why don't you know where she is? You have Marlo the Magnificent, yes?"

"I'm sure she's known most of our moves for months – it's a game to her."

"Of course it is. She is the cat and you are the mouse, my friend. She won't kill you outright. She wants to play with you first and you have something she wants."

"She is not going to get me or my abilities."

"As you absorb more gifts you only become more valuable."

"What do you mean?"

"You can't fool me. I know you've got Miles and Stephan in there."

"If I could get Kraeghton out of here, I would," I said emphatically, thumping my chest.

"You're doing it wrong. Don't try to shove him away and don't try to cut him out; embrace him."

"Are you crazy?! I can't trust him. He keeps trying to take control."

"In this you can. You have a common enemy. I bet he's done nothing but help you. You just don't recognize it for what it is. He sends you dreams, right?"

"I'm afraid to let him take over. It doesn't... go well."

"I'll take that as a yes. You need to consider the risks out there that are nastier than Kraeghton. You and Miles live happily together. Try letting Kraeghton loose."

"Kraeghton is not Miles."

"No, but you could think of them as the angel and devil on your shoulders."

"Great, I feel lots better now."

"You should, I went to a lot of trouble to see you."

"You went...? What did you do?" All of a sudden I could see it. It was his style. "Did you poison Marla's staff? Why would you do that?"

"See, I knew you were smart. They'll be fine. It's just the stuff you give patients to clean them out before surgery. It's not permanent. I'm not that cruel."

"Really?" I was pretty sure you could cut the sarcasm with a knife.

"I'm offended. I'm here to help you."

"You are here for you. How'd you know he was sending me dreams?"

"I know him. I know he wasn't always dark. If Lucie and White Eagle pulled the dark out of you, then what's left? Maybe the darkness *is* you?"

"No… I.."

"Owen?" Marla called.

I turned my head toward her voice and back, but he was gone.

"There you are. Please go get the extra pan of enchiladas from the van. We're running low. It's a hungry crowd."

"No problem. I'm on it."

"Thanks," Marla said with a sigh, she really didn't look well.

"Are you okay?"

"I will be. I must have gotten the bug that everyone else did. They started getting sick yesterday. I need to get back."

"Feel better," I said to her departing back and then I headed for the van but I wasn't alone.

The Gypsy rolled around the edge as I opened the back. "You didn't choose this but you should make use of it," he said softly.

"I'm working on it, okay!?!"

"You have evil in you, but you need it to fight Evilia."

"Am I strong enough to not let it take me?"

"Think how many people you could save. It's worth the risk."

"And die trying?… great," I huffed as I lifted the tray.

"Perhaps. You've been ready to die before… what's changed?"

"Maybe I found my line and I won't cross it."

"Bob's view would be to win at all costs – including the loss of you. Kind of makes you think, doesn't it? Who is really the greatest evil ever known?"

"Well, I think…" damn. He'd done it again. I was alone.

I lugged in my tray, prepped it and shoved it in the oven. *How was I supposed to find someone who didn't want to be found? Getting clues from The Gypsy was like trying to decipher a riddle.*

I started cleaning the kitchen while I waited on the enchiladas so I had time to think. Lucie hurried through to refill her coffee pot. "What's up?"

"Nothing," I lied. "I'm good. Tired. Maybe I'm out of practice with the whole catering thing."

The wrinkle between her brows told me she wasn't buying. "Well then, how about brewing some more coffee while you're in here. I'll be back."

She hurried back out with the last steaming pot and I sighed again. My life was too complicated.

When we finally slammed the doors on the back of the van a couple of hours later, I still had no real answers and lots of questions. I was glad to get home. Maybe tonight I was tired enough that I could actually sleep.

When my alarm went off on Monday it felt like I'd just fallen into bed. I would have to remember not to schedule any 8:00 classes when I went to college next year. I realized I wasn't the only one who was tired when Marlo picked us up for our ride to school. I shoved the tracking device over as I slid into the back seat.

"Why haven't you put this back under the car?"

"Why bother? So what if they know? We might as well make them a little uncomfortable for once. At least Mica has been smart enough to stay away from us. I'd like to give her a piece of my mind. Every time I look at Neil, which isn't often these days, I just want to hug him and tell him how sorry I am that he fell for such a mean…"

"It's not all her fault," Lucie defended Mica.

"How's that?" I asked, feeling immediately resentful.

"She's not against us. She wanted Kraeghton. They don't know everything but they know we had something to do with his disappearance. Saul and White Eagle made everything go away. I don't even know if she knows he's dead. She feels hurt and left out. Maybe she bought into us being the bad guys – I could see Bob doing that."

"You are way nicer than me, Luce," I huffed.

"Or me," Marlo added.

I sat through class, keeping my head down, trying to get good enough grades for Portland State but not do any more work than I had to. When the bell sounded, I felt like I was escaping something. I jogged to the shop in the rain, listening to the distinctive sound of tires on a wet surface. Like I'd noticed the last few days, a car followed me to the neighborhood behind the shop and another picked me up as I got closer. I wondered again why they thought I was worth it.

I got dried off and checked in with White Eagle. Nothing was out of the ordinary here, thank goodness. I could relax a little. I turned on some music and set to work on my "to do" list. My cell vibrated. I sighed. Maybe I should be thankful. I'd been looking at the same chain saw for thirty minutes and hadn't made a bit of progress on its repair or restoration. I looked at my screen. I didn't know the number. I started to set it aside and ignore it but... what was it? I felt pulled, so I opened the line and listened. I muted my end, putting it on speaker and then I turned up the volume. I didn't want to miss a word. I started up Marlo's work computer and opened the tracking program. I plugged my phone in and waited...

"What do you want?" Evilia asked in a bored voice.

"I want to make a deal," The Gypsy replied.

"You don't have anything I want."

"Ah, but I do. I can get you Owen Ryer." My stomach clenched in response.

"Well, well, Kovac. Who knew you could be bought? I thought you were against doing business with me."

"All business, no; some business, yes."

"I might be interested. What do you want in exchange for young Mr. Ryer?"

"I want to know about Stephan Kraeghton," The Gypsy replied.

"My sources told me that you were working with him. I'd think you'd know plenty."

"You want Owen, but you don't come right out and take him. I think you don't move on him openly because you want to play with him first but you also know that Robert Bowman is playing with him too. I think you are more afraid of Bowman than you are of Owen. I could get you Owen from under Bowman's nose."

"And for that piece of assistance you want to know what I know about Kraeghton. Interesting. Let me think about it," she replied. I could sense her greed.

"You just let me know when you decide and I will make the appropriate arrangements."

Marlo's program continued to narrow in until the line went dead. Judging from the cell towers used in the triangulating program, The Gypsy, Kovac, was in Beaverton.

Now I didn't know what to think. He'd done it on purpose – giving me a clue and an in with Evilia. I couldn't locate her but he could. If he'd given me her location would I have been ready to use it? Maybe we couldn't find her because we just weren't trying hard enough. Maybe I really wasn't ready to face her. Perhaps I needed to be backed into a corner before I would fight and what about Kraeghton? I'd gotten pretty good at shutting him down. Did I have enough skill, courage and control to let him out – should I?

Instead of worrying about all that, I pushed it to the back of my mind. Valentine's Day was coming and I wasn't up for the best boyfriend award this year so I better do something spectacular. At least it gave me something else to worry about; something that I had a chance of doing something about.

I got back on Marlo's computer and started researching. I put in every search term I could think of. Why was this stuff so easy for him? I couldn't quite find what I wanted. I knew I didn't want to get her the usual go-to gigs. I didn't want flowers, chocolate or even jewelry and I sure couldn't afford to buy her a car. I gave her all the time I could carve out of my schedule so what was left?

Marlo caught me before I could clear the screen. At least it wasn't Lucie.

"What are you doing?" he asked.

"I wanted to do something nice for Lucie, you know, for Valentine's."

"You should cook her dinner with candlelight and flowers and stuff."

I gave Marlo a look of distrust. "I should trust your opinion on women because why?"

"Because I Googled it and I'm the king of research," Marlo came right back with a snap, snap, snap of his fingers.

"And you were Googling Valentine's Day because...?"

"Well duh, I've been dating Caitlyn off and on for a long time. We're on again and I need to make a statement this year."

"Ah. So your majesty, what do you suggest?"

Marlo smiled. "I told you, you should cook, but the venue is critical. Make it memorable my man."

Memorable. What could I do? I had a week. I could get candles and flowers, no problem, but what should I cook? Marla would be swamped. It would have to be fairly simple but pulled off with flair. I wasn't as good as Marlo, but I could garnish with the best of them. I didn't have a lot of time, so I could go with a packaged salad and then I could focus on the main course. I could do the dessert ahead...

Lucie came through the swinging door so I gave up on my dinner plans and switched over to practice mode. I missed working out with Adrian but I still managed to spar with both Neil and Mitchell occasionally. When I worked with Marlo it was mostly for his benefit but Lucie could hold her own now.

I smiled at her.

"Uh oh, I don't like that look in your eye.

"What?" I tried innocently.

"You're up to something. I can tell."

"I'm not up to anything. I just thought we could spar."

"Oh boy!" Now she sounded like me.

217

SIXTEEN

I went over the plan in my head. White Eagle was taking Sarah to Amadeus and then to a concert so I could use the kitchen and get set up for her. As a special treat, Lucie and Sarah went to get their nails done; giving me plenty of time to put up the LED lights around Sarah's back patio and bring in the special dishes and glassware from the shop that Lucie had been collecting.

I hefted it on to the counter and gave it all a quick washing. I mixed up my first ever Red Velvet cake using Marla's recipe. I put it in the oven with a couple of bakers I quickly scrubbed and poked and started in on the cream cheese frosting. I pulled out the salad mix when I put the frosting in the refrigerator, gave it a toss and put it back in beside the frosting.

Next I pounded chicken breasts, dipped them in egg mixture and dredged them in flour. I lightly fried them but pulled them before they were done, set them on a parchment covered baking sheet and put them in the oven to finish while I mixed up the white wine sauce.

I pulled the cake pans and set them aside to cool and got the frosting out to warm. I turned the oven down and finished my sauce. I realized two things: I was having fun and I was feeling pretty good about myself.

White Eagle came home while I was frosting the cake. "You'll get more points but my way is easier. Next time just make a reservation. Here…" he continued as he began rinsing dishes to go into the dishwasher, "My Valentine's Day gift to you."

"Thanks, White Eagle." I pulled out Sarah's parmesan cheese grater and set about creating some white chocolate curls for the finishing touch on the cake.

"What are your folks doing tonight?"

I laughed. "With kids at home? They're having pizza and watching a movie."

"Well, good for them."

"Yeah, I think that may be my 'go to' for next year. I don't know how Marla does this every day."

"She loves it. Well, that's about all I have time for right now. I need to go change."

"Thanks for the help."

"You are very welcome." I watched him go, shaking my head as he cha cha-ed down around the corner while whistling.

I admired my cake as I slid it into the fridge and thought about how much I'd learned from Marlo's mom over the years just by watching and later from working for her.

I heard the garage open a little earlier than I expected. I hadn't had time to change, so I guessed she'd have to take me like I was. I dusted the flour off my old Evanescence t-shirt and worn Levis.

Lucie stepped through the back door and stopped. Sarah almost ran into her. Lucie looked surprised but Sarah's face lit with a huge smile.

"Earl, honey," she called, "it's time to go."

They were gone in a flash. Lucie looked around and then at me. "Wow."

Wow was right. She looked... amazing. Maybe it was her new haircut or maybe the Portland Bohemian chic thing she had going. Since becoming a *watcher* and her mother's death, she'd changed. She wasn't so… rigid, so mini executive – the child protégé was gone. She still wore the blazers, but now she rolled the sleeves to show off her many bracelets, bangles and bands. She wore jeans and leggings way more than skirts these days and balanced the boots we wore for fighting with girly tops.

The change had been gradual but tonight it smacked me over the head. She could pass for a college student in her black leggings, black riding boots, deep dark cherry blazer and white, lacy, low cut top. Of course the sleeves were rolled up so that the white, clear, pink and deep red glass beads on her wrists sparkled.

"You look beautiful, Luce. I like your hair all twisted up like that."

She smiled the smile I loved so much. "What's beautiful, is this: Candles, flowers, real dishes, silverware and actual flutes."

"I skipped the champagne but I bought sparkling cider."

"You thought of everything."

"I was thinking of you."

"How did you set all this up?"

"I had a little help and I pay attention. I know you set aside this stoneware that came into the shop and have been paying it off; just like you hold back the nicest pots and kitchen stuff. Your passion is glass, but you're practical. I've watched you polish these flutes more than any others. You like them and you dream of having your own place one day soon just so you can show everyone you're not a victim and that you can do it."

"I don't know what to say. You really do pay attention. I think you know me better than I do myself."

"I love you Luce. I'm sure I don't deserve you yet here we are. No one knows me like you do and nobody else would put up with me."

She kissed me. It was what I was hoping for. I had been tough on her. I hadn't appreciated her and she really was amazing. She had asked me lots of times what she would do without me, but talking to Kovac made me realize that it was all backwards – I couldn't make it without her.

I held her close and spoke into her ear because I couldn't stand to watch her face. Maybe I was a coward. People were fools to believe I was anything more. "I want to tell you something. I'm sorry... for the way I've been... for everything."

"Then choose to change."

"I... I can't."

"You can, but you won't – You've been pushing me out."

"I don't mean to. I'm afraid to let Kraeghton get too close to you."

"It doesn't have to be this way. You don't have to let the darkness win. Choose the light. I'm not afraid of Kraeghton anymore because I believe in you."

"I can feel the evil inside me – I've changed – there is no going back."

"You can always change, Owen. You just have to choose it," Lucie whispered, tears glittering in her eyes.

"You don't understand."

"I do. Remember when you saved me at the lake? You wondered how I held my breath so long. Well, the truth is. I didn't."

"What?"

"When Kraeghton and I fell into the water. I struggled and then... I closed my eyes and let go. I saw a flash from behind my closed lids. Kraeghton released me and then... it was like I was suspended. Someone else was there."

"I jumped in and…"

"Before you were there."

"Luce, no one else was on the dock."

"Not on the dock – in the lake."

"No, no one was there – there couldn't have been anyone. We'd been searching. I would have sensed…"

"Not someone… something. Something was trying to help us."

"You never said anything before."

"It was a blank at first. I thought I'd suppressed it or something, but as time has gone by… it… I've seen more and more of the event in flashes. I've seen it in my dreams."

"If you've seen it in your dreams how do you know it's real?"

"How can you ask me that?"

"Okay Luce, point taken, but what does this have to do with…"

"I get it now. It was The Gypsy. He helped us. I don't know how but he did. Now tell me. What did he say to you?"

"I… wait, how do you know he's been talking to me?"

"I felt his presence at the reunion job and I'm done waiting for you to tell me about it."

"I can't tell you all of it," I said trying to show her with my eyes that I wanted to but couldn't.

"Why?"

"Much of what he said was a warning to me."

"Then let me help you!"

"You are and you do but this…"

"I could help you better if you'd tell me what's going on. If I understood…"

"Luce, I want to tell you but I can't. Please trust me. I know it's frustrating but I'm trying to protect you."

"Well don't. It's not me that needs to be protected. It's you. Let me take care of you for once."

"Aw, Luce." I wrapped my arms around her and held her close. I twisted my fingers into her soft hair. Her lips touched my neck and her breath moved over my skin. We stood there – the seconds gliding past.

"You don't have to do this alone."

"It seems like I do. When I don't, people I care about get hurt and that's worse than anything they could do to me."

"But when you try to go it alone, you get hurt. Guess what happens to me when you do? Trust us, please."

"I want to but…"

"You know what? Forget that for now. Let's focus on finding out everything we can about The Gypsy."

"The closest I got was Beaverton. He called me the other day so I could listen in on a conversation he had with Evilia."

"Really. Then let Marlo help to narrow the search area. Call…"

"Kovac?"

"Call Kovac and let Marlo help you run the trace again. Also have him look into the name."

"I don't know if it's his first or last."

"It doesn't matter. If I've learned anything from Marlo, it's that patience is usually rewarded and narrowing the field can yield some surprising clues."

"Okay, Lucie but right now, how about if you enjoy your dinner before it's ruined?"

"Let me say one thing first." She waited until I made eye contact and gave her a nod before she continued. "The Gypsy, Kovac, he's offered us a way in. He cracked the door, maybe it was all he could do for now but its him we need to go after first. He wants to help you and he has a history with her. Follow him and he will lead you to Evilia. Thank you for cooking dinner."

Lucie helped me bring everything to the table despite my trying to get her to sit and enjoy.

"Everything looks really nice. I can tell you worked hard and I appreciate it."

"I wanted to do something you would remember. I'm sorry the chicken got a little overdone."

Lucie laughed softly. "Maybe you just need more practice."

"Yeah, that's it. My second career can be as a caterer or chef."

"It could be if that's what you wanted," Lucie said turning serious.

Now was a good time to change the subject. How could I plan a future when I didn't know if I had one?

"So tell me. How's your project coming with Alex?"

"Slow but steady. At first I thought maybe they worked for *her*. Sometimes it feels like it's all related but it's not. She doesn't have control over everything; it just feels that way sometimes."

"I know what you mean. Why do you think they got involved with gangs?"

"You know what? I truly believe that it all started as innocent fun. They had this image of gang stuff being really cool, you know? They didn't appreciate the danger. So many things in games, on TV and in life are blown up to be so much better than they really are. They were lost and confused, Owen. They aren't really bad kids at all. Alex's friend Tyler has started hanging out with us after school. Those boys are becoming friends and turning to safe activities. We're bringing them in, one by one."

"Good for you, Luce. That's magnificent. I'll be sure to tell Alex how proud of him I am… magnificent… Kovac called him Marlo the Magnificent. We call him that. How did he know? How does he control everything and know everything?"

"I don't think he's who he wants us to think he is."

"I really want to call Marlo right now but he's on a date."

"He deserves to have a normal life."

"So do you, Owen."

I leaned over our plates and kissed her. Kraeghton was quiet so maybe he was asleep, either way; I planned to enjoy my normal moment.

Lucie helped me clean the kitchen and restore it to its preValentine's state. When she put the leftovers in the fridge she found the cake.

"You baked too?"

"It's Marla's Red Velvet cake with white chocolate cream cheese frosting."

"It looks so good and it smells amazing. You know I have a cake weakness. If one piece is good, then half the cake is better. Do you know how far I'm gonna have to run to burn that off?"

"Are you telling me you lack willpower?"

"You know I have it at the store, but at home? Nope."

"That's so weird; you're one of the strongest people I know."

"That may be true but my Achilles heel is cake."

Sarah and White Eagle came home three hours later and found us on the couch making a halfhearted attempt at our homework with a movie playing on Netflix.

"Did you guys have fun?" Lucie asked.

"It was lovely, dear."

"How about you?" Sarah asked.

Lucie shared a look with me. "It was great."

"I overcooked the chicken."

"No one expects you to be perfect all the time," White Eagle said. His look clued me in that he was talking about way more than just my cooking.

"Sarah, what all do you have access to now that Bob has cut you off?"

"I have brought Bob to the attention of his boss. It was a gamble. It may cost me my job completely but for now, I am just on leave. I can't use official channels but I still have friends. Bob originally put the team together to work on special cases. We looked for people like you and tried to help. Back then I didn't realize what a user he was. When Neil came clean and let us know what was going on... well, let's just say I've been very leery of Bob ever since."

White Eagle sat on the love seat next to Sarah, put a huge slice of cake with two forks on the coffee table and then put a hand on Sarah's knee. Apparently Lucie wasn't the only one who was a glutton for cake.

Sarah smiled at White Eagle and took a bite.

"This is really good, Owen."

"It's Marla's recipe."

"Always humble. Never change. Back to access. While Bob was busy with his own agenda I was cultivating relationships. I was careful with the favors I did for people and I kept track. This whole time I have been watching and testing people. I think I know where all the players stand. I've asked for as little as possible so that when we have a real emergency I can start pulling favors from the right people at the right time."

"You can almost read people like my mom does, can't you?"

"Now that I know what I am and what I'm looking at… yes. I've also spent a lot of time with your mom. We've been working together. She and I were never meant to be frontline folks like you. We are support a team all the way."

I had a sudden realization. "You're like Marlo."

"No one is like Marlo." Sarah smiled at me, big and warm, with her heart shining in her eyes. We all laughed but not at his expense. Marlo is magnificent.

"Why are you asking about my resources?"

"Lucie had a brilliant idea. We can't seem to find Evilia, not even Bob can do that, but we have found someone who knows her. We thought we'd try something new and track him."

"Ah. But you don't want to use Marlo?"

"No, we do. We just thought he might need a little help."

"It would pay to be very careful," Sarah said. "I wouldn't be surprised if every person who has helped us along the way is being monitored to some extent. Bob wants things and when he does, nothing stands in his way."

"I believe that we are standing in his way," I replied firmly. *Now I was even more anxious to get back to the shop where I could have some exclusive Marlo time. I needed his brain.*

I headed home feeling positive for the first time in a long time. If my luck held it would even be a nightmare free night.

I was up before my alarm, thinking about all the things I wanted to get Marlo going on.

He was not entirely happy with me when I couldn't stand it anymore and called, waking him up.

"What!"

"Morning, Sunshine. I thought you could help me with a project."

"And this couldn't wait until a reasonable hour? I was out late. I'm tired."

"Come on, you know you love a good investigation!"

"Ugh, chipper in the morning. What's wrong with you?"

"Mars, Lucie had a great idea. I want to go with it. We've been stuck for months. Let's go."

"Fine. I'll meet you in an hour."

"Can't I come over now?"

"Seriously?"

"Well, yeah."

"I guess. Bring coffee."

He clicked the phone off. He hadn't cussed or hung up on me. *That had to be a good sign, right?*

I was at his door ten minutes later, coffee in hand. He'd unlocked the back door and sat slumped and rumpled at the kitchen table. His hair poked out all over his head making me wonder what he used to tame the multitude of cowlicks during the day. He had on fuzzy socks, Muppet pjs and a shirt that read, "I take life in gigabytes."

"You ready?" I asked, wondering if I shouldn't have given him a little more sleep.

"I'm good," he mumbled, taking the cup of coffee from me and heading to the man cave.

I gave him everything I had on Kovac and Lucie's big idea. He was unilaterally unimpressed. I even tried calling Kovac who didn't pick up, so Marlo barely got more than his number.

"Well?" I prodded.

"You're kidding, right? You know it takes longer than this to get anything. Go away. Don't go away mad, just go away and I'll tell you when I've got something."

I admit it, I felt let down. I didn't dare bug Marlo anymore so I did the only thing I could do while I waited for the rest of humanity to catch up to me, I went for a run. When I got back he still had nothing. I had gotten so used to him performing miracles on a regular basis that I didn't know what to think.

SEVENTEEN

Days went by and I found myself getting antsier and antsier. Each day I'd give Marlo the look and each day he'd give me a shake of his head in return.

Finally, Marlo came into the shop looking a little less haggard. Clearly I'd been too hard on him. Guilt washed over me.

"I'm sorry, Mars, I won't ask today. I'll leave you be."

Marlo laughed. "Funny thing is, I got it."

"You did? What did you find?"

"I traced the phone."

"I thought it was a burner."

"Wait for it, would you?"

I took a breath and tried to wait. Fortunately, Marlo didn't let me suffer as long as I probably deserved.

"I found out where he bought the phone. He finally turned it on and I got a ping. Then I looked at all the Kovacs in a mile radius of the purchase point. I have a house for you to look at. Kovac is his last name by the way."

I hugged Marlo. "Road trip?"

"Not this time. I need to do my shop work and then head home. My mom is on my case."

"Oh? Need help?"

"It will blow over. It always does. She just doesn't understand why I'm so busy all the time."

"Thanks for your help, Mars."

"No problem."

I headed up front, Kovac's address in hand and kidnapped Lucie for a drive by and spy mission.

Kovac's house was small with a neat yard. Unless he kept his ride in the single car garage, he wasn't home. Marlo was right, the place he'd bought the phone was in walking distance. We drove around the neighborhood hoping for a hit but we didn't get lucky.

We repeated the routine as we had time for two weeks before we caught him walking around the block. It was barely misting and nearly dark, so we decided to park and hoof it. We watched him go in and decided to use his abundance of shrubbery to hide and spy on him for a while.

From the kitchen window we saw him make egg salad and fix a microbrew of some kind. We followed him to the next window as he took his plate into his dining room or was it an office? It was the chandelier that gave it the dining room feel. The tacky, cut glass behemoth was totally inappropriate and out of place in the otherwise classic office set up with a dark wood desk and lots of shelving filled with an impressively eclectic variety of books. Nature photographs decorated the deep terracotta painted walls. An expensive looking leather coffee-colored desk chair and its matching companion completed the room. We watched him sit down at his computer. I pulled out the mini notepad I kept in my cargo pants pocket and tried to write down what I saw without taking my eyes off Kovac.

"He's gonna mumble the password," I muttered.

"He will not," Lucie hissed back.

"Bet you a buck, he will."

"You're on."

We spied some more while his computer ran through its warm-up routine. His Windows login came up and sure enough, he mumbled as he typed in his login and password.

"He did it. He mumbled the password under his breath as he typed it. How'd you know that would work?"

"I didn't for sure, but it's human nature to say something aloud you want to remember or when you're struggling to do it correctly. It's a complicated series of numbers and letters, so he mumbled."

"You are something else."

"I have my moments. Let's wait him out and see if he leaves."

"He won't. He just came home. It's dark; he won't go out again tonight."

"I feel like he will."

Kovac read through his emails and then stood up.

"Wait, you're not making him do that are you?"

"I don't think so. I am thinking about it but I don't really feel Kraeghton right now."

"Stay here. I'll check the kitchen window. He picked up his plate. Maybe he's just tidy."

She moved silently away. A moment later she was waving me toward her. Kovac had gone out the back door and was smoking a pipe. It was an interesting choice for him. The warm scent of cherry wood drifted our way.

"So much for compulsion," Lucie breathed next to me. "Should we break in now?"

I shook my head and Kovac's cell began to ring.

"Yes… yes… I will."

He set the pipe into a holder on the table and walked back into the house without locking the door. We eased back along the house toward the front in time to hear the door slam and then watch Kovac head away from us down the street.

"Now, we break in."

We headed straight for the back door. It was still unlocked.

"He left the pipe. That means he won't be gone long," Lucie warned.

I felt the house but I got nothing. I moved into the kitchen. Kovac had put his dishes in the dishwasher. The counters were spotless. I checked the fridge and opened a few cupboards.

"What are you doing? I just said we didn't have much time."

"Lucie, whose house is this clean?"

"Who cares? Come on." She moved into the office but I opened a couple more cupboards. What was it?

I followed Lucie into the office where she was quickly thumbing through a stack of mail.

"Luce, do you feel anything?"

"Not really, why?"

"Do you hear anything?"

"No," she huffed at me and moved to the filing cabinet. She looked at me standing there. "Look, while you ponder, at least be useful. See if you can get into the computer and copy some files for Marlo."

I sighed and did what she asked. I pulled a thumb drive from my pocket and plugged it in. "It's weird. There isn't much here. Call it a weirdly unusual lack of files. It's also strange that we don't sense anything. Most houses have something to tell us." I started moving files to the drive.

"There is something here, but I don't recognize it. It's almost as if the house is warded but it isn't against us. At least I got a first name," Lucie said holding up a utility statement. "Vandilo. What kind of a name is Vandilo Kovac?"

There was a sound and Lucie stopped talking. We held very still and listened. I watched the download bar crawl across the band and wondered if it would make it. Nothing else happened and Lucie moved on to a hutch.

"Ah ha, we have a laptop, my friend. Now why would he have that and a tower? Do you suppose he travels? He sure doesn't look like he has a lot of money."

"Good, I'll be right there." Another sound made us freeze.

"What is that?"

"I'm not sure I want to stick around and find out."

"Can he tell we're here?"

"I'm not sure. It almost seems like it."

"He let us in, didn't he?"

"I have no idea but let's get this to Mars," I said pulling the laptop from Lucie's fingers.

"It's only breaking and entering right now. If we take that…"

"I know, come on."

We headed through the kitchen going slow and listening carefully. I moved on to the back patio with Lucie right behind me. We edged back into the bushes and through the neighbor's yard. It felt like I held my breath until we got back in White Eagle's truck.

"You are giving me an ulcer," Lucie groaned.

She called Marlo and I drove.

"Do you know how many favors we're going to owe after this little adventure?" Lucie sighed.

"Yeah, and I'm ready to pay. We had to do something."

We pulled into the shop and headed straight to the back where a grumpy Marlo was waiting. I pulled out the notes first and handed them over. Marlo was quiet while I set the laptop on the counter.

"What is this? It looks like crap. I can't read it," Marlo fussed, sounding frustrated.

"Oh for the love – give me a break would you? I wrote it in the dark."

"Why didn't you just text me?"

"Light up screen? We didn't want the neighbors to see us or Kovac for that matter."

"Oh…. Oh! Well, could you at least decipher it then?"

A heavy sigh slipped out. "Yeah, I could do that."

"Parts of emails and his password to his computer. That's what you got?"

"No, the laptop is his too."

"Is it password protected? Is it the same password? People do that sometimes. They should use different ones."

"We haven't opened it, Mars. We saved it for you."

"Oh."

"Two computers. He's more like you than we thought," I laughed and then I stopped. "Like you... what was that password again? tn3cifingam... tn3cifingam."

"What? What are you thinking?" Lucie asked.

"tn3cifingam, it's magnificent backwards with a 3 in place of the E!" Marlo yelped and then covered his mouth with his hands, realizing that he'd shouted.

"No way!" Lucie exclaimed. "He wanted Marlo to find this?"

"Yeah, I know, I'm pretty awesome."

"Not that. He's communicating. I mean, you are awesome but that's not the point," Lucie sputtered.

The laptop screen flashed, drawing us all to look.

"He sure is! Look at that," Marlo hissed.

"What?" All I could see was a list. It meant nothing to me, in its current form.

"It's everything he knows about Evilia. At least it's everything he's willing to share. Which is way more than we knew by... well, it will take me days to decipher.

"I still don't see it."

"I do," Lucie said softly. "We're looking at global time stamps." She moved closer to the laptop and pointed.

"See. Here are the latitude, longitude, numerical date and twenty-four hour clock, along with activities," she said in awe as she touched each item on the screen.

I was beginning to see her reasoning when my cell vibrated in my pocket. I considered ignoring it but I couldn't. My gut was telling me not to. I pulled it out slowly as if it were about to bite.

"Hello?"

"Is Marlo happy with his gift?" Kovac asked me, a smile in his voice.

"Yes… I don't understand you? Why didn't you just give me a flash drive last time I saw you."

"That would have been too easy. You have to earn it."

"I don't like games."

Kovac turned serious. "I know you don't, Owen, and I really don't either. I couldn't be seen handing you anything. You had to take it. You're not the only one who is watched. I'm about out of time. Come meet me."

"I thought people were watching."

He sighed heavily. "Just meet me at the Starbucks by Best Buy in fifteen minutes."

"I'll be there."

"Come alone."

"No."

"Come alone or I won't help you anymore."

"I'll be there. Alone. Happy?"

"Not yet."

The line went dead. I made note of the time and picked up my jacket.

"You're not going!" Lucie grated, her jaw clenched.

"I am, but you can go too. Just stay back and stay hidden. I'll meet him and you may spy, Sunshine." I reached out and gently touched her face.

"Ugh," she growled at me. "I'm calling M…"

Her phone buzzed. She showed me the face of her phone, opened the line and hit speaker.

"Hey, Mitchell, you're on speaker, go."

"Where do you need me?"

"I knew this was going to be bad. Meet me at Arawan right now. Order us two Thai coffees and I'll fill you in. I'm on my way." She closed her phone and gave me the evil eye. "I hate it when he does that. I hate it that you're doing this."

"Do you want me to go too?" Marlo worried.

"No, Buddy, you stay and do what you do best. We'll handle it."

"Sure, Owen, 'cause you did such a great job last time."

I just gave Marlo a look. He threw up his hands in response. "Fine, have it your way; you always do. One of these days it's going to bite you in the butt. For now, I'll look for patterns in *her* movements. May karma smile on us all."

Lucie put on her jacket and headed out the front while I headed out the back door. I took White Eagle's truck and drove to Starbucks. I felt for Kovac before I left the truck. As far as I could tell he was the only one waiting for me.

He was waiting in the pickup line for his drink. I placed my own order without looking at him. A moment later he was out the door and standing by one of the trees out front. As soon as my name was called I grabbed my tall house blend and met him.

"Walk with me." He turned and didn't even wait for me to follow. He knew I didn't have a choice. Well I did, but not a good one.

"Why did you want me here?" I asked as we crossed the parking lot towards the baby store.

"Because the game has changed."

"That's not an answer."

He stopped for a moment and looked at me. I could see sadness, pain and hope in his eyes. "I can't give you a direct answer."

"Why?"

"Maybe it's a curse. Maybe it's why I go by many names. Maybe I am bound by rules you cannot see."

"Look, Kovac, I appreciate what you did, but I don't trust you."

One corner of his mouth quirked up, "Of course not – no one does – it's part of my charm. I find it interesting that the darker side is always a little more ready to accept me for what I am. Though maybe they're more desperate."

"I am willing to listen but that is all I'll promise."

"All I really want is to be left alone to do what I do without interference. It is not good for me either if things get too far out of balance, so I have a gift for you if you will accept it."

"My mother always told me to be wary of gifts from strangers."

"But we're not strangers. We've met many times and I've only helped. I've never tried to hurt you."

I raised one eyebrow at that. He took my elbow and pulled me on towards the street that ran behind the mini-mall.

"Not so trusting and not one for free gifts or surprises. Mmmm, I see that you are not," he said as he looked thoughtfully at me while stroking his goatee. "Here is the truth then - You must kill Evilia Malvada. I want to help you but I can't. You understand?"

I wasn't sure that I did but apparently I didn't need to say anything.

"I've already done more than I should. Let Marlo work out the information; he will do it quickly, I know. I will provide you with something that will help you. If *she* wins then my life will become... difficult, and so will yours. You must win and that is why I am helping you."

"You're not a *watcher* and Kraeghton's not here to foot the bill, so why help?"

"Do you assume that because I do dark things I am on the side of darkness? I am on the side of... balance. Look at me again Owen Ryer; I am neither a *dark* nor a *light watcher*. I am a true *secret watcher*. You and a handful of others know of my existence. I am neither completely good nor evil. I believe that there is a certain order to things but that we should leave nature alone. She wants... she wants too much. Look at me closely with your other sight..."

In truth I wasn't sure what he was. I had never encountered any-one else like him. He looked... like nothing. It was weird. Even normal people showed me a little something. I could see him with my eyes but when I looked at him with my gift it was as if he wasn't even there.

"Now do you want the gift or not? Trust me when I say that Marlo's help will not be enough."

"I'm still not convinced that I should trust you. You had me kidnapped and you show up unexpectedly. You tricked us into breaking into your house."

"You will never know if you can or you can't but I think you will find that you don't have a choice."

"You don't own me."

"I am perhaps the only one who isn't trying to 'own you'. I have saved your life twice. Once when you rescued Lucie from Carmichael and again when you faced Kraeghton. I chose you over him and I most certainly choose you over Evilia Malvada and her wheedling lackey, Carmichael. Kraeghton I could at least respect and understand. He thought he could gain enough power to get back the love of his life. Carmichael has given himself completely over to Evilia. He doesn't know what we know."

"And what's that?"

"She will use him up completely and then throw away the husk."

"I've suspected as much. She only loves herself."

"And she wants what she can't have."

"And maybe you're just reading my mind and feeding me what I want to hear in hopes I'll do what you want."

"I'm not that powerful."

"I wonder. Lucie thinks you saved her at the lake, back when Stephan Kraeghton tried to drown her."

"I have some magic and it wasn't her time. He was blinded by rage. He didn't see the bigger picture."

"What's the bigger picture?"

"We all must work together to bring down Malvada."

"Even Robert Bowman?"

"Everyone."

"How do I know what you say is true? Besides, there is always a choice."

"For you there is not. Not anymore."

"I like to think I make my own choices."

"Yes, you like to think it, but you don't." He laughed. "You have been a pawn since you were a small boy, if not from the day you were born. Maybe even before then." I started to argue but he waved me off. "I like you Owen Ryer, defender of the weak and innocent. I am not a *dark watcher*; my mentor was of the light. You know her as Nadie Black Feather."

"You can't be that old."

"I have many secrets and sometimes I trade them for things I want. Stephan Kraeghton was not in his early forties when he died. He was almost seventy. Evilia Malvada wanted that secret but I will not share it with her. That is a truth for you to ponder. You are the second person ever to receive anything from me without a price. Usually I only give people what they pay for."

"What they pay for... you make that sound like they don't always get what they expect."

"You are finally becoming wise. Think of me as neutrality. Remember that I am neither inherently good nor evil. You may not think I'm your friend but I am not your enemy. It doesn't mean you can't trust me. Evilia is our common enemy - do not become mine. Be wary of me but do not fear me unless you have done something to cause the fear."

"So Evilia should fear you?"

"Evilia has become... too much. She wants desperately to drive you to her side and that I simply will not allow. Be cautious of what you do for your side. Always think before you act."

"How will I know where the line is?"

"You will know. You will feel it. I sense that although you are inherently good you are not one to abuse power. Learn from Miles, but don't become him. Never believe that you must hunt down every last bad thing in this world. That is not balance. It is ultimate control and that is NOT how things are meant to be."

"Why me?"

"I did not choose you."

"You didn't? Then who?"

"Miles and White Eagle of course."

"Let's say that I believe you. How could Miles choose me? He's gone."

"Is he? Perhaps he had a debt to pay to the side of good."

"Then it's paid back now – let him go," I said emphatically.

"You think *I* hold him here?" He laughed.

"You're the reason he was in the watch. It stands to reason... why not you?"

"You have an interesting way of looking at things, young Owen. I guess White Eagle knows more about me than I thought... well here is another truth then about your watch. I did once give Miles a gift. I taught him how to make the charm he so desperately wanted but I taught Kraeghton too. I guess you could say that is my talent," he said as he opened his duster to show me a myriad of them hanging inside the lining of his coat and from his belt. From there my eyes flitted to his bracelets and other jewelry.

"I liked Miles. He understood me. Of all of us, I am the true *watcher*. Miles saw that. Evil is winning and we can't let that happen. You have the remains of two of my charms now but you only know how to use one. To fight her you need to go back to your roots. You need to understand what you are and how you got here."

"Yeah, whatever that means. Tell me... I thought the term "gypsy" was considered rude. Don't your people prefer Romani or something?"

"I am unlike any other and names carry meaning. Perhaps there is something the name is meant to convey other than my lineage."

"You are talking in riddles like always."

"And you are beginning to frustrate me."

"Then don't help me. Kill her yourself."

"I told you. I can't"

"Can't or won't?"

"It isn't allowed."

"You are talking in circles again. If you couldn't kill her then why take the job from Kraeghton in the first place."

"I can't do it but I can help. Besides, it got me what I wanted. I couldn't see you but he could."

"See me? What do you mean?"

"You were hidden from me, but once Kraeghton led me, I could always find you again.

"Help me understand. You let Kraeghton hire you so that you could get to me? How'd you even know about me?

"Yes, I used Kraeghton. I heard the stories and rumors of a young man who can do… unusual things even for a *watcher*. You may be an irritating gnat to someone like Madame Malvada yet people believe you will one day be a much bigger problem for her."

"What are you saying… stories about *me*? I couldn't help but laugh. "Yeah, right. I'm like Batman. There are legends and everything." I laughed harder.

He just looked at me, expressionless.

"No way!"

"Prophecy is a funny thing. Often people see what they want. Something is predicted and then we start seeing all the signs pointing to it or so we think. Is a glass half full or half empty? It is all in the perception of the thing. It was foretold that one remarkable young man would be the downfall of evil. People believed it and so they make it come to pass. There is always a price – any choice you make has consequences. Haven't you heard the saying that risks are the price you pay for opportunity?" He did not watch me as he spoke. He watched what little traffic used the back road as if gaging every driver.

"So the risks I've taken helped to put me here?"

"Yes." I would have to ponder that one.

"Tell me about the thing of Kraeghton's I broke."

"They go by many names depending on the lore. I call them charms."

"But Kraeghton used black magic."

"I did not teach him that!" Now he sounded angry but he still wasn't looking at me. Now he was looking into the past.

"Okay, okay," I said in a soft calm voice. "I'm just trying to understand."

Kovac took a breath. "The watch and the phylactery; they're both charms and they both hold power and memories."

"Surely Kraeghton did not make his for me?"

"Of course not. It was an insurance policy. In the beginning I'm sure he wanted to collect someone and perhaps he did many times. It was part of how he stayed young."

"But I'm aging."

"You are not fully grown. Once you reach about twenty-five that may change or it may not. You did not collect anyone; you came by them... accidentally."

"I don't want to live forever."

He snorted. "Then figure it out. Stop it."

"I don't understand."

"You will."

"Let me guess… this is another one of those things you can't answer directly."

He nodded at me. I hate guessing games but it was the only game right now.

"I think he didn't use his gift like he promised you he would. He corrupted it and if that's true, then why did you help him again?"

"I saw his end. We both know Evilia would never let him win. I should have taken care of her when she was young and weak but I misjudged her and then it was too late. It was out of my hands."

"Oh, so you admit you made a mistake."

"I've made many of them. You better not be one."

"And if I am?"

"Then I shall be very disappointed."

I couldn't decide how to take him. He wanted to help and I could see the strain of something holding him back. It was almost as if he tasted words on his tongue before he let them pass his lips. I was trying to figure out what I needed to ask next but he beat me to it.

"I can't tell you any more but I can give you one thing."

I took a deep breath, looked him in the eye and nodded. He was right; my back was up against a wall. What did I have to loose. I held out my hand. "You are filled with nothing but riddles and no real answers. I give up. You win."

"I usually do."

He reached into one of his many pockets and pulled out something small. I held very still.

"You are brave, youngling. This is for you. You will know what to do with it when the time is right." He opened his hand and an ancient arrowhead fell from his grasp, bounced to a stop and then swung from a leather thong. He reached toward me and I allowed him to hang it over my head. When I looked down I realized that a white feather was suspended with the arrowhead. I looked up to thank him but he was gone. I saw nowhere that he could have disappeared that quickly. Now that was a trick I could use.

The arrowhead vibrated and hummed at my touch and soon my head was filled with drumming and chanting. Next images rolled out. I could see White Eagle's grandmother meeting with The Gypsy and he looked just like he did today except for the clothes. His hair was longer and he wore round wire-rimmed glasses. He still held the same cocky confidence and a smile that said he knew a secret. He wore sandals, raggedy jeans and an old tired t-shirt with a peace sign painted on it. Even back then he wore a bunch of leather bands tied around his slender wrists.

"He's not ready," Nadie said sadly. Her gray hair looked like it was thinning. What little there was she had scraped into a crooked bun. A few strands had escaped and even those lacked shine.

"He will be when the time is right, Nadie."

"You don't understand, Vandilo."

"Yes, I do. I understand more than you know."

"I need time to make him understand and to teach him but I'm running out of it."

"I can help you but you have to help me in return."

"What do I have that is of value to someone like you?"

"Ah, Nadie, do not underestimate your worth. You are more than a trainer of watchers. You are a medicine woman, a keeper of histories and secrets."

She laughed. "Nobody believes that stuff anymore."

"But you do, because you know it's true and so do I."

"It is against our laws to share. They are tribe secrets."

"In for a penny, in for a pound, Nadie – I can sense you don't have much time left. Call me when you really want my help."

The scene changed.

White Eagle's grandmother looked even more frail and ill. They were in the same location, but clearly time had passed. Nadie Black Feather's clothes were too big on her frame. The bones and blue veins in her hands and wrists stood out in stark relief.

"You win." Her ravaged voice held pain.

"I usually do."

"What do you want?"

"Teach me to bind power into a charm."

"You swear you'll help me?"

"You teach me and I'll teach you. Everything you know will pass to him. I can make that happen. He has denied his destiny and the balance must be restored. You can fix this Nadie and it's time you did, don't you think."

"Yes," she sighed, "past time."

"Owen! Owen, can you hear me?"

I opened my eyes and then blinked. Where was I? I was wet and cold. My brain seemed to snap into place. I was wet and cold because I was on the ground behind the strip mall, back where the cardboard waiting to be recycled and the dumpsters lived.

Lucie's eyes shifted from my face and she focused on the leather thong around my neck. Her hand moved and I grabbed her wrist but not before she connected to the arrowhead.

What was around us swirled and we were elsewhere or maybe *else-when* was a better descriptor. Miles and Vandilo Kovac stood before us.

"I did what you asked." Miles sounded resigned.

"Good. We can't have any mistakes. Your mentor is not ready to take the next step."

"He's tougher than you think. He has survived a lot," Miles insisted.

"He still has to survive you so that he can train the chosen one. You are just practice."

"You really believe all that hoopla?"

"You haven't seen what I've seen."

"The spirits gave you a how-to guide, did they?"

"I wish it was that simple, Miles. Now be a good little watcher and do your part. Darkness will rise and you must help to ebb the tide."

"You understand I'm only doing this because I've got nothing left?"

"I understand that revenge is all that gets you up in the morning. I also understand that we all have our parts to play. Now buck up and do yours. It doesn't pay to make us angry." Kovac's eyes shifted from Miles to us. "You shouldn't be here." He held up his hand palm out and we were thrust back into the present.

I blinked hard and took a moment to make sure I was okay. It felt like I'd been hit with one of Kraeghton's power blasts. I looked at Lucie, still on her knees and panting. Nothing around us looked disturbed. The only change I could discern was that the water had wicked a little further up our pants.

Mitchell's pounding feet and then voice cut through the moment. "What the heck just happened?"

"Nothing," Lucie covered quickly, getting to her feet.

"It's not nothing," Mitchell denied, reaching out a hand to pull me to my feet. "I felt the power surge."

"Look Mitch, you're a sweet guy and I appreciate the backup but I made a mistake. You shouldn't be here." Lucie took his hand, clasping it urgently.

Mitchell swung his gaze from Lucie to me. "I got a message, our kind of message, that I needed to be here."

"It was a mistake," Lucie insisted.

"I don't understand." A wrinkle appeared between his brows as he dropped Lucie's hand. He spread his feet a little wider and crossed his arms.

I shifted my gaze to Lucie and saw that she had her feet spread and arms crossed too.

"We got into something we shouldn't have," I tried. "We don't want you to get hurt."

Mitchell laughed harshly. "'Cause our line of work is so safe."

"You're right. It's just that…"

Mitchell interrupted me, his body rigid and his eyes closed. "There's a presence here that wishes to remain hidden. You were chosen. I was not. It doesn't want me here." Mitchell blinked and then swung his head in every direction looking for a source. "What is that? I've never felt anything like that."

"It's him," Lucie explained, "the person who wanted to talk to Owen. He's really powerful and he was very clear that he didn't want us here. We should go."

"Whoever he is, he's scary. Are you sure you should be dealing with him?"

"He's helping with Evilia," I said feeling resigned.

"At what cost? Surely he wants something."

"Leave it alone, Mitchell," I reminded him gently.

Mitchell threw up his hands in frustration. "You're riding with him I assume?"

Lucie nodded and Mitchell left, grumbling to himself on his way back to his car. I took Lucie's hand and lead her to White Eagle's truck. Her warmth next to me on the drive home was more than just body heat. Lucie rested her hand on my knee and her head on my shoulder. Something had happened when she touched the arrowhead and it was more than just the image. I just didn't know what yet. Whatever it was, I felt... safe.

EIGHTEEN

Marlo was still at work when we returned to the shop. He glanced at us but kept at it past closing time. We finally had to drag him out and force him to go home when his mother called for the second time.

A week passed and then two. Marlo barely spoke to us. Lucie, White Eagle and I couldn't seem to stop talking about Vandilo Kovac. After our last meeting, I couldn't decide if I was happy or sad not to have heard from him. Every day we researched lore and magic. Every day we practiced old skills and worked on new ones.

Mom convinced the principal to let her finish the year half time and they found a long term sub to cover the other half of the day. Mom came to the shop more and more to train and work with us. Having her was a plus but I worried about Lucas who was around more because of it. He and Alex learned new skills and practiced old ones with us and in their free time took over all the shop cleaning and simple maintenance. Mom learned the register and store computer systems.

Sarah was around more too. Bob might have been able to fire her temporarily but she still had a pension. Money was tight for all of us but if we were careful, we would be okay. White Eagle even warned Mitchell that the house needed to go on the market to free up some cash. Mitchell admitted that he wasn't jazzed about maybe having to move back into my room but he'd deal. He understood and acknowledged that he would have to move back to Fallon sometime between graduation and the end of summer anyway. He was at the shop when he could be but he was clearly avoiding me. It was as if he was saying goodbye before he even left and it made my chest hurt in an unexpected way. I finally owned that he meant a whole lot more to me than I had ever realized.

Still Marlo worked on, ignoring all of us and even his shop duties in this quest to understand the comings and goings of one Evilia Malvada. He had a map up on the board with pins and string strewn all over it. He attached articles he'd printed off the internet that might have something to do with it but he never had time to explain it to me.

On Friday when Marlo picked us up for school he was practically vibrating with pent up angst. "I can't take it anymore. My mom is driving me bat…" Marlo cut his eyes to Lucie, "poop crazy."

Lucie turned her lips in and pressed them together. I could tell by her expression that she was biting down hard on a laugh but she didn't interrupt Marlo's rant.

"She wants to know where I am all the time and what I'm doing. She keeps popping her head in my room. I can't get any work done. I have to tell them! I have to do it so that I can work!"

"I understand, Mars. Do what you think is right."

"You're leaving me to do this alone?" he screeched.

"Okay, okay, how can I help?"

"I don't know," he vented, as he backed out of Sarah's driveway fast enough to scrape the undercarriage of his car.

"How about dinner with Sarah and White Eagle?" Lucie suggested.

"Yes, please." Marlo sounded tired yet relieved.

"I'll set it up. You just focus on your driving." Now it was me that had to try not to laugh.

Marlo's parents showed up with a bottle of wine and big smiles. I prayed we would get them to a place where they could smile when they left.

Before their backsides had even fully connected with the couch Marlo blurted, "I have... news. I'm going to Portland State University in the fall with Owen and Lucie." Marlo held his chin high.

"Why, son? You were accepted to Harvard. Why..."

"Dad, I can't go to Harvard. I have to stay here. This is where I'm needed. I understand now. I have a gift and it isn't the one you think it is. I have a special ability and I have to use it. I'm a *watcher*, Dad – a *secret watcher*. My place is here with the people I serve and protect."

"What?" Marlo's parents said together.

"Show them, Marlo. Show them what you can do," White Eagle suggested gently.

"What about Adrian? Is he staying too?" Marla interrupted.

"He's gonna go be a duck at University of Oregon. They offered him a great sports scholarship. He has helped us over the years but he's not like us."

"What do you mean?" Marla begged, desperate for us to tell her it was a joke. "You sound crazy."

Marlo sat very tall and straight. Then he closed his eyes and lifted his chin as he took a deep breath. "Darkness is gaining in power. Evilia is going to do something to draw us to her. Her cult of *dark watchers* has swelled and she's almost ready."

His parents were giving him strange looks while Marlo's words had left him shaking.

"I don't understand," his father said. "What was that supposed to show us?"

"Let me try," I offered, taking Lucie's hand. I looked over both Saggios hoping for a hit. Ah ha. "Melvin, you had a meeting with your boss today. You are being forced into a new position and you don't like it. It will mean travel and time away from your family but it... it's that or..."

His mouth fell open and Marla gave him a sharp look. "Why didn't you tell me?"

"I thought one crisis for today was plenty."

"So it's true?"

"Yes, but how did you..." he asked looking at me.

"I could see that you were distressed. You are wearing the shoes and pants you wore to work when you became distressed. They showed me the story in images."

"Unbelievable," he said with wonder. "How did this happen to you?" he asked turning to his son.

"By the way, Dad, I'm not a crisis. This was a gift. How I got it was an accident but I always had a touch of... something. You might too or I might have just been lucky." Now Marlo sounded like he meant it instead of sounding sour like he used to.

"Accident? When? How could you let this happen?" Marla burst in, her angry eyes turned on me. "You promised me you'd watch out for him!"

Marlo scowled at her.

I sighed and told our story. Marla seemed to grow angrier with each word that passed my lips and then she began to cry. By the time I got to Marlo's gift being awakened, they sat hunched on Sarah's sofa. Marlo's dad had his arm around Marla. I wanted to tell her it was going to be okay but I knew it wouldn't be. I owed it to them to catch them up to the present.

"What will you study?" Melvin asked his son. I could tell he was trying to absorb everything, be understanding and overcome his enormous disappointment.

"I still plan to study computer science. Lucie wants to study bio-chemistry and Owen is going into criminal justice. We plan to cover our bases. We are a team. If all goes well, then we will have jobs waiting for us when we graduate. In exchange for what I'm giving up, I will work for Sarah and will begin an official intern-ship with her. I know I'm giving things up but..."

"Like Harvard or MIT," his mother nearly wailed.

Now, Mom, don't be upset. I have a guaranteed job and a paid internship. That's worth something."

"So were Harvard and MIT. I want you to be happy but... this... I don't know."

Lucie touched my hand and asked in my head, "Does Marlo know that Sarah got fired?"

"He's hoping we'll get that fixed. He feels like it will," I murmured by her ear.

She squeezed my hand and spoke again without words, "Well, good. 'Cause no job, no internship."

I turned my attention back to Marlo. "This is the way things are – it sucks but I'd better get used to it. I can't deny it anymore. I'm not like everyone else."

"We never thought you were. This is just... unexpected," Marlo's dad said softly.

"You thought I wouldn't be upset if you told us here?" Marla asked, her voice cracking.

Sarah went and put an arm around her shoulders. "Marla, it's not like that at all. Your son is meant for more than Harvard. He is going to do things that no one else can. The down side is that most people will never know, but in your heart, you will."

"Really?" she whispered.

"Really," White Eagle answered for his wife. "All this time I let you believe that I was just a pawnshop owner. My real job is to find people like Owen, Lucie and Marlo and train them to be *watchers*. It is their calling to fix what's broken. There is always more going on in the world than anyone ever knows."

"Oh my Lord, you're vigilantes," Marla sobbed.

"We're not," Sarah said in her most soothing voice.

"Then why does it have to be a secret," Marla sniffled.

"It is for your protection as much as ours," White Eagle took over again.

"You don't do anything illegal do you?" Marla asked, still worried.

"Certainly not!" Sarah lied.

"Promise me, you won't let anything happen to him – he's all I've got."

I couldn't stand it anymore. I love Marla but today she was drama central. Lucie and I excused ourselves to put the finishing touches on the meal and check the table. I took it as a good sign that no one was shouting in the other room.

Dinner was one of the most uncomfortable of my life as we struggled to help them accept us and Marlo's fate. There was lots of talk about closed doors to opportunities and this being a whole new path. We talked about the good we'd done and steered clear of any subjects related to Evilia Malvada. Marlo admitted that he mainly did research for us. They went home at nine, without the smiles I'd hoped for, but at least they were less upset.

Lucie gave Marlo an extra big hug before he followed them out the door. "Have courage. It's going to get better."

"I sure hope so," he mumbled and left.

Sarah and White Eagle had disappeared. I found them quietly talking as they cleaned the kitchen.

"You're worried," I stated, probably unnecessarily.

"Damn right," White Eagle groused.

"You know it was time. He had to do it. They were driving him crazy," Lucie said softly.

"Yes." He said it on a sigh. I swear I could almost hear his heart breaking. "It wasn't supposed to be like this. I don't like to hurt people and I don't want to ruin lives."

"Marlo would say that he is where he's meant to be. He fought it for a long time but now he feels it even more strongly than I do." I knew it in my heart, I just couldn't explain it.

"I just want someone to tell me that everything is going to be okay," Lucie lamented.

"I think that would be more Marlo's or Mitchell's department," I said, hoping a little levity would lighten the mood.

"Go watch some TV. Go be kids. We've got the kitchen. Put it out of your mind, Lucie. We've done all we can for now."

It made me sad that White Eagle was so grim. I decided it just didn't pay to think about it too much.

Lucie pulled out a book, but not even she could concentrate. "There are only ten weeks left of school, it's Senior year but all I want is for it to be over. What's wrong with me?"

"It's a strange feeling isn't it?"

"There are things about high school I'll miss but mostly I just want to leave. I think college will be easier, at least the scheduling part."

"I think so too. It's just so strange. It feels like it's just the three of us, you know? Some people I'll miss and some I won't but we've been with them since grade school and now it all ends."

"I'm hoping it's not the only thing that ends."

Lucie put her head on my shoulder and closed her eyes. "Deep breaths and enjoy the small moments, right?" she whispered.

"Yeah, that's it." She sat there taking comfort in my presence. I wished that I could do the same, but not tonight. Thoughts pinged around in my head, elusive as butterflies. What should I do about Evilia? Marlo needed to explain what he'd learned from tracking her. I needed to understand what he was doing. I needed to do something about that table. Marlo had gotten so busy with Madame Malvada that he had let that one slip. Then there was Bob. What should I do about him and Dr. Moretz? Had Sarah really scared him off? And what about the team? Was he treating them okay?

Lucie slipped her arms around me and under my shirt. She slid gracefully around me. "They left and you didn't even notice."

I snapped my head around and looked over my shoulder. Sure enough the kitchen was dark. Lucie took my face in both hands and moved it around to face her. She watched me for a moment and then moved forward to rest her forehead on mine.

"I want everything to be okay, but I'm scared."

"Me too, Luce."

I closed my eyes and felt her lips move over mine. Thinking about her was way better than worrying about everything else.

"You need to go. It's almost eleven."

"I know," I sighed. "I'd rather stay with you."

"Me too."

"I'll see you tomorrow." I kissed her one last time and headed home.

I thought mom had left the light on but I found her dozing in her chair. It reminded me of old times but it was different too. The lamp picked up something new in her hair that I hadn't noticed. A few threads of silver were now mixed with the caramel and gold. The hand that held a used cozy mystery reminded me of Nadie Black Feather. I had never noticed Mom's hands but they didn't look the same. They weren't old yet but they didn't look like Lucie's anymore. The smile lines around her eyes were even visible as she slept. I had done this to her. I was making her old. I felt a lump swell in my throat. I needed to take better care of her but I could barely take care of myself.

"I love you, Mom," I whispered. I moved in to kiss the top of her head but I woke her up.

"There you are," she mumbled.

"Yes, here I am. Let's get you to bed. You didn't have to wait up."

"Yes, I did. I can't sleep until you get home unless I know where you are."

"You knew I was with Lucie."

"Yes, I mean, I knew you were coming home."

I hugged her. She was cute and fuzzy when she was sleepy.

"Whaz that for?" she asked in that same sleepy voice.

"I just wanted you to know I love you."

"Love you too."

I dropped her at her door and headed for my room. I looked in on my brothers. Alex had twisted his long, skinny frame into a ball and Lucas was spread out. He practically reached from one end of his twin bed to the other with his arms thrown over his head. When had that happened? I remembered reading to him. Where had that little guy gone? I closed their door gently behind me and walked into my own room.

I sat on my bed and pulled out the arrowhead. I needed something and I didn't know what. I stared at it hoping it would give me a message. Miles and Kraeghton were silent as well. For the first time in a long time I felt utterly alone. I flopped back on my bed, suddenly too tired to even get up and brush my teeth.

I was still there, not awake and not asleep when dawn slithered into my room. I wished I could put my finger on what was wrong. Who was I kidding? Everything was wrong and it felt like very little was right.

I wrote a note for my mom, changed into running clothes and headed for the shop. If I was lucky something there would speak to me. The White Eagles' was still dark as I ran past. Pink streaked the sky and traffic was nearly nonexistent in the early surreal light. I had no sense that I was being followed. Maybe even bad guys need rest now and then.

I unlocked the back door to the shop and turned off the alarm. I checked Marlo's other security equipment and then pulled out Kraeghton's phylactery. I held it with the arrowhead and finally tried it with the watch. Nothing was working. I begged. I cajoled. I even considered going all pulp fiction, cutting myself and bleeding over the top of them but I didn't think it would work and I was sure I shouldn't dabble in dark magic. I set them all aside and tried running through every karate kata I knew.

White Eagle was startled that I beat him to the shop. Knowing he isn't a morning person either, I helped him go through the opening routine without a word. I didn't know what to say anyway.

I was relieved when Marlo and Lucie showed up an hour later. Turns out the silence was killing me.

"Why didn't you wait for me?" Lucie asked, the minute she was in the door.

"I didn't want to wake you."

She gave me a more careful once over. "You didn't sleep, did you?"

"Guilty."

"Oh, Owen..."

"I got a hit," Marlo interrupted excitedly.

"Oh?" I asked.

"Since we had nothing on Grolier I started researching the family line and checking every name. I think a family member's antique shop is worth a look. Don't you?" Marlo wore a huge grin and waggled his eyebrows at me. *Who could resist that?*

Lucie broke in. "Speaking of the table, I've been working with Meegan to decipher the images we saw. Ze really wanted a look at the table, but confirmed that it is marked by dark magic by looking at the photos Alex took. Ze was surprised to find us because ze says that no one really believes in magic anymore. Ze teaches classes on the occult, but most take it out of curiosity and many people think ze's kooky. Ze says it fits the image and I guess that makes sense. Think about it. We do the same thing - hide in plain sight."

"Hide in plain sight... I wonder... I think I need to go look into that antique shop on Sunday while most folks are at church. It's just a preliminary look. I could go alone."

"No, you should not, but I've got adventure hounds to turn to the side of good with Alex," Lucie lamented. "Now is not a good time for me to be a no-show with the board warriors. We can't afford to lose any of the ground we have gained with them."

"And Marlo will be covering home base and doing research," he said referring to himself in the third person. "But I suppose I could go with you remotely to keep an eye on you."

"Deal."

"No deal. Didn't we agree that none of us would go anywhere alone?" Lucie said with a scowl worthy of any teacher.

"I'll have Marlo remotely, so no big deal. Besides, I'll stay out of trouble. It's just a look. I won't do anything stupid."

Lucie wasn't smiling. The look she sent me, screamed *idiot* and *I don't trust you* all at once. Too bad, this was my call, not hers.

NINETEEN

I took the Max downtown so that I could get lost in the crowd and jump trains if I needed to. It seemed like Bob's boys were still on me because I caught sight of them now and then. He had resorted to sending regular guys after me when it became apparent that I could sense our kind a little too easily. Either Evilia had figured that out too or she was busy with other projects.

I made it all the way to Northeast Portland, when my radar pinged. How the heck were they tracking me now? I'd ditched my watch and I was being careful. *Come on! Not today. I'd used just about every trick up my sleeve to avoid having Bob's boys follow me.* I missed the days where either Sarah or Rick gave carefully worded, weekly reports to Bob and he mostly left us alone. With a sigh, I plugged my earbuds into my phone, but only popped one in so it would look like I was listening to music and then I dialed.

"Mars. I think I'm being followed. I'm at the corner of 13th and Glisan. Can you catch a glimpse?"

"I'll give it hell. Give me a minute." I could hear keys clacking madly in the background and Marlo mumbling into his headset. "Keep walking east. I've got a few cameras. Now head north and make your way to the hospital. At Lovejoy you can cross under 405."

"Copy," I said into my phone and tried to catch sight of my tail in any of the windows I passed. I tried to keep walking and playing it oblivious.

"Scratch that. The next block is Kearny. Take that to 23rd and then that to the hospital."

"Copy."

I paused to take a look at a reflection in the nearest shop window. Someone's movement had caught my eye and made the hair on the back of my neck stand at attention. There was no mistake. I was being followed. I recognized the body language. When I stopped, they stopped, they kept their head tucked, hidden under a U of O ball cap and held a smartphone constantly within their field of vision. I stepped into the nearest shop doorway and peered out the front glass. Whoever it was, they never once looked at me directly. With the ball cap pulled low and a bulky plaid flannel I couldn't tell for sure if they were male or female.

I couldn't distinguish any facial hair but the feet were large for a female and were encased in black Danner boots. Slim hips pointed to male. He looked up revealing dark glasses and a male jawline. I couldn't tell for sure if he'd made eye contact, but the face returned to the screen, so probably not. Time to make my move.

"Mars, I've got a plan. I'm gonna ditch my phone. I think they're tracking me by my GPS and not the actual me."

"They better not be. I worked hard on this system."

"Someone has got to be. The guy following me has not looked directly at me, not even once and I left the watch at home. I was completely clear of a tail until about ten minutes ago. It makes me think while I was dodging them on Max, they went by car."

"If someone has cracked my system again..." I could hear the clatter of keys.

"Never mind that now. I'm near Johnson and 21st. Look for a male twenty to thirty years-old, slim built, about five feet ten inches and around 160 pounds. He's got on black Danner boots, tan cargo pants, a green and blue plaid flannel shirt and a Ducks lid. I'm at a market - didn't catch the name. I'll plant my phone on a shopper and see what he does."

"Then how will I communicate with you?"

"I'll be fine. Watch me on whatever cameras you can snag."

"I hate to have you burn the phone. They don't grow on trees you know."

"Thanks, Mother. I did know. Maybe I'll find a Good Samaritan who'll return it to the store. Look, I just want to find out about this guy. If I go head on, he may bolt or whoever he works for will find a way to follow me in a way that's harder to identify."

"Fine, fine. Do it, but I don't like it."

I turned my attention to the market's clientele for a few moments.

Marlo began mumbling over my earbud. "I've triangulated your position and have global coordinates. I've got a camera on a building to the east and I think I see your guy. Go ahead."

"Roger that," I mumbled back. An older lady caught my eye. She wore a dark purple trench and expensive leather shoes. She collected her reusable fabric shopping bags complete with celery and French bread poking from the top, grabbed her credit card receipt and looked like she was ready to roll. As she walked toward me, I began to walk toward her. At the last moment I dodged, bumping into her just enough to distract her, as I slid my phone into the celery bag.

As I bumped her, she released a small surprised puff of air, but didn't look too concerned as she paused to look at me. I watched her adjust her load and could almost see the wheels turning in that split second. I imagined her calculating the weight of her groceries and purse.

I turned my palms out in a gesture of peace. "Pardon me ma'am. I'm so sorry. Are you all right?"

I watched her relax. "Yes, I suppose I am. Good day." She continued toward the door.

I glanced around and no one seemed to be paying any particular attention so I let her pass and returned to the window. My tail looked confused for a moment and then began to follow her down the street. I moved back out onto the sidewalk and positioned myself in the tree line. With the jumble of parked cars, bus shelters, and real estate flyer boxes, I had plenty of urban camouflage. I had to trust that Marlo could track me, but not flannel shirt guy. The lady turned a corner.

Now he was following too close making me think he had to be new at this. He looked around and then stared at his cell. I could feel his confusion. I watched him almost run into the woman, he was so focused on his phone. She must have sensed him in her personal space because she picked that moment to turn. Her eyebrows went up as she moved her head back on her neck. He looked at her angrily. Not the reaction I'd expected.

"Where is he?" I could hear his voice drift to my location behind a tree.

"What?" she asked, perplexed.

He grabbed her upper arm and pushed her into an alley. She only had time to utter a gasp. This was not the plan. I put her in this position, so I'd better get her out of it. I sighed and ran for the alley. He had pushed her against the wall, her bags forgotten on the ground by her feet.

"Where is he?" my tracker snarled again.

"I don't know what you're talking about. Who?"

"Where's Ryer?"

Could he not tell her body language plainly shouted she knew nothing.

"Stop!" I yelled from the mouth of the alley.

His head snapped around in my direction. "You!"

"Who are you?" I growled at him.

"Help me," the woman begged. Her voice was barely above a whisper and we both ignored her.

He didn't look inclined to answer the last question so I tried another. "Who do you work for?"

He smiled.

"You work for Evilia?"

He snorted. "They said you were smart."

This guy was no *dark watcher* but he had some skills. I decided to try agitating him. "You're not too smart. If you were, you wouldn't be tracking me by my phone."

His eyebrows rose and then lowered into a scowl. He clenched his jaw, squeezing her arm tighter, making her whimper. He turned his shoulders toward me, his body tense, but his feet were out of position – he was off balance. He had enough strength to shove the woman to the ground. He turned and stalked toward me. How predictable. I watched his movements. He was confident but he moved slowly. He went to grab me but I evaded his grasping hands.

He snarled and swung. I side-stepped at the last moment, delivering a blow between his shoulder blades as he passed. He stumbled and spun to come at me again. I could faintly hear a siren. It might not be coming this way, but I couldn't risk getting caught. The way Bob had been treating me, I was pretty sure he'd leave me to rot. I ducked flannel's kick and punched him in the throat. He grabbed his neck as he bent and coughed. I flung my leg out to kick his temple. He dropped in a heap and lay still.

The sirens drew nearer, their volume increasing. The woman sat, stunned, on the dirty ground. I left her and checked the guy's pockets. I snagged his wallet and cell. Then I turned to her and dumped her celery bag in her lap, retrieved my phone and sprinted further into the alley. I ran toward the back wall increasing my speed as I went. I ran up the wall and caught the edge of the fire escape. I swung and flipped myself onto its catwalk, ran to the end and leapt for the neighboring window ledge. I hoisted myself up and used the building's decorations to make the top. I lay panting on the roof as the sirens grew louder and then stopped. Definitely time to go.

My hand was stinging, my fingertips scraped and one knuckle bloody. I'd even lost part of a fingernail. That was gonna hurt when the shock wore off, but I had no time for that now. I opened the cell I'd stolen and pulled the battery. I turned off the GPS on my own phone and then ran to the far end of the roof and jumped into space. I rolled as I landed on the neighboring building. The view helped me see where I needed to go - my own personal Google map. I still needed to head north and east. I found a way down to the street level and eased back into humanity.

I dodged into a café where the after church crowd was just picking up. I walked up like I was getting in line and then edged past and headed for the back hall, hoping for a bathroom to wash up before someone noticed the blood. Sure enough, back hall bathroom. I guessed it wasn't used much since the old tile floors in the hall were stacked with boxes for cups, lids and other restaurant essentials. There was no mirror to check my face and the old sink was cracked and rust stained. They got points for the lack of stench, but the lemon air freshener was a little overpowering. I washed my hands and wiped up my face with a clean paper towel.

I reconnected with Marlo. "Hey man, you got me?"

"Are you nuts?"

"I couldn't leave that poor lady with flannel shirt after I got her into it."

"Ugh, you are killing me. You've got eight blocks to go, but I think you should just call it a day."

"No."

"Owen!"

"Don't make me hang up on you."

"Fine," Marlo snarled back.

I checked both ways before I left the bathroom and then I headed out the rear entrance. I walked on and on, taking a crooked path, my senses on high alert, but I felt nothing unusual. Just down the block, a black sign with lettering bright as fresh blood swung from a rusty chain. It squeaked with menace like you'd hear at a haunted house. I resisted the urge to run the other way and approached cautiously. I watched for a moment from across the street. Someone's cat and a lone motorist were my company.

The windows were dim and dirty. A red neon sign claimed the store was "pen" the "O" having long ago burned out or broken. With no other company, I opened a line to Marlo and pushed off the wall I'd been leaning on to head across the street.

"I would like to repeat that I don't like this at all. You should have waited," Marlo groused, sounding a little calmer if no less angry with me. "Leave the line open so I can record what's going on. The second this gets out of hand, I'm sending backup and who-ever it turns out to be – they're gonna be grumpy."

I said nothing. I left the line open and dropped the phone into my side pocket. I opened the door. An old fashioned notification bell let anyone who was interested know that someone was inside the murky dim. Mustiness fell over me in a thick layer, clogging my nose. I resisted the urge to cough. For the moment the shop was silent as a tomb. A small scrape alerted me to someone else's presence.

I squeezed my eyes in an attempt to see. Herbs underlay the mustiness. Then the tang of a freshly lit match wafted by with the scent of clean wax. Another scrape and the creak of the floor told me someone was drawing nearer. My *watcher* sense was telling me things I couldn't comprehend, but one thing was for sure, I was being scanned.

"You're not welcome here," a scratchy old voice intoned.

"Excuse me?" I still could not see the speaker.

"Your kind. You're not welcome here."

My eyes were adjusting and shapes were beginning to take form in the cluttered shop. I could finally make out that a stooped woman was not an old chair or a mannequin. Her wispy gray hair barely covered her scalp, which I could see plainly because of her diminutive size. She finally raised her gaze to mine and I was startled by her white eyes shaded by heavy black brows.

"I'm sorry ma'am, I don't know what you mean. Are you talking about my age, heritage, school or what? The sign said you were open. Is that a mistake?" I ended with a shrug she probably couldn't see.

"Don't play coy with me, boy. You are no ordinary child. You are disrupting my energy. Did you not see the sign? No *watchers*."

I felt Kraeghton rise up within me. I had a sudden, overwhelming urge to take a back seat on this one. Everyone told me to give him a chance, but I was afraid. I felt his power swirl and surge like a bad case of indigestion. I took a breath and let him loose.

"What sign?" I asked with the last of my control.

"Master, why do you hide in this boy?" she asked in a much kinder tone.

Kraeghton seized control of everything and all I could do was helplessly watch, a passenger within my own mind. When had he grown so strong? Why did he choose now? He had let me think I was winning. I was an idiot. He had always been there – waiting.

"It is not for you to question. It is for you to serve," Kraeghton chuckled. *Was this a game they were playing?* "I am here and in need of your special talents," Kraeghton said with my voice. *Not just an antique shop – I knew it now. Dark magic lived here with the potions and poisons.*

She bowed her head as far as her dowager's hump would allow and turned to walk toward the back of the shop. I struggled but Kraeghton held me in check and still let me watch. Either he needed me or maybe he wasn't as powerful as I first thought. Maybe he was a magician with tricks up his sleeve.

As I followed behind her, Kraeghton sent me flashes of their time together. He thought of her as a crone, a seer and mostly a pur-veyor of darkness. If you stayed on her good side, she had a heart of gold and a mile-long streak of irritation. As for her bad side, well, it did not pay to go there. Things were done her way or not at all. It was better to beg forgiveness and hope for the best than it was to ask permission. This tiny woman was extremely danger-ous, Black Mamba sneak-attack dangerous.

Dark dusty, musty cobwebs covered the small dirty windows. I could barely see. She moved around fairly well considering the hunched back and arthritis riddled fingers. I kept watching. She barely mumbled. There was no real sound, more a moving of her lips as she moved. She was counting. She was doing everything by feel. What I had taken to be clutter was engraved in her mind and in an order that she could find again.

"Tell me what you seek, Stephan."

"I must face an evil greater than my own. I need the projection crystal."

"You picked a pretty package this time, Stephan."

"I took what I needed," Kraeghton said with my voice.

"You always do." She sounded pleased, almost proud. "You were a good student."

"What will you trade for the use of the crystal?"

"You're joking," she scoffed.

"You know who I face. You need me as much as anyone. Not even you can take her on."

"Where have you been for almost a year then?" she snarled sounding angry.

"Doing what had to be done."

She was around the central table, where a black candle burned low, in a flash, grabbing my wrists with hands dry as parchment but with amazing strength. "Tell me where you've been!" she hissed.

She squeezed and I felt my wrist give a little. She watched me with her creepy white, sightless eyes. "Hmmm," she breathed and then she reached up to touch my face. I tried not to gag as her fetid breath washed over me.

"He is more than meets the eye," Kraeghton pushed past my lips.

She released me with a sound of frustration. "So he is. Fine, don't tell me."

She moved back around what I now saw was a butcher block and over to a cabinet. My eyes were adjusting to the even deeper darkness and various states of decay back here. The smell of herbs was more pungent and looking up I could see thousands of sprigs hanging in bundles over my head. I shifted my gaze to the floor and then back toward the rows of shelves along the far wall and realized that what I'd taken for canning jars of food actually held chicken feet, teeth from various species of predators, feathers, granules, powders and liquids from murky opaque to clear in a rainbow of colors. I found myself both fascinated and horrified.

The bell over the front door rang. The crone froze and sniffed the air, then she grunted and returned to her rummaging. A light tread headed toward the back of the shop without hesitation. I turned from her to the doorway.

"You've met my son, Julius."

The hair on the back of my neck did its thing as a chill raced down my spine. The man we'd been looking for stood calmly just inside the open doorway. Julius was Abner Grolier.

"We have not officially met," Kraeghton said in a bored voice.

"This is my old student Stephan, though he wears a new guise. He had a wonderful proclivity for the dark arts and soon outdid his teacher." I was half afraid she was going to pat my cheek with her withered hand.

"Mmmm," Grolier sneered. I could feel his power pushing at me in a way that made me think of a hundred snakes slithering over me. "You shouldn't have come, Stephan, especially in this form. These are dangerous times. You should have made yourself known to me the first time we met."

"You know that wouldn't have been wise," Kraeghton answered for me.

"Mother, he should leave."

"Go fix us some lunch. He's just leaving."

Grolier turned and left. I heard a door creak and slam in another part of the shop.

"He gets testy when he doesn't get his way." She tossed the crystal to me and nodded when she heard it hit my hand. "Kill her for all of us. Don't come back. I can't have you leading her here."

The crystal grew hot in my hand. Kraeghton turned me around without so much as a thank you and marched me to the door. The moment I cleared the threshold, memories of her were a fireworks display bursting through my mind. She had taught him. He was there when she was blinded by a spell gone wrong, but it was a price willingly paid – in exchange for power.

The series of vignettes burst forth faster than I could understand as her voice chanted in my head. "Words are power. Rituals are power. Actions are power. Items can hold power."

I could see her arms gnarled like old tree branches moving around in intricate patterns as she cast a spell. It hit me full in the chest, slamming me into the bricks of her store. I couldn't move and then her voice was in my head. "The time has come to choose. Help us and we spare you, your friends and family. Don't and we kill you and the rest and wait for the next one to come along. I know what you really are, Owen Anthony Ryer. Tell Stephan Kraeghton he does not fool me. By the way, your brother is looking like a fine candidate for second choice if things don't go my way."

Whatever held me was suddenly gone and I slid down the wall to catch my breath. The moment I could move, I was up and running. What started as a sprint wound down to a jog and finally a walk as I hit the Max station. I took the first train; I didn't care where it was going.

It took three stations before I was calm enough to realize I was headed for Beaverton. I got off at the next stop. I hopped the red line and took it to Gateway where I could switch to green and head on home. At Clackamas Town Center I got on my bike and rode straight to the shop.

White Eagle, Lucie, Marlo, Mom and Alex all stood arms crossed waiting for me to come in. The two browsing customers in the shop looked from them to me and left. Who could blame them, this wasn't looking good.

"Your phone died," Marlo said sounding deceptively calm.

"Oh?" I took the moment it took to pull it out to collect my thoughts. "Um, yeah, so it is... dead that is. Did you, ah, try to call me or something? I got the cell of the guy who was following me. I took the battery out so they, whoever they are, couldn't track it."

Still their faces were grim but Marlo took both phones, the battery and the guy's wallet.

"You took the wrong train." Lucie's voice was stiff.

"Uh, yeah, could happen to anybody."

"Not to you."

"No, I guess not. She had me a little rattled."

"Good!" Mom shouted. "Next time get scared BEFORE you go in a place like that and then don't go in. You about gave me a stroke as I watched you on Marlo's hijacked surveillance feed. What's wrong with you? You could have been killed and..."

"Lila!" White Eagle's calling her name stopped the tirade but now I was afraid she'd cry.

Lucie took over again. "And the people in the shop just let you go?"

"Yep."

"Just like that?" she pressed.

"They thought Kraeghton was in charge."

"Was he?" Alex asked.

"Sort of?"

"Oh Owen," Mom wailed.

"I can explain."

Their arms were still crossed and not one of them looked happy. White Eagle sent a hand signal to Alex who went and turned the door sign to "closed" before he locked it.

"Where's Sarah?"

"In a meeting with Bob and his boss."

"Oh, boy."

"Don't worry about that right now. Tell us what happened"

I took a breath.

"From the beginning," he added when I started to open my mouth.

I began from where I first thought I was followed and ended with the spell the old witch had cast on me. Although they listened without interruption their faces were grim.

Silence followed my story until Marlo cleared his throat. "So I ah, recorded what I captured on the street cams." He slid a glance to the others but he couldn't hide his grin as he cued up the video. "You look like Spiderman. How do you do that? Life is so unfair."

Marlo made me feel like smiling again. "Who are you to talk? Think about what you can do with a computer. Talk about awesome. When I grow up, I want to be you, Mars."

"We all do," Lucie added, "but I believe we are best at what we practice – it's not just learning a skill that counts – you have to be willing to put in the time."

"Hear, hear, Lucie. When did you get so philosophical?" I quipped.

"I've been hanging out with someone whose net memories add up to over 100 years of experience - though you wouldn't know it from today."

"It sounds so creepy, when you say it that way," Marlo shivered.

"Try living it," I huffed.

"I'm sure," he said back.

"I'm not surprised," White Eagle cut in. "It was bound to happen. Miles was reckless too. You need to be more careful."

"I didn't realize I was in trouble until it was too late. Today it was a good thing that I had Kraeghton in here. It's the first time I've felt that way. Mostly I keep hoping that one day it will all just go away."

"Why?" Marlo asked, curious.

"Because I keep having mini arguments with myself and their voices all the time, Miles, Kraeghton and I just don't get along.

"You hadn't told us that," Mom said, sounding like she was back in control.

"Well duh, do you think I want to look crazy or paranoid?" I asked, feeling frustrated.

"I'm just glad you're back. Alex has a competition, so we need to go. You… you be more careful, like White Eagle said. I love you, but I will kill you myself if you do that to me again."

I hugged her and watched them leave. Lucie came and stood next to me as White Eagle returned to sign to "open."

"You know it's gonna happen again, right?" I sighed.

"Sadly, yes. Go help Marlo, I've got work to do."

"Don't hate me," I begged.

"I don't hate you, Owen. I love you. You are just so incredibly frustrating! I totally understand your mom today." *Now I was in real trouble.*

I headed for the back to see Marlo. I didn't want to deal with the emotional stuff anymore today. I was fried. White Eagle looked at me and just shook his head. The shop bell rang and he left the back without a word.

"So Mars, tell me about all this Evilia stuff you've got going on here. I don't get it." I could hear movement in the main shop and hoped no one needed us.

278

"Well, I have color coded her activities by year. I didn't go any further back than five years because we want to get a good picture of what she is currently doing. I can see the impact of our work and that's exciting. Her trafficking here has slowed way down and she has shut down her San Diego operations. The bad news is that she's picked up her activity in Arizona and New Mexico. She still has holdings all along the eastern seaboard."

"And she's still here."

"She spends most of her time here."

"Then I'm not crazy," I said feeling relieved.

"You are. Then add delusional, manipulative and murderous." A new voice intruded.

I snapped my head around, startled. I looked right down the barrel of Mica's Ruger LC380.

"Do you think I'm stupid?" Mica demanded. "How long did you think it would take before we found him?"

I wanted to respond but something held me back. I felt Kraeghton and clamped down on him for all I was worth.

"On your knees, both of you and put your hands where I can see them."

Marlo looked at me and I nodded. He moved slowly toward the practice mat, never taking his eyes off Mica.

"Let him go, Mica. You know Marlo has nothing to do with this."

"And have him go for help? Forget it!"

"What about customers?" I asked, stalling for time.

"You're closed."

"Was anyone up front?"

"Lucie and your lying mentor won't be bothering us."

"What did you do?" I growled.

"Walked right in but I forgot about the stupid bell. They're not dead. This is your fault. They got in the way so now they're collateral."

"Listen to yourself. What's happened to you?"

"You did!" she screamed. "I hate you."

"What did I do?" I asked feeling a little perplexed.

"You know."

"Say it out loud." I watched her eyes; they were constantly moving. My peripheral vision picked up the slight tremor in her body. She was losing it.

"When he killed my sister, I swore I'd get revenge. I've spent years... years... looking for him. I know where Kraeghton is. I found him. He's a John Doe at Riverside Cemetery. You're not as conniving as you think. You thought you could dump a body and keep it in-house. You made him look like a homeless person and no one thought any different but I didn't give up."

I couldn't help it. My jaw dropped. "I didn't know."

"You were there!"

"I was there when he died. I was... not myself afterward. I didn't know."

"He was mine. Not yours. What did he say to you?"

"Mica, it wasn't like that."

"You would have had a confrontation. You would have taken him on. I know you found him. They told me he escaped."

Movement caught my eye but I kept my attention on her. She was beginning to sweat. Rick burst through the swinging door and laid her out with one blow to the back of the head. He kicked her Ruger away and cuffed her before he sat next to her unconscious form. "Damn, I'm gonna be in so much trouble."

Marlo sat hard on his backside as I lunged to my feet.

"White Eagle and Lucie?" I barked.

"They'll be fine. They're with Saul. Don't worry, she just tranqed them."

"What is she doing here? What are you doing here?"

"I promised Sarah I'd keep an eye on her. She's Kraeghton-crazy anyway and she's been meeting with Dr. Moretz."

"Oh, no."

"Oh, yes. I'm not supposed to be here. I could hurt Sarah's case but I had to make sure you were okay. Sarah is back on administrative leave. She is unfired but not fully reinstated pending a thorough investigation and that may take months. Dr. Moretz has been arrested; somehow Bob put it all on her."

"He's not being investigated?"

"He is, but he gets to keep his job. I don't want to risk mine. I'm the only mole you've got right now."

"What about Saul?"

Rick laughed. "Bob doesn't see his value. He put him on another team. He is helping us in his off hours."

"Bob let you keep your team?"

"The players have changed and I can't trust them. For now I hold my position."

"What are you going to do with Mica?"

"I have help. I think a good cover is that she slipped in the shower and hit her head. She'll need to stay at home and recover from her concussion." He shot me a huge white toothy grin that gleamed in his dark face. "I'll lock her up at Neil's."

"Neil is your help?"

"He knew she was spiraling. He loves her even with her faults. We'll get her the help she needs. I trust him."

"You guys really are on my side."

"Of course we are."

"I had gotten overconfident when I knew that you, Melody, Joy, Saul, Mica and Neil were there. When Bob really turned and then set Dr. Moretz on me... well, I've already got Evilia and lately I was beginning to feel paranoid and like everyone was against me."

Rick smiled and I could feel his compassion but it was Marlo who spoke, "Geez, Owen, don't be dumb. When you're being hunted, paranoia just plain makes sense."

"Oh, okay, Marlo," I half-smiled at him, complete with eye roll, so he could feel the sarcasm and Rick laughed.

"Ya know kid, he's right. Stay paranoid; it could save your life. Let me get her out of here. Bob is still watching but it will be dialed back after Sarah's visit today. Just always expect it. I still don't know what Bob really wants but he's trying to make you look like the problem."

Rick pulled his car up out back and waited for us to open the bay door. He cautiously backed in and we put Mica in his trunk.

"She is gonna be pissed when she wakes up."

"She had extra tranq serum on her. I think I'll put that confrontation off for at least twenty-four hours."

"Keep us posted."

"You too, kid. See ya."

We waved him off and listened to Lucie and White Eagle complain about Mica getting the drop on them. At least they couldn't be mad at me anymore.

TWENTY

I plopped onto a stool next to Marlo but something in my pocket pinched. I pulled out the crystal. "Oh yeah, anybody want to check this out with me?"

Lucie and White Eagle looked at me with expressions that I'd never seen before. It was as if they were moving forwards and back at the same time.

"What did you do?" Lucie asked as White Eagle spoke, "You brought something from that shop here?"

"I forgot I had it. What's the big deal? It's just a crystal."

"You… you don't know… can't you feel that?" Lucie's voice held both fascination and alarm.

"What? It's uncomfortably warm when I hold it in my hand, but so what? It's something Kraeghton wanted. It was his idea that I accept it." I paused, waiting for the explosion that I knew had to be coming. They just stared. "I guess I was expecting more of a reaction," I added after a few uncomfortable moments of silence.

White Eagle took a slow deep breath, "I'm waiting for the rest of it."

"He took over but let me watch. He asked for the crystal. Not a crystal, *the crystal*. He called it a projection crystal. I didn't get anything else before I was kicked out."

"Did it speak to you?"

"It grew uncomfortably warm in my hand and I felt suspended for a moment as a burst of memories raced through my mind. He thought of her as a crone and in his mind he called her that when he was angry. He was repulsed by her but he knew he needed her. She taught him about poisons and medicines. She also taught him some black magic. He was there when she tried a powerful spell that went wrong and blinded her. Except she's not really blind. The stuff she did was weird. It made me think of the way that Daredevil sees."

"Who?" Lucie asked.

Marlo clued her in. "He's a Marvel comics superhero who was blinded by chemicals but has such amazing hearing that he can *see* sounds."

"Good thing that's not creepy," Lucie cringed. "Why couldn't you pick something from our local Dark Horse Comics like Hellboy or Buffy the Vampire Slayer?"

"Those two didn't fit what I experienced. That old woman... Kraeghton's right, she's a seer. She knew where things were in the shop, she didn't bump into anything and she knew things about me she shouldn't have."

"The point," White Eagle reminded us.

"Her blindness is no curse as far as she is concerned. Her shop was jammed with decaying junk. I don't think it's junk to her though. I think they're spell components. Look, she knew my full name and she thinks I can talk to Kraeghton. Over and over in my head I could hear her chanting, 'Words are power. Rituals are power. Actions are power. Items can hold power.' She wanted me to remember. Kraeghton told her that he had to face an evil greater than his own. He admitted that he takes what he needs and she reminded him that he was a good student. She wanted to trade for the crystal but in the end just gave it to me. She wanted to know where he'd been for the last year. He wouldn't tell her and

285

she tried to read my mind to get it out of me but that part was blocked to her. She admitted that she needs me."

"Was the table there?" White Eagle asked when I paused.

"What? Yeah. That's what you care about?"

"No, but it's what you cared about when you went in."

"I didn't think about it at the time but, yeah, it was in the main part of the shop."

"Did it speak to you?" he pressed.

"Everything in there was yelling at me."

"Ah, so you were distracted." I could almost see White Eagle's wheels turning.

"I guess. What are you thinking?" I asked.

"Later. Tell me about the crystal growing hot."

"Um."

"Can I see it?" Lucie interrupted.

I held it out to her. It changed from its original pale almost clear aspect to darkness as something swirled inside. As her hand drew closer, redness bloomed inside like the glow of dying embers.

"Whoa," Lucie exclaimed drawing her hand back.

White Eagle reached for it next. The reaction was similar and even stronger.

"This is something only Kraeghton or at least only someone of darkness can control. I cannot help you."

"Is Kraeghton tricking me? I feel like I can trust him."

"Maybe you can in this, but should you?" I'd never seen White Eagle look so worried.

"As a last resort then, but I don't know what it does or how to use it."

"He asked for it. He must know how to use it." White Eagle looked at me with his other sight. "That's when she first saw you for you. She touched you and the crystal but not at the same time."

"That's right."

"Hmmm," White Eagle said, touching a finger to his chin in thought.

"But she let me have it anyway. Why?"

White Eagle gave me a sad look. "The seer doesn't want Evilia to win."

"Is it evil?" Marlo asked tenuously.

"It's not the fault of any object. It is all in how it's used. Objects are neutral until they aren't." I had spoken but it wasn't my idea. It was Kraeghton's. I was flustered for a moment so I changed the subject. "Hey, I almost forgot, I learned something else – Abner Grolier is her son – except she called him Julius. He didn't want me there. He recognized me."

"So what is our job? How did he know to take the table from us? What is written about stuff like this?" Marlo began to babble excitedly.

"Leave it alone!" White Eagle said, sounding alarmed. "If they aren't bothering us we won't bother them. Don't kick the hive, Marlo."

Marlo looked taken aback. "Um, okay. What else did the shop tell you?" He turned back to his computer where he was recording everything.

"Nothing I could understand. Let me see…" I thought hard but I couldn't separate all the images. "I wish I could take Lucie with me but…"

"No!" White Eagle exclaimed so loudly we all turned to look at him. "Focus on the crystal, nothing else. Whatever it does, it's Kraeghton it wants to talk to, not us."

"But it's not telling me anything."

"It will." He turned and walked away. For the first time in years, I felt lost, alone and scared.

I looked to Lucie and Marlo. They were both watching the door to the main shop swish shut.

"He just needs time to think," I defended.

"Of course he does," Lucie agreed.

"Mars, where are we at with Evilia? If I'm gonna use this rock, we need to know where she is."

"I've narrowed it down. She's here, but I can't tell what she's doing or where exactly around here she is. I can tell from the info Kovac gave us, when she activates an account. I've been following the money."

"Good job," I said meaning it.

"Tell me that when we get her."

"Is there anything we can do to help you?"

"Nah."

"Okay, Mars, I'll lock this up with the other stuff and we can call it a day. Maybe if I don't think about it, what I need to do will come to me."

"We can always hope," Marlo fretted.

I took Lucie's hand as soon as I secured the crystal in the safe. "What do you think? Ice cream? A movie?"

It's still daylight. Let's go for a walk. Mount Talbert Nature Park is close. Let's go there."

"Whatever you want, Luce."

We took the almost two mile loop hidden right in the middle of the suburbs. Whether or not she planned it I wasn't sure but breathing in the fresh cool air, scented by the Douglas firs, ferns and mulchy decaying leaves was wonderful. The deciduous trees waved at us in the gentle breeze with their bright new leaves and I could almost forget all my worries. Almost.

We went home as the sky was deepening and the few clouds that hung around were turning pink. We had taken the bike and riding it home made me feel free. I kissed Lucie at her door and headed for home.

My parents were discussing the trip to Cuba again when I walked through the kitchen door. "Come sit with us," Dad encouraged.

"I've got homework." It was sort of the truth. I did have some but it could wait. I just didn't want to talk about a trip I'd probably never get to take.

"Sit." He said it more harshly this time.

"Brad," Mom warned but he ignored her.

Lucas' eyes had grown huge but Alex looked like he was about done with it all.

"Why do you have to treat him like that?" Alex burst out.

"You will not speak to me that way. Now go to your room until you learn some manners."

Alex gave me a secret smile as he slipped past. He was getting skilled at pushing Dad's buttons. I slid into his chair and prayed for patience and wisdom.

Dad droned on about the trip and mom got up to start cleaning things in the kitchen that didn't need it. He was focused on me so he didn't realize that Lucas had a game going on his new PlayStation 3D under the table. A half grin touched my lips.

"So, I see you're excited about the trip too," Dad enthused, misinterpreting my smile.

"Uh yeah, sounds great. Now do you mind if I go hit the books?"

"I guess."

"Me too," Lucas blurted, trying to catch him while he was in a good mood.

"Fine, your mother will help me."

Poor Mom, but she was tough. She could stand up for herself.

Lucas and I headed upstairs and went our separate ways. I pulled out my books and tried to read but I was soon dozing in boredom. My nightmares came back.

The sun was kind enough to wake me. I thought about calling Marlo but I didn't see any point in bugging him. He was in his own little world of pain. The images melted like shadows in sunlight but the words stuck with me, "Secrets and lies – I hurt people – I protect them."

I showered, made a quick breakfast and headed down to Lucie's to wait for Marlo to come pick us up for school. He was running unusually late. I watched him drive up and he was clearly agitated. During class I realized he really was disintegrating before my eyes. I left school for the shop and decided that we would have to talk soon.

Each day I tried to work with the crystal and other objects I'd collected. I tried them individually and together. I even tried getting Lucie's and Alex's help. Nothing was working. Each day Marlo grew more nervous and White Eagle more distant. I wanted to talk to him but I didn't know where to start.

After almost two weeks, I couldn't stand it anymore. I decided that Marlo and I had to have that talk. I couldn't let things go on like this. White Eagle would talk to me when he was ready and I could only deal with one of them at a time. As soon as he came into the back with Lucie, I jumped him. "What's up with you, Mars? You've lost weight and you're fidgety.

"Evilia is close. It's having an effect on me. I can feel her. It's like she's looking at me. I think we gotta hit the eject button – this is too dangerous. She could get us anytime so why doesn't she?"

"Because we're not worth it," Lucie added.

"Please don't make us worth it," Marlo almost whined.

"You've been scared before but not like this. What happened?" I asked Marlo.

"She got to Adrian." I could plainly hear the worry in his voice now.

"We don't know for sure it was her," I replied trying to ease him back down.

"But we do. I found a transaction. She had the stationary and envelopes purchased under one of her business accounts. It's the same stuff Adrian got."

"She has left him alone for quite a while," I reasoned.

"That's because she got what she wanted. He's avoiding us. She wants him out of the way."

"Now you're being paranoid. Relax. You think better when you're calm," Lucie added.

"Why am I always outnumbered?"

"Because you're the brains and we're the brawn," Lucie smiled.

"Don't sell yourself short, Luce. You're both. Him, I wonder about," I laughed.

Marlo's lip twitched into a half smile. "I'll try guys, but I'm scared."

"We all are, Mars," Lucie said, putting her arm around him.

Lucie and I had him relatively calm by the time Alex showed up. By mutual agreement we didn't talk about any of it in front of him. I didn't need Alex buying into the unease that was eating at Marlo.

I set aside my work as Alex stretched and then got out our gear to spar. We only went a few rounds before Alex's eyes closed and he rubbed his head.

"It's hurting again, isn't it?"

"Yeah," he sighed.

"Have you told Mom? Maybe…"

"Come on, Owen, it's not medical."

"How do you know?" *How could he be so certain? What if something was really wrong with him?*

"He knows because I told him." White Eagle interrupted, sounding exceedingly calm and almost zen as he pushed through the swing door. The urge to yell welled up inside me. This was the same man who had virtually cut me out lately.

"You need to manage your rage." Alex spoke to me as if he was suggesting a new brand of soap.

"What?" I figured I had to have misheard him.

"I can see your anger, confusion and worry. It shimmers over the surface of your skin."

"Of course I'm worried," I snapped at him.

"What do you mean, you can see it?" White Eagle asked.

"Can't you?" Alex asked back.

"No," he drew out the word slowly. I knew he was busy thinking. "You're changing," he continued as he looked at me. "Your abilities are going through another growth spurt. What is it with you boys?"

"I don't know," Alex answered the rhetorical question, "but I can also see that good and evil are at war inside Owen. Good is barely ahead an it's two against one. He has to learn how to work with Kraeghton and stop fighting him,"

"Don't talk about me like I'm not here," I snarled.

"Dude, right now you're flickering. You're light but then shadows move over you like rainclouds covering the sun. Find the part of Kraeghton that was once good and work with that part. If you use your common hatred of Evilia then the darkness will not win. You need another angle 'cause rage is not doing it."

"You don't understand. Kraeghton is like an itch I can't scratch."

"Owen, slow down. Ridding the world of evil is a marathon, not a sprint," White Eagle added. "Remember, you don't get to choose who you are. You were chosen. You didn't even get to choose your side. You may make some adjustments along the way but this path was chosen for you long ago. This is just another challenge you must face. You are in the crucible. Let the heat do its work in the right way."

"Now you sound like him."

"Who?"

I sat on the nearest stool. It was time to come clean. "I need help – guidance. I don't know who to listen to anymore and I don't trust myself. I've been meeting with The Gypsy," I watched White

Eagle's jaw clench. "I should say, he's been finding me and he gave me this." I pulled the arrowhead from my neck. "I see now that I've done it all wrong. I didn't want anyone to know how truly screwed up I am."

"It's never too late to turn a corner. Lucie knew about this, didn't she?" White Eagle asked sounding weary and resigned.

"Yes."

"She wanted you to tell me?" White Eagle asked but it came out sounding more like a statement.

"Probably," I admitted.

"I did," Lucie answered from her stool next to Marlo.

"Why didn't you?" White Eagle asked me.

"Because he felt guilty and … dirty or bad… no ashamed," Alex answered for me.

I looked at Alex and wondered when he had become so… intuitive – probably while I was wallowing in self-doubt and pity.

"Ah," White Eagle almost sighed, like a long-wondered question was finally being answered. "You feel torn between being unworthy and righteous indignation. You feel like you have to beat them all alone – you're wrong." He touched me and the present flew away.

White Eagle and Nadie Black Feather stood before me in some dense woods I didn't recognize. "Owen, this is my na-ahk."

"I know who you are."

"Yes you do boy, and you are playing a dangerous game. My grandson wanted me to tell you that you have been marked by The Quartet."

"The Quartet?"

"He did not know who they were either at first, but he recognized the magic. Be wary of them."

"Who are they?"

"They go by many names and wear many guises. You will know them by their power."

I blinked and I was back at the shop. "I don't understand."

"I learned that Bob has found out about some kind of great power source. Something bigger than Evilia and he thinks you're the key. He wants a seat at the table. He thinks he will get it by blocking you."

"What table."

"All I know is it is known as The Table of the Quartet. Whoever they are they are more horrific than Evilia. You are dabbling in dangerous things. You shouldn't be there. It's beyond anything I've trained you for. We're not ready. I asked my na-ahk for help. It's the first time since her death that she has answered. That alone should scare you as spitless as it does me."

I nodded. What should I do? Let it go or work it out, despite their wishes. I waited for everyone to get busy with their own tasks and pulled out Kraeghton's phylactery one more time.

I stood in a place I'd never seen before. It must be dry here, the grass is golden and the trees are pine not fir. They are also much further apart. I can almost detect a hint of dust in the air. It's not the loamy, moist smelling earth of home. Sage; I can catch a tinge of it.

Big rough rock is pushed up through the dusty earth making it seem like it must have hurt to do so. I had to be on the outskirts of town. Why was Kraeghton here? The dreams he sent me, made it feel like there was a purpose in everything he did. He – I leaned against the fender of a Ford F250 super duty mid 90s model. Today Kraeghton wore jeans, a t-shirt, ball cap and cowboy boots. This Kraeghton felt strange and alien like he wasn't quite comfortable in his own skin... Yet. That was it! He wasn't comfortable. I could feel another presence struggling within him. He had taken a necklace from this watcher – as he rolled the medallion over in his hands – images burst forth – as if it were in my own hand.

But they weren't from the necklace – I had never been able to use my ability in these Kraeghton memories – it was Kraeghton's own memory of the kill. He was smart, clever, wily, all of that and more. He was dangerous. Now I knew why he had wanted me so much – before things had gone so terribly wrong. It was the secret that Evilia had tried so hard to get out of him. Kraeghton had put together the teachings of Nadie Black Feather and The Gypsy. But there had to be something else. He reached through the open window of the truck and pulled out a lacquered box. The surface was covered with sigils. He opened the lid and dropped the necklace inside with many other mementos. I cringed at the sheer number. He had used black magic to bind it all together. He had taken three different lore, put them into one deadly spell and used it to drain watchers of everything.

He no longer needed a vial or other items to store watcher gifts in – he was the receptacle, the vessel and it kept him from aging. It was incredible and frightening. He had changed himself – he had taken what was good or neutral and corrupted it to evil. The side effect was youth but the price was high. I thought he'd sold his soul to Evilia but I was wrong. He'd done that long ago. He'd sold it for evil.

I felt sadness well within him as a young woman came into view. I felt his heart begin to beat faster. Emotions swirled in him. He loved her and he shouldn't. I could feel her watcher gift, new, young and inexperienced. He wanted her for that and for so much more. He was confused. He felt guilt. All of a sudden she noticed the truck. Her body language changed. She was happy to see him. She ran forward and I went cold. I knew this woman. I'd watched her end her life on a bridge.

"Jim!" I could hear the happiness in her voice.

"Erika, how've you been?"

"I've missed you!" Her enthusiasm was plain. She reached up and hugged him tightly. He took a deep breath of her hair and I felt his body react. I wondered what had happened. How could things go so wrong from here that she felt she had to end her life? "Come on in," she continued, interrupting my thoughts.

Hand in hand they walked into her house. She chatted on about horses and chores. Kraeghton felt happy and at peace. Possibly the best he'd ever felt. This was where he wanted to stay – this was home – but it was also an illusion. His hunger for power drove him. Once again I saw her teetering on the edge of the bridge before she jumped without so much as a scream.

White Eagle touched my shoulder. "I thought we agreed."

"We did, I guess. I'm just trying to understand Kraeghton. I was hoping he'd talk to me."

"All this time you said you wanted to shut him down and now you don't."

"In that shop, when I met the seer… there was a mark by the door. I didn't recognize it. I don't communicate very well with Kraeghton as you know. I think he knew what the mark was and he was both trying to protect me and encourage me to go inside. I can't explain it but something changed in that store."

"I can't believe you trust him."

"I do and I don't, but you know what? I believe when it comes to Evilia I can. He didn't like me, but he respected me in a way. I never lied to him. I truly believe that he hated her way more than he ever did me."

White Eagle pulled me to my feet. "You just need to survive. Quit pushing the string."

"Yes, Master Yoda."

TWENTY-ONE

Several days crawled by and Kraeghton would say nothing else to me no matter what I tried. No one made me angry enough to make him pop out either. Except maybe my dad, who was pushing my buttons to the limit. The only thing getting me out of talking about the trip to Cuba this time was that I was needed at home to guard my brothers. I shouldn't complain, my grandfather was paying, but it wasn't where I wanted to spend my last summer before college. He considered it my graduation gift. I would've rather had a laptop. It would have been cheaper too.

The weather took a strange turn. Okay, so yeah, you have a fifty-fifty chance of rain around here in May but big storms are unusual. They do happen and tonight was a good one. Heavy rains were joined by wind as my parents left to visit my grandfather to finalize the arrangements for the dreaded trip to visit family in Cuba. All this time and I still barely understood him. I was much happier staying home with Lucie and my brothers than I would have been visiting my grandfather. I knew I should be able to visit with him; it was childish of me not to, but there was so much pain between us. Lucie put a hand on my shoulder as I watched my parents pull out of the driveway.

"It's going to be okay. You don't have to be perfect all the time, you know."

"It feels like I do."

"I worry about you. You're so intense. You take on everyone's problems as if they are your own. They aren't, Owen. Let them go."

"Let what go… Kraeghton? Carmichael? Evilia? They are my job and my duty. I am responsible for Kraeghton's death and I will be responsible for Evilia and Caleb's. People tell me that it's my destiny. I've got to learn how to use the tools I've been given to weaken them."

"The fate of the world does not have to rest on your shoulders."

"But it does. I told you, it's my destiny. It is what I'm meant for."

"I wish we could go back to the way things were. I've had to share you with Kraeghton ever since he hijacked you. You're different - darker."

"I'm never alone."

"You've got to talk about it. All this has been brewing inside you for months. You know I love you and I would do anything for you, but I will not encourage your fatalistic attitude. It isn't in your best interest and I can't stand to see you get hurt. We make our own destinies, they don't make us."

"No, Luce, I have to do this – with Kraeghton."

"This is wrong. You can't fight darkness with darkness."

"Why not Luce? What we've been trying isn't working. I've drained *dark watchers* by mistake. It's time we learned to do it intentionally or we will never survive."

"We'll find another way. Didn't you understand anything Kovac told you?"

"No, I think you don't understand. Don't you see, his message is not about the battle with Evilia… it's about what we do with our lives after we defeat her. He can't let her win. If she does, she'll be too powerful – but we can't get too powerful either."

"If you do this, then *you* will be too powerful – you'll be like her and he will come for you. He is pushing you to do something that puts you at risk of crossing the very line he drew in the sand." Lucie's throat seemed to seize up. As she stopped talking I became aware of the pain that rose inside her, searing her chest and her throat, as she fought to hold back the tears. To hold them in she also had to hold in her words. She was afraid, afraid for my life and my soul.

"Lucie, I don't know if I can change the world, but I have to try."

"I just don't want to lose you," she whispered.

"It would be worth it. Me for them."

"You're wrong," she choked out and the flood gates opened. I pulled her into a hug and held her.

"It's okay. Let's just enjoy the time we have."

She shook her head and held on tighter. Over the wind and driving rain I thought I heard some strange thumps but it came from… the roof? Lucie saw my eyes roll skyward. "What is it?" she asked through her tears.

"I don't know - tree branches hitting the roof? Something doesn't feel right but it isn't *dark watchers*. You stay here with your cell ready to dial. I'll check it out." She gave me a crisp nod as I headed for the stairs. I hit the landing as a series of crashes and the unmistakable shattering of glass assaulted my ears. I knew this house better than anyone and no one would get the drop on me. I kicked open my door, front flipped to my window, kicking the intruder in the head as another window exploded behind me. I dove at his prone form and smashed his head against the floor before I ripped his communications device from his unconscious form and jammed it into my own ear to listen… several voices spoke almost at once.

"…the girl," the first voice said. *One.*

"Two minutes," a second voice informed. *Two.*

"The middle boy needs medical attention. He fought back," the third voice stated. *Three.*

"Leave him," Two instructed.

"Where's Ryer?" One asked making me think he was in charge of the on-the-scene side of the op.

"Check in!" Two shouted.

"Girl, ooofff," a new voice answered as the sound of blows came over the com.

"Baby Ryer," answered Three.

"Jerome, copy?" Two asked.

"Uhng," I grunted into the mic since I was pretty sure that Jerome was the guy on the floor. There hadn't been enough feet marching around for there to be too many more. I glanced back at him. They didn't look like Bob's guys. Dressed in black, cargo pants and boots, with no visible weapons - who were they?

"Check Jerome. He may be down. That means Ryer is loose. Baby Ryer secure."

"Copy, Leader," One said.

I crept out the window avoiding the lights. I heard cars pull up out front and chanced a peek - two SUVs, a van and a pickup. A bundled up Lucas was being hauled toward an SUV.

"Cars in position. Loading the hostage," a new voice, said. Was that five?

"Move! We've attracted attention," Two, the leader, shouted.

Time to move. I glanced both ways and lightly sprinted to my parent's room and felt the area again. How many and where were they? My gift was telling me nothing. A soft thud sounded on the other side of the wall, alerting me. "Jerome down, sir."

I quickly scanned for a weapon. I saw nothing and then my eyes landed on Lucas' yo-yo. He'd broken a lamp doing tricks so now it was on a timeout on Mom's dresser. I picked it up, put the string over my finger and held it snugly in my fist.

"Load him up. Time to go."

"His headset is gone."

"Radio silence." My line went dead so I threw it aside.

I did not see a way to win this one. No matter what I did I couldn't protect Alex, Lucie and Lucas. I'd have to trade myself for him. I couldn't do this with my feet and fists. This was going to take my mind and I was going to use all the experience I had at my disposal. *You hear me Kraeghton? I'm giving you a chance. Show me you're worth it. I'm putting his life in your hands. Well, mostly.*

Mom's bedroom door began to slowly open, so I melted out of sight into the shadows of the darkened room. The minute his head cleared the door I attacked. The yo-yo popped out of my hand, struck him in the bridge of the nose and zipped back to my hand.

"Son of a bitch!" he yelled as blood gushed from his damaged nose. I knew that voice, I'd just found Four.

In the moment of stillness I heard Lucie snarl and the smacking thud of landing body blows. She needed help, but I had to get past this guy first. I needed to check on Alex too. In the moment I hesitated, Four shouted, "I've got Ryer."

I flung out the yo-yo again as he spoke. He tried to evade but I nailed him in the cheekbone. Keeping the yo-yo, I decided in a split second this was going too slow and I smashed my foot into his chest with a powerful front kick. It sent him back through the door and left him grasping the frame.

"It's funny that you think that you do," I snarled.

He used the doorframe to leverage himself forward and fling himself at me. I could hear another set of feet pounding up the stairs and fighting still raging in the living room. He struck at my side. I used that to spin toward him and connected with my elbow. Fists flew faster and the second guy was in the room. They struck at once, making something crack and I fell to my knees.

"Back, back!" someone yelled from downstairs.

Four kicked me, hitting my chin and toppling me backwards. A sloppy block was all that saved me from being knocked out. I was a little slow getting to my feet but I was after them. They pounded down the stairs. Lucie stood in their way but they had momentum on their side. The lead guy smashed into her but instead of being flattened she summersaulted backwards. I chased them on out the door. They jumped in the back of the idling pickup and pulled out.

Lucie and I skidded to a stop in the street trying to make out the plate, make and model. The rest of the vehicles were gone and the rain was washing evidence away.

"Alex!" I started to run for the house.

I collided with him in the entryway as he came down the stairs. He fell into my arms. "I'm sorry," he croaked.

I could see bruising appearing all around his neck where someone had held him in a chokehold.

A noise alerted me to turn but it was only Lucie and White Eagle. Sarah was on her phone arguing with someone and only a few steps behind them.

Where was Marlo? He always appeared as if by magic any time the uglies were going down. As if on cue, Lucie's cell vibrated. She twisted around searching for it. Just as it quit, she found it under the edge of the couch. She froze, still bent, reading the screen.

"Oh my God! They've got Marlo."

"What? How do you know?"

Slowly Lucie turned her phone so I could see the screen. "It's a trick. Help me," I read aloud.

"No!" Lucie nearly shouted with tears in her eyes. "Above that."

About forty minutes ago Lucie had missed a text. "Someone's in the house. Going into lockdown." Followed by, "Where are you guys? What's going on up your street? Does it have to do with this?" And then, "They're coming up the stairs. Dumping the drives. You know how to get it back. They're coming for me!"

"They took Lucas too," I said roughly. Alex still held onto me mumbling that he was sorry.

"It's not your fault. What happened to the alarm?"

"They knew," White Eagle replied. "Nothing went off at our house either. We were in the back watching TV. It took us a bit to realize... I'm sorry too."

Suddenly I was aware of Sarah's rising voice, "Why won't you help? They have Lucas... It most certainly *is* your problem. This is your fault!"

She stopped to listen and then began signaling to White Eagle. I didn't understand the pointing and arm-waving but apparently he did because he whipped out his own phone and moved into the kitchen. I turned my gaze back to Sarah who was coming in the front door.

"Draw her out?! Yes, I can see it worked... Of course we'll hunt her down. Tell me you are at least tracking... And just how are we supposed to do that? She has Marlo too, you idiot." Sarah jabbed "end" on her phone and threw it at the couch with enough force to make it bounce. I thought she was going to burst into tears but she straightened and looked at each of us.

"Call your mom. Consider the appropriate authorities notified. I'm headed down to the Saggios. That power hungry son of a bitch I sometimes work for knew this would happen. He knew Evilia has been watching us for weeks. He thought we'd get her here, tonight. He's disappointed in *us*!"

"She wasn't here," Lucie whispered.

"I know that. She's smarter than Robert Bowman," Sarah raged and then turned and stalked out the door, slamming it behind her.

Lucie looked at me and then after Sarah. "Go," I said and she snatched up Sarah's phone and sprinted out the door too.

I dialed Mom.

"Hello?"

"You need to come home. Evilia is ready to finish this. She just took Lucas."

There was a long stretch of silence. "I'm on my way," mom vowed solemnly.

In less than fifteen minutes White Eagle was off the phone with Rick, and Mom and Dad were pulling into the driveway. It took fifteen more minutes to calm my dad down enough to listen and get my parents the information they needed. Rick and Joy showed up as we were finishing our strange story.

"I can help," Joy surprised us.

"Of course you can," I replied.

"No, I mean Marlo has been working on something and he contacted me about it about a week ago."

"What?"

Mom's phone vibrated, interrupting us. Joy quickly opened a case she was carrying and told Mom to answer the phone, put it on speaker and then set it on the pad inside the case. Mom gave her an odd look but did as she was told.

"Hello?" she asked tentatively.

"Mom?" It was Lucas and he sounded scared.

"Lucas?!"

"Mom, it's me. Can you come get me? I don't want to be here by myself."

"Where are you?"

"I'm at the zoo."

"What?"

"They just dropped me off and left without saying anything. Two men picked me up, tied me up like a package, carried me out and threw me in the back of an SUV. They drove off and came straight here. They didn't even talk. Can you come now, please?"

"On my way." Mom flew out the door with Dad right behind her. Rick nodded at Joy and followed them.

"So it looks like the cell was Lucas'. Maybe he can give Rick more information to help us. He knew I was working with Marlo on the side. Marlo has been working on a way to amplify the GPS he's been using. He would get all upset when he thought someone was out-teching him." Joy paused, making a strangled sound, showing me how truly worried she was about our friend.

"He's been working on some triangulation to boost the GPS. We need to get to his house and see about hacking his system," she finished.

"Lucie and Sarah are already there."

I turned to White Eagle and Alex. "Don't worry about us. I'll take care of him and secure the house. We'll meet up later."

Joy packed up her gear and we walked through the rain to Marlo's.

"What do you think happened? None of our security worked." Something was going on here that I didn't understand.

"He's been tracking her, right?"

"Yes."

Joy cleared her throat. "Well I think that she used what he was doing to follow it back to him and I think Bob helped her do that."

"What?!"

"This is pure guess but he has kept the old team really busy. When Mica got sick…" she sent me a wink.

"Yeah, I know."

"With Mica out of the picture to spy on us, he must have thought he needed to step up his game. He has been watching someone watching you. He let some intel on Marlo slip."

"I thought he was under review by his boss."

"He was but he covered his tracks. He had to take Sarah back, but he's dispersed the team and he has some new people working for him that… okay, I'll say it, my gut tells me they are not okay."

We were at the Saggio's driveway so we quit talking. Every light was on it seemed. Joy and I let ourselves in the back door.

"Is Marlo with you? Usually when he disappears he's with you," Marla begged.

"No, Marla. He's been taken."

"How could you let that happen?!"

It broke my heart to watch her weep while Melvin patted her on the back. Joy edged past me and headed upstairs. I was only partially surprised that she knew where she was going. I thought about my earlier conversation with Marlo's parents when we had to break it to them that he was a *watcher*. If that was bad this would be... devastating. We gathered around their kitchen table. I just didn't know how they ever could be normal again. If we could get Marlo back he would never be the same either. Emotions rolled off the Saggios in waves. It was easiest to see the anger, fear and overwhelming sadness but I could see the guilt and hope too. They thought that if we were working on it, then Marlo was as sure as found. *Please God, let us be up to the task.*

I thought that Lucie showed real courage to sit by Marla. I was afraid to get too close but she must have sensed me looking at her because Marla looked up and shocked the hell out of me. "Owen, I apologize for yelling at you. You've been Marlo's friend since kindergarten. You've always protected and defended him. I just can't believe he's gone and... that... that woman... why would she take my boy? What will we tell everyone... and school... he was set to be..." a hiccup escaped. "Valedictorian."

"I swear to you, we will do everything we can to get him back. For now we have to cover up that he's gone," I said, using the calmest voice I could muster.

"Why would we do that?"

"To save his life."

"It's wrong. We should go to the police."

"Normally we would agree with you but this is different," Sarah said softly.

"Why," Marla begged, desperate to understand.

"The FBI has been informed. People we know will protect Marlo but we can't let just anyone know. It has to do with the job he does for us…" Sarah stopped talking and looked at me. This was the hard part. "Marla, Melvin, your son hacks for us."

"What?" they both yelped.

"I'm sorry, it's true, but know he does it for the good guys."

Joy burst in. "I've got something!"

All eyes turned in her direction. Joy proudly held up a laptop. "They took and or damaged most of his equipment but I knew where he kept this." It was the old special, hi tech, laptop with the hardened case that Sarah had gotten him a couple of years ago.

Lucie's cell buzzed while Joy was booting up the laptop.

"It's Marlo, he sent me an email but it doesn't make any sense."

"It tells us that he is alive. That means there is hope," I said firmly. "We have work to do. We'll be in touch and if you hear anything from Marlo, please let us know."

"I'll stay here for now," Sarah informed us. "You three go see what you can get out of that laptop."

Joy put it to sleep and tucked it back under her arm. Lucie, Joy and I walked back to my house. My parents were just pulling in. Lucas hopped out and ran over to hug me.

He immediately began to babble, "They broke through my window and grabbed Alex. I hit him but he kicked me aside. He did one of those choke things with his arm to Alex and then tied me up. He threw me in an SUV and I rolled around while they were driving. I watched the whole time. They went left to 7-11 and over the tracks. Then we got on the expressway. I knew when we headed to the zoo. They untied me in the lot, tossed me out and sped away while I was still rolling. No one would help me. It was weird but I can tell you what they looked like and everything. Why would they do that?"

"Maybe they thought no one would listen," I guessed.

"Well, that's dumb," Lucas shot back. "They told me not to talk or they'd sell me. Why would people… sell children? They talked about Marlo and something about hacking some money. Maybe it's Marlo she wanted all along – He's the smartest computer guy I know."

I started to discount him but paused. People don't listen to little kids because they don't understand them or assume they're fibbing. Sometimes they do stretch the truth but sometimes what they say can be profound. I looked to Rick. "Did you get all this?"

"Every word. Lucas is really quite observant."

I smiled at my brother. "I'm sure it will help."

"Is Alex okay?" Lucas asked.

"Let's go see him."

We headed in. "Where's Beggar?" Lucas asked.

I froze. I'd let her out in the back yard just before my parents left. Lucas and I headed around the side of the house since the front door was open.

She didn't come to my call but she did come to Lucas. "They tried to catch her but she's too smart for them. Look, she got a piece of someone's pants too. Who's my good girl?" he crooned to her.

Lucas handed me the fabric and looked her over. "They hurt her but she'll be okay."

"I never heard her bark."

"It was raining. She hid. She doesn't like her feet to get wet."

I didn't know if she was talking to him or if it was his vivid imagination. Alex stumbled out the back door. "I've been run over by a truck and you're worried about the dog?"

"You look like it too," Lucas flipped back.

"Now that's appreciation," Alex said sarcastically.

We settled in for the night, letting Rick take over on Marlo until the morning. Lucie, White Eagle and I needed to be ready at 'go' time.

TWENTY-TWO

Lucie and I had slept on the couches in the living room, Sarah had stayed with the Saggios and Rick's crew had gone with White Eagle down to their house to use Sarah's office and secure system.

I woke up first and started with a patrol of the house. In the daylight I could tell that White Eagle and Alex had cleaned up all the glass and boarded up the windows. I peeked in on my brothers and found Beggar curled up under Lucas' arm. She wagged her tail for me but didn't move. The boys slept on.

By the time I was dressed and headed for the coffee maker, Mom was already on the phone with a contractor. Lucie handed me a cup of steaming joe.

Her phone buzzed and she looked at it. "Again? Doggone it Marlo, I want to help you but I don't get it!"

"Let me see," I asked as I reached for her phone. It was another email. "We need to print these out."

We headed to the den and hooked up Lucie's phone. She printed out both emails and we scanned them carefully for clues.

"He's getting this to me by embedding it in something he's doing for her."

"How can you tell Luce?"

"She'd never let him just email and I know he knows how to do it."

"So what's he saying? It doesn't look like much to me."

"I don't… wait… it's a game we've played."

Her phone pinged again. Looking over her shoulder I could see it was a screen shot. She printed it.

"Do you see now?"

"He's showing us an account that belongs to Eve Malone."

"It's her account, Evilia's. Come on. We need to show this to Sarah!"

I scratched a quick note to Mom and we ran for Marlo's house. I was not surprised to find them once again in the kitchen. I figured it was the place that Marla was most comfortable.

Sarah had barely opened the back door when Lucie burst out, "Marlo got a message to us. He turned it into a puzzle, like he's been teaching me. Madame Malvada coerced him to steal money electronically and put it into an off-shore account under one of her shell corporations."

Marla looked thoroughly confused. Melvin clenched his jaw, "Let me see."

Lucie pulled up the message from Marlo time stamped earlier today and laid the printout on the table. She decrypted Marlo's code as she ran her finger along the line while Melvin watched. *I hate what she's making me do. I am working under duress. It doesn't excuse me and I am willing to take my punishment but don't want to die. What I'm doing is wrong but I don't have a choice. She threatened me bodily harm and even death before she said she'd kill my parents. Evilia Malvada is forcing me to steal money and dump it into an account she's holding under the name Eve Malone. See Screen shot. Please save it so that I can go back and fix this! Forgive me, Mars.*

Melvin took the phone from Lucie. "I can track this."

"You can?" Sarah asked. "Not even…"

We all looked at each other.

"I believed Bob when he said it couldn't be done. I believed that Marlo was virtually untraceable. He's our tech guy and we have no one on the team like him. I should have known something was up," Sarah snarled. "Melvin, you figure out where that signal came from and we will go get your son!"

We took the Saggios to Sarah's after securing their place. While Melvin went to work in Sarah's system with Rick and Joy, Sarah took Marla to the kitchen to make tea and calm her down.

I checked in with White Eagle. "What do you think? Do we go in soft and quiet or with a bang?"

"What does Kraeghton say?"

I was taken aback. "He hasn't spoken to me. For all I know he's dead, gone or dormant. Why?"

"I don't like surprises. We'll go in small and quiet. I don't want this leaking to Bob."

"Agreed."

"Let's get the van ready while Melvin does his thing."

"Deal," I said brightening. Work is always better than worry.

Lucie and I helped White Eagle pack the gear locked up in the garage and loaded the van. I was having trouble imagining this rescue without my friend on the other end of the com. It had always been Marlo. He'd been with me from day one.

"We'll get him back." Lucie had put her hand on my back and was looking at me intently. "I love him too."

"I know, Luce. I'm glad you're here. All this time I've been running around protecting you and my brothers but I had it all wrong, didn't I. You really can take care of yourself, but not him. He is the behind the scenes guy." I bit my lip to hold everything in and then I took a breath and shook it off. "I think Joy's right. Bob let this happen to push me to get her. He used Marlo to motivate me. I hate Robert Bowman."

Lucie hugged me. "That's a lot of pain you're holding."

"Yeah, and you don't?"

"I don't blame myself. You do."

Melvin came out wearing a hopeful look. "I've got an area and the ring is closing with the help of my son's triangulation software that Joy showed me."

"We're ready here. Let's go."

"We've got work to do," Lucie finished for me.

We slapped on the fake insect control logos. *Have I mentioned how much I love those magnetic signs?* Melvin and White Eagle got set up in the van. After a brief debate, Rick and Joy stayed with Sarah as she watched over Marla. We couldn't blow our hand yet. Not that they would tell Bob, far from it, but they could work remotely and be ready if we needed them. Marlo's poor parents were getting a much closer look at our lifestyle than any of us ever wanted. I began to pray for Marlo, for them and for us.

Melvin guided us to a house in Oregon City. It was in the old part of town and the neighbors weren't close. He was good, but he was not his son. White Eagle drove past the house and then we came at it from the back side.

A shiver ran down my spine. I had experienced this before – we were getting close to Carmichael, but I also knew Evilia would sacrifice him in a moment. Her only loyalty was to herself. She held control through fear. I sucked in some slow deep breaths through my nose. I closed my eyes and put out my feelers. "She's not here."

White Eagle looked me dead in the eye, "Then we wait on the backup. You got this?"

I nodded. "Let's go," I said to Lucie and we hopped out of the van.

This was the craziest, least planned... I forced myself to take a breath. Lucie and I approached the neighboring house, and then quickly slid around the side and over the back fence. We each took one side of the property. The windows all looked dark but Marlo could be anywhere. Shrub to tree, we moved using the natural cover until we could get up to the house itself. I felt for Evilia and still got nothing.

"You look great from here. We'll give you twenty minutes and then move out front of the house," White Eagle said through the com.

"Copy," Lucie replied softly.

"Copy," I repeated, checking my watch.

I rolled under a huge azalea that was right under a window. I rose up tight to the window and peeked in. I was at a dining room. There was a chair tipped over on its side and a partially eaten plate of food on the table. No flies buzzed and no mold was present. I crept to the next window. The kitchen held a half empty two liter of Pepsi and a takeout pizza box. Crumbs were on the counter and still no flies or ants. I tried the window. It wasn't latched so I eased it up, listening hard. I pulled myself up and teetered on the edge, listening again. I could hear the creak of the floor overhead and nothing else. I pulled myself on in, careful not to rattle any dishes in the kitchen sink.

I caught movement and dropped below the island in the kitchen. I peered around the edge and saw Lucie. I went to the door, checked it for an alarm and opened it for her. I signaled for her that someone was upstairs and to take the right side of the house. She left on silent feet. I quickly scanned the kitchen and pantry and then went back to the dining room. I put my hand on the table, there was still a warm spot. It was just the right size for a laptop. *Gotchya!*

I snuck into the hall and felt the space. Something in me squeezed tight. There was something familiar about that evil signature. I turned, ready for anything.

"She said you'd come." Carmichael stepped from around the edge of the living room where he'd been waiting.

"Where's Marlo?" I growled.

Carmichael didn't answer. He was different today. Maybe I could figure it out if I could just... He didn't answer my question but he did speak, "You don't see it, do you? She weakened his powers – she made him desperate – he wanted to steal your power, but then she turned the tables on him and used him to get to you. You work for Evilia and do what she wants or you die – she punishes us to help us learn. You have to admire her. She learned from him all she could. I'm sure she knows all his secrets. You should be afraid. She is better than all of us."

I kept my mouth shut but my mind was racing. I didn't kill Kraeghton. I knew that now. Carmichael had let it slip in anger. He was wrong about one thing. She didn't know all of Kraeghton's secrets. They weren't his to share, they were Vandilo Kovac's and he only gave them to those who paid the price. Evilia had not wanted to pay... Kovac had shared with me only the things he thought I should know. If Carmichael was trying to see if I knew Kraeghton's secrets he would be disappointed. I knew that Kovac would only ever let out the things that were to his advantage and the fact that I knew more of Kraeghton's secrets than anyone was only because Vandilo Kovac had allowed it.

Carmichael was staring at me, clearly waiting for a response.

"You sound like you worship her."

His anger flashed. "Not worship. I respect and admire her. She is the most powerful woman I've ever known. It is an honor to serve her."

"You mean, be her slave."

He was on me in an instant and the slap he delivered turned my head to the side and left my teeth rattled. I leapt back, bent and yanked the hall runner out from under his feet, dumping him onto his back. "Where is Marlo?" I snarled.

"Not here."

I started to strike him but he held up a hand. "You don't want to do that. If you hurt me, she will hurt him."

"Tell me where he is."

"It's not going to be that easy."

"I know he was here," I growled.

"And now he's gone."

"You're stalling."

I heard a step behind me. I turned, ready to fight but it was too late. A dart *thunked* into me. Even as I reached to pull it out I could feel paralysis seize my body. I started to topple. Carmichael caught me and laid me on the floor. "Today is not your day," he hissed and then he and the woman left. At least it sounded like they left.

The chemical wore off almost as quickly as it had come on. Feeling returned in reverse, starting with a tingling in my fingers and toes.

Lucie raced down the stairs. "What happened to you?"

"Caleb Carmichael."

"Someone locked me in a room upstairs and then they blocked the com." Lucie helped me sit with my back to the wall.

"Crap. White Eagle?"

"I'm on my way and so are Mica, Neil and Melody," he snapped over the com.

"What? How'd they get free of Bob?"

"Maybe they'll tell us when they get here," White Eagle replied abruptly.

"Look at this," Lucie interrupted. "I found it upstairs." She held out the smashed up bits of Marlo's phone.

"Oh hell," I sighed, "how are we going to find him now?"

"Come on, get out of there before someone comes," White Eagle urged.

"I need help with him," Lucie said distressed. She was right; my legs weren't acting right… yet. "Come in the back door," she went on.

White Eagle burst in and yanked me to my feet. "Somebody called the cops. Did you touch anything?"

"Just the table."

"I'm clean," Lucie answered.

"Lucie, you get the table wiped and then come help me. Melvin, start the van and leave it back there. Meet us at the back fence."

"Shouldn't I bring the van around?"

"No, I don't want anyone to see it."

"Got it."

We limped through the back door. Lucie was right behind us. I glanced over my shoulder and saw her give the doorknob a wipe before she followed. "It's locked. It will waste a little time before they get in."

Lucie and White Eagle boosted me over the back fence and Melvin helped to steady my fall. I was almost back to normal.

We piled in the van and White Eagle sped off. He kept it seven miles an hour over the speed limit all the way home. One of Bob's black SUVs blocked the driveway behind us.

Sarah came out on the porch and then marched in our direction.

Mica hopped out slamming the door behind her. "See, this is why Bob can't trust you! You lie, hide, cover up and twist everything."

"So that's what he has you believing now," Sarah said coldly as Neil and Melody got out of the vehicle.

I felt Kraeghton move for the first time in weeks. "Mica Michelle, you are just like your sister, always listening to the wrong people. I'll tell you where I am. Right here in Owen. He's changing and so am I."

"I knew it!" Mica crowed. "You'll never be free of Bob. He sent us to control you."

Movement caught my eye. It was Melvin sneaking away with Marlo's laptop under his arm. I quickly moved my gaze back to Mica. Neil was right behind her and then she went limp.

"Sorry, Babe, you're on the wrong team."

"What happened?" Sarah asked Neil.

"She tricked me. She's been off her meds and conspiring with the enemy. What could I say, when Bob brought over Melody and told us to get to work?"

"Not much I guess."

Melody spoke for the first time. "He still doesn't know for sure what team I'm on but he was counting on Mica," she said with a jerk of her head in Mica's direction. "Bob is really angry with you and Owen, Sarah."

"Yeah, I'm always in the way – except when I'm not – like when I work directly for him."

"Now what do we do?" Lucie asked.

Sarah took charge. "Let's lock her up here and get back to work. Earl, honey, take the kids to the shop and bring back anything useful. Mel, get Joy and go grab Mr. Saggio and bring him back here. We need that laptop."

I resisted the urge to salute. Since it was still running, we hopped in Bob's company SUV and headed off on our mission.

The shop was sad, dark and empty. We were never closed at this time of day. I sighed, my heart heavy. My phone pinged.

"Hey Mitchell," I said listlessly.

"I've been trying to call you. I've been out of cell range. Is Marlo okay?"

"We don't have him yet."

"Hold on... he's scared. There are... lots of trees."

"What kind?"

"Douglas fir."

"Anything else?"

"Not now, but I'll let you know, okay?"

Lucie and White Eagle looked at me, waiting. "He's still in the Pacific Northwest."

Their shoulders moved down simultaneously and then they headed for the back door of the shop. We went inside.

"It's clear," Lucie said almost immediately.

I hadn't even thought to feel the shop. I just stood looking around at all the maps and everything Marlo had attached to them. Lucie came up behind me to hug me.

"I miss my friend." I could feel my eyes begin to burn, my vision blur and my chest and throat grow tight.

"Don't give up." I could hear the tears in her voice too.

"Give up? I always said I'd go down fighting. I just don't know what to do anymore. What we're doing isn't working. We're missing something. I'm talking to Kovac."

"If he wanted you to know something, he'd tell you," Lucie insisted.

"I think he was waiting for me to be ready. Let's see…" I entered in the last known number we had on him and listened to it ring.

"Hello, Owen. You must be ready." I gave her my best I-told-you-so look.

"I am." This was the most confident I'd felt in a long time but Lucie was busy shaking her head *no* at me, so I ignored her. "When and where?" I asked Kovac.

"How about now? Meet me at Pietro's Pizza. I'm hungry."

"Give me twenty minutes to make a delivery and then I'll be there."

Lucie and White Eagle were not happy with me, but sensing my resolve they let it go. We grabbed as much as we could at the shop and jumped back in the truck. We dropped off White Eagle and all Marlo's notes and left again before anyone could stop me. We ordered our favorite, a Bartender's Special, and found a table away from the games and a large crowd watching baseball. I left

Lucie with our order number and went for drinks. I was filling Lucie's glass when I felt someone behind me.

"Let's go."

"We just ordered pizza."

"Now, Owen."

"Let me just…"

"Now! Without her. Hurry."

I set the plastic cups aside, pulled out my cell and followed him, texting Lucie as I walked. He led me to an old partly rusted Jeep. "Get in."

I hopped in the passenger side. Lucie was gonna be hot. I rode in silence watching every turn. At first I thought he was headed back to my house but then he turned left onto Linwood and headed up the hill. He pulled into a trailer park I'd never noticed before called Zeida's. He parked in front of one of the trailers. "Come on."

I followed him inside. I recognized a few items from the house, enough so that I could believe it was his. "What happened to the house?"

"I can't have her finding me. You've been careless and you don't know what she's been doing but we do. We do and it's almost too late! I'll let you in on a little secret. Right now – we need you and we need you to be smart."

"I assume, she, is Evilia. Who is we? I thought you worked alone."

He didn't even respond but continued on as if I'd never spoken. His movements were jerky in the small space as he paced four steps each way.

"You know enough – I can lead you to a bit of lore. You must enter her place of power as Kraeghton – touch her tools of the trade…"

"Who are you talking about now? The Crone? I can only *see* the items in her shop. I should take Lucie."

"No. The shop will sense her goodness and will protect itself. It will be closed to her. The Crone is the dark side of order. No one as pure as Lucie can enter."

"You know her. Is she the other part of we?" I asked.

"Be quiet. You need to listen. We don't have much time. White Eagle's grandmother was the representative of good."

He stopped speaking and tilted his head like he was listening, but I could hear nothing but a few passing cars a short distance away. "I don't understand."

"You've watched the Wizard of Oz. You know, four corners."

"I don't know. You aren't making any sense. Have you been drinking?"

"No! I'm trying to explain. Have you played D&D?"

"Some. It's mainly Marlo's game."

"There are things you don't know about how the world really works."

"Okay?"

"Evilia has systematically been drawing power toward evil and chaos. She was chosen to be the Black corner but she wanted it all and with no White corner to hold her off…"

"Black corner?" I asked, still feeling confused.

"Don't you see? I must balance it all – I was once a *secret watcher* like you, but not anymore. I must guard my own corner now."

The arrowhead grew warm against my chest and I saw Nadie Black Feather training him. She was not teaching him to be a *watcher*, she taught him to represent his corner. My hand had moved to the arrowhead. I sat hard on the built-in love seat and stared at Kovac.

"I'm known as The Traveler or The Gypsy. I represent chaos. Sometimes I lie, but I mean well."

The door next to me burst open.

"Don't hurt the boy," Kovac yelled, throwing up his hands, palms out. I felt a wave of energy push past me.

"Vandilo! What's he doing here? What have you told him?"

"I work with Stephan Kraeghton and so should you, Eboleen."

"Evilia has made me a really nice offer. Seems you let her down."

"You didn't take her offer either. You know she wants it all. You know when she is done with you, she'll throw you aside just like everyone else she uses up. You believe that there is an order to things and that all things must remain in balance, for the system to work. If the system is to work, she has to go!"

"A gift has fallen into my lap. She offered to make me her partner."

"You know you mustn't accept."

"What do you offer instead?"

"I offer wisdom and confirmation of what you already know. He is the one. It will be Owen who restores things to how they should be.

"And here I thought you were all about fun."

"There is a difference between letting things come and rolling over to let Evilia Malvada have it all and rule the world. Read him, see what I've seen," he pleaded. "We are of balance."

"We are a relic of the past," she insisted.

"We can be whole again. Someone needs to be the governing body."

"We have no fourth. Clearly we are incapable of governing anything as we are."

"We will have. He is the key to making things right. You know it's true."

"So *you* say."

"Robert Bowman wanted the White chair and we've held him off. He thinks he can handle it and that he can control Owen."

The old woman burst out laughing. "No one controls this boy. He is the wind running across the prairie – the ocean beating relentlessly against the shore – the rock unmoving in the river."

"So you have looked."

"Stephan chose him, yet even he does not have full control. Owen is in charge of Owen but he was never meant to be the fourth chair either."

"You're right, he is not. He is the sword of goodness, the warrior and knight. He was never meant to hold a corner. Can we agree that Robert Bowman and Evilia Malvada are also not good candidates?"

"Yes, Kovac, we can," she sighed.

"I'm so confused." I whispered aloud. They both turned to look at me. I think they'd forgotten I was there.

"It is of you and through you, but not you that must make things happen," Kovac instructed me.

"I've always been a pawn."

"A pawn with a conscience," Eboleen added.

"A pawn who had choices. You know who you are. You have good instincts. Listen to them," Kovac said as he reached for me, pulling me to my feet. Before I could step away, the Crone touched me as well. My world shifted. I could see Kraeghton to my right and Miles to my left.

"The tool is forged," they intoned together. I could see it now. I knew what I had to do.

"I have darkness to extinguish," I said in a voice not quite my own.

"Yes, you do," Eboleen encouraged.

I blinked and she was gone. I felt dizzy and confused.

"What happened?"

"Did you really think that when the clock struck midnight all your troubles would just go away like a puff of smoke?" Kovac asked.

"I don't know. Why am I here?" My head felt fuzzy, thick and confused. I was forgetting something.

"We had a meeting but you're not feeling well. It's time to go home."

"I'm not feeling well," I said back, knowing it was true.

Kovac opened the door and pushed me out. Lucie, Alex and White Eagle stood by his truck looking dangerous.

"He's all yours," Kovac said, giving me a little push.

He slammed the door behind me. White Eagle charged the door but instead of being locked, it opened easily. They went inside and I brought up the rear. Kovac was gone. I heard his engine catch. The Jeep was gone before we could get back out the door. Apparently there was a back entrance to the park because he never turned around.

"What were you thinking?" White Eagle raged.

"I'm so tired of everyone acting like I'm the bad guy. What did I do? I did everything I could to make things right, to make the correct choices and make the best out of bad situations and yet... here I am and everyone is mad at me again."

"You are being reckless."

"We needed information. I got it."

"What did you get?"

"People are people and things are rarely written in stone. I may be going down but I'm going down fighting."

"And?" White Eagle prompted.

"I feel like nothing is what it seems."

"Yeah, yeah and Jimi Hendrix says, 'Knowledge speaks, but wisdom listens.' What did you learn?"

Why was White Eagle so frustrated? I was telling him everything. "You had me convinced I was broken. I'm not. I may be damaged but I'm in control."

"Sure you are. You're more dangerous and untrustworthy than ever."

"White Eagle!" Lucie hissed.

They pushed me into the truck and we drove off, headed back home.

"Did you save me some pizza?" I asked hopefully.

"What's wrong with him?" Alex sounded concerned.

"He's spelled," White Eagle answered sounding both worried and angry.

"What does that mean?" Alex inquired.

"His friend Vandilo Kovac crammed more in his head than he can sort out right now. Give him a while. I'm guessing it will take until morning for him to sort out all the debris flying around in the cyclone of his thoughts."

They remained quiet, so to be helpful, I continued to answer White Eagle's essential question, the only one I could answer – what did I learn.

"It's simple, I just need to take all the horrible stuff and put it together and smash it into Evilia's brain."

Lucie looked at me helplessly.

"Too bad we can't reboot him," Alex bemoaned from the front seat.

"Yes, reboot. Start over," I found myself saying.

"Is he telling us that we should put him to sleep, White Eagle?" Lucie asked.

"Maybe. Let's get home first."

"The Gypsy and The Crone, they hold two of the four corners," I told them.

"Alex, grab the notebook out of the glove box. He really is telling us, we just didn't get it. We've got to write it down!" White Eagle spat.

Alex started rummaging so I continued, "Bob is denied a seat at the table."

"What table?" Lucie asked.

"Evilia is too much darkness. She is dangerous." I said rolling over the top of her with my voice. I had to get it all out.

"Don't ask questions," White Eagle advised. "Just listen."

"They could be part of a trifecta instead of The Quartet, but they cannot function with less. I will be the white knight when the corner is restored. Decisions are made by a vote of three out of four."

"I'm trying to get it all down but I feel like I'm translating from a foreign language. Here Luce, help me." I watched Alex hand her some paper.

I reached out and touched her so she would take me seriously. "The gray knight or order is Eboleen's son, Julius Abner Grolier."

"Okay, Owen," she replied soothingly.

"The Traveler has yet to choose."

We pulled into Sarah's driveway and got out of the truck. Lucie lead me inside where I was nearly overcome by a kaleidoscope of color and sound. I covered my head with my arms and hunkered down.

"It's too much for him. I'll take him to my room to rest." Lucie pulled me to my feet and led me to her room. The quiet dark was soothing. It helped to calm my mind. I sat on her bed and waited. At midnight, I was to go to her shop and touch the tools of her trade.

Lucie had left at some point. She returned with Saul who looked me over.

"Just let him rest," Saul advised.

I listened to the sounds of Marlo's search ebb and flow.

Lucie checked on me periodically, but she didn't stay. It was just as well.

I needed to get to the garage.

Lucie came in again. "Mitchell's here."

"He will tell you where Marlo is."

"He doesn't know."

"He will know."

"Oh, Owen, how can I help you?"

"Time will pass. It will all be over soon."

"When will it be over?"

"Vandilo will tell us."

"He'll tell us when it's over?"

"I have a job to do."

Sarah knocked gently on the door. "How is he?"

"About the same."

"I'll get Earl. We can't leave him like this. I thought he would have snapped out of it by now." I watched her leave.

White Eagle entered and together he and Lucie slowed the swirling in my mind…

TWENTY-THREE

I opened my eyes and then blinked. It was still pitch black. Lucie sighed and I knew where I was. I smoothed back her hair and kissed her forehead. "Come find me when the time is right," I whispered.

I slid out of bed and felt around for my clothes. Someone had helpfully stripped me down to my boxer briefs and t-shirt. I dressed and snuck out of Lucie's room. I could hear Sarah and Rick talking to a sleepy Mitchell behind the nearly closed office door. I checked the alarm and let myself out.

I hurried home and let myself in. I grabbed my keys and walked my bike out of the people door of the garage. I pushed it down the street and started it at the corner. I rode to the pawnshop and collected all the items from the safe. I put my old watch on my wrist, leaving the newer working one I'd been wearing behind and then I put the crystal and Kraeghton's phylactery in my pocket. I locked up and got back on my bike to ride to the Crone's shop. It was a good three hours until dawn so traffic would be nonexistent.

I pulled up out front and boldly moved to the front door. There was no point in hiding now. I was doing exactly what Bob wanted but I wasn't doing it for him. I touched the symbol by the door I had not recognized before and the door unlocked for me.

I entered the shop. The eerie glow of a street lamp gave me enough illumination to make it to the back room. *Touch her tools.* I looked around the back room. I put my hands on the butcher block. It had all kinds of stuff to tell me but none of it mattered now. I was not looking for *watcher* jobs; I was here to defeat Evilia.

I tried her mortar and pestle, but that wasn't right either. My arrowhead vibrated. I needed the crystal, the watch, all of it. I needed them here. I pulled each item out and set them on the butcher block. I took off my watch and the arrowhead and laid them there as well. I lit her black candle with the matches she'd left next to it. I waited a beat. Somewhere in my jumbled brain was the recipe. I picked up the arrowhead again but dropped it when it cut me. Blood dripped from my finger as I reached for it.

The moment my fingers connected, I could hear Nadie Black Feather in my head. I needed fire, rain, wind and earth. I also needed a map. Eboleen had left one for me, neatly rolled on the counter to my right. I cleared the butcher block for it and unrolled it over the top. I set all my items on it and then paused. No, one in each corner. What had Kovac said? Wizard of Oz. Wicked Witch of the West. I put Kraeghton's phylactery in the West. If I was right, then the arrowhead was Nadie and it went in the East. Where did the watch and crystal go? Kovac had been guiding me for a long time. He was balance. He was my compass. He went in the North. That left the crystal to go in the South.

I looked around the shop. I had fire from the candle, but what about the rest. Eboline had a sad looking aloe plant in the window. I took some soil and put it in the middle of the map. I opened the back door to a small courtyard. A gentle breeze blew in and sure enough, by the downspout was a small puddle of water. I scooped some up and drizzled it over the dirt. Part of me believed it would work and part of me thought it was utter craziness. This would have been so much easier with help, but they weren't supposed to interfere and Lucie couldn't enter. I wondered briefly why White Eagle's grandmother could, but then dismissed it because she wasn't really here.

Eboleen's voice came back to me, chanting in my head, "Words are power. Rituals are power. Actions are power. Items can hold power."

I repeated the words aloud as I held one thought in my mind. I need to find Evilia. I waited. Nothing happened. Fire, I needed fire. I repeated the words and held the thought as I touched the candle to the damp earth. Instead of snuffing the candle, the little mound burst into flames and the door slammed shut on a gust of air. For a brief moment the entire map was engulfed in flame and then it wasn't. The dirt was gone and the map was whole except for one tiny burned-out piece, just off the Clackamas river.

I collected my four pieces and put them in my pocket. I realized it was getting lighter. Where had the time gone? I needed to be on my way. I rode toward home and marveled at the crazy people who were already up and about. Didn't they know this was going to be the last day of my life? I hadn't even told anyone a proper goodbye. The Crone and The Traveler had seen to that.

My thoughts might be becoming my own again but I could not make myself take a side trip home. I shied to the east, my heart tearing in two. I could imagine my friends and family starting to wake up and beginning to panic but I couldn't change course. I was locked in to a map burned into my mind.

I followed my virtual map closer and closer to the river as I got further and further from the city. Highway changed to two lane road and then to dirt. It became increasingly dangerous as it narrowed and moved closer to the cliff's edge. The blind corners made me nervous, yet I didn't slow. I'm coming for you, Evilia! Winner takes all this time.

It was difficult to hear other engines over the roar of my own. An old truck and a steeply canted curve took me by surprise. The driver honked but didn't move over – the bend tilted toward the cliff edge but curved away from it at the same time. I wobbled slightly at the horn's sudden burst. *Hang on*, I yelled at the bike in my mind, but it was no use; I was losing control. I slid toward the edge. I tried to turn into the slide but I only succeeded in moving faster toward the edge and then I was slipping. I laid the bike over and skidded to a halt, tangled in the shrubbery near the edge. The truck never stopped. The man's startled face and wide eyes flashed through my mind.

I glanced at my arm hanging down into open space, teetered for a breath and then slid off, head first. I grabbed desperately at roots and branches. They popped from the very earth slowing my decent but not stopping it. As if in slow motion I watched each root rip from the earth showering me with dirt until I hit the water. I grabbed at the muddy, slippery river bed trying to pull myself back towards the edge of the cliff. The squish of the mud in the shallow river's edge was slick and disgusting. Finally my fingers bit in deep enough to draw me toward the bank. After what felt like an hour, but was probably only minutes, I was on my knees.

Hand over hand I clawed my way to standing and then I began to look for footholds as I clung to the vegetation. I enjoyed rock climbing – this was not rock climbing. On the plus side, the loose sandy dirt hurt a lot less than rock on the way down.

Making my way to the top was agonizingly slow. My muscles screamed in protest as I clawed my way back to the top. When the top was within reach of my fingers I wanted to cry with relief. I hauled my torso over the edge and lay there panting for a few minutes. I crawled over to my bike and gave it a quick check. I would have to collect it later; it was of no use to me now. I'd killed it, but with some love, a few parts and some elbow grease I could resurrect it. If I lived.

I checked my pockets to see what had survived my fall. I still had all four spell components or whatever they were and other than bruises, scratches, scrapes and broken nails, I was still intact but my clothes were headed for the rag bag for sure. My mom crossed my mind. She worked so hard and I had ruined everything...

again. I sighed as I checked the compartment on my bike. I left the first aid kit, wrench and flashlight, since I would have to carry them on my hike to Evilia's. I pocketed the screwdriver as a weapon and began limping up the road.

I hiked and worried, my stomach twisted in knots. Reinforcements were coming, Vandilo had promised. Could I trust him? I should have left a note at the bike to let whoever came behind know that I was still alive… for now. Oh well, I wasn't going back.

She would think I was coming to give myself up but I was taking her out. Plan… what irony. I had no plan – I was running on gut instinct and sheer will.

Part of my brain was nearly paralyzed with fear. Part of it was distracted by the color and texture of each leaf and blade of grass. At least my near swim in the river and climb up the bank had done one thing for me – I was camouflaged.

Up ahead nestled in the trees was Evilia's latest estate. The house itself was surrounded by fields, but here at the edge was dense forest, just like Mitchell said. I moved from tree to tree watching and then I froze. Someone was bringing Marlo out. It looked like they were prepared to walk him like a dog on a leash.

My fingers clenched on the bark of the tree I hid behind, the roughness biting painfully into my scraped and bloody fingertips. In a choked whisper I mumbled, "I'm so sorry, Mars. I did this to you. Please forgive me. I should have been a better friend – smarter - wiser. It should be me… it will be me. I may have blown Valedictorian for you, but you'll still graduate. You earned it."

Even from here I could tell he didn't look well. He needed a shave, a haircut, clean clothes and a good night's sleep. By the way he was squinting he also needed his contacts or his old glasses. Up and down, up and down, Marlo's daily exercise. Up, down, up…

Marlo froze and appeared to almost sniff the air. Uh oh, he knew I was here. *Don't give me away, please.* I sank to one knee. I felt the fear and anguish settle on me like a heavy, rain-soaked blanket. The very weight of it pressed into my back and shoulders – alone – I must go on – alone. I would lose everything or I would die. There was no winning this time. I had been tricked. I was the sacrifice or was I?

Evilia told me that I would no longer be able to tell what was real and what wasn't. She was right, she had confused me to the point I wasn't sure anymore. I could see her hand in everything I'd done – in everything that had happened to me – in every choice I had made. I was born a human and reborn a *watcher* because of her. She manipulated me, my family and my friends, but that was nothing – she had addicted, tortured, sold or killed many others. She had to be stopped. What was one, compared to many?

Now I was caught between impossible choices. I'm not afraid to die – I'm just not ready quite yet. Marlo is an only child and my parents have other children. Better me than Marlo but I had to save him first or it would mean we'd both be dead.

A breeze brushed over my skin and for a moment I thought I heard a faint drum beat. No, it was only my heart pounding in my ears. My fear was taking over and stealing everything except my basic instinct to survive. I hung the arrowhead back around my neck and checked my watch. In one hand I put Kraeghton's phylactery and in the other I held the crystal.

I swallowed hard and rose to my feet. I rolled my head around on my neck and shook out my arms. One deep breath and I stepped out from behind the tree. I kept my eyes on Marlo but every sense was in overdrive. I walked slowly forward, my arms loose at my sides but away from my body. This moment should be epic. Movie music should play and I should go in with guns blazing. Instead I was praying I wouldn't pee my pants and I was shaking so hard it was visible.

I kept telling myself that Evilia's hunger for me would keep her minions from striking me down before I could cross the open field. I sensed the area, knowing that if I could sense them, they could sense me, but I had to know where they were. Every hair on my body stood at attention and I swallowed hard. My breath caught and I felt like I was suffocating. I was surrounded with the darkest energy I'd ever encountered. *This is what drowning must feel like.* It was black and endless like a deep cave with no daylight. It was difficult to find the small fissures marking the end of one *dark watcher* and the beginning of the next. Maybe it wasn't that it was the darkest dark. The most evil of all was Evilia. It was the quantity. She had wanted to raise an army. Did the numbers here qualify? Compared to Marlo and me, it was one. There were more *dark watchers* here than we had ever faced. I had come to a slaughter.

Maybe if we could just take out one or two enthusiastic wingman some would surely be scared enough to run. That's what *Jack Reacher* says, right? Wishful thinking.

The guard noticed me. He moved closer to Marlo and spoke into his com. He listened a moment and then shouted to me, "Stop there!"

I paused and watched wondering if I dared move closer. The *dark watchers* I'd felt began to gather on the back patio. I counted ten, but more had to be nearby. A tall one stepped out pulling another chain; attached to the other end... was Jon. Madame Malvada stepped out. Her midnight hued hair was scraped back in a tight knot like I'd seen ballerinas wear. Today she was dressed in an all-black track suit with black running shoes. She looked ready to fight and here I'd never taken her to be one for the action. Control it yes, but participate? No.

Caleb Carmichael moved from behind her and stepped to her right like the obedient dog he was. No one moved. I felt her power crash over me, testing and then it receded.

My eyes slid back to Marlo. He was now standing behind Evilia Malvada and Caleb Carmichael. The chains that linked his hands and feet clinked in the near silence. This close I could see there was a smudge of something on his cheek, and his hair looked like it had a monster case of bedhead. He had to be terrified, yet he stood tall, his gaze locked on Madame Malvada. Scorn rolled off of him in waves. I hoped the same look was mirrored on my face as I moved my gaze to her as well. I knew that to appear weak or even doubtful would be deadly. None of them were to be trusted. They would kill Marlo in a heartbeat the second they believed he was no longer of use.

I was amazed again by how tiny Evilia was. She barely came to Marlo's shoulder, but her malevolence radiated out at us as if she were fifteen feet tall.

"I would be careful, boy. Very careful," she sneered.

"Or what? You'll kill me?" I asked in a snarky voice.

"You're already doing that to yourself by defying me."

"We all die a little each day until the end," I quipped bravely, my voice surprisingly steady.

A ripple moved through the air. Did I see Marlo flinch? What had changed? I took a shuddering breath – citrus and wood smoke tickled my nose. *Citrus meant Lucie, but wood smoke? White Eagle?* I took another breath and detected pine and the desert. *Everyone must be here... somewhere... gathering. Just as Kovac had promised.*

"I saw what you could be. Things couldn't have gone better if I'd orchestrated it myself. I learned from my mistakes. You found your way to me the first time we met. I couldn't let that happen again until I was ready. I've been drawing you in for over a year. Do you know how tricky it was contacting Alex and hiding from you."

"You ruined Alex."

"Collateral damage and so what? His life will be short, but extraordinary. Consider it a gift from me."

"He was a child."

"So?" she asked and I could feel that she truly did not care one whit about anyone but herself.

"You're a monster."

"I've been called worse by better than you. I see the look in your eye - that's rage! Come on! Lose it – I dare you – all it takes is once and you'll be mine. It's an evolution."

She waited and I waited.

"Marlo stole lots of money for me. He's pretty handy to have around once you motivate him properly."

She waited but I said nothing, sensing that the key to information was to let her blab it all out. I also wanted to be sure my friends were in position.

"I'm disappointed that I didn't learn the secret of extending my life from Kraeghton but the money helps to ease my pain."

No one moved. I squeezed the phylactery, feeling it bite into my hand. Where was Kraeghton?

"It's time for you to choose a side, Owen. What will it be?"

"I will never, ever, join you." As I spoke, I felt a shift. The darkness was pushed back and *light watchers* began to appear among the trees.

"You brought company. It doesn't matter. I have the home court, little *watcher*. Come here!"

I felt the pull of her power but it was nothing more than the pull of a receding wave. She looked a little taken aback but she tried to cover it quickly.

"So you have brought it to this. I have been persuasive, forgiving and far more patient than I've ever been and still you deny me. You would have been a powerful ally but I'm no longer sure that you're worth the price I've paid. You may think you've won but I have one last card to play. You won't turn? Fine. Your choice is made. You will die and those who choose to stand with you will share your fate. Any who wish to turn to my side shall be spared. Anyone?"

One by one my family and friends stepped from the trees. None spoke. The silence grew and consumed everything from bird song, to insect chirp, to the rattle of the leaves.

"Well then, Owen, you shall watch them fall."

Her hands twitched and her face contorted with rage. "I have never hated anyone like I hate you."

No one moved, not even a fidget as the silence stretched on and on. Then the very air seemed to take a deep breath and the world imploded as she snapped her fingers. The *dark watcher* holding Jon jerked up his chain and snapped his neck. Someone screamed. It was over so fast, all I could feel was shock and then the *dark watchers* were advancing. Sight and sound became a jumbled mix. Figures twisted and blurred. Screams pierced my ears in an unending, painful succession as chaos spread like flames though dry kindling. I could not protect everyone and save Marlo. It was a scene from my worst nightmares and perhaps I *had* seen this coming in my dreams.

We had finally brought the fight to Evilia but now I saw that was what she had wanted all along. She didn't care how many her side lost, she could get more *dark watchers* to follow her. But I cared deeply about every good *watcher* and as they fell, I felt the pain of their loss. I couldn't even fully process the maelstrom of destruction pounding around me. I would feel later – for now, my focus had to remain solely upon Evilia. I watched her across the field of battle. She was my target and my goal. A fist came at my head. I ducked to the side and put an elbow to the offender's jaw with a sickening crunch. I didn't pause to check my work, that was the job of the team. Evilia was my sole objective. I could feel waves of her power spread out and over me but she could not touch me.

I sped up my pace. Two *dark watchers* converged from either side, one going high, the other low. I leapt into the air at the last moment and kicked out to the sides. I caught one in the face, the other in the solar plexus. I barely noticed Adrian right behind me to clean up what I'd left behind. Adrian, who'd been absent for months was here when we needed him most. I jumped past the downed men to run toward Evilia. One of them tried to make a grab for my ankle. I yanked my pant leg free and kept moving, diving over another *dark watcher* who barred my path. Mitchell came in from my right to take her on. He tackled her to the ground where I could see them wrestle in my peripheral vision.

Evilia was not far from me now. She opened her mouth and appeared to scream as she clawed at the air in front of her. I felt waves of her raw rage crash into me before she released a blast of pure energy. I couldn't avoid it so I threw up a shield hoping to send it to the sides instead of through me. I stood braced but it did not rush at me… it oozed and slid. Fear ensnared me. I didn't know how to fight this. It gripped and slowed me, like her tentacles in the dream world. As the wave rolled past I felt the tone of the battle change. I heard screams and moans from the *good watchers* intensify and amplify. I had to tune them out and focus or I'd lose it. The sounds of suffering beat at me regardless and she could see it.

She smiled a sickening smile and waved me forward to my doom. I caught a flash and ducked as a blade whirled past where I had been a moment before. I felt my senses shift into hyper-drive. Suddenly Carmichael stood between me and Evilia.

I could see him preparing for his own power blast so I reached out and grabbed his arm, yanking him forward as I turned to throw him off balance. Before he could recover I jumped and drove my knee into his head. He wobbled for a moment. I saw Evilia release another energy blast. I dropped to the ground but she wasn't after me. It blew harmlessly over my back and stuck Carmichael. I paused, amazed that it didn't hurt him – in fact, it seemed to regenerate him.

I gulped and sprung to my feet, away from him. While I had hesitated Evilia stepped back and smiled at me again. "Get him Caleb, but don't kill him. When no one is left but him, he will turn to me before he gives up his life."

"Don't count on it," I replied through gritted teeth. Evilia just smiled.

I watched Carmichael for clues to his intent as I kept half an eye on Evilia. Adrian came in from the left. "No!" Evilia snarled and lunged at him, dagger in hand. I feinted toward Carmichael and went for her. I spun and dropped to one knee to hit her in the kidney with my elbow when she passed. As she arched back from the blow I grabbed her knife arm and yanked her off balance. Adrian was on her in a heartbeat but Carmichael was ready. While I was distracted he closed in on Adrian, kicking him in the head. He dropped like a stone and lay still.

Oh God, please let him be okay, I screamed in my mind. Carmichael snarled at me and attacked. Behind him I could see Evilia getting to her feet. I took ahold of Carmichael's arm and pulled down on it as I kicked at his head. With his free arm he managed to get hold of my leg and we toppled to the ground. I know White Eagle's *dark watcher* rule, "When you get them on the ground don't stop pounding until they stop moving."

Evilia screeched and tried to peel us apart. She even tried to drain me but I threw a quick fist up over my shoulder, smacking her under her chin. She fell behind me. Carmichael couldn't get in a good hit. Evilia reached for me again, but I twisted away and she fell onto Carmichael. I hit at both of them to give me space to move away. I caught sight of Lucie, fighting her way toward me.

She pulled a *dark watcher's* arm toward her as she kicked his leg back, sending him to the ground where she kicked him again for good measure before she resumed her sprint toward me. Another *dark watcher* blocked her path and she sent two fists straight up through her adversary's chin, snapping their head back and then I lost sight of her as movement caught my eye.

A fist was hurtling toward me. I twisted, caught it and used it as a lever. Carmichael was on the ground again. I quickly dropped to one knee and power drove two fists into his gut. I jumped to my feet as he crawled to his. We stared at each other. I saw his eyes flicker but it was too late. Evilia seized me from behind, locking her fingers around my temples as she forced her will upon me. Everything warped and skewed into blurry focus. Images ripped through my mind faster than I could process. I felt the pressure building and my nose began to bleed.

I opened my eyes and the scene before me was all wrong. *Damn it!*

"You won't know what's real anymore," she hissed.

"Yes, we will," Kraeghton stood to one side and Miles to the other. The three of us faced Evilia and Carmichael.

"What have you done?" Evilia actually sounded scared.

"We stand with the boy. Your reign of terror is at an end. You tried to take my *watcher* gift. You wanted to manipulate people even more than you already do. No one should hold that much power," Kraeghton all but snarled. "You took everything from me and you shall pay. You are going to join me in Hell."

Evilia tried to laugh. She only twitched a hand but I was yanked up by one arm and thrown aside like a rag doll to land with a crash. I felt my shoulder give way and agony almost took me under. I blinked and saw Kraeghton lunging at her as Miles took on Carmichael. Carmichael dodged to the side in one last-ditch effort to save Evilia, causing Kraeghton to barely bump her but where he did, her skin appeared to sizzle and burn. Carmichael took the brunt of it, whatever *it* was, but instead of a normal reaction, the three men came together with a flash and my allies passed right through.

I blinked again, sure I'd lost my mind, but I was back in the field. I scrabbled to my feet in time to watch Carmichael fall straight over backwards – his eyes staring up at the sky turned nearly black with heavy clouds. Rain began to fall. My arm hung useless at my side while blood dripped from my fingers and nose.

Evilia stood transfixed, staring at Caleb Carmichael. I saw my opening, lunged and put my good hand to her chest. I ripped her power from her, collected it with all the hurt and pain around me, thrust it into her mind, forcing her to feel all the destruction she had caused and then collapsed over her as the darkness took both of us.

~ ~ ~

Bright light struck my eyelids. I tried to squint but the light burned. I could smell citrus in the air and the rain had stopped. I tried cracking my eyes again. I could make out a form bending toward me and threw up my good arm defensively. Hands closed gently over it and warmth infused my body.

"You did well. I'm proud of you." The voice was familiar, welcome and safe.

"Miles?"

"Thank you for fulfilling my dream. Thank you for releasing me."

"What? I didn't do anything. I don't understand. "

"You will. You hold *watcher* gifts that you got from both sides of your family tree, mine and White Eagle's. You are the child of your biological parents, myself and White Eagle. You have a lot to pass on and you will, but Evilia still wins if you don't go back."

"Where are we?"

"This is the in-between. You have been here before with White Eagle and Lucie. After today you won't find me here anymore. My family is waiting for me."

"Why are we here?"

"Because you have a choice and I couldn't help but assist you in making the right one after all you have done for me."

"What have I done for you? I think you're mistaken. You have done everything for me."

"That's not true. You have beaten the three most powerful *dark watchers* that we know of. Can't you feel the peace swelling around you?"

"I… I guess, but the price tag was too high. We lost Adrian and I don't know how many others. I'm afraid to go back and find out," I said brokenly as tears began to run down my face.

"Owen, those who gave their lives did so, so that others could live in peace. They knew what they were doing and they wouldn't change a thing. Neither would I."

"What happens now, Miles? What is my job if Evilia's gone?"

"Owen, you are brave and strong. There will always be problems for you to solve. You may even get big ones now and then. Who knows? I think it is for you to decide. If you want, your next adventure may be just around the corner."

"So I'll never be normal?"

"I would like to think that you are going to be… more. Have a wonderful life, Owen. You are everything I hoped you would be." Miles became filmy and translucent.

"Wait," I begged but he vanished. "How do I get out of here?"

"Owen?"

"Dad?"

"I was wrong about you. This is what you're meant for. I'm proud of you."

"Dad, why are you here? You shouldn't be here. You have to go back."

"No, Owen. You do. I'm here to show you the way."

"No, Dad. I'm sorry. I should have done things differently. I should have listened."

"Owen, you did what you were meant to do. I always loved you even when it didn't feel that way to you. Now, let's forgive each other and get you back where you belong. People are waiting for you."

"Dad, no."

"Yes, Owen. Go do your job."

"Come with me."

"I can't. I made a promise. I have to go."

"What promise?"

"I made a trade. You and Adrian for me."

"NO!"

"The Gypsy gave me something to show you. If I go willingly you can have this. I owe it to you. Trust me."

"Noooo…"

Images and colors swirled around me and settled. *A dark haired man stood before me. I looked over his shoulder and saw Lucie in a hospital bed looking tired and worn. Her hair was in a messy braid going down her back and there were dark smudges under her eyes. Lucie... when she looked up and smiled at the man, I realized she was bending over... a small bundle that wiggled in her arms. The door swung silently open and Mom walked in with a huge bouquet of flowers. Balloons bobbed behind her held by... Lucas? Except he looked like he was in high school. Behind him came a more grown up version of Alex holding the hand of a red-haired girl. Behind them were White Eagle and Sarah. I felt my heart sigh, but yet I still worried. My gaze shifted back to Lucie who was passing the baby to the man so she could hug everyone. I felt my heart tug and looked at the bundle in my arms.*

"Hello, little person. Are you here because of my dad?" The baby looked at me, almost as if it could see my soul which I know is crazy because I know babies can't focus when they're that small and then the door opened again to reveal Adrian and Marlo. I smiled and looked again at the baby in my arms.

TWENTY-FOUR

Pain raced through my chest and I moaned. Everything was dark and I could hear crying. I heard beeping… an electronic heartbeat. "He's alive," someone shouted in a too loud voice.

"Owen? Can you hear me?" Lucie asked, her voice thick with tears.

I slowly opened my eyes. There was Lucie with the same raggedy braid and dark smudges under her eyes. "Where's the…" My voice came out broken and cracked.

"Shh. It's going to be okay," Lucie said softly as she took my hand.

I closed my eyes. "Yes, it is." I whispered.

Saul ripped the pads from my chest and everything came rushing back. I opened my eyes wide. I was lying on Evilia's deck. I tried to rise but Lucie pushed me back.

"Where's Marlo?"

"Helping with the other injured *watchers*."

"How'd they get here? I wasn't expecting so many."

"Even Bob is here. Sarah is making sure he doesn't step over the line but it was Kovac who alerted the *watchers*. They began showing up at Sarah's at dawn. We figure the first one appeared about the time you left the crone's shop."

"I'm sorry, Luce."

"I know. I'd blame Kovac but he led us to her just like he told you he would."

"Is… is Adrian okay?"

"Yes, but…" I watched her bite her lip and a fresh tear slide down her cheek.

"My dad is gone, isn't he?"

"I'm so sorry. It looks like he took a blast of *dark watcher* energy to the chest. There was a burn mark on his shirt right over his heart and… and nothing else."

I took her hand and closed my eyes. I started to move my other arm and searing pain tore through me.

"Take it easy with that one. Saul just put it back. It was dislocated."

"Who else did we lose?" I asked wanting to know and wanting to never find out at the same time.

"Two watchers I've never met, the one who tortured me that Bob managed to turn and… and Julie."

"Julie…" I could feel the tears burning at the back of my eyes begin to spill. "What about Evilia? And Carmichael?"

"Dead, both of them." Now her voice was firmer.

"And Bob's here?" I asked not really believing what I'd heard.

"Taking credit and making arrests," Lucie answered sounding disgusted.

I sighed. "I want to go home."

"He'll want a statement," she warned.

"He can get it later. Take me home, please, Luce."

We found my mom sitting by a form covered with a sheet. I watched her pull the ring from his finger and slowly slide it onto her thumb. She picked up his hand again and then she seemed to realize we were there. She swallowed but she couldn't seem to speak. Tears coursed down her cheeks and her nose dripped. Blood ran down the side of her face from a gash and she never looked more beautiful. She closed her eyes for a moment, shook her head and looked at me again. "It's going to okay," she croaked.

I nodded and then found my own voice. "We're going home. I'll see you there."

"Yes," she whispered. "I'll see you there."

Lucie drove and I did nothing but look out the window. When we pulled up, my house was dark and empty. Plywood still covered my window and color had washed out of the world.

"Where's Lucas?"

"Your mom sent him to his friend's house. That one he always goes to, um, Tyler Donaldson's or is that Alex's friend and I'm mixed up?"

"You're mixed up. Lucas' bestie is Nick Moore."

"Oh, yeah."

"I'm glad he's safe. I'm going to take a shower."

"You should go to the hospital."

"I've got you and Saul. I'll be fine."

Lucie sighed.

I struggled with the seatbelt and door handle but I had it open before she could come around and help me. I did let her take the key from my pocket when I couldn't reach it with my off hand. Beggar was happy to see us so the house had to be safe.

I trudged up the stairs avoiding the mirror in the hallway. Ron, our cat, gave me a wild-eyed look and scurried into Lucas' room. I grabbed clean cargo pants, boxer briefs and a t-shirt and headed to the bathroom.

Suddenly I was desperate to get the blood off my skin. The metallic smell of it and the sickly sweet odor of death filled my mouth and sinuses. Visions of the carnage swam before my eyes, twisting my gut. I stripped out of my sticky, stinky clothes and wondered if they were even salvageable. A metallic thud hit the floor. My watch lay there, lonely. Hadn't I been wearing it? When I picked it up, I saw that the crystal was broken. "Miles?"

I couldn't hear him. "Miles?"

I couldn't feel him. "Miles, no."

I sat on the floor and went through my pockets. I still had the screwdriver. The crystal from Eboleen was nothing but dust as was Kraeghton's phylactery. Him I would not miss, but what had he left behind? The arrowhead still hung around my neck. I looked at it. The feather was gone, burned away and it was cracked straight up the middle. It would be a reminder and it was broken, just like me.

I pulled myself to my feet. The mirror caught an ugly reflection, one I couldn't ignore. I stood for a moment, transfixed. I had dried blood and things I didn't want to identify stuck to my hair. More blood was splattered over my face, neck and arms but my hands were the worst. They were coated in a rust brown layer. A drain mark stood out ugly red above my heart and bruising darkened the skin over my ribs, shoulder, along my check and one eye.

My stomach gave an urgent roll. I emptied the contents into the toilet. At least the smell of the acid covered the smell of blood and death. I grabbed my toothbrush and adjusted the water temp in the shower.

I let it beat over me until the water ran clear but no matter how much shampoo I used I figured I'd never feel clean again. A sob caught in my throat as I thought of my dad. I remembered when I wished him out of my life. Now he was. I leaned on the wall of the shower and finally slid down and sat in the tub, water pounding on my head.

Lucie knocked and when I didn't answer she opened the door. She pulled back the shower curtain to make sure I was okay. I just looked at her and shivered. She shut off the water and covered me with the bath towels hanging on the rack.

She helped me step out of the tub and dry off. I pulled on my underwear and she pulled the t-shirt over my head.

"Your Mom's home."

"Okay," I whispered trying to pull myself together.

Lucie handed me my pants. I pulled them on and followed her back downstairs. I found Mom, hair still wet from her own shower, slumped in her chair. She slowly opened her eyes when she felt me enter the room.

Now what do we do?" she asked softly.

I cleared my throat to get my voice to work. "We keep getting up each morning and keep putting our feet on the floor. We keep breathing."

"We need to talk about what happened."

"Tomorrow, please. Tomorrow will be soon enough." Not that I would sleep. It was more that I didn't want to think. Saul had relocated my shoulder while I was unconscious. It hurt like bloody hell now, but I'd be doggoned if I was going to take anything for it. The pain kept reality in place. After four years of having voices in my head, I was afraid I was finally crazy because I couldn't stand the silence.

I sat next to my mom and took her hand. Lucie got out the makings for tea. I heard footsteps and then a key in the lock but I was too drained to care. I never again want to see the look I saw on Melody's face when she rounded the corner with Alex. Her eyes were misted by tears and she was pale and disheveled. She made it real.

"You don't have to stay," I said when she pulled out at chair. "There is no one left to hurt us."

"Evilia may be gone but I'm not leaving. I'm here to watch over you. I owe you that."

"Fine. I understand. Thank you. I think I'll go to bed then."

I lay on my bed with Lucie curled into my side, staring out my window. Guilt and moonlight poured over me. My chest and throat were tight but I felt too numb to cry. Every time I looked at my clock the numbers had marched a little closer to dawn but that was the only thing that changed.

I awoke to a pounding both inside and outside my head. I glanced at my clock. 5:30 am. I rolled out of bed and hurried to the front door where Melody already stood with her arms crossed and her jaw clenched.

It was an agent showdown. The two on the other side of the door looked just as surly. Their eyes were hidden behind dark glasses but their heads moved in my direction as I came down the stairs.

Melody turned to glance at me over her shoulder and that was all it took. The shorter, sturdier black-suited agent pushed past her and tackled me to the floor – sending fresh waves of pain through my head, neck, shoulder and arm.

Melody's feet moved past my line of sight. I heard a sound on the stairs and then felt the prick of a needle.

"Why?" I croaked. No one answered. The pain dulled but so did my senses. I couldn't make my body cooperate so I lay in a heap unable to do anything and not really caring that I couldn't. Not anymore.

Melody, Lucie and Mom were arguing but I didn't really understand it. The tall agent pushed my mom. A feeling like anger burned in my chest. Alex jumped on the back of him and then more agents were pouring in the front door reminding me of little black sugar ants after a cookie. Lucas ran down the stairs and tried to get to me but one of the many agents picked him up and held him off the floor where his little legs and arms couldn't connect with anything worthwhile.

Everyone in my house was being held and I was carried out. I was tossed in the back of an SUV like yesterday's trash. I tried to notice where we were but I couldn't seem to focus. The vehicle stopped. I knew this place. I'd been here before. My chest felt funny again. I think it was telling me to be scared but that would take energy I didn't have. I was carried down familiar concrete halls with utilitarian lighting. Bad things had happened here. I needed to leave.

This time I was put in an interrogation room. It was all I could manage to crawl to the chair, get onto it, and put my head on the table before I passed out.

The click of high heels brought me around and I focused my bleary eyes on Dr. Moretz.

"What happened?"

I said nothing.

"How do you feel about your father?" she tried again.

Her questions came faster as her frustration grew, "How did you kill Caleb Carmichael? How did you kill Evilia? They were to be captured."

Her foot began to tap as she tried a new line of questions, "What do you know about Miles Malone? Where is Stephan Kraeghton?

Mica thinks she's found his body. Did he disappear because of you?"

I listened but I did not speak.

"What do you know about Vandilo Kovac?"

She waited a beat and tried again, "We can try you as an adult, you're eighteen."

"No one will believe you," I finally croaked in response to something.

"Of course they will. We're the government. It wouldn't be the first time someone has falsified records."

I groaned and pulled myself upright in the chair.

"What happened to your father?"

"You seem to have all the answers; why ask me anything?" I queried back.

"We want to understand."

"I don't understand. How am I supposed to explain it to you?" I said listlessly.

"We want to know what you know."

"Why?"

She just stared at me waiting. I gave up and tried another tactic. "Don't I get a phone call? An attorney? Something?"

"We aren't the police."

"But you are the FBI, right?"

"I am not. Now quit stalling and talk or I'll help you to do it."

"Fine," I sighed. They'd figure it out anyway.

"Tell me, who is Vandilo Kovac?" she asked again.

"You don't know?" I asked, surprised.

"No."

"Well, I don't know either, other than he is sometimes called The Gypsy."

She looked at me really hard, measuring and evaluating. "You really don't know anything. Were you knocked out the whole time? You are less useful than I thought. I believed that you were more resourceful. So... here it is. The team is being broken up and moved all over the world. The threat is gone. You're done. Go back to your life. We don't want you anymore."

"Just like that?"

"Just like that." She snapped her fingers and two agents came in and hoisted me to my feet.

"Wait," I said. "I'm curious. I thought you were arrested."

"Turns out Bob didn't have the evidence he thought he did," she sneered. "And, Owen."

I turned back to look at her. "Stay out of our business or we will get right back in the middle of yours."

She flicked her hand at me and they led me out. I glanced over my shoulder one last time. She met my glance and told me without words that she would be watching.

I was hustled out of the building and shoved back in the SUV. This time I got an actual seat. I sat sullen and silent, watching our route and trying to decide my next move. I was surprised when it became clear they really were taking me home. I saw White Eagle come flying out of his house as we passed. The agent sitting by me, turned, and pointed a finger at the door. I looked at it and then at him but he'd drawn his weapon.

357

I pulled the handle and almost fell out of the moving vehicle. I caught myself before I fell and the driver could run me over. White Eagle was nearly clipped as they passed but he knew better than to stop a moving object like that with his body. He did not stop but merely turned out of the way. I felt my throat tighten at the thought that I meant more to him than catching my captors but he'd been here before – he knew what to expect. They had done their job and they would leave.

He grabbed me tight in a painful hug. "Are you alright?"

"I will be."

Mom, Alex, Lucie and Sarah burst out the front door and ran toward us.

"Why?" It was all my mom said.

"They wanted to know what I knew. They should have asked me nicely."

"He was paying you back for not sticking around," Sarah huffed.

"Can't we get him for that?" Mom asked.

"It's our word against his," Sarah answered.

"Dr. Moretz questioned me. I thought she was gone."

"I did too," Sarah said sadly.

"She said they're redistributing the team."

"Just some of them," Sarah answered. "How did you hold the doctor off? Did Kraeghton help you?"

"Kraeghton is gone. So is Miles. The voices are silent." Everyone but Lucie looked stunned.

"I still have some memories but they're fading, just like normal ones do."

White Eagle took ahold of my good shoulder and looked at me with his other sight. "He's right. He looks like the old Owen, just not as bright. How about your *watcher* gifts?"

"I don't know yet. I think I can only *see* things. I feel fuzzy and weird. I don't know."

"You need rest," he decided.

"How did you avoid telling the doctor everything?"

"I really don't know, but she believed that I knew nothing. They would never believe the truth anyway."

We went inside and I tried to figure out what I was going to do with the rest of my life.

"How's Marlo?" I asked Lucie when the hub-bub died down.

"He's worried about you."

"Me?" I asked.

"He can tell you're different."

"Lucie, we're all different."

"I know," she said softly as she touched my face.

"He's gone. My dad is gone and so is Miles. What do I do now?"

"You are not alone. Remember that," she said and I knew she meant it.

The part of me that could still reason knew she understood. "I feel like I have a hole in my chest."

"You do and it's okay. It will heal, I promise."

I put my head on her shoulder and closed my eyes. I let the darkness take me.

~ ~ ~

I awoke to quiet voices at the kitchen table and stumbled in that direction.

Mom looked up at me. "Sit. We need to talk."

"Okay," I said looking from her, to White Eagle, to Sarah, and then to Alex and Lucie.

"I got a sub to finish out the year for me."

"Okay."

"I called your principal and I have arranged for you to miss your finals and for your teachers to accept your current grades as your final ones."

"Oh?"

"Are you ready to take your finals tomorrow? Have you even cracked a book in days?"

"No."

"It's settled then. Your grades are good enough for Portland State and the district will let you graduate. You passed enough credits. We'll start slow and figure out how to rebuild our lives."

"Thanks, Mom. How are we going to stay here and what's the cover story on Dad?"

"I don't know where we will live, but we will survive this. As for the story..." She looked to White Eagle.

"The best way to explain the burn on his chest is an electrical accident. Saul used the AED on you. The story is, he had a heart attack, the machine was used on him and it... failed. It was raining."

"Yes, but don't those things have fail-safes?"

"Accidents happen," White Eagle repeated.

"What about the others who died?"

Sarah took over the answers, "Each has their own story. It is in everyone's best interest to leave it alone and let Robert Bowman handle it. It's on him, not us."

"If he was there, he knows what happened. They'll be coming back for me."

"I doubt it. He has bigger fish to fry. Between all the arrests and questioning of Evilia's people and hiding the bodies, he'll be busy for a long time. He came late to the party and you were already on the ground so maybe you really didn't see anything." Sarah sounded confident, but I wasn't.

"I thought he was in trouble with his boss."

"He is and he isn't. There is what we know and what we can prove. There is enough to have him looked at, but he is covering up faster than evidence can be found. He'll get his. Karma if nothing else will see to that," Sarah ended.

TWENTY-FIVE

Lucie, Marlo and I parked at the University of Portland, our venue for tonight's graduation. Our caps and gowns waited in a garment bag on the back seat. Marlo sported Converse and a garish tie, in a feeble attempt to recapture the old Marlo. Lucie and I were way past that. We were so far from the people we had been that it was too much struggle to even fake our way anywhere near our former selves. No one tried to leave the car.

Marlo rested his hands on the steering wheel and stared straight ahead. "We should be happy, right? Maybe we should be relieved or even giddy. I for one just feel… empty."

Lucie leaned forward from the back seat and hugged him. "It's not a good time for any of us. Just remember, for better or worse, we are done with this part of our lives and now we can move on."

"To what?" Marlo's voice cracked. "I never trusted Bob, but he promised me all this stuff, a future, a career… I always had hope and now… he dissolved the team, we're not allowed to talk to each other, I'll never see Joy again and I gave up some really good colleges." He leaned forward and put his head on his hands. "I sound selfish."

"No, you don't. Marlo, we love you. We are a team. Together we can do this. It's not fair and it never has been. I know it feels like he took everything, but you still have us. That will never change. You still have your parents and most importantly you have YOU. You are the smartest and most talented person I know. Keep remembering all the good we did and how many lives you saved by bringing down Evilia," I said, resting a hand on his shoulder.

"I didn't, you did."

"No, Mars, we did. I could never have done any of this without you, Lucie and the team. None of us stands alone."

Marlo took a deep breath and raised his head. "Well then, onward. Let's go get our damn diplomas."

The lining up and mini-practice flowed around us. Most kids were happy, silly almost and in the mood to party. Adrian, having taken one look at us, stayed with his jock friends. He had no idea what had been sacrificed on his behalf and if I had anything to say about it, he never would. The ceremony rolled on. Time seemed to both speed up and slow down. I was just counting the minutes until it was over. I could pick no one out of the enormous crowd and at this point I didn't care. I could barely make my facial muscles smile when they handed me my diploma and took my picture. I sat staring at it as everyone in my row fidgeted with excitement and then we were marching out. I felt like it was all a dream and I'd never been there.

I met up with Lucie and Marlo who both looked like I felt, dazed. We let ourselves be pushed by the flow of graduates moving out the doors toward the courtyard and then we wandered through the throng of people, hugging friends and family, searching for our own relatives. Marlo saw his parents first and moved toward them with Lucie right behind him. A shiver went down my spine, making me turn.

"Congratulations Owen."

"Thank you," I answered stiffly.

"It seems that everything is going your way," Kovac whispered.

"It was," I snapped back sarcastically, irritated that he was interrupting our special day.

"I have helped you get rid of the greatest evil that has existed since Hitler. Now you are the greatest good. I wanted to say thank you. I came to help you celebrate."

"Nothing personal, but no thanks. My family is here. They're all I need."

"Too bad they *all* couldn't be here."

I clenched my jaw. Tears burned at the back of my eyes. I wanted to strike out.

He did nothing but watch me for a beat. "I will always be watching."

"So will I," I replied in a rough, constricted voice.

A hand landed on my shoulder. I turned to see Bob. I glanced back toward Kovac but he had been swallowed by the crowd.

"Congratulations," Robert, Bob, Bowman said, slick as a greasy salesman.

"No thanks to you," I growled.

"The way I see it, you have plenty to thank me for."

"Bull..."

"Now, now, language," he interrupted. "I still have a job for you when you graduate."

"No thank you."

"No thank you, sir."

"Sorry, you haven't earned it and after what you've done to my friends and family. I don't see that changing."

"You just don't see the whole picture. One day you will."

"Owen, there you are," Mom interrupted. "Mr. Bowman, what an unpleasant surprise. You'll excuse us, won't you? It's a special day for our family and we need to take some pictures."

Mom's gaze was steel, her face like stone. Bob looked a little taken aback. "Of course, Lila."

"That's Mrs. Ryer to you. Please leave my family alone or I'll call security."

"You know they won't arrest me."

"Maybe not, but it would burn up some of your valuable time, right?" Mom took my arm and turned us away to head over to Lucie and Marlo. Alex was right behind her. He had fooled even me by changing his posture and blending with the crowd. As we passed him, he didn't take his eyes off Bob, ensuring our safe passage.

When Alex rejoined the group, I hugged him tight. "Thanks," I whispered.

"He left. I watched the car leave." I nodded in acknowledgement. "Dad's here you know, he'll always watch over us." I looked into his eyes, startled. We didn't need words. He knew my thoughts and had answered my unasked question, but how did he know? His eyes told me that he completely believed that it was so.

Lucie's father and brother approached with Lucie's new step mom in tow. Sam moved forward without hesitation to give her a big hug. "Congratulations, sweetheart! You look beautiful."

"Thanks, Sam. And thanks for being here. It means a lot."

"I'll always be your brother, Lucie." His voice was so earnest it almost hurt.

Ted Ness cleared his throat. "Congratulations, Lucie Beth, I'm proud of you."

"Thanks, Dad." Her voice sounded soft, hopeful.

"I haven't always been easy on you. I really did want what was best. Well, the way I saw it anyway. I ah, wanted you to have something for this milestone. I should have given it to you sooner but well, anyway, here." His hand stretched out, he opened his grip a little and part of a key chain released.

Lucie's eyes went wide. "Keys?"

"To a car, a Kia Sorento, actually. It's for college. It's in your name. Sam helped me register it at the DMV, all in your name. You just have to call your insurance company. And this..." he said, holding out a check. "It's for the first year of insurance. As long as you are taking college classes and maintain a B average, I will pay for the insurance. It's what I did for Sam."

"I don't know what to say."

"It's not new, it's used," he faltered.

Lucie moved forward and hugged him. He looked momentarily surprised and then he held her tight.

"I'm sorry, Lucie Beth."

"Me too, Dad. Thanks for coming."

"Ah, yeah, well, we need to go. We've got, um, business in town."

"I understand."

"Oh, I almost forgot. Sam has the title for you and um, good luck." He turned and walked away with his bride. It was brief but it was a start I guess.

Sam hugged Lucie again and I lost track of them when Adrian and his folks came over for a picture of us. I ended up smiling so many times that my cheeks hurt. It was kind of an irony because even with the cheek cramps I still didn't feel any real joy.

~ ~ ~

A month had passed since I had traded my father for the downfall of evil. I hurt inside every day. We all did, but Lucie and I had decided to celebrate his sacrifice and those of the other good *watchers* by taking the bike to the beach. It was a beautiful day. The sun was shining and the breeze was light. We drove to Cannon Beach because it had always been one of my family's favorite spots. I parked in the Tolovana Park parking lot so that we could walk the beach. Lucie and I strolled hand in hand in the sand. I felt happy and sad all at the same time and wasn't sure what to do with all the emotions that rolled through me.

Lucie turned in front of me. "You're going to be okay. I promise. I've been there. I know."

"I know, Sunshine, and I have you."

"Maybe you do and maybe you don't," she laughed, giving me a shove, and then sprinted down the beach. I shook my head, smiled and chased her, finally tackling her on the sand. She giggled and kissed me.

"You're my favorite," she laughed and then got serious about the kissing. She sighed and pulled back. I don't want them arresting us, so we better get moving. I don't look good in mug shots."

"How do you know?" I asked laughing.

She pulled me to my feet and then hopped on my back so I could give her a piggyback ride. Maybe she just wasn't ready to stop touching me. I walked on for a bit and then I pulled off her shoes and socks. "What are you doing?"

"I want you to have the full beach experience. You've got to get your feet wet in the ocean."

"I've done that before."

"Not here."

"No, but in Hawaii."

"Yeah, but you were there for a competition. It wasn't a real vacation. Today you are here for no reason other than to have fun."

"Okay, smarty, have it your way, but then you have to feed me or I'll get grouchy."

I laughed as I let Lucie slide off my back so that I could remove my shoes and socks and roll up my pant legs. I took Lucie by the hand and we rushed into the water. "It's cold!" she squealed in delight. She squeezed the sand with her toes and watched in fascination as her heels sank into the saturated sand.

"When I watch the water pull away from me, I get the sensation that it's me moving backwards," Lucie commented. I could feel her curiosity and fascination.

"Yeah, it's cool, huh?"

"I'm glad it's not too late to discover things," she said softly, smiling at me in a way that made my heart beat faster.

I took her hand. I could look at her all day. I took a deep breath of the cool, moist ocean air and began to walk again, still holding her hand. Occasionally she would pick up a rock to study. We skipped a few of the better ones as the water snuck away from us and then would watch the next wave try to get back at us. Her smile, her sparkly eyes, her hair messy from the breeze – what could be better? I still remembered eighth grade but today's background was perfect.

Lucie shifted her gaze from the ocean to me and looked almost surprised that I was still watching her. "Enough, my stomach is growling like a bear. Can't you hear it?"

"Not over the rush of the waves. I guess you want lunch?"

"You bet!"

We collected our shoes and drove into town to walk around and find some chowder. Later, Lucie and I strolled the main drag so she could window-shop. When we reached the ice cream store, we stopped for a cone, then got back on the bike and headed south so that she could see more of the coastline.

I stopped at a lookout so that we could watch the ocean. I wrapped my arms around her from behind and held her close. "Thank you for today. If I'd stayed at home I would have moped. I need to be thankful for everything my dad and the others did for us and appreciate the good moments."

"Me too. You mean everything to me and when you hurt, I hurt."

"Love you, Luce."

"I love you too, Owen. So very much."

I lost track of how long we stood there, just being. The sound of distant waves and passing cars, the wind in our ears and our sight full of beautiful, endless ocean, sand and crookedy beach trees bent out of shape from the wind, made for a perfect moment in time.

A retired couple came by and offered to take our picture. It was a great opportunity and a wonderful background.

We rode on and found a rustic restaurant with a good view for dinner. We talked about everything and nothing. The best part was, it felt like even nature was giving us a day off. Neither of us felt even the slightest *watcherly* twinge.

We found a quiet, scenic spot to watch the sun go down and then we searched out the perfect log to rest against. The colors started with the barest hint of lavender and were growing steadily brighter and redder as we settled in.

"Owen, your eyes are like melted chocolate. I could fall right in. I'm liking the stubble too, you look *hot*. I could eat you up. Melted chocolate. Yum." The look in her eye was both playful and intense.

I needed a bucket of ice water dumped right over my head to hold myself back from this side of Lucie, but how could I resist such cuteness and charm? She reminded me of a pixie or an elf. She'd had so much fun today. I still couldn't believe her parents had never taken the time to bring her to the beach just to play. The same sunlight that she thought made my eyes look like melted chocolate brought out the highlights in her hair. I brought my hand up and pushed back a lock that had escaped from her clip in the light sea breeze. If I was melted chocolate, her eyes were surely sunlit waves. "You are so beautiful," I breathed softly.

Lucie leaned in slowly keeping her eyes on mine. Her lips touched mine, my eyes drifted closed and the usual fireworks began to explode within me. Lucie leaned back a little and my eyes popped open. She was still looking at me intently as she rolled gracefully to her knees. She turned her body so that she was facing me completely then she slid a leg over me and sat straddling my thighs. She slid forward, watching my reaction. She placed her hands on my shoulders and leaned forward to nibble my ear. My weak spot. *Lucie, you're killing me.* "Luce, I thought you wanted to watch the sunset," I said in a hopeless effort to save the situation before... .

"I'd rather watch you," she said while her lips trailed down my neck. Oh Boy.

"Aw, Luce, you are playing with fire."

She sighed and rested her head on my shoulder. I slid my hands from her knees to her hips. She moved my sweatshirt hood and t-shirt away from my neck so she could rest her cheek against my collarbone. I thought I was doing really well until she started kissing my neck. She moved her hips and my whole body burst into flames. There was no hiding it, she'd know exactly how I felt.

"Lucie," I groaned

"Someday... ." she mumbled against my lips as she moved a hand over my hammering heart. She closed her eyes and tilted her head back as she moved again. "Someday soon," she whispered again. Then she moved back in to kiss me. "I won't ever forget today," she said between kisses.

I slid my hands from her hips to touch the warm skin of her waist under her sweatshirt. I moved one hand to her back and the other to her ribs. I knew I should stop. It was a public beach, though no one was around. I had to stop while I could still think but I didn't want to. I moved my hand up and she shivered but didn't stop kissing me. Lucie moved her hands under my sweatshirt to travel over my overheated skin. Don't stop. She kissed her way along my jaw and went back to my neck. Electricity seemed to flow through me. I remembered the narrow space at the adoption agency two years ago when Lucie had run her hands over my body, the time at Sarah and White Eagle's wedding and that time in San Diego when... .

Lucie pulled back a little. I started to drop my hands but she shook her head at me. Her face was lit by a brilliant smile. "How could two wrecks like us be happy?"

"What?" I asked perplexed. What were we talking about? Our damaged bodies and psyche were not on my mind at the moment. Lucie pulled her hands from me and unzipped her sweatshirt. She let it fall open showing her fitted t-shirt that barely met her jeans. She pulled down her low-cut neckline to expose her shoulder and the fading pearly white fingerprints over her heart that she had gotten forever ago when a *watcher reaper* had tried to completely drain her gift and get to me. Before I could stop myself I leaned in to kiss her damaged skin.

"We've been through so much. How do we know what we have is real? We're so damaged on the outside and worse on the inside. Maybe we're afraid to let anyone else see the real us."

"Lucie, everything that has happened to us makes us who we are. I have plenty of scars inside and out. A few on you don't scare me at all," I mumbled against her sweet skin.

"You're a guy. It's different if you're a little damaged on the outside – it makes you look tough and you don't let most people see the inside."

I tilted my head back to look at her. "It's not different. I suffer but both my mind and my body are healing. You are alive. That's all I care about. In time the nightmares will go and so will the guilt. Just know that I would love you if your mind didn't recover, your whole body was scarred and you were bald. I still loved you when you were a brown-eyed brunette, right?" I moved back in to kiss the spot and any other skin I could reach.

Lucie made a strange choking sound. I looked at her, alarmed for a heartbeat, and then she threw back her head and laughter bubbled up.

"You say the best things! Bald, please no, not ever! We're going to be okay, you know. I shouldn't have doubted us. Now, kiss me!"

"Okay, Lucie." I moved my hands to her face and pulled it down to mine. She was right, it had been a good day and we most certainly would be okay. I would never forget any of it. Ever. I don't know what happened with the sunset. It was setting and then it was dark. I had missed it, but I didn't care. What I hadn't missed was better by far.

THE END

Life moves in positive and negative ways – whether we want it to or not. Dance when there is dancing to be done – smile and laugh often but most importantly, never forget who you really are because you are on the brink of becoming someone extraordinary.